Brides of WYOMING

Brides of WYOMING

3-in-1 Historical Romance Collection

S. Dionne Moore

BARBOUR BOOKS
An Imprint of Barbour Publishing, Inc.

Print ISBN 978-1-63409-799-4

eBook Editions:
Adobe Digital Edition (.epub) 978-1-68322-054-1
Kindle and MobiPocket Edition (.prc) 978-1-68322-055-8

All scripture quotations are taken from the King James Version of the Bible.

Published by Barbour Books, an imprint of Barbour Publishing, Inc., P.O. Box 719, Uhrichsville, OH 44683, www.barbourbooks.com

Our mission is to publish and distribute inspirational products offering exceptional value and biblical encouragement to the masses.

Printed in the United States of America.

Contents

The Shepherd's Song

Dedication

To Renee, for paving the way of arthritis, menopause, wrinkles, and bodily malfunctions for your MUCH YOUNGER sister. Still love me? And to Sharon, thanks for being there for mom. I'm so glad we've united. Finally. Love you both!

Chapter 1

Renee Dover lifted her head to peer over the rock she hid behind. Excitement pumped through her when she saw the four men sprawled out on the ground in various stages of rest. Only one of the four showed signs of wakefulness, his attention glued to the stick he whittled. A small pile of shavings covered his lap and peppered the ground around his thighs.

The easy motion of the knife against the wood worked another curl from the stick. He lowered the knife and raised his head. Renee ducked behind her rock, her initial thrill oozing into an uneasy feeling that snaked through her veins. All at once, she recognized the foolhardiness that had led her to bait her brother into the hills to try to find the hideout of the Loust Gang. Now that she had stumbled upon their camp, the knowledge that her brother was in the hills on the other side of the valley reinforced the fact that she was alone. With four outlaws. And a gun she had shot only three times before.

Stories of the Loust Gang's deeds swelled in her memory. Her pa worried that their ranch was too close to the Loust Gang's new territory and might be visited by the outlaws, prompting in Renee all types of romantic notions about finding the gang and collecting the reward. And now here she crouched, looking right at them. A shudder trickled through her as she slowly backed away from the rock.

"Renee?"

She inhaled sharply at the sound of her brother's voice, distant, calling from the valley floor. She glanced back toward the men to see if they'd heard Thomas's call. The man with the stick lifted his head. Renee ducked down and shifted to the right where a large, prickly bush with no leaves allowed her to see the men but shielded her from view. The lanky man's eyes probed the area where Renee hid. He stared for a long minute, bent one knee, propped his arm along it, and continued to whittle.

"Renee? Shoot your gun so I know where you are."

Thomas's voice was closer. Louder. Renee squeezed her eyes shut. If she didn't answer, he would continue up the hill and get caught. She had to warn him away, but how could she without risking her own safety?

The lanky man rose to his feet this time. He buckled on his guns and toed the man next to him. "Rand, get up. Someone's coming," he hissed.

"Let Lance take care of them," the portly man mumbled before releasing a yawn.

The slender man kicked the man harder. "Get up. I don't know where Lance is.

He shouldn't have let anyone wander this close."

"Maybe he fell asleep," Rand mumbled as he frowned up at the skinny man. "With you hollerin', he'll wake up and take care of things. Stop your worrying."

"Renee!"

Thomas's voice rang clearer, closer than before. The tall man's head jerked and his eyes narrowed. Renee's heart slammed. Even Rand lifted his head then elbowed himself to a sitting position.

The slender man's head rotated one way, then the other, eyes scanning, before he started in the direction from which Thomas's voice had come. He drew closer to Renee, so near that if she so much as twitched, he would notice. Her heart thundered now, ears roaring with the fear that swelled in her throat. His hand hovered over his right gun. Behind him, Rand marched to the other two outlaws and barked at them to get up and buckle on their guns.

Renee huddled into a tighter ball, afraid to move and afraid not to. She closed her eyes and strained for the sound of Thomas's horse. If they spotted him, she would jump up and hopefully divert their attention while Thomas used his six-shooters. He'd been practicing with his new guns and was good. Much better than she. But if the outlaws got off a shot first. . .

She held her breath and waited.

"Ya seen Lance?" Rand's voice whispered, close at hand.

"Guard the gold," the slender man growled back. "Tell Lolly to keep watch to the west, and Dirk to the east."

Sweat trickled down Renee's back, her ears primed for any hint that the slender man had spotted someone and was going to draw. She could see his cruel face in her mind's eye, and she had no doubt whatsoever that he knew how to use those six-shooters on his hips. She exhaled long and slow, haunted by the memory of the article in the latest edition of the town newspaper, already two weeks old when her pa had brought it home, that reported the latest body count as a result of the Loust Gang's thievin' ways was six.

A shot rang out, and Renee gasped and jerked her head up.

"Got 'em, boss!" a deep voice barked up the hill. A new voice.

Thomas! Renee's stomach rolled. Her fault. All her fault. The distant sound of a galloping horse came to her ears then disappeared. Probably Thomas's horse, riderless, returning to the ranch. Pa would be devastated. Her throat burned and tears collected in her eyes. Her body tensed.

"Thought you'd fallen asleep on us," the lanky man said, his hands relaxed at his sides now. She could see the cruelty of his mouth. He scratched along his jaw, his eyes sweeping the rock-littered hillside.

A horse whinnied, and the clop of hooves alerted her to the movements of another man, probably the Lance Rand had mentioned. She would be trapped. And it didn't matter. Not with Thomas dead. She deserved to die, too. Renee slid out from the bush, her back to the camp, her legs stiff from the hunched position.

She heard quick footsteps behind her, just as a horse trotted up the hill into view. Two more seconds and the man on the horse would see her. She didn't care. She stood and faced the lanky fellow just as the horseman hollered out from behind her.

"Boss!"

The lanky fellow's head whipped her direction and a gun appeared in his hand, the cold eye of the barrel pointed at her chest. "Get over here where I can see you. You have a gun; shuck it now."

She grabbed the lone gun in the holster awkwardly buckled around her hips. For the journey into the hills, she'd begged Thomas to let her wear a pair of his pants.

Lanky's jaw clenched, though she thought she saw amusement in his eyes. "Got ourselves a boy." His eyes raked down her. "Correction. A girl playing like a boy."

At her back, the clop of hooves stopped and she heard a sardonic laugh. "Prettiest boy I ever seen. What you going to do with her, boss?"

A low whistle rent the air, and Renee followed the movement of Rand and the other outlaws coming toward her. She didn't know which had whistled.

"Fine catch, Marv," Rand said. "Mighty fine."

The lanky man didn't move. She felt his gaze on her but kept her eyes averted, chin high. She would not cry.

"You must be Renee," he finally said.

She refused to look at him and stared, instead, at the horizon, where the sun's color touched the bellies of the clouds, turning them pink. She heard the crunch of his footfall and the blur of motion before a painful vise clamped her arm.

"Look at me when I talk to you," he snarled.

Renee gasped as pain shot up her arm. She faced him, beating down the fear that worse treatment was to come, even as anger flushed through her. "Leave me alone."

A smile shot across his face and he let her go. "Anything you wish, m'lady. Shall I have a noble knight show you to your chambers?"

The men bunched in closer, sharing a good laugh over their leader's wit. Her breathing quickened and her scalp tingled. She did the only thing she knew to show her disgust. She spat, just like Thomas had shown her, and the nasty wad landed right on Marv's shirt.

Silence fell over the group as Marv stared down at his shirt then back at her. His eyes flashed cold and she tensed, waiting for his wrath to fall. But he only stared, muscles trembling along his jaw.

"Well?" she said, her voice sharp, unable to stand his silence a moment longer. "Aren't you going to shoot me?"

"I don't pull lead on a lady." His eyes narrowed and a smirk curled his lips. "Unless I'm provoked or there's something in it for me. . ." He lifted a hand. "Rand!"

The potbellied man stepped forward, eagerness to please evident in his demeanor.

"Take the *lady*"—he drawled the word—"to the cave and stay there with her until I decide what to do with her. Do whatever you need to keep her under control." He pivoted and took two steps, his head whipping side to side. "Lance, get back on watch. Lolly, Dirk, pack things up. We're moving down toward the valley."

Chapter 2

Tyler Sperry patted the grungy, smelly hound and pushed the rabbit he'd just shot closer to the dog. The hound didn't hesitate, his floppy ears waving, mere ribbons from the many fights he'd had with the coyotes and the snakes. Alerted by the hound's return to camp, Tyler's sheepdog, Teddy, woke and began to move, goading the sheep to their feet. Tyler loved the rhythm of the two dogs. The hound hunted and kept predators at bay, seldom coming into camp, and Teddy worked the sheep daily, ferreting out those that had wandered during the night and moving them when needed. Exactly what Tyler was needing now as he led the herd into the mountains where it would be cooler in the summer months.

Tired, Tyler shuffled to his horse. He stooped and ran his hands down the horse's legs and over her hocks, feeling for the telltale warmth that spoke of pulled tendons. The horse shifted her weight and craned her neck to playfully nip at Tyler's shoulder. "On with you now, Sassy." But the horse's playfulness brought a smile to his lips. He stood and brushed his hand down the horse's back. "You take a swipe at me again and I just might leave you to the bandits. They'd like a horse like you."

Indeed, few cowhands possessed long-legged, powerful horses like Sassy. He'd thought of selling the animal for a smaller horse when he took the job as sheepherder, but he chose to keep her because of the history between them. He ran a finger over the scar on her right shoulder, and his lower knee ached at the reminder of the bullet that had grazed the horse and lodged in his leg.

Tyler saddled his horse and walked Sassy around the camp. "Go ahead and let it out, girl. You know I'm going to cinch you up tighter."

Sassy nickered, and Tyler stooped to tighten the cinch strap where the horse had finally let out her breath. "Can't play the same trick day in and day out and not expect me to catch on." He grinned as he mounted and picked up the reins. *But you do try.*

Lifting his head, he gave a low whistle, and Teddy appeared from the bunched flock. He nodded in satisfaction. "Good boy, Teddy. Go easy on them, now."

Tyler twisted in his saddle and kept a sharp look as Teddy zigzagged behind the sheep, always keeping them moving forward with quiet efficiency, though the young lambs challenged Teddy's efforts. Satisfied that Teddy was working well, Tyler led the herd toward the taller grasses where the sheep would spend much of the morning munching and drinking water from the streams.

As they approached the verdant hillside, the sheep spread out. The old hound trailed Teddy by a few hundred yards. Tyler knew the dog's instincts would drive him to disappear among the trees and hills that surrounded the herd to look for signs of predators. He cast his eyes over the herd, satisfied to see Teddy setting an invisible boundary where he patrolled the sheep to prevent them from escaping on the side opposite the stream.

Tyler dismounted and climbed onto a boulder to survey the sheep, especially the three pregnant ewes. The other mamas had delivered, but these three were late. He kept his eyes on the herd but allowed his mind to wander. The sunshine warmed him and deepened his weariness. Tomorrow he would need to break camp and move the sheep farther uphill, a good four miles.

As always, the silence both soothed him and made him restless. He loved the peace of the sheepherder's life and hated the isolation. Yet it was the path he had chosen. Had been forced to choose. And he had only himself to blame.

A distant bark brought his mind back to the sheep. Most of the flock went about their grazing, not spooked by the sound, though Tyler knew if the dog continued, the sheep would begin to react. Before he could move to investigate, the hound appeared on a rock ledge above the herd, tongue lolling to one side.

The animal usually howled at coyotes, gaining enough of a response from the predators to enable him to find their location. This was different though. Tyler climbed off the rock, his palm scraping when his foot slid. He took a moment to remove a leather sack from the pack behind Sassy's saddle. From the pack he took out a piece of thin linen and awkwardly wrapped it around his palm to stop the bleeding. He pulled his rifle from the scabbard and set out.

❧

Every nerve in Renee's body tightened. The stone bit into her back as she shifted to try to see where Rand had wandered off to. Since their arrival at the new location three days ago, he had hardly said two words to her, not that she minded. His rotten teeth repelled her, and the oily glances he sent her way stirred fear in her stomach.

Though he had not tied her, she could see that he was a man—that they were all men—who would let their guns rule any situation. Rand would not be sweet-talked, and she would be crazy not to try to escape. Long into the night she had considered and dismissed several options. Rand stuck close to her. She would have to be careful.

On quiet feet, she moved to the mouth of the shallow cave that had become her new home and peeked out. Rand stood some distance off, his arms loose at his sides, his gaze on some point distant, as if he was listening to something. Or for someone. Was Rand expecting Marv and the rest of the gang? The dawning of opportunity stacked tension along her spine, but the sight of Rand's guns gave her pause.

She owed it to her pa to at least try. Better for him to find out about Thomas than to agonize when neither of his children returned. Even now, she knew he must be sick with fear, if only for Thomas. She doubted he would grieve much over her disappearance.

Renee closed her eyes. She blew a frustrated breath and continued her study of the area. She had to focus on her mission. As they had traveled, she'd tried to keep track of the direction they'd gone, but the constant switching back had left her confused. Regardless, she would escape first and then worry about getting home.

A bush rustled beside the cave entrance where she stood. She tensed for the appearance of a snake, but the blur within the branches seemed larger. A brown mottled face poked out of the brush. A dog.

Stunned, Renee could only stare at the animal. Where had he come from? When he emerged, she saw his shredded ears and the scars along his face and shoulders where hair did not grow. The dog sat down, gave one short bark, then turned tail and scampered back through the brush and emerged as a black blur on the other side.

"That stupid dog." Rand's footsteps closed her window of opportunity. She wanted to hate the dog for his bark, but at the sight of the sorrowful mess of his ears and face, sympathy stabbed through her. The poor mongrel was probably skulking about looking for food.

"Mutt came sniffing around the other night, too. Heard a coyote in the distance and it took off running. Probably scared silly."

Renee doubted it. Maybe the dog was hunting coyotes and smelled them in the form of Rand, Marv, and all his cohorts. The thought plucked the first smile she'd enjoyed since being captured. It slid from her lips, though, when she recalled all that had happened and the way Marv had looked at her that first night after her capture. She shuddered. If she couldn't escape first, she would have to fight hard against their lecherous attempts in hopes they would shoot her dead.

With nothing left to do, she went deep into the cave and lay down. She didn't know how long she slept, but when she woke the sun had dipped farther toward the west. Rand remained in the same place, dozing by the looks of things, but she didn't want to get too close, realizing that his inattention afforded her an opportunity.

She surveyed the area around her again. Purple lupine contrasted the yellow orange of the poppies to create a riot of color. Such a contrast to the ugliness of the situation she now faced. Other than a few scrubby bushes, the lupine and the curved branches of the prickly cactus, she had no other coverage on the hillside.

Rand's guns would find her long before she put enough distance between them to feel safe.

Renee turned to stare at the tangle of brush—the same direction the dog had taken earlier. Her heart slammed hard and perspiration beaded along her back as she considered the more densely populated side of the hill. Time was of the essence, for she knew that Rand could come alert at any moment and realize his mistake in not keeping a closer eye on her. From where he sat, the cave would cover her disappearance for a few minutes at most.

With a steadying breath, Renee ducked beneath the thick bush and followed a strange, low arch formed in the branches, as if wild animals knew of the tunnel of brush and traipsed through it often. She debated staying there, hidden from view, but just as quickly realized the folly of simply hiding when she had the chance to put more distance between herself and her captor. Branches snarled her hair and tore at her clothing as she pushed forward. She gasped at the pinches of pain from the poking branches and squinted her eyes to protect them against damage. When the sunlight brightened, she realized the branch cover was thinning. She paused for a moment at the end of the arching tunnel to collect herself for the run down the rest of the hillside and said a prayer, out of desperation more than faith, that she wouldn't feel a bullet in her back. That the Lord might, just this once, give her the desires of her heart.

Chapter 3

Tyler followed the hound from a distance. He had no doubt that the animal's instincts had picked up on something out of the ordinary, but he also wasn't fool enough to stick too close to the animal should the problem be bigger than one man could handle. He knew outlaws used the mountains and valleys as cover, places to elude capture, and he had no desire to walk into a hill of fire ants such as that. Shutting the mouths of anyone who would discover their whereabouts would be their first reaction, and the rocky ground and spring flowers would mark the site of his final resting place.

The dog halted and crouched. Tyler stopped as well, sighting up the hills on either side of him for any signs of wildlife, either the outlaw variety or the four-legged kind. Seeing nothing, he glanced back at the crouched dog just as the hound lunged forward and snapped his teeth. Tyler understood at once what the dog was doing. The long, limp body in the hound's jaws didn't surprise him at all. Long ago, he had learned of the animal's prowess at killing rattlers, though he'd also almost lost that battle a number of times.

When the dog spit out the body and gave it a sniff as if to assure himself of the serpent's death, he moved forward. At one point, he paused and glanced over his powerful shoulder, and Tyler knew the animal was making sure he was still keeping up. Interest piqued by the hound's behavior, Tyler picked up his pace to close the distance between them.

He skirted a large boulder, his eyes roaming the landscape, when he became aware that the hound had stopped. Tyler's eyes narrowed as he scanned up the hill. He immediately picked up on movement and raised his gun. His quick assessment determined the target to be a woman. He followed her path down the hill. The hound stood at his side, hackles raised, though he remained quiet.

Tyler flung himself behind the rock and readjusted his aim, his finger on the trigger, tense but loose. The woman kept coming. She lost her footing on the rocks and skidded, catching herself and pushing upward again. And that's when it came.

A shot rang out and the woman went down, whether from fright or because she was hit, Tyler didn't know. His gaze darted along the ridge of the hill, pinpointing a lone figure. He squinted down the barrel and returned fire, aiming low, his intention to maim rather than kill. The man jerked and disappeared, and Tyler set aside the gun and dashed up the hill to the fallen woman. She lay in a heap not two hundred feet away and began to move just as Tyler dropped down on his knees beside her. Seconds ticked by as he picked her up in his arms, knowing a bullet could crease him, or worse, at any given second.

He skidded to his knees a couple of feet from the boulder, the woman in his arms just beginning to thrash her protest. He released her and snapped up his Sharps, leveling it at the ridge again. He could see nothing. Satisfied, he scanned the woman from head to foot, searching for blood or signs of injury. "You hit?"

Her stormy eyes sparked of fear more than the bravado her crouched position and clawed hands threatened. Her chest heaved with the rapidness of her breaths. Tyler had seen that look more times than he wanted to count. It was the stance taken not by the hunters, but by the hunted.

❧

Unshed tears of panic filled Renee's eyes. She tried to slow the quickened slam of her heart and ease the rush of fear as the strange man picked up his gun and fired. He had asked her something, but the words were lost to her in the cloud of gun smoke and fear as she waited for the moment when he would turn the gun on her. Truth fought to insert itself in her mind. Why would a man shoot at her after carrying her down the hill and away from danger?

He straightened, glancing her way. "I'll take the fact you're still on your feet as a no."

Moisture bunched in her eyes, and she blinked to clear her vision.

He picked up the rifle and she flinched, wondering what such a long-reaching gun would do to her at close range. She stiffened and opened her mouth. He never raised the gun, instead holding it out to her.

"I'm going up the hill. Cover me."

She wanted to tell him not to, that Rand waited up there, but the words knotted in her throat. He moved out fast and scampered up the hill even faster. A dog ran at his side and some vague familiarity scratched at her mind as she watched the tattered ears flop with every step.

The man slipped on the steep slope but caught himself, his hand catching in a nearby cactus. She winced for him. When he righted himself, he kept low to the ground. Renee raised her gaze to the place where she'd emerged, afraid Rand would appear at any moment, his gun aimed at the stranger.

She stretched against the rock and lifted the weapon to her eye. She was no perfect shot, but maybe she could dampen Rand's desire to nail her rescuer. Grateful for the steadying effect the boulder offered to her shaking hands, she continued to follow the line of the man's advance up the hill. When he reached the ridge, he disappeared over the crest. She waited in silent expectation. Horror swelled as minutes passed and he didn't reappear. Only the fact that she heard no gunfire kept her from giving in to her nerves. If Marv had heard the two gunshots, he would rush to the cave. The stranger would be ambushed. Killed. She would be alone again.

She kept her eyes hard on the place where the blue of the sky met the curve of the hilltop. She debated making a run for it. Here she was, again, hiding from the Loust Gang when an opportunity to flee was open to her. But she couldn't leave the stranger. He had rescued her. He counted on her. Just as Pa had counted on her to stop her wild ways and become a lily-skinned do-gooder—a daughter he could be proud of.

Renee lifted her head and relaxed her hold on the rifle. If the stranger got caught, he at least had the hound. If she got caught, she had the gun. But she was more vulnerable to a gang of men than he was. They would hang him or shoot him dead, but they'd do far worse to her before finally putting a bullet into her heart. She couldn't think about it. Wouldn't. Instead she leaned forward against the rock. She would give him some time.

He would return.

He had to.

Chapter 4

Tyler scanned the area at the top of the hill from right to left. A small fire struggled for lack of new fuel. He shifted his gaze to the hound that stood a few feet off staring at the empty campsite, frozen by duty, muscles tensed to bring down any enemy sighted. Only a soft breeze ruffled his fur. Tyler knew the animal's senses were keen, probably much sharper than his own, so when the dog finally turned and trotted back down the hill, Tyler knew whoever had shot at the girl had disappeared.

He took his time gathering what little information he could from the signs left behind. Footprints circled the campfire. Boots. Narrow toes and deep heel marks gave clue to the man's weight. He found, too, the place behind the boulder where the man had sprawled, the outline of his body deeper in the middle where his belly lay. Tyler also made note of the depressions where the man propped himself before raising to the rock. On the right, the blur wasn't as deep and the indentation larger. Right handed. He had shifted weight to his left elbow to settle the gun or check the load.

Armed with enough information about the girl's enemy, Tyler tried to make sense of it all. Outlaws? He'd not heard of a group hiding out in these mountains since rumors of Big Nose George and Frank Cassidy. He raised his hat to wipe the sweat from his forehead as a sickening burn lanced his stomach. Could be nothing more than a lonesome band of drifters up to no good.

Tyler picked up a stick and used it to scatter the fire, waiting for the flames to dwindle, then kicked dirt on the remaining embers until the smoke dissipated. With one last sweeping glance, he took in the vacant area before starting down the hill. He wondered if the girl had taken off back toward her home, or if she'd waited for him as he'd suggested.

His foot skidded. His right hand skimmed the ground. Fire stabbed his already-raw palm as the rocks and gravel bit deep. He winced and pushed himself upright, swiping his hands against the rough wool of his trousers. His breath caught as the raw wound burned. He glanced behind him at the hills that gave way to the Big Horns as his palm cooled, then to the relatively flat land spread out west and north of where he stood. In the distance he could see the hound, already on its way back to its duties. He marveled at the animal's instinct and loyalty. With more cautious steps, Tyler continued down, pressed by the idea of the man returning to the camp, bent on vengeance.

As Tyler neared the bottom, the young woman's head popped up from behind the boulder, her eyes huge. She held out the gun to him, and he noticed the tremor in her hand and the vacant glaze of her eyes. She was going to cry by the looks of it.

Tyler took the gun and broke it to check the load and to avoid watching the girl's distress. Probably a reaction from what she'd just endured. He'd seen it all before, but it never ceased to churn nausea in his stomach.

"I'm Renee. Dover's my last name."

Her voice trembled, but a hard note showed the determination with which she tried to hold on to her composure. Tyler snapped the gun shut and shoved it into the scabbard. Now that he'd done his duty by her. . . What now? He had to return to his flock, and he doubted very seriously she would be placated at the idea of going with him.

Bracing his arm against the saddle, he leaned against Sassy's warm side and stroked her neck. "You live 'round here?"

"I did."

Something in her tone made him straighten and pay attention. She turned her back to him and walked a few paces, hugging herself. Her head dipped, and quiet sobs grated against his need to put distance between them.

He stared up at Sassy as if the horse could offer a solution to his dilemma then took up the reins and mounted. "Needing to get back, ma'am."

She spun with a gasp. "You can't leave me here."

Of course he couldn't. But neither could he bring himself to offer to take her along. Wasn't right for a single man to be gallivanting with a single woman. Especially a woman like her.

❧

Across the distance, Renee saw his gaze dip to his hands resting on the pommel. She didn't care how it might look; he couldn't leave her here with only her burning anger to keep her warm, no food and no horse. Renee didn't want to beg but she would if she had to. Surely he could see her problem and understand the precariousness of her position.

"I've got a flock of sheep to tend. You'll have to stay in camp as I move them." He lifted his gaze to hers. "With me. Alone."

Were his words a challenge? If the man rescued her, surely it meant he had a healthy sense of honor.

"Your. . .flock?"

"I'm a shepherd. A sheepherder."

She never would have guessed it by his looks, but then, what could one really discern by something so deceiving? Her pa had mentioned a rancher taking on sheep over by Sheridan. It had been a vague comment made many months ago, and she remembered little else other than her father's contempt for any man trying to run anything other than cattle.

Renee wished she could see the man's eyes, but they were shadowed by the brim of his hat. His angular jaw and the bristle of beard gave him a hard appearance, not unlike the men he'd just rescued her from. But a gentle face did not a gentleman make, although the reverse was also true. That much she knew.

Still, what choice did she have? She wished mightily that she had not surrendered the rifle to him—or that she still had her own weapon. The man swung the horse away. A chill swept over her at the thought of being alone. She stepped closer to him and reached a hand to stroke the horse's nose. The animal stretched out her neck and nibbled Renee's sleeve.

"I can walk," she offered, not wanting to give overtaxing the horse as more reason for him to leave her behind.

The man didn't argue and gave the horse a soft jab. Open mouthed at his quick dismissal of her, and his failure to even offer her a chance to ride, she could only watch as the horse put distance between them.

Chapter 5

Surely she didn't expect to be treated like a lady. What woman would wear pants and then expect preferential treatment? He still believed a woman should look like a woman and not gallivant around in trousers or buckskins or anything other than a dress. Besides, it was her idea to walk. Still, the dusty memory of gentlemanly ways and manners taught to him by his mama made him purse his lips and frown. He fought the silent battle for about half a mile, haunted by images of what the man might have done to her. The horrors she might have endured. It was the mental picture of his mother's disapproving frown that goaded him. With a sigh that was more a moan, he stopped the horse and slid to the ground. "You ride."

"I can walk."

A burst of quick, hot anger shot through him. "Get on the horse." Her horrified expression made him bite back the flash of his temper. He should know better than to speak so roughly. She was, no doubt, tired, and by the way she dressed, a bit willful. Commanding her to do anything would not hasten his return to his flock. "Please," he added. "That man can still follow our trail. It's best we move fast."

"Men."

He could only stare at her.

"There was four of them, maybe five. They'll kill us."

"Best get to it, then." He patted the saddle.

"Shouldn't you ride as well?"

Deciding to seize the moment, he heaved a sigh and toed his boot into the stirrup, sweeping back into the saddle. He kicked his foot out and reached out his hand to offer aid in her ascent. She grasped his hand and hauled herself up. For the first time he realized what a gift it was that she did not wear skirts. The saddle was crowded enough with her presence. When she placed a tentative hand at his waist as he wheeled the horse, the shift in wind direction brought a light, sweet scent to his nostrils. He frowned, the smell mocking somehow, evidence of what he'd missed by not settling down at a young age with a good girl like his mama had wanted.

Her slender hand gripped his shirt harder when he dug his heels hard into Sassy's sides and took them to a ground-eating gallop. When he figured they'd gone a mile, he stopped, wheeled the horse, and studied the terrain behind him. No signs of dust rising into the air to indicate pursuit. Behind him, Renee remained quiet, yet he was more aware of her presence than he wanted to be every time he caught that sniff of sweetness.

An hour had passed when he relieved Sassy of the wicked pace he'd set and they began the climb up the eastern slope of the mountain. Within an hour the sheep finally came into view. All seemed well, though the sheep had scattered a bit, even under Teddy's watchful eye. He stopped at a boulder. "This is where we stop. We've put a few miles between us. I'm moving the herd up this mountain. It'll take a couple of weeks, maybe more, depending." He did as much as he could to help her dismount smoothly, unsettled by the need to touch her hand, and the feel of her hand brushing his shoulder then gripping his forearms. "Stay here."

He could tell by the stiffening of her spine and her dark frown that she resented his command. Tough. He had a herd to move, and that she got herself into trouble wasn't his fault. He would protect her, even try to get her back home safe, but she'd have to wait. It might be a long wait, too, but if he told her that, she'd probably stomp her foot and pout.

He stole a look at her and wondered how she would feel about staying in a camp with nothing but sheep, nature, two dogs, and a horse to keep her company. No doubt she'd not like it too much. But he'd chosen his path for a reason, and he'd sooner stick to his reasons than leave the herd defenseless and let down Rich Morgan.

In the small camp, he let Sassy drink long from the bucket of water he'd fetched that morning. As the horse drank, he took down his tent. He rolled his coffee, sugar, flour, dry beans, and salt pork into two bundles and stuck them into his saddlebags. His pan, plate, fork, tin cup, and blanket were rolled up in the center of the tent, and the entire bundle covered with oilcloth. The familiarity of the work soothed him and made him forget the girl. At least until he glimpsed her movement along the perimeter of the campsite. When he motioned to her, she started his way. Teddy came to his side, as if sensing the tension. Tyler picked up the last thing left at the campsite, his Bible, and gripped it hard as he prepared for what he knew would be a verbal showdown.

❧

Renee could only think of home. Of Thomas. She wanted, no, *needed*, to go home. She set her jaw and moved forward, directly into the milling sheep that moved away as she drew near. The small dog beside Tyler came alert as she approached. Not unfriendly, but his tail didn't wag either, and she wondered if getting too close might be a bad idea.

"If you're heading higher into the mountains, then it's best to get me home now."

Tyler stared hard at her. "Should have stayed home then and not gotten caught by that band of brigands."

"It wasn't my fault, they—" Her oft-repeated phrase held no conviction. It *was* her fault. Adventure was something she always longed for and never failed to find. Her mouth turned sour at the realization that her wild imaginations had helped to lay Thomas out cold. He hadn't wanted to go, but she'd persisted and gotten her way. Again.

Renee closed her eyes and clenched her fists. Face to face with her hardheaded ways. Thomas's words of caution rang in her ears. He often pleaded on behalf of their silent pa on the matter of her willfulness. Words she often chafed at and always ignored.

Now, when tears of repentance should come, she felt nothing but a dusty, arid emptiness.

Chapter 6

Tyler's hand sweat against the cover of the Bible as he watched her, captivated by the shifting emotions that at one moment pinched Renee's features then shifted to stark vulnerability. She was a young woman. Alone. And he had been a man alone, too. For too long to deny the appeal of having another person to talk to and interact with, even if only for a few days.

"I can't take you home. Got to stay with the woolies and get them to higher pasture before the hot temperatures get on us."

She blinked at him like a newborn lamb testing the light of the world for the first time.

"You mean you're staying *here*?"

He allowed himself a grin. "Well, no. Not *here*." Her pique was evident in her stormy gaze. He smoothed his hand down Sassy's side and opened the saddlebag to slide the Bible into its little niche. "As I said, I need to move them higher." There was no choice in the matter. Not for him. Not now. He'd already crossed the narrow bend of the path that was one of the most dangerous. If he left the sheep now and they wandered back to the familiar, he'd lose some over that ledge, and he held a stake in this herd. When Rich Morgan sent out his camptender to deliver supplies to Tyler in another couple of months, he could send her back then. Let Rich deal with figuring out how to get the girl home.

"I can't just stay out here. With you—"

He jerked her direction, working to bite back hard words. She would not understand the isolation he was forced to endure. And why would she? She was a young woman wanting to go home after being held by a band of men probably not fit for human society. "That's the way it's got to be, Renee." He tripped over her name. Saying it seemed so strange. A woman, here, in his camp. An event beyond his comprehension.

"If I leave the sheep alone, they will scatter and die. I watch them for a man by the name of Rich Morgan, and I've a stake in the herd, too." He gathered Sassy's reins and led the horse to the boulder. "Need help getting on? Four miles is a long way on foot." She didn't look at all happy with him. She stared around as if trying to figure out the direction she should go. Wide eyes met his, and he felt compelled to apologize. "As soon as someone comes, I'll send you back. But not until then."

She brightened, and he knew she misunderstood the promise inherent in his words.

"That could be two months. Maybe more."

Her expression crumbled. "You can't make me go with you."

"No. Frankly, it's easier if I don't have you with me."

"Then I'll make my own way."

"And risk becoming prey to the mountain lions or those men all over again? Who's to say they aren't looking for you right now?"

Her eyes settled on him. He could see the flecks of gold in the smoky gray expression. Strange eyes. Yet beautiful. He shook himself. No use letting his mind go soft just because he had a woman in camp. He stabbed the pointed toe of his boot into the stirrup and mounted up. When he glanced over his shoulder and raised an eyebrow, she remained rooted to the spot.

"You left them to come get me."

"No. I left them to follow the mutt. You just happened to be part of the bargain." No need to tell her she was only partly right. Following the dog usually meant finding evidence of coyotes or other predators who might hunt the sheep. When the dog had led him so far out, sheer curiosity had made him follow. He'd begun to wonder if the dog was getting too old for the work when he'd discovered Renee. How he'd wished then he'd yielded to his instinct to break off trailing the mutt. No use fretting on it now, though. What was done was done.

Tyler urged Sassy along, throwing over his shoulder, "Go or stay, it makes no difference to me."

❧

How dare he leave her standing there. He gave a long whistle and the little dog came to life. It skittered out in as wide an arc as possible around the edges of the flock. Renee's anger drained as she watched in fascination how the dog prompted the sheep to their feet and into a rough column. A few times the dog disappeared, only to reappear with two or three sheep moving reluctantly along in front of him. With each passing minute, the man rode farther and farther away and the column of sheep grew longer, until the last one straggled behind the others baaing in protest and running to keep up. The dog trotted up beside the long column, tongue lolling from exertion, though its eyes never strayed from the sheep.

For the first time, Renee realized she had no idea what the man's name was. He looked tough. His movements were easy. She scanned almost straight up the mountainside and then back to the east at the path from which they entered the grassy meadow. With a sinking heart, she realized she had no way of knowing in which direction her home lay.

A rattle in the bushes to her right jerked her attention that direction. Cold fear coursed through her veins and she froze, heart thundering. Snakes would be awake with the warm weather. Or cats. Even bears might be ambling around.

Without pausing to think, she dashed off after the band of sheep, running for all she was worth along the edge of the herd, fanning them out off to the side and into the undergrowth. "Help! Please stop."

She sensed whatever lurked behind her moving closer. She imagined that at any moment she'd feel pressure on her back as whatever it was pounced and shoved her to the ground. Her foot caught and she stumbled and cried out.

Chapter 7

Tyler heard the cry for help and pulled Sassy around. He scanned the column of sheep and saw where they had plunged off the path and into the rocky ground and dense underbrush. What now? It would take him, Sassy, and Teddy awhile to get the sheep rounded up and back on the trail. With a grunt of displeasure, he backtracked along the column and whistled for Teddy to wait for commands. No use having the dog try to control things until he knew the reason for the girl's distress.

Alert for movement or threat, he frowned when he heard nothing out of the ordinary and saw nothing move. He pulled the Sharps from the scabbard just in case. About two-thirds back along the column of sheep, he spotted the heap on the ground, the elusive hound lying a few feet away, obviously guarding the woman. Apparently the mutt had centered his affections on Renee. His heart rate picked up as he nudged Sassy to a trot, fear rising that Renee had hurt herself. As he drew closer, he heard her sobs. Gut-wrenching cries that scared him with their fierceness. He shot one more distance-eating glance around and slipped the gun into the scabbard. He slid to the ground and knelt beside her, aware that the mutt also chose that moment to disappear into the underbrush. When Tyler touched Renee's shoulder, she didn't move.

"Are you hurt?"

She shook her head, her cries softening.

"Renee?" He wanted to be angry. All he needed now was a hysterical woman to slow down his progress.

"I thought—" He helped her to her feet, and she brushed at her cheeks. Her knees showed grass stains; her hands were embedded with small gravel. She brushed them together.

"You thought you heard an animal."

She nodded, and the meek vulnerability in her gaze twisted him up inside. He'd seen that look before. That mix of fear and hope. Pleading.

He clicked his tongue and Sassy came up beside them. Without a word, he cupped his hands. Renee needed no further invitation. She settled back as he swung into the saddle. He did his best to shut his mind to her presence, but then his shirt tugged as she grabbed a fistful of the material to hold on to. Tyler swallowed hard and nudged Sassy toward the column of sheep. He whistled and saw Teddy swing into action at the farthest edge of the herd. He shifted Sassy's position to the other side of the herd and began working the sheep forward from the rear of the herd as the dog darted into the underbrush to draw out the sheep Renee's screech and flight had scattered.

Tyler fought hard with every clop of Sassy's hooves to draw his mind back to the sheep and away from the troublesome woman at his back. He scanned for predators and encouraged Teddy to keep the line moving forward. Time passed in a slow wave of receding heat as the sun passed its zenith and began to sink over the tip of the mountain, though he knew daylight would still exist for several hours.

Only when the tightness of his shirt loosened somewhat did he dare hope Renee might be relaxing into the rhythm of Sassy's gait. But, minutes later, the soft, sagging pressure against his back told another story.

He drew rein and shifted in the saddle. "Renee?" Immediately the pressure of her against his shirt released. He couldn't help but smile. "If you fall asleep, you risk falling off."

"I wasn't asleep," she assured, yet the rusty sound of her voice gave her away.

" 'Course not."

"Can I walk?"

Not waiting for an answer, she put her hands on his shoulders and shifted her right leg over. Without a word Tyler turned to brace her and held onto her forearm as she slipped to the ground. "Stay close so you don't spook the sheep again." He watched her begin the trek, taking a place beside Sassy. The nearby sheep shied from her, already having had one experience with her screeches, but he spoke to them, telling them over and over it was okay. Finally, and with no little embarrassment, he used the method that worked best to soothe the animals. The first few notes of song were rough with the nerves he felt singing in front of her. He could feel her eyes on him, but he kept his face forward, leading the herd along like the fabled pied piper.

As the words of the song slipped out, he imagined her exhaustion must match his own. Events of the day spiraled into a tight knot of weariness between his shoulder blades. And still there would be more work to do once they arrived at the new campsite. He finished the song and called out. "We're two miles out."

No answer. He breathed deeply of the cool air and started another song.

Another mile passed before he looked back. Renee still walked, though her stride had diminished to a shuffling stagger toward the back of the long line of sheep. This girl was going to make him crazy. He whistled to Teddy to keep the line going and stopped Sassy to wait for her to catch up. She seemed not to notice his presence and gasped when he planted himself on the ground in front of her.

"You ride," he said, his voice a growl. "I'll walk."

To his surprise she didn't fight him or protest. She leaned heavily on him as he caught her booted foot and raised her up.

"Another mile at most."

Her shallow nod acknowledged his words.

"It won't take me long to set up camp. Then you can sleep."

"Thank you."

At first he thought he'd heard wrong, her voice so low, the words little more than a whisper. "You're welcome, though I'm not sure how thankful you'll be come tomorrow."

If she wondered what he meant, she showed no curiosity. Tyler wondered how long it would take her to come to despise the solitude and crude life of a shepherd. And even as Sassy carried her that last mile to the next camp, he questioned his decision to continue the ride to summer camp with Renee in tow.

Chapter 8

Fear tugged Renee toward wakefulness. Thomas's face flared in her mind; then a gunshot rang out and he disappeared. Her breath came hard and fast, her heart beat the thunder of a thousand wild mustangs. She cradled her face and pulled air into her starved lungs. Like someone sawing through ropes with a dull blade, the dream released her one cord at a time. Despite the open sky above her and the light blanket, she expected the face of her captors to appear over her. Taunting. Daring. Thomas, too, his face a mask of pain, accused her.

She became aware, first, of the baaing of sheep. Of the snap and crackle of a fire. Then of the man who had rescued her.

He sat on the ground two hundred feet in front of her, his back to her. An animal lay in the thick grass beside him. She rubbed at her eyes. His presence cut the last strand of her disorientation. The animal beside him baaed again. She shuffled to her knees, chilled by the sweep of cold against her blanket-warmed skin. He had settled her on the ground and given her a blanket in the early evening of the previous day. She'd slept long and sound, until those last, vivid stabs of memory.

What would she do here? What was there for her? If this man wouldn't take her home, she'd have to find a way to go by herself. But the thoughts filtered away as the sheep's legs stiffened and the animal's neck extended, a powerful *baa* pulsing from its throat. She sat up taller and could see that the man stroked the side of the animal, speaking in low tones, though she could not understand what he said. She watched as he moved, hands gentle on the animal's side.

Mesmerized, she stood to her feet and moved closer. He worked over the animal, sending her a startled glance when he caught sight of her. The animal lay on its side, straining, and Renee realized the sheep was about to give birth. The man motioned her away with a violent slicing of his hand. His dark frown discouraged her even further. She retreated back to the blanket and sat.

He still had his back to her, yet she could see that the birth must be difficult, for the man assisted the animal diligently. The bunching of his shoulders and movement of his head, and above all else, the gentle tone of his voice continued as the long minutes stretched into a ball of tedium. She shifted her position a dozen times, wondering how he could sit so still and be so patient when every nerve in her body pulled taut. Eventually the sheep stretched its neck and pulled almost to a stand. The man sat back on his heels.

When he turned and caught her gaze, he put a finger to his lips. But she glimpsed the burst of a smile as he again faced the new mother and baby. He ran his hand over the newborn animal's face until it wheezed and air filled its lungs. A black lamb. Wet. He lifted it and brought it to the mother, and she began to nuzzle the baby. Renee couldn't take her eyes from the dark form struggling then resigning itself to its mother's nuzzles and licks.

"It's her first lamb." He did not look at her, his eyes on the mother as she cleaned her baby. Something sad slashed across his features. Her heart tugged at the wistfulness in his expression. The sight of mother and child must remind him of family. Way up here, in the mountains, she could see where he would get lonely, perhaps for his own home, wife, and child, for what did she know of him?

"What is your name?"

His eyes flicked over her, euphoria over the lamb's birth morphing into something piercing. "Tyler Sperry."

His gaze held her in its grip until she blinked, confused over the unexpected hostility in the thrust of his jaw and the coldness of his eyes. Before she could respond, or even begin to grasp the reason, he pivoted and waded into the herd. Renee stared after him, feeling more alone than she had in a long time. Weighted by the grief of Thomas's death and her guilt, she curled into a knot by the fire. Hunger bit at the pit of her stomach, but the ache of her loss, of her inability to return home, eclipsed everything else.

Tyler worked among the sheep for hours, checking their feet, patting them as if they were his friends. The sight of him coddling the animals angered her. She needed to go home. How could he worry over such dumb, ugly animals when her need was obviously greater?

The anger burned through her reserve and she burst to her feet, the pinch of placid muscles fueling her anger as she walked about, working the kinks from her back, her gift from sleeping on the hard ground. Her stomach growled, and she railed at Tyler Sperry in her mind for not having at least the sense and hospitality to offer her something.

He continued his work, oblivious to her raging temper and, for the lack of someone on whom to vent her rage, it bled from her in a thin stream that left her exhausted and empty. Not knowing what else to do, Renee plopped down on the ground and hugged her legs to her chest. She buried her head in her arms and must have fallen asleep, for when she lifted her head, she not only felt the heat from a fire but smelled food.

Tyler nudged at something in the skillet then nestled the pan back into the hot coals. He rose to his full height and turned to the crude tent, snatching up a hammer. "Watch the griddle cake while I finish up here. There are a few pieces of salt pork to fry when it's done."

Renee frowned hard. "I'm not a good cook," she bit out. Mama had tried, but nothing Renee put her hand to in the kitchen ever seemed to match what her mother could produce. Or maybe the memories of her mother's cooking were so distorted through years of missing her that she couldn't discern reality from imagination.

"I'm sure you'll do fine."

Heat rose to her cheeks. "Am I to be some sort of slave, then?"

Tyler stood still, his back to her. Her heart slammed hard as she waited for his response. She half expected him to hurl the hammer, but he didn't.

"A little help is always appreciated, Renee."

His soft words flushed her with shame, and her throat ached. "I want to go home."

His head sagged between his shoulders, and she heard his long sigh. "A shepherd doesn't just leave his flock."

She understood. Deep down inside she knew she was being unfair to ask this of him again. "How can I stay here with you? Unchaperoned? It's not. . .right."

"It's not the best situation."

Somehow his concession didn't comfort her. He moved then, toward the tent spread out on the ground and began pounding the stakes. Renee rose to her knees and used a cloth to pull the griddle from the fire. A finger to the top of the griddle cake seemed to indicate it was done. With a fork, she pushed it onto a tin plate. She found the slab of salt pork and sliced some into the griddle, nestling the pan into the hot coals. Settling back on her heels, absorbing the warmth of the fire, she looked up. Tyler's gaze was on her. A small smile curved his lips.

Chapter 9

It was the time of day that Tyler usually dreaded, when the loneliness of his occupation ate at him most. Renee's presence seemed odd, yet exciting. What he hadn't realized was that being a sheepherder had chiseled away at his ability to carry a conversation. Or maybe he was just too afraid he'd give himself away. Even mentioning his name had rattled him. He'd feared it would bring instant recognition and fear, something he would expect even if he hated the effect. Regret had become a powerful and very real force in his life.

Tyler stretched out on the ground across from where Renee sat by a pool of water a short distance from the camp. He had debated with himself about interrupting her solitude. He had questions. She had all the answers.

"Maybe we should talk some more."

He cringed at the way it sounded. Desperate. Awkward. She didn't react, and if his presence irritated her, she didn't show it. Her eyes remained riveted on the smooth surface of the water. Birds flew overhead, chattering and challenging each other. The sheep baaed in the background. Pastoral. Very Psalm 23, Tyler reflected, except for the presence of the woman and the problems it created.

"How did you manage to be taken captive?"

She bowed her head and squeezed her eyes shut.

He regretted the question. Her distress could only mean. . . "Did they hurt you, Renee?"

She sobbed. Once. And then shook her head. "No. Not really. They. . ."

He waited. Knowing something more, darker, must be shadowing her memories.

"It's my fault." Her statement drowned beneath a bank of sobs that shook her shoulders and seemed to rip every bit of strength from her.

He hated the helpless feeling her tears evoked. He glanced at the sheep, incredulous at his earlier vision of pastoral peace. Her tears tinged everything with gray. He was sorry he had rescued her.

No.

That wasn't quite right.

He was sorry he couldn't get her home.

Would they come looking for her? He knew little of the circumstances that placed her with those men. If they were holding her for ransom, they would come after her. If she were a hostage, they might let her go, unless they feared her being able to describe them. In that case they would either run to avoid capture or try to find her trail.

"They shot my brother." Her breaths came hard. He digested the words, fresh anger consuming him. "I wanted him to come with me to find the gang."

"A gang?"

She nodded and brushed her hand across her eyes. "I thought it would be fun. Thomas didn't want to go."

"You thought it would be *fun*?"

"I didn't expect to really find them."

He couldn't believe his ears. This young woman went after a gang because she thought it would be fun? That she'd been foolish to set off after a gang, to even desire such a reckless thing, spotlighted her immaturity. He judged her to be about eighteen. Probably spoiled by parents who demanded nothing of her. If she expected words of consolation, he had none to offer.

"It was a foolish thing you did."

Her eyes flashed to his, angry. "You don't think I know that?"

"Having a person's blood on your hands is a terrible thing."

She swept to her feet, spun, and ran away, scattering the sheep in her path. He let her go. So much for a conversation. But her revelations withered his estimation of her. Still, he'd had his say. He would not coddle whatever insecurity made her go off on such a foolhardy quest and drag her brother along, only to get him killed.

A lamb toddled his way, pausing, its mama close by but its curiosity leading the baby to forget her for a moment. Tyler wondered how many lambs he had rescued in the last three years, their desire to explore their world leading them down a narrow path that separated them and sent their mothers into a frenzy. At least they were innocent of their wrongdoing. Unlike Renee. Unlike himself.

Chapter 10

She'd wanted her freedom, curling her lip at the idea of being a wife and mother, of being tied to a ranch and all the hard work when there was a world to see. Places to go and things to do that had nothing to do with horses or saddles, cows or fencing. Thomas would have been alive if not for her. Tyler was right to call her a fool, though it hurt her pride to admit it.

From a safe distance, she watched as he hauled a lamb onto his shoulders and walked it back through the herd to its mother. He knelt by the little one, stroking its head and ears. He went through the flock, touching a random sheep, petting a skittish lamb, or checking the feet of some animal, for what, she didn't know.

He didn't scold them, but his low tones were soothing and gentle even if she couldn't make out his words. He was a strange man. Content to lead a flock of sheep in the middle of nowhere with nothing more than a dog and a tent.

At some point, the wind carried a low humming to her. Tyler was a distant speck, at the lower half of the herd scattered along the meadow. The sheep seemed to enjoy his attention. She tilted her head to catch the source of the humming. A bee? But it was too indistinct beneath the baaing of the sheep and the twitter of birds.

When Tyler had gone through the herd he returned to his spot next to the cook fire and pulled out a small book. Relieved he wouldn't ply her for more answers or want to talk, she studied him from the distance that separated them, realizing anew she knew nothing of this man who refused to take her back home, or even to a nearby ranch. Instead she was at his mercy. Should she try to leave, she would not get far, not in the rocky terrain, steep slopes, and narrow trails. And the dog, that scarred hound with the tattered ears. . .she shuddered. If Tyler was intent on holding her captive and discovered her missing, he might set the dog on her. She squeezed her head between her hands, desperate with the sudden worry of it all.

"Renee?"

She raised her head, wary. Tyler lifted the little book and gestured to a spot on the ground near him, posing an unspoken question. She shook her head and glanced away, more than content to maintain her distance, even as her hands slid up to rub her arms. The temperature had dropped sharply. The warm fire beckoned her closer.

Her legs were stiff from sitting so long on the large rock. Chilly air bit through her thin blouse, and she ventured a tentative step toward camp. The collie caught her movement and lifted his head. She expected to see his teeth bare, but his intelligent eyes were merely alert, aware for movements out of the ordinary.

Tyler glanced up and motioned her closer again. "You must be cold." With a confidence she didn't feel, she took the next steps.

"It's too cold to wander far from the fire. Tomorrow will be warmer," he said as she drew into the circle of light. He smiled into the sky as if he understood something she didn't. "I can feel it."

"Maybe it's because you're so close to the fire."

Tyler laughed, and the sound reminded her of Thomas. Laughter softened his face and erased the severe expression she'd grown accustomed to seeing. He always seemed so intent on his sheep and his "duty" that her well-being appeared nothing more than a second thought. She winced inwardly. And why shouldn't it? A sharp wind beat around the hill and pierced through her thin shirt. She shivered.

"No use trying to stay warm out there. Come closer. I'll get a blanket."

She obeyed without protest and angled her body toward the flames. She felt the moment when he lowered the blanket to her shoulders, its weight a welcome shield. In short order he had a pot of something bubbling over the fire. Between the smell wafting from the pot and the warmth, the tightness in her stomach eased. Food sounded good.

A movement to her left caught her eye, and she jumped and turned. Her heart slammed at the shadowy dark figure now crouched next to her before she realized it was Tyler's dog.

"Come here, Teddy," Tyler called. "You know it's supper time, huh?"

Tyler rustled in a sack and threw something. The dog caught whatever it was in his mouth, gave two chomps, and swallowed. She heard Tyler's low chuckle and another piece of food flew through the air.

"Where's the other dog?"

Tyler glanced her way and threw another morsel to Teddy. "You mean the mutt? He kills his own dinner usually. You won't see him much unless there's some trouble he can't handle."

"I saw him on the hill before you got there." She fingered the blanket around her shoulders. "The trail I took down the hillside was the same one he had taken. It was like he was showing me the way."

"He's a good dog. His howls usually mean he's onto a coyote or something, but that day. . ." He shrugged.

"Do you think they'll try to find me?"

Tyler squinted at her, and a hard glint flashed in his eyes. "If they're outlaws."

"I saw the wanted poster on them."

Tyler's nostrils flared. "Outlaws don't like people to interrupt their plans or steal from them, and that's exactly what they would think. But I doubt they'd ever find us. The Big Horns are vast."

Something he had said niggled at her, but she couldn't quite bring it into focus as the fire worked its magic and made her drowsy. She would remember tomorrow.

❧

Tyler didn't sleep well that night, his mind occupied with the dilemma Renee's presence posed and the impact it would have on the safety of the sheep. The woolies seemed more restless than normal, some lying down but most on their feet. One in particular, his boundary walker, found a crevice between two rocks that led to a rough patch with long, dry grass. It took him a while to encourage the ewe back into the pasture. For twenty minutes he worked in the dark to block the crevice by stacking stones.

He meandered back through the herd, noticing that more were on their feet, as if sensing the ewe's escape and fearing they would somehow be in trouble as well. As he strolled in their midst, he hummed, the soft strain of music his gift to them. Tyler stroked the faces of a little lamb and its mother. Their trust in him satisfied on a level he had never experienced.

Not that he'd ever been a man worthy of trust before becoming a sheepherder. What Renee did not know of his past she would be better off not knowing. The girl seemed troubled enough, as well she should be. Still, the death of her brother must weigh heavily on her. He hoped the event would rattle some of her wayward tendencies—setting off after a band of outlaws for fun? He shook his head in the dark, disgusted with her all over again.

As the sky lightened, the sheep began to rise for the morning graze. Teddy went to work at Tyler's command, walking passively along the perimeter of the sheep, ever watchful for those that might stray too far.

Lambs nursed from their mothers as they cropped the lush green grasses of the flat, wide section. His throat grew thick at the idyllic scene, and he wished he could absorb the peace and imprint it on his soul. What he would give to remove the blight his own reckless youth had left. Tyler retreated to the camp and found Renee still asleep. He recognized himself in her. That burning, youthful need for something more. A desire to be different, though unsure of what that difference entailed or what it would cost. Adventure replacing caution and common sense.

He shuffled to the blanket spread on the ground and rolled himself into its warmth. Tyler rummaged in the sack he used as a pillow and pulled out the Bible. He wondered if God could redeem a robbing murderer.

Chapter 11

Renee's eyes snapped open. She became instantly aware of the fire and the man encouraging it to flame higher. The sun was just skimming the horizon, and the sheep baaed as they moved about the grassy area. The picture brought back her mother's stories of serenity and peace. Scriptures she often quoted from the Bible about men in trouble and women who went beyond the edges of what was considered proper. All directed at her. To tame the wild streak that even then her mother had sensed.

She pulled onto an elbow and ran her free hand through the tangles of her hair. She needed to wash it and considered how good it would feel to sink into a tub of hot water.

Tyler poked at something in a pan and put it over the fire. "Got some time before food will be fit for eating."

She nodded and stretched.

"There's a pool of water down a ways if you've a need."

Renee moved in the direction he'd pointed, following the stream as it meandered away from where the sheep grazed. It widened at a point about eight hundred feet away, emptying into a pool deep enough to cover her knees. She gasped at the icy cold clearness and cast an eye back toward camp. She could see the tendrils of smoke rising from the fire but nothing else. If it got hot, the pool would be a refreshing place to bathe and scrub her hair. She raised her hand to scratch at a spot over her ear, chagrined that the idea of washing her hair seemed to make all the itches pop out along her scalp.

With a sigh she lowered herself to the ground, grateful for the material of the trousers covering her knees to protect them from the rough rocks scattered along the shore of the pool. She leaned forward as much as she dared. Her hair swirled in the water but not enough to get wet. With a huff she flipped her hair back and formed a quick twist to secure it with the few hairpins that hadn't slipped out during her captivity and rescue. She would have no choice but to wait until Tyler was out of camp; then she could wade into the pool. Soap, too, would be nice.

When she returned and sat at the fire, Tyler handed a plate over to her. She felt his eyes scan her. "Pool's a good place. Get yourself a cake of soap from my saddlebags. I'll take the sheep down to water after we eat."

She watched as he returned to his spot across from her and sat on his heels, perfectly balancing his weight and the plate of food. He bowed his head for a moment, and she looked down at the food on her own plate wondering what he saw that was so interesting. She scooped up some bacon and chewed, enjoying the rich saltiness of the meat. She'd have to say that the man was a much better cook than she'd ever be. Bacon had been something their cook despaired of having her master.

The thoughts of home, of her father and Thomas, clenched her stomach hard. If Knot Dover didn't love his daughter before he would never love her now that Thomas was dead. She lowered her head, the plate growing blurry as tears collected in her eyes.

She pictured her father's grief-stricken expression, the same one he'd worn since the death of his wife, except this time it would be worn because of Thomas. She wondered if he even missed her. A little voice tried to pry reason into that thought. Her father hadn't always been so remote. She still remembered his tenderness toward her mother. That first time she had caught her father hugging her mother and had laughed out loud at the delight of seeing those two shapes merge to form one big lump. It brought a smile to her lips even as tears squeezed through her eyelids.

Tyler cleared his throat, and she raised her head. He stood a few feet from her, his hands working around the edge of his hat. His downcast eyes showed his awkwardness. "I'll be taking those sheep downstream. Be gone for quite a while." He held out his hand, and a cake of soap sat on his wide palm, a gray-white lump against the roughness of his calloused skin.

She swallowed hard and accepted the gift.

"You can clean up the plates."

She could only nod her head, the urge to protest against the work far away. She didn't know how he cleaned up in a camp, but she'd figure something out.

Tyler said not another word but turned and gathered the reins of his horse, mounting up and whistling for Teddy as he dug his heels into Sassy's sides.

❧

Tyler adjusted his position in the saddle, casting another glance over at the huddled form of Renee Dover. Her rich, thick hair. Her clear skin and smoky eyes. He nudged the horse hard with his spurs. Rich would send a camptender in six more weeks. He would be at summer camp in the mountaintop in two. He'd already given thought to having the man stay with the sheep while he returned Renee home. Six weeks was a long time for the girl to wait. He toyed again with the idea of letting her take Sassy down but knew she would never be able to find the way. He groaned. *Dover, Dover. . .* The name was not familiar, but that didn't mean anything. More people were coming out to the Big Horns every year.

The sheep were lying down. Following a hand signal, Teddy began a slow and wide circle behind the animals. In response to the dog, the sheep rose to their feet and headed off toward the rocky pool a mile downstream. Besides having to bring in Punky, the wayward ewe who always led a few in rebellion down impossibly narrow paths or out onto ledges, all went smoothly. As the sheep drank of the cool water, lambs, finished with their breakfast milk, began to frolic and play, running and stopping, legs splayed, before they bounced into the air and repeated the actions.

He used the hours with the sheep as a means to give Renee space. As he checked over several of the ever-growing lambs, the sheep spread out more. He rescued a playful lamb that got stuck in brambles. Tyler carried the injured lamb on his shoulders back to the hill that looked out over the stream and sheep. Teddy sniffed at the lamb as Tyler swiped blood from the lamb's cuts and applied a thick salve. When the lamb finally stood on his own legs, the dog nosed the baby and it began bounding around, eventually heading toward a clump of ewes.

Several ewes kicked out at the suckling lamb, refusing to accept its presence as their responsibility. The moment the baby found its mother, the ewe chewed its cud placidly and the baby nursed, little tail flapping in joy. Tyler assessed the two ewes yet to give birth. Most lambs were already thirty days old.

With the herd settled for a while and his long, sleepless night wearing heavily, Tyler stripped off his hat and lay back on the grass, eyes closed against the warm sunshine. His last conscious thought was of glossy dark hair and gray eyes pooling with tears, and of his fingers reaching to wipe those tears from her soft cheek.

Chapter 12

Touching the cool water froze Renee enough to make her scalp prickle. Undeterred, she plunged into the refreshing liquid. The icy cold snapped up her spine. She gasped and splashed, laughing at the spectacle she was making for any animals watching her antics. The water streamed in rivulets down her neck and back and over her shoulders. With brisk strokes she worked the soap over her hair and body, invigorated by the idea of being clean again. Loosening the trail dust with warm bathwater always cheered her back home, though Thomas usually taunted her to "hurry it up" through the curtain that surrounded the wash tub.

The memory of her brother evaporated her joy. She clutched her forearms and pressed her lips together to keep from crying out. *Oh Thomas.* She dipped her head beneath the water and for a fleeting moment she stayed there, tempted as she'd never been before to inhale and let the water fill her nostrils and lungs. No one would miss her or be disappointed.

A muffled sound caught her attention and brought an immediate picture of a mountain cat to mind. She'd seen only one, and at a distance, but despite the animal's small size, she had also seen the speed with which it moved and the ferocity with which it killed. She jolted upright, squeezing the water from her eyes and pushing her hair back to clear her vision. A bark sounded, and she released a hard sigh. The dog stood in front of her. The mutt with the tattered ears and strange eyes. Pressing a hand over her racing heart, she sank to her knees in the water, too weak to stand.

The dog barked again. Sharp, hard yaps that seemed to send a message she didn't understand.

Her flesh crawled. Had the dog gone mad? His amber eyes appeared sure and steady in their intensity. The dog barked once more. Renee pulled in a steadying breath and swiped the water from her hair then tied it in a loose knot. As she approached the edge of the pool, the dog ran off a few yards, turned around, and sat back down to maintain his watch. But what was he watching for?

She dressed in her still-damp clothes, glad she'd washed them first. Chilled to the bone and worried about the dog's strange behavior, she moved. Tyler would know what the dog was trying to communicate, and she suddenly wished she were not alone.

Another bark from the mutt and the animal ran off another few feet, looking over his shoulder as if begging her to follow. "I'm coming, I'm coming."

Her ankle turned on a rock, and she scraped her arm against the surface before she caught herself. As she got to her feet, the dog barked at her again then took off and plunged into the brushy, thorny vegetation.

❧

Tyler awoke with a jolt. The mutt sat down across from him, panting heavily, his yellow eyes alert and staring. Tyler touched his hand to the ground and came to his feet in a smooth motion. He saw that the horse's ears were pricked and she stared hard in the opposite direction.

He yanked the rifle from the scabbard. "Easy, girl." He stroked the horse's neck and mounted, his eyes on the mutt. He gave a sharp, long whistle and Teddy circled off to his left, telegraphing to the sheep that it was time to move. At times like this Tyler wished he had more than one dog to handle the herd, for he knew the mutt's sudden appearance could only mean the sheep were in danger.

The tatter-eared dog leaped through the air at a run, diving into the underbrush. Tyler could trace his path by the occasional fluttering of the low branches and thick vegetation.

And that's when he heard it. The scream. Tyler gripped the rifle as his eyes roved the rocky outcroppings to his right, the direction in which Sassy was looking. The mountain rose almost perpendicular, a climb he knew he would have to make over the next couple of days. The mountain lion would be up there, more than likely, eyeing the sheep and sizing up the kill. Sassy's ears swiveled back and forth. Steady as the horse was in a crisis situation, the one thing Sassy had no fondness for was mountain cats. He tightened his hold on the reins and patted the horse's neck.

He glanced at the sheep. Teddy knew his stuff and worked the sheep with a calm confidence that reassured rather than frightened. Those ewes that had wandered away from the main body of the flock were loping out of the woods and over toward the majority.

Tyler noted two things—the oddity of a cat prowling at this time of day and the desperation that must be driving it to do so. Neither bode well for the flock. The mutt would instinctively go after the cat—had, in fact, probably sensed it long ago. Tyler made his decision and raised his head to release a warbling whistle directing Teddy to move the sheep forward. Then he nudged Sassy forward. They skimmed the far edge of the flock at a fast walk as Teddy began pushing the sheep away from the water back to the bedding ground of the previous night. A mile away. But they could spread out there, and there was a rise where he could see for miles in every direction.

Renee!

Her name struck fear. There would be no way to alert her. Nothing he could do but hope she at least knew the danger when she heard the cat's distinctive scream.

If she stayed near the fire she would be fine. He spurred Sassy into a canter.

Punky tried to push away with about ten other sheep, but Tyler cut them off and got them turned while Teddy worked to keep the other side of the column in line. Tyler kept a sharp eye on the rocky ledge overhead as the sheep moved, expecting at any moment to see a cat leap down onto the helpless back of some woolie.

Short, sharp barks rang out, followed by another low scream from the cat. Tyler brought his rifle up and sighted down the barrel. Nothing moved on the ledge. He heard the mutt growl low in his throat. Tyler's heartbeat skittered upward. Every muscle in his body tightened, and he longed for the sight of the cat, knowing how vulnerable his herd would become should the mutt get killed. He'd lasted through some tough battles with rattlers and coyotes, but a cat...

A sickening mewling, gravelly with menace, rose and fell as the two animals squared off. The dog's barks, consistent and fierce, were sharp and harsh, not as high pitched as usual.

Tyler measured his options. The mountain lion would do its best to scare off his unexpected opponent with a series of snarls. The mutt, though, would be no match for a cat. Tyler had but minutes to make his move.

He traced the path up to the ledge with his eyes. Scaling it would take too long. He lowered the rifle and stabbed glances at the rocks surrounding him. Boulders lay along the path of the stream. With a modicum of strides he pushed Sassy toward the farthest boulder, dismounted, and skipped to the lowest of a trio of boulders. Using them as stepping-stones, he clawed and pulled until he stood on the biggest. He raised his gaze as he settled the rifle, gratified to have a clear view of the ongoing battle. But his new dilemma slammed into his gut as he viewed the scene. The cat had the higher elevation to his advantage, with the dog holding lower ground, legs braced wide, showing his teeth, eyes locked with those of the cat's.

Tyler raised the gun to his shoulder and took careful aim. To miss would mean pandemonium. His finger tensed on the trigger just as the cat sprung toward the dog. Tyler lowered the gun to gauge the fight and the dog's chances, helpless to do anything now that the two animals were engaged. He swallowed hard against the burn in his throat.

He had always known the mutt to be a sweet animal, though he'd seen it fight, coming alive with the rage and instincts of his ancestors. The mutt enjoyed his job as guardian of the herd. Rich Morgan had trained the animal well.

The cat rolled the dog to its back and took a swipe at its neck only to roar with anger and draw back when the dog kicked out with its hind feet and lowered its jaws on the cat's nose. Back and forth the battle went. Blood ran from a deep gash in the dog's shoulder. Tyler raised the rifle to his shoulder again, steeling the trembling in his hands to make his aim more sure. The animals would tire of the fight and break apart. He had to be ready for that moment.

The hound rolled the cat down a rocky incline and the animals both scrambled for their footing, placing them a few feet apart. Tense with the opportunity, Tyler tightened his finger on the trigger and the gun fired. A howl rent the air. For a minute the air was heavy with silence. Tyler sucked air into his lungs and took aim again at the cat. The shot found its mark. Writhing and twisting, the animal fought the new, invisible enemy for seconds before pushing to its feet, only to fall to the ground again and lie still.

Hands shaking, Tyler felt the coldness of shock begin to take hold of his body. He fought it and pushed to his feet, moving while the opportunity allowed and before he could think about what he'd just done. He had eradicated the enemy. But there was no sign of the dog, and his mind painted the picture of what the howl after his first shot meant.

Chapter 13

Renee saw the column of sheep, their bleats filling the air as they made their way in her direction. They fanned out as the narrow trail broadened, but the momentum of the sheep behind them pushed those in front. Minutes passed as the sheep galloped onto the ground just outside the campsite. The rear of the column came into view, with Teddy weaving back and forth behind the herd, keeping them moving. She expected to see Tyler, but he was nowhere.

A terrible, scratchy scream shattered the clamor of the sheep's hooves against the trail and dulled the baaing of the animals. She knew that sound for what it was. She wondered if the tatter-eared dog had sensed the animal's presence and come to her at the pool as a means of warning her.

She stood frozen, eyes scanning, not daring to leave the sputtering fire even for a minute. Above the din created by the milling sheep, she thought she caught the sound of snarling. A shot rang out, and she tensed and clasped her hands around her knees, curling tighter into a knot, unsure what to do. Never again would she allow the man to leave her without at least the protection of a gun. She hated the fact that she didn't know where Tyler was or the reason he discharged his rifle.

In tense silence she waited for the inevitable return of Tyler, or the mutt. Teddy trotted to camp and sank to the ground, tongue lolling with the effort of his herding. She stooped to scratch the dog's head.

"What's going on out there, Teddy?"

The dog stared at her, ears pricked.

Her throat knotted with fear. If anything happened to Tyler she wouldn't even know how to survive or where to go. Her sole hope would be the arrival of the man Tyler had called the camptender.

She squeezed her eyes shut and rested her forehead on her folded arms. Her mind churned with the possibility of being attacked by a bear. She would have to gather wood to keep a fire going to fend off wild animals. The sheep, though . . . She didn't know what they needed or what to do for them. She'd heard Tyler whistle to the dog on several occasions, each whistle apparently meaning something different to the animal.

Her head began to pound, and she pushed against the tears that burned for release. Another thought taunted. What if Tyler had been hurt and couldn't move? She lifted her head, the idea sending waves of panic coursing through her body. She swept to her feet and knelt by the saddlebags and the pack that seemed to hold so many of the necessary staples. Surely the man carried something for wounds.

Renee pulled items out one by one. A bag of beans. Flour. Sugar. Coffee. She dug deeper and discovered a salted ham. The other bag held personal items. Books. The Bible she'd seen him read on the previous day. A clean shirt and trousers. Strips of leather and clean patches of cotton material. A tin of a thick cream that she raised to her nose. Some type of salve, she hoped.

She took the cotton material and began ripping it into strips, rolling them as fast as her stumbling fingers could manage. She tied the leather around the rolls of cotton and jammed the salve into the middle of the last cotton strip before she rolled that, too, into a tight wad.

She would need water, but she gave up the idea of hauling the heavy pail. She would have to move him to water. But if his injuries prevented him...

Renee shook her head, gathered her treasures into her arms, and turned. If she didn't add more wood to the fire it would burn out and leave her without a place to retreat for safety.

She dropped her cache of bandages onto a grassy patch, her gaze shifting over the wide space in front of her. A small grove of trees offered some possibilities. She glanced around for the small hand ax she'd seen Tyler use on many occasions but couldn't find it. She used a long wooden stick to poke at the fire and threw on another log. The last one. She could only hope that the flame wouldn't consume the dry wood before she could get Tyler back to the campsite. If she could get him back.

She turned at the dull vibration of the earth. Squinting in the direction from which the sheep had come, she saw a small dot of movement. Relief rolled over her when she recognized Sassy, with Tyler sitting upright on the horse. She strained to make out his features, afraid to see them pinched with the pain of a wound. She ran out as Sassy came closer, slowed to a trot now by Tyler's guiding hand. He raised his hand to her. Anxiety peeled away.

"I was afraid you were injured."

Tyler stopped the horse, his brow pinched with something she could not define. "Guess you heard the cat."

"I heard the shots," she admitted, her body quivering with relief so powerful she feared she might fall in a heap.

He said nothing as he dismounted, pulling the reins over Sassy's head and leading her through the sheep to a boulder where he picketed the horse and removed the saddle and blanket. He gave the horse a pat on the neck.

His silence stoked her temper to a white-hot flame. How dare he ignore her. She retreated to the fire, miserable that she'd burned so much energy worrying over a man not the least bit troubled by all the turmoil he'd caused her. She glared at him as he moved among the sheep, oblivious to her.

She poked at the fire; the flames caught at the old wood and leaped up a few inches. He cared more for the sheep than he did for humans. It was absurd. How could she be expected to stay in this camp for who knew how long with a man who couldn't see beyond the end of his own nose?

She flopped onto the ground and drew her legs up to her chest. As the flames grew in height, she refused to move back. She was hungry, too. She stabbed another glare at Tyler's back as he ran his hands over some of the sheep searching for what, she didn't know.

He worked over the sheep for what seemed an eternity. Lulled by the heat, Renee never noticed when he returned, awakened by the sound of grease in a pan and the smell of something delicious.

When she blinked her eyes open, it was dark, and Tyler sat across the fire from her, his Bible spread on his lap, his expression far away. Without moving she studied his face, noting the crease on his forehead that showed tan beneath it and paler skin above, a product of Tyler's preference to wear a hat as he worked. For the first time she realized his face was not that of an old man. Her best guess put him in his late twenties. Creases at the corners of his eyes spoke of a man who squinted or laughed often, though she suspected the former as he'd only once cracked a smile since her arrival.

And again she had to ask herself the question. What kind of man secluded himself away in the mountains of Wyoming for months on end with nothing but sheep, a horse, and two dogs for company?

❧

Tyler felt her eyes on him. She'd awakened at some point between the memory of his wasted youth and his moment of redemption. If, indeed, that moment had come at all. Maybe it never would. The Bible in his lap nudged him to cling to the hope of a better day. A new day. And it reminded him of the sheep.

He rubbed his hands together, distributing the oil on them from the new growth of the sheep's wool, which was still short since they'd just been clipped. If he'd known at the age of seventeen what he would be doing at twenty-six, he would have laughed. Much as he suspected Renee laughed at the idea of being in the mountains, alone with a herd of sheep and a hard-edged, silent man. His silence upon his return had irritated her, he was sure, but he'd needed time.

Sheepherding had been a way for him to cut himself off from all the painful things he'd done—to himself and to others. He'd welcomed the retreat into the mountains offered to him by Rich Morgan, a rancher who'd taken a chance on a broken-spirited man with no heart for living another day.

Rich had told him his wound wouldn't kill him, but his broken spirit would grind him to dust if he let it. Despite Tyler's desire for death, Rich had helped

Tyler's body along the path of healing. And then Rich had offered him a stake in a herd of sheep and sent him up into the mountains. Tyler had spent the first month of that first trip surrounded by more silence than he could take, thinking he would go crazy with nothing but the sheep and the sheepdog for company. He'd been forced to leave Sassy at the ranch to heal.

"She'll be needing some extra care," had been Rich's argument. "That shoulder wound is pretty deep. She's too good a piece of horseflesh to let her go lame."

Tyler had set out on the trail up the mountain with no illusions about the job, having heard too many stories from the other herder Rich employed. Rich had turned up at the end of that month, checking on the herd, he'd said, but Tyler suspected the man was checking up on him as well as the herd.

It had been on the tip of his tongue many times to bark his complaints, but Rich's kindness to him, and his compassion and willingness to help a stranger at a time when Tyler had felt himself beyond help or hope, meant he could not let his friend down. Plus the herd was his investment. All the money he had was wrapped up in the timid little animals.

Tyler pulled himself from the wrappings of memory and set the Bible aside. Renee watched him in silence, though he couldn't be sure that she wasn't watching the flames. He got to his feet and stuck the fork into the chunk of meat in the pan. The water was simmering it slowly, making a nice broth in which to boil the beans that he'd left soaking that morning.

"I'm hungry," were her first words.

He nodded. "It'll be awhile. Take some coffee."

He filled a tin mug for her.

"Sugar?"

A precious staple, sugar. He preferred to drink his black, but if sugar soothed the lady. . . He spilled some from the large sack into another tin mug and took it back to her. She dumped most of it into the coffee and swirled it around.

At least sipping the brew would keep her occupied until supper. Good thing since he had more work to do.

"That dog barked at me."

Tyler lifted his gaze to hers then glanced over at Teddy, who lounged at the edge of the herd.

"Not that one. The one with the fringed ears."

He frowned, unsure of the direction of the conversation. Could it be that she resented the dog barking at her, perhaps scaring her? "He does that to get your attention."

"I heard the cat later on." She sipped at the coffee, made a face, and dumped in the last of the sugar. "Was he warning me, do you think?"

The mutt had a sixth sense about danger. There had been so many times when Tyler hadn't heard or sensed anything amiss with the herd but the mutt had. He'd often taken off under cover of dense shrubs, guarding the sheep as if they were his own pups. "Probably."

"You don't talk much, do you?"

He nodded her way. "Don't mean to be rude. Guess I'm not used to having company."

"You shot the cat?"

"In the neck or head."

"Did the dog find him?"

"Found him and picked a fight. It was a young cat but it outweighed the hound." He squinted out toward the sheep. He would need to set some fires around the perimeter of the herd to help keep predators at bay. He'd shoot a rabbit for Teddy while he was out. "Keep an eye on the meat. Beans are soaking over in that pan. Add them and put a lid on it. Should be back by the time they're done cooking."

Chapter 14

The sheep seemed calm despite the extra movement brought about by the presence of the cat. Tyler winced at the memory. How could he have missed the cat that first time? His hands must have been trembling more than he realized. He'd nailed it with the next shot, though, even as the reality of what his first shot had cost him sunk deep into his mind.

It had taken him awhile to climb the incline where the mountain lion lay dead within a few feet of the mutt. Mercifully he'd shot the dog in the chest, its howl probably the last sound its starved lungs could gasp. He'd dug a shallow hole with a sharp-edged rock and buried the animal, agonizing over the loss. Rich Morgan wouldn't be too happy with him, but the man would read the situation for what it was and hold no blame.

At least the mutt had sired a litter of pups the past winter. They'd be old enough to train by summertime. The loss of the dog cut deep for numerous reasons. Tyler put complete trust in the animal's instincts to track and keep predators away from the herd. It meant he would have to be more on guard. Ever watchful in his hearing as well as his vision, and even then his instincts would never be as refined as the hound's.

He scrambled together some twigs and leaves and used them as kindling for the small fires. He crossed between the four that he set, working them until they were hot enough for the greener wood that would produce smoke.

When he returned to the camp, he gave the rabbit to Teddy. Renee sat cross-legged, peeling the bark off a twig one strip at a time. He passed her without comment, understanding all too well the boredom she must be feeling. Getting involved working the sheep would be good for her. Time would fly faster if she had chores and responsibilities.

He bent over the pot, satisfied to see the beans had been placed inside as he had requested.

"Were you afraid I would forget?"

Her voice held an edge. He ignored the question. "I'll get the plates." When he handed her a plate, she took it, her eyes searching his. He met her gaze head on, unwilling to let whatever attitude that brewed go unchecked. "Work will be good for you, you know. It will pass the time, and with the loss of the dog. . ."

❧

Renee lifted her eyes from the plate of beans and the strip of meat. Tyler's words sank in slowly, and there was no missing the catch in his voice. "The dog? You mean the mangy one?"

Tyler ran a hand over his mouth, the material of his sleeve catching on the coarseness of his stubbled chin. "Shot him by mistake."

As far as she could see, the loss of the dog wasn't anything that terrible.

"He was a fine animal. Brave. Smart. Could track a coyote and kill a rattler in an instant. And his loss means more work. I don't have him to drive away predators, which leaves the sheep more vulnerable."

It was the longest stream of words she'd heard from him. "Why do you do this? Get stuck out here? For them? Doesn't it make you crazy?"

Tyler's eyes glittered in the firelight, and she thought she saw a slight smile curve his lips. "I felt the same way the first month. Rich kept telling me to pay attention to nature and I wouldn't be bored. Then he gave me a Bible."

Renee's laugh was harsh. "Did you get religion or something?"

He seemed to mull her question, taking a bite of beans. "I don't know what happened. Things change so much. The sky, for example—have you ever paid attention to it? The colors?"

A laugh rose in her throat, but the sincerity with which he spoke made mirth seem folly. He was serious.

"The sheep are gentle creatures. I hated them at first. Thought they were dumb animals." He paused and stared out at the flock.

"What changed your mind?"

"It was all about me. I hated being up here. I hated being alone. I hated them because they were the reason for my isolation."

Renee let his words sink in, unsure what it all meant. "Then why come at all?"

"Because I had no choice."

Chapter 15

At first, she couldn't think of anything to say. Ideas that explained his reason for becoming a sheepherder rolled around in her mind. Maybe he'd been jilted by a girl. He'd said he blamed the sheep for his isolation, but how could that be?

He shifted his weight, and the flames of the fire caught the strong cut of his jaw. His eyes seemed paler in the brightness. His expression always appeared on the brink of becoming surly and hard. She shivered at the idea of feeling the heat of his anger. She set aside her plate, hunger dulled by the hardness of the beans. She would have to add them sooner next time.

Tyler had never been anything but a gentleman. Terse, perhaps, but what man wasn't when working hard at a job? Her pa never had much to say when there was work to be done, which was why the evenings seemed such a special time for her as a child. At least, before her mother had died.

When he spooned the last of the beans into his mouth, he pushed to his feet. "If you'll wash the plates, I'll check the herd one more time."

"What do you mean that you had no choice?" She blurted out the words, curiosity overwhelming her. She'd had a choice to drag Thomas into her little schemes, never considering the consequences of those actions. Surely Tyler had more options open to him than being a shepherd.

He stopped in his tracks and turned. His hand scratched along his jaw then fell to his side. "Some make bad choices. Others make good. It's all about what we learn from our experience. You're not the only one to make a bad choice, Renee. And if that group that caught you does find us, we'll have to make some more choices. Real fast."

Tyler turned and walked off. She bit her lip and picked up the dirty plates, never having considered the danger she put him in if the Loust Gang found them. Kneeling by the bucket of water, she used an old rag to rinse the plates, eyes lifting along the herd of sheep, content and peaceful.

❧

Renee Dover was a troubled girl. The desire to draw her out both surprised and annoyed him. Getting involved in the girl's problems wasn't his business. Teddy waded with him into the midst of the sheep. Tyler stilled and listened hard for sounds of predators. As if in answer to his unspoken question, a coyote howled, and a series of yips answered. Tyler gave a grim smile. Most of the sheepherders in the region would have taken note of those sounds. These were far off. About a mile by his guess. It was the silent stalkers, bears and cats, that raised the hair on the back of his neck.

He checked his smoke screens and relit one that had gone out. The smoke was feeble at best, but it was all he could do tonight. Weary from the day, Tyler left Teddy at the edge of the pool and stripped down. The cold water shattered his weariness and sharpened his mind. He worked the soap over his back and down his arms. He scrubbed the bar over his head and down his face. If he'd given it more thought he would have brought his razor and shaved off the scrubby bush. He'd do it in the morning. Lingering in the pool of water in the dark was risky with it being a perfect watering hole for the very predators he hoped to avoid. Tyler left the cold water reluctantly, invigorated, but anxious to get back to the warmth of the fire.

Teddy growled low in his throat, and Tyler hurried into his trousers and poked at the sleeves of his shirt. He knew better than to leave camp without his rifle, and his detour to bathe was more than foolhardy when unarmed.

Whatever had alerted Teddy moments ago didn't seem to bother him now. Tension ebbed from Tyler's shoulders and he hastened back to camp, not bothering to tuck his shirt.

The sheep were quiet, and Teddy curled up in his spot overlooking the herd, ready in an instant to splash into the midst and get them moving.

"Good boy, Teddy."

He patted the dog and scrubbed his fingers down through the thick fur to scratch at his rump, an attention Teddy particularly loved. From his vantage point beside the dog, he looked into camp, expecting to see Renee. When he couldn't make out her form anywhere within the ring of light, his breath caught.

"Renee?" he whispered.

He stalked the perimeter of the fire, keeping his face away from the bright light lest he ruin his night vision. Her bedroll lay on the ground where she'd left it that morning. The plates were gone, the skillet beside the fire where he'd left it. He told himself not to panic. He would embarrass her and himself if he traipsed after her only to discover she'd left to take care of personal needs.

He squatted beside the fire and held out his cold-stiffened fingers. Time weighed heavy on his mind. He kept expecting her to step into the camp, plates in hand. Duty done. He stood, buttoned his shirt, and stuffed it into his pants. He would not wait another minute. He grabbed his rifle and marched to the perimeter of the camp, not quite willing to leave just yet. Renee obviously needed schooling in camp life. She should never leave camp at night unless she took the rifle or Teddy. The irony that he'd violated his own rule made him clench his teeth hard. He moved into the stretching shadows. Something skittered out from beneath a shrubby patch to his right. Tyler tensed, but the small animal scurried away.

He gave a low, quiet whistle, and Teddy loped to his side. The collie was not a guard dog, but the sensitivity of his eyes and ears could mean the difference between life and death.

Night sounds seemed loud now, taunting him with his inability to find the girl. He'd never been fond of wandering the mountains at night. Too many risks. He tightened his hold on the rifle. He didn't do vulnerable.

Teddy went still, his head cocked, ears pricked. Seconds passed. Tyler wished the moon would show its face, but the thick clouds seemed slow to scoot. He heard a new sound. Slow. A creeping *whoosh* that exploded his chest. The sheep were moving, panicked by an enemy. A scream rent the air.

Sweat broke out on Tyler's forehead as he tried to remain steady and grip the direction of the sound, sure this time the sound was not the ladylike scream of a mountain cat, but Renee.

"Renee!"

Teddy lunged forward, a blur of white moving along the edge of the herd. The sheep were bunching away from the threat. Tyler raised the rifle to his shoulder as a panicked whimper rent the air.

"Renee!"

He could make out her outline now. Another dark blur moved behind her. Loping along. The sheep broke into a run. Tyler aimed the gun at the blur behind Renee, sucked air into his lungs, and then pulled the trigger. The animal growled and kept moving. He shot again, and then again. Rage-filled roars filled the air, and the dark mass fell and remained still.

Tyler stabbed through the dark to find Renee's figure. He saw nothing. "Renee?"

"Here." Her voice trembled. "I'm here."

Teddy bounded out of the darkness. Tyler whistled and the dog took off. Tyler's limbs shook with the shock of the ordeal. He found Renee on the ground, head in her hands. He heard the deep sobs that wrenched through her and knelt beside her. "Hey." She shuddered a breath. "I forgot to tell you to take the rifle when you leave camp. Or Teddy."

She didn't answer, the sobs clawing out of her. He touched her shoulder, and she raised her head. He wasn't sure who moved first, but she was in his arms then, her back shuddering beneath his hand.

As they sat there the sheep returned. Slow, spooked, more bunched than normal. But his presence seemed to soothe them and they began to spread out again. And still he held the fragile form in his arms, unable to let go though her tears were spent, her terror diminished.

Chapter 16

Renee clung to him. His presence something secure and stable. His solid strength pushed her fears back to manageable proportions, and still she couldn't make herself let go. Didn't want to move away from the safety of his arms or the beating of his heart that soothed with evidence she was not alone.

If it hadn't been for him, the bear would have killed her. She'd wanted to die earlier, at the pond, even welcomed it, but instincts for survival had made her run from the bear. If she hadn't looked up and seen it lumbering down off an outcropping, probably coming for water but having its eye on the sheep, she would never have made it. And if Tyler hadn't been there with the rifle. . .

She shuddered and his arms tightened around her.

"Let's get you closer to the fire," he whispered into her ear.

She nodded against his shoulder and pulled from his embrace. As he helped her to her feet, she felt the muscles in her ankle protest.

"Lean on me if you need to."

Renee shook her head. "I've been enough trouble already. I can walk."

He didn't argue but neither did he let go as he led the way back to camp, Teddy joining them at some point. He patted the dog's head and scratched its rump. The campfire burned low for lack of fresh fuel. Renee lifted a log as big around as her leg and lugged it toward the fire. Sparks shot up into the air when she dropped it, and Tyler laughed.

Turning to him, she pressed her hands to her hips. "What?"

"You'll have to get something a little smaller to build the fire up first." With that he grabbed a few slender branches and broke them with his hands into short lengths. He used the long stick to roll the heavy log off the fire and placed the smaller branches on top. The flame caught the dry sticks immediately.

"I have a lot to learn."

Tyler nodded. "We all do."

"I guess my first lesson is not to wander at night."

He shrugged, and a slight smile seemed to play at the corners of his mouth. "Wandering at night is sometimes necessary. The lesson is not to do it without a gun or dog."

She stared down at her fingers, cramped from the cold, her palms bloody from her fall, and she realized when Tyler turned away that his shirt showed stains from her hands. She shuddered. Terror tightened her throat. The bear had moved more swiftly than she had anticipated.

"Lesson two."

Tyler's soft voice brought her attention back to him.

"Don't run from a bear. Your best bet is to scream and flail your arms until the bear backs off. If that doesn't work, drop down and pull yourself into a knot."

"And wait to be eaten."

This tugged a smile from him. It transformed his face and lit his eyes.

"You should smile more often."

His smile wilted, and she wished she could take the words back.

He glanced away. "We need to be getting some sleep. I was going to shift the animals off, but the grass is holding so we'll stay put tomorrow."

She had no idea what all that meant, but he didn't explain further and she didn't want to ask more questions. Her body seemed to deflate all at once and it was all she could do to roll out the blankets and crawl into their warmth before drifting away into velvet slumber.

❧

Tyler lay awake long after she slept, troubled by his reaction to the woman. She tugged at emotions he hadn't felt for a long time. Hadn't wanted to feel. Renee wasn't his type. Their embrace had been nothing more than a means to soothe her overwrought nerves. But her observation about his smile was different. It both pleased and embarrassed him. He'd not thought of himself as attractive since Anna.

He rolled away from the fire and onto his back. Anna had just begun to love him. The few times they'd been together had been magic. She would have been everything his mother would have loved in a daughter-in-law. For Anna he would have given up the wayward life and become someone she could respect. He had been ready to do just that, too.

Renee was none of the things Anna was. She was younger, for one thing, more. . . What? Selfish? Who was he to judge? But she'd suffered. Something haunted the girl, and he wanted to drag it from her. Talking about the deep down things had helped him. Rich Morgan had been a patient friend. He could do the same for Renee, but he had no inkling of how to do that. He was no healer, and his best attempts with talking to people proved clumsy.

It would be so easy to ignore her. He could use her help in camp. It would be good for her to be busy, just as he'd suggested to her, but he wouldn't get involved.

He closed his eyes, settled on the matter, but sleep wouldn't come. The feel of her in his arms. The frailty of her frame beneath his hand. The harshness of her sobbing gasps. A longing for a closeness he'd denied himself came alive despite his efforts to the contrary.

Chapter 17

Renee woke up shivering. The crackle of fresh wood on the fire beckoned her closer. She climbed out, gasped at the chill air, scooted her blankets closer to the heat, and dove back inside.

Rich, male laughter made her squeeze her eyes harder.

"Playing possum won't work. Breakfast is almost ready anyway."

She wiggled her toes and debated abandoning her blankets to help with breakfast.

"I could leave it for the bears."

Renee lifted the covers over her head.

"I'm sure they'll come running when they see you, their old friend."

He wasn't going to leave her alone, but she had to admit that the sparkle of humor in his words delighted her. Even his rare burst of laughter seemed a gift. She swept the covers back in a pretend huff, immediately wishing she hadn't been so hasty when the cold air slammed against her.

"Do you have those plates?"

"I'll get them." She stretched her body upward and tried to tame her hair. Tyler stood, drawing her attention and making her gasp. It was Tyler, but it wasn't Tyler. He caught her stare and ran a hand over his jaw.

"Tired of looking scruffy. Meant to do it last night."

The line of tan skin beneath where his hat rested on his head grew pale again along the newly shaven jaw and chin. But the clean-shaven face peeled years away. Despite the strange coloring of his skin, Tyler was a handsome man. His lips full. A cleft in his chin. Square jaw. She gasped air, not realizing she'd been holding it as she perused his new look. "You—you look..." *Handsome* was the word she almost spit out, but she clamped down and finished with an awkward, "younger."

"How old did you think I was?"

Renee glanced away, heat creeping into her cheeks. "Late twenties. Early thirties." She hugged herself, remembering, against her will, how he had held her in his arms and what protection and comfort truly felt like. She'd had too few of the latter in her life, and a gun was generally her protection. "Let me go get those plates."

His chuckle caught her attention. "I'll get them while you finish waking up."

She watched him lift down the plates then turn, catching her eye, his expression serious. Sober. She didn't know what to think about him or about the feelings he stirred. Was it wrong for her to enjoy the comfort he so freely had given during a moment of crisis? She didn't think so. He had saved her life.

His eyes slid away from her gaze, and he picked up a paper-wrapped piece of meat. "The bear left us with a few good things."

This surprised her. "How long have you been up?"

His grin went huge. "Longer than you."

"If you'll show me how, I'll try and do the cooking."

"Your mama never taught you?"

His casual assumption rattled something deep down. "She died when I was eight."

"I'm sorry."

There it was. Simple comfort. His tone conveyed a deep empathy. She stared out at the herd, moving now in the cold gray of morning light. Peaceful. Quiet.

" 'The Lord is my Shepherd.' " Her heart raced at the voice, and she thought for a moment that God Himself was speaking to her. Tyler, his face turned toward the grazing sheep, too, continued, as if reading her thoughts. But she recognized the words of someone else entirely. " 'I shall not want.' "

He didn't continue, and in the stillness Renee heard her mother's voice; she'd often quoted that psalm late in the evening. Her father had been there, too, listening as she read, a tender smile lighting his eyes as he would pull her closer to him. Renee hadn't recalled those nighttime Bible readings in years.

As a child she had accepted the words because they were read by the mother she loved so much. When had she begun to doubt? She knew the answer. Her mother's death. The change in her father had been jarring. He began to shuffle her and Thomas off to neighbors when he had a cattle drive. She hated every minute of being away from him, plied from his side for reasons she didn't understand and had stopped trying to figure out long ago. How she wished for someone to take care of her with the same tenderness with which Tyler cared for his sheep.

"You're their shepherd."

He rubbed his jaw, as if he couldn't quite get enough of the smooth feel of his skin. "I suppose I am."

She made a face. "You didn't know?"

"I don't think about it much. I do what needs to be done to keep them content."

"You *are* a religious man, then?"

❧

The way Renee said it gave him pause. Did he read the Bible? Yes, but he read other books, too. Did that make him religious? Caring for the sheep had begun as a job. He realized now that it was a calling, one he'd been ill equipped to take on at first, but something he had grown into. That first month he'd resented the position, resigned to being alone because it was his safeguard against those who would seek him out.

"I began to see the sheep for what they were. Helpless, dependent animals who needed care and attention." His throat closed over the words, and he dipped his head beneath Renee's gaze. Waxing poetic about sheep seemed silly.

"You mean you enjoyed bossing them."

He wanted to laugh, but she hit too close to the truth. Though bossing wouldn't have been the word he would have used, it would have appeared that way to anyone watching him at the beginning of his training. "Bossing doesn't have anything to do with it. You lead sheep, you don't beat them. I found it was less about me and my needs and more about responsibility than anything else. Like I said, you just do what needs done because it needs doing." He paused to gather his thoughts. "Some sheep aren't easily led. They get it in their head to bolt off every chance."

Renee moved beside him back to the camp, her silence weighing on him, until, finally: "I guess there are a lot of us like that."

He didn't respond. He understood the deeper meaning of her words all too well. For a second, he considered sharing his story. It would prove to her how far he'd come, or at least, how far he felt like he'd come since his wild youth.

In camp, Renee picked up the heavy iron skillet and sliced some of the meat into the pan. Her hands worked in jerky motions. To his eye she seemed upset, but he refused to pry. Could be she was thinking of her brother or missing her folks. Lord knew even though he was a grown man, he still missed his ma and pa.

"What now?"

Her question startled him, and when he met her gaze, her expression seemed more relaxed. He nodded toward a small sack. "Flapjacks. I'll show you how."

Days settled into a familiar rhythm. Renee's cooking did nothing to aid his digestion, but she was learning and he refused to criticize. Besides, he'd eaten worse many times. The task of herding the sheep up the mountain to summer camp became easier now that he had help, and he enjoyed showing Renee the right way to work with sheep; all the lessons he had learned along the way. At least most of them. At night he would set the small fires and return to camp to whatever Renee had cooked up. She hadn't said much over the last few days, and he hadn't prodded. With days beginning at three in the morning, conversation became a luxury neither indulged in, too tired at night to find words.

But he enjoyed watching her work, and the gentle hand she had with the sheep was rewarded by their trust in her. Where once they had run when they saw her coming, now they calmed and skirted around her, vying for attention.

The last leg of the journey led through patches of dense sagebrush on a narrow ledge. Getting the sheep through would be the challenge it was every year. That night he made a point of opening a conversation, lonely with the silence between them and needing to outline his plan for the next day.

"You've been quiet."

Renee's spoonful of stew didn't make it to her mouth. She set the spoon down. "I didn't think you were much for talking."

He shrugged. "Guess silence has become second nature to me."

"Is the camptender going to arrive soon?"

The question pierced him. So she was only biding her time. He'd thought she might be coming to enjoy tending the sheep, maybe even enjoying. . . What? A silent man incapable of reading a woman's heart and mind? Irritated, he snapped, "He'll get here!"

Renee's eyes flashed. She bit her lip and looked away. "My father. . ."

Whatever she'd been about to say was lost. The strength of her emotion was evident in the way her jaw worked and her lips tightened. She angled her face away from him, toward the night sky. The campfire danced along her cheek and neck but left her eyes in shadow.

"He'll be looking for you."

"No." Her shoulders sagged and she pulled her knees to her chest and rocked. "He probably hates me."

To his ears the words were raw with emotion. "Not as much as you hate yourself."

She was shaking her head, and he heard the tears in her voice. "With Thomas gone he'd have no one. . . ." She shrugged. "It was to be an adventure. I'd gone to town and seen the poster and thought it would be fun to search for the outlaws. Thomas didn't want to go."

It was the perfect time to ask, yet Tyler didn't know if he was ready for the answer. Still, there were outlaws by the dozen. Gunslingers who thought themselves fast and wanted quick money. But he had to know for sure.

"What was the name on that poster?"

She tilted her head at him. "Name?"

"Of the men after you. The gang."

"The Loust Gang."

Tyler's focus narrowed as he replayed what she'd just said. *The Loust Gang.* He swallowed, but his mouth remained dry. "They were in Cheyenne." And he had hoped they would stay there or go back to South Dakota. Why trail him after all this time?

He was aware of Renee's silence, of the strange expression on her face as he pushed himself vertical. Stumbling to the edge of camp, he darted out into the blackness of the night and welcomed the cold darkness. Muscles in his shoulders bunched and placed an automatic pressure in his head, stabbing behind his eyes.

Chapter 18

Renee followed Tyler's path out of camp but stopped just inside the circle of firelight. Through the haze of her tears she hadn't been able to make out his expression, but his surprised, "*They were in Cheyenne,*" begged to be explained.

She returned to the fire and cleaned up the mess, rinsing the plates in a pail of water. With nothing left to do, she rolled out her bedding and lay down. She'd so wanted to share with him about Thomas. Her little brother. It made her throat ache to remember. For days she had agonized over how to get home to explain to her father. Until a week ago when she realized returning to her father would only rain down more of his anger on her head. Somehow she had hoped the camptender might never show up, that she could wander the hillsides and work beside Tyler forever. Safe in his silence.

He'd been nudging along her education in sheepherding. Opening her eyes to the colors of the sky and what cloud formations portended. Then there was the sheep and how he would run his hands through their wool to check for bugs or cuts when they'd landed in thorns. He encouraged her to do the same, and she came away disgusted by the natural oils from the sheep's wool that coated her hands. She learned the reason behind some of the lambs not having tails or missing an ear—born in the dead of winter and incurring frostbite.

She'd begun to understand the logic behind herding sheep into the mountains where the air was cooler during the hot summer months. Words hadn't been exchanged much, but what conversations they did share were meaningful learning experiences.

It culminated in her need to understand what Tyler meant when he said he'd learned from the sheep. She thought she might be starting to understand what he meant. Every time he took charge of a small lamb, carrying it on his shoulders back to its mama. Or the times when he guided an animal away from a dangerous patch. Even the patience he had shown when one of the sheep had lain down in a hollow and rolled onto its back. She had wanted to laugh at the flailing animal, but Tyler had been serious about the work of rolling it back to its feet. He stroked along its back and sides for long, patient minutes until the sheep's feet could hold its weight again.

His ways with the animals touched a deeper spot within her. One that ached for the same gentleness she saw him lavish on the sheep. It rolled questions about the man through her mind. She wanted to ask about his past and the wild days he had alluded to, but she never mustered the courage, and with the early mornings, sleep had become a precious commodity.

Renee must have dozed, for the next time she opened her eyes it was to see Tyler across the hot coals of the dying fire.

"Sorry. Didn't mean to wake you."

She elbowed herself to a sitting position. "I was worried about you."

He caught and held her gaze, eyes searching hers, before he looked away. "No need."

"What happened? Why did you leave like that?"

Tyler's right arm rested across his bent knee, the other leg straight out in front of him. He looked, in that moment, weary beyond his years. He scrubbed a hand down his face then raked his fingers through his hair. "Might be best for you to get some sleep."

He was putting her off. "I want to know, Tyler." If she expected more hesitation, she didn't get it.

"I used to run with the Loust Gang."

She gasped. "You were an outlaw?"

"Might be the less you know the better."

Renee weighed what he was implying against her need to understand. This gentle man who cared for sheep as if they were his own precious children had been an outlaw? She searched his face, admitting to herself what had tickled her senses for days now. She was drawn to Tyler Sperry in a way she'd never been drawn to the gangly cowhands on her father's ranch. She'd always felt their respect for her to be nothing more than a thin veneer. They were not men she would count on in times of trouble. More than that, none of them twisted her heart quite like the russet-haired man across from her now. Without putting a name on the emotion she was feeling, Renee crossed the distance that separated them and sat beside Tyler. "I need to know."

❧

Tyler told her then about his mother's struggle to survive raising two restless young boys. When she'd remarried, he'd left home, anxious to experience all the things he knew his mother would frown on.

"I fell into the gang because I wanted quick money. They sent me on odd jobs at first; I guess to test my loyalty to them, or to ensure that my heart was just as black as theirs. We stayed in the hills of South Dakota, robbing miners of their placer gold. It made us money but not much, and the others got bolder. I could tell they weren't satisfied with seed money. Especially Marv."

He glanced at Renee and saw the light of recognition in her eyes. "The leader of the gang," she noted.

"Rand?" he said, testing her.

"The one who kept watch over me." She smiled. "Until you came along."

Lolly, Dirk, Lance. They'd been his friends at one time, until. . . "Marv started planning a big raid. I didn't want to do it. The Homestake was shipping to Cheyenne, and the money promised to be more than we'd ever done before. It was a big risk because Marv had never done something like that before. He sent me and Dirk in to scout the route to Cheyenne and scope the town. Took us about a month. Got to know the people. Pretended we were new hires. Even had a name of a rancher far enough out that no one would question if we said we worked for him." He pulled in an unsteady breath. Raoul Billings was the man's name. Never did meet the real man.

"But. . .something happened."

He jerked a glance her way, amazed at her perception. Him, a man who prided himself on not showing his emotion or feelings. At some point this woman had learned to read him. "I started having doubts about it all—the life, the robbing. Tried not to let on much since Dirk was with me, but then I met Anna."

"Ah. Was she pretty?"

He caught the glint of amused humor in her eyes, relieved, somehow, that she hadn't taken on in a jealous rage. Jealous? Of him? He dismissed the thought. There wasn't anything between them. He exhaled. "Yeah. She was pretty. Good hearted. I thought maybe I'd go straight then. Get a job as a ranch hand and court her."

He shifted his position to relieve the ache in his bent knee. "But it was time to head back to camp and give our report. I don't know what happened then, how Marv found out about Anna. I decided I'd ride on the job and make like I was going to go in then head out of town."

He'd been so mixed up inside. He had wanted nothing more than to break off before they hit town, but it would have meant a bullet in the back, and his desire to see Anna had squelched the idea. He'd have to play his hand quietly, quickly.

"I don't know if Marv knew I was up to something or not, but I was never left alone. Never got the chance to make an escape." He let his head fall back. The stars shone bright and he reached a hand upward, pretending to grab at them. Embarrassed at his foolishness, he chuckled and shot a glance at Renee.

She laughed, too, her head dipping backward, the glorious spread of her hair falling nearly to the ground. "They're bright tonight. I've often wondered what it would be like to hold one in my hand. Thomas and I used to—"

Her voice broke and Tyler watched her struggle for composure. He knotted his hands together over his upraised knee to keep them still. How he wished he could turn back the hands of time for both of them. He clenched his teeth. Mistakes were often hard to live with, but mistakes brought on by one's own bad choice were gut-deep impossible.

They sat in silence for a long time before she spoke.

"So you went through with the robbery?"

He cleared his throat, the cobwebs of silence making his throat dry and his voice raspy. He cast back over those days, sharing with Renee as much as he could.

Among the gang, he'd felt just like the prisoner he was. Even though none of them acknowledged they were watching his every move, he knew Marv had warned them to keep a close eye on him. He didn't dare try to get a message to Anna through Dirk. Friend or not, Dirk was as much an outlaw as the rest.

The day of the proposed robbery broke hot and grew hotter with every hour. Marv ordered him to ride into town with Dirk one final time before they hit the bank at noon.

"It'll give them the feel that you're just one of them. Then, once you've bought some supplies at the store, mount up and leave. We'll meet you on the north end of town and ride in together."

He'd thought it might provide his opportunity to break free. With only Dirk on the trail beside him he could pull out and make a run north or east, to get lost in the Basin or the Big Horns.

Dirk made easy talk along the trail, and Tyler let down his guard. Maybe his friend would let him go. But something deep down told him not to trust the man. As they rode, he noticed Dirk always rode in back and a little off to the side of him. He had told himself he was thinking too much.

If he kept to the trail and went into town, he might see Anna. If he could get a message to her, or to anyone in authority, they might be able to warn the bank before it was too late. He held on to the hope of becoming a hero for the duration of the ride, mulling over and over ways to get a message to someone.

They trotted straight to the store. Tyler tied his horse and followed Dirk inside. Tense moments swelled when the first person he laid eyes on was the town's marshal, a little man with big eyes that seemed outsized in his small head. Outlaws' gossip said the man's appearance wasn't to be underestimated. Sheriff Walt King was pure poison with a gun.

Dirk played it easy with the man, while sweat had formed between Tyler's shoulders and dripped down his back. Walt's demeanor matched Dirk's in ease, the two exchanging words like old friends.

The storekeeper finished up with a woman and leaned over the counter, a kind smile on his face. "Reckon Anna will be glad to see you. You back for a spell?"

"Just in from the ranch for a few provisions." He feared the man would continue to question him about his intentions toward Anna, but the conversation drifted to talk of ammunition, flour and sugar, bags of beans, and coffee.

"You wanting this delivered?"

"No," he said, too quickly. The storekeeper's eyes narrowed. "Thought it strange Mr. Billings didn't come to order supplies himself."

"We're leaving. Tired of breathing dust and repairing fences."

The floorboard squeaked and Dirk appeared beside him, his manner still easy. "We're hoping to go up and try our hand at gold in the hills. Supplies are cheaper here than in any mining camp."

The storekeeper seemed to relax at that and turned his attention back to filling the order.

That was when events became a blur of activity. Dirk had crossed to the front window of the general store, looked out across the street, and then checked the pocket watch he always carried. But it had been the look he'd given Tyler that brought a wave of fear. That, and the door of the general store opening. . .

Tyler sighed, the telling of the story exhausting him. Renee shifted her weight, and he realized she had moved closer during his talk. He straightened his leg and relaxed back against the rock, feeling the hard poke of the rough surface. The fire had begun to blaze again. Almost as an afterthought, he realized she had thrown more wood on it.

"Tyler?" she asked, the sound of his name a warm whisper in the night.

He nodded to indicate he was fine. His memories of what happened next remained clear. The events must have taken place in seconds, yet each one seemed to last minutes in his mind.

He massaged his temples, almost feeling the stabbing pain of fear he'd felt when Dirk gave him that smirking glare.

He heaved a sigh and continued to unroll the sequence of events. "Somehow when I saw Dirk's sneer, I knew I'd been tricked. I moved to the window and stared across at the bank. Saw Marv's horse, and Lance's, and felt certain they were both inside, holding up the bank. I knew then, plans had been made to exclude me because I'd shown myself untrustworthy, and it made me both mad and relieved at the same time."

"What happened?" Renee asked.

"I went for the door, but Dirk drew on me and told everyone to stay right where they were."

Tyler exhaled and closed his eyes. The next memories were the hardest and always the ones that kept him awake at night with the burning shame of what he'd done.

Chapter 19

Renee recognized that Tyler was in the grips of something powerful. Though she wanted to know what happened next, she stopped pushing. He would tell her in his own time.

"Anna entered the store then. She had no idea what was going on, or that Dirk had a gun on everyone."

Tyler struggled to continue, his Adam's apple bobbing hard. "She saw Dirk first, then the gun, and then her eyes went to me. Dirk, too, stared at me. And then..." He blew out his breath, long and slow. "And then he gave me a little grin and I knew...." She watched him struggle to keep his emotions in check and placed her hand along his arm. "Anna ran toward me, her face full of terror, and I saw Dirk level the gun...."

Though Tyler's eyes remained dry, his face appeared haggard. Renee could see the pulsing of his heart in his neck and noticed the wetness in his eyes before he dug his fingers into them to clear the moisture.

In the silence of night, wisps of cool fog seeped toward them. She didn't like fog; it always seemed to rob the day of something. She sat in miserable silence, wishing she could ease the burden of his hurt. His grief mingled with hers in a silent twist, much like the shifting, burgeoning clouds of the rolling fog. She shivered as the fingers of the mist roiled and shifted, swirling around her body and laying a coat of silver across their shoulders.

"Tyler?"

He finally shifted and rose to his feet. Using the long branch, he stoked the fire to a blaze. "Stay close to camp. It will burn off by midmorning." He cast her a sideways glance. "Be glad we're just on the west side of the mountain now. If we were on the east, it could stay for days."

She couldn't fathom paddling around in fog for days, and even the idea of having to do so made her scalp prickle with fear. "What about the sheep?"

"I'll take Teddy out and we'll make sure they're not straying. The dampness will make them miserable but it'll limit their movement somewhat."

She didn't know why a damp fog would bother sheep, but she did know she sure hated it. Worry that Tyler might get lost niggled at her mind, but she kept her silence. He'd seen these things before; that much was obvious to her. She had no doubt he knew exactly what to do and when to do it. Still, when he disappeared into the thick fog, her insides squeezed in an agony of fear. With nothing left to do, she lay down on the ground and closed her eyes, replaying the story of his past.

Her heart ached for Tyler's pain.

Deep breaths eased her, and she noted, too, a freshness in the air that hadn't been there before, or maybe she hadn't noticed. She likened it to the scent of mountain mahogany, or the air scrubbed clean after a heavy rain, or. . . She fell asleep trying to decide.

❧

Tyler could feel the moisture penetrating the sheeps' wool, weighing it down. The first rays of sun were lightening the sky, though blocked by the mountain peak for now.

Teddy, his nose guiding the way, had bolted off after a few ewes that had strayed out on a narrow trail. Tyler made note of the area, knowing he would have to return when the fog lifted and stack rocks to prevent future wanderings. A subtle lightening of the oppressive air relieved his mind. The fog was moving out, and the dark silver of the mist was brightening. The familiar work tending the sheep kept his mind occupied and away from the specter of Anna that would have, he knew, stolen sleep from him even if he had tried to rest.

Teddy led the way back to camp, the fog still a heavy presence. Tyler stoked the dying fire and checked the blankets to assure himself Renee hadn't wandered off. He knelt to touch the soft spot his feet found. "Renee?"

In the thickness he heard no rustle of response or soft whimpers and shuffles of someone waking. "Renee?"

He stretched his hand out farther. Empty. And that's when he heard the rush of feet and the half-choked sobs. He angled back toward the fire and bumped hard into something. A choked gasp identified the object.

"Renee?" Her exhale was forced and shuddering, and he placed a hand on her arms, feeling the quivering terror of her breathing. "What is it?"

"A monster."

He chuckled and pulled her closer to the fire where he could finally see the vague outline of her face. "There are no monsters. Was it a bear? A cat?"

The same shuddering cries rocked her shoulders. "Tall. Small head. Long arms."

It was balanced on his tongue to deny it again but he thought better of it. "What were you doing?"

"I—"

Her hesitation told him all he needed to know. "You went to. . .'talk to the neighbors.'"

She gaped up at him then away, smudging a hand across her cheeks.

The fog hid her expression, but if he'd been a betting man he would have bet her face burned as hot as the fire. "You saw your reflection in the fog. It happened to me once before in fog this thick. I'd gone out a few paces from camp and saw this apparition. It was just like you described. Took me a few seconds and a couple of bullets to realize what I was dealing with."

He could almost feel the tension draining from her. Her expression, clearer now through the thinning fog, sported a sheepish grin. Flickering flames licked shadows along the side of her face closest to the fire. His eyes followed the dancing light along the curve of her jaw then down the column of her neck. A powerful longing to draw her close rose within him. With every ounce of willpower, Tyler removed his hand from her arm and took a step back. "I'm going to catch some sleep."

Chapter 20

"What are the black sheep for?" Renee asked later that day.

The sheep had watered and were moving back toward the bedding ground. Tyler and Renee stood atop a ledge that allowed full view of the herd, which made the summer pasture easy to manage. Welford camp, as it was called, had a stream that ran the length of the boundaries, which also eased the need to push the herd from bedding ground to watering sites and grazing places.

"Markers," Tyler replied. "One for every two hundred sheep. If I'm missing a black sheep when I go to count, I can assume I'm missing white sheep and do a search. It might mean predators or that they've strayed off trail."

"It's quite a system."

Tyler nodded, completing a silent count as they stood there. Six black sheep. He stood for a moment, Renee a few feet off, and watched the sheep mill, some lying down as others chewed cud and a few grazed. The littlest of lambs bounced and played. A light breeze blew against his face—cold air, the promise of a cool night, like most of the nights while summering herds.

"Let's hope there's no snow tonight," he said out loud, not realizing he'd spoken his thoughts until Renee replied.

"Should we put up the tent?"

He turned, wondering if she was more worried about him or herself. The last several nights, he'd allowed her to use the tent while he slept under the stars. "Frostbite isn't so bad."

She stared at him for a few seconds then reared back her head, her hair snaking along her shoulders, her laughter punching the air. God help him, she was beautiful. He looked away until her laughter died. "Tyler?" She tilted her head back in the direction of camp and cocked an eyebrow. "Do I need to gather more wood? I'd hate for you to lose toes to frostbite since I'll be snug in the tent."

Tyler lifted his face to the sky, all desire to tease leaving him. "We'll be good for tonight, but there's a cabin down a ways from camp if you'd like to move in."

She tucked hair behind her ear. "Your cabin?"

"Trapper built it long ago. It comes in handy when bad weather threatens."

He shuffled down the face of the rock, turned, and offered a hand up to Renee to guide her descent from the rough surface. Her touch seemed too warm against his palm, and he let go as soon as she was steady. His heart pounded in his ears, and he forced himself to concentrate on something other than the woman at his side. "I'll show it to you and you can decide. I've got to pick up the traps and set them before night."

She stood in front of him, her eyes sober, and he wondered what she was thinking. Hoping to reassure whatever thoughts of impropriety might be running through her head, he added, "I'll stay outside in the tent."

❧

Renee wondered if Tyler knew what a handsome man he was or if any thought of himself had been trampled beneath what he perceived as his failure with Anna. "Have you tried anything other than herding sheep?"

"No."

"Maybe you could get work with cattle or something."

"Rich Morgan had a job to do and it fell to me." He pivoted away from her and she felt dismissed.

"Do you think they're after you?"

"I don't know, Renee."

She dared to ask the question that had been plaguing her since their conversation. "Are you risking my life by keeping me up here when they might be coming up the mountain as we speak?"

He stopped in his tracks, his back to her. She could see the hard line of his lips. "Take the horse down tomorrow. Find your own way home. I've got a job to do."

Tyler's words bit hard, and for the first time in a long time she felt the claws of shame against her conscience. She hadn't meant it to sound so. . .selfish. Like she was laying the blame for whatever might happen to her at his feet. There was irony in her question, too, when only days earlier she had entertained the idea of never going back to her father.

She opened her mouth to repair the harm she'd done, but his long strides took him swiftly away from her. Renee stood there in silent misery, watching as the sheep lay contentedly among the rocks and patches of grass. Hundreds of them. Content because they knew Tyler would protect them.

A shiver trickled down her spine. She had wanted to believe her father would protect her forever. Her mother's death had shown her that her father simply did not want to be bothered with her. As he'd grown, Thomas had become the one to bridge the gap between father and daughter. She'd resented the silent arrangement at first, imagining Thomas's every reasonable suggestion as the voice of her father. When she'd decided to go off on a cattle drive, Thomas, caught between the warring opinions of father and sister, had come to her.

"You've got to stop this, sis. You're killing him."

She'd known immediately who "him" was and tried her best to tune out her little brother and continue her preparations to ride over to the rival ranch. The rancher's son had taken a shine to her, and though older by ten years, he'd given in to her pleas to ride with them during the drive. "Maybe Pa'll come with me. He can be my protector."

"You know he can't."

"You mean he won't."

"No, Renee, don't you ever listen? He can't. Pa's got his own cattle to round up and send out."

"Well I won't get in his way then."

Thomas had squeezed his eyes shut, his frustration showing in the way he worked his jaw back and forth. "Renee, you're wrong. You are so wrong about Pa. He does love you; he just has a hard time showin' it. Please don't do this. Nathan Potter is not a gentleman and you'll be the only woman. Don't think for a minute that he'll protect you from. . ."

She'd drawn up short at his choice of words, a little stunned to realize the scope of her brother's knowledge of women. "What do you know of such things?"

Thomas had cracked a little smile. "I hear the hands talk all the time."

"They should be more careful."

"Why? You'd protect me from that talk but ride right into a situation that puts yourself at risk?"

His heartfelt plea and pointed question had turned her away from the folly. She had even tried to make amends with her father after Thomas's pleading, trying her hand at cooking and learning to keep house. But other than an occasional, grudging thank you, Pa had never seemed to notice.

Renee stepped into camp, deflated by the memory of her failure to gain her father's affections. By her words and Tyler's reaction, though, she almost couldn't blame him for taking offense.

The camp was empty, though the fire had been stoked and the rifle left behind. Tyler either forgot his promise to show her the cabin or had been so irritated he'd decided against it.

Restless, she moved to the canvas-wrapped haunch of meat high in the tree, lowered it, and hacked away a nice piece with a huge knife. She could at least make him something to eat. Settling the skillet deep into the hottest part of the coals, she wondered at the wisdom of Tyler leaving so late without the rifle. Even though it was still daylight, the shadows were growing long.

She browned the mutton and added the beans Tyler had left soaking that morning. He had no fresh vegetables and very little flour and sugar left. The low sugar supply had been her fault, and she felt the twinge of guilt for her selfishness. In those first few weeks, he had always offered it to her, never seeming to mind how she mounded it into her coffee while he drank his black. Now she saw how he must have cringed as she dug selfishly into his supply, never once denying herself but claiming the sweetness as if it were her right. As the days had progressed and weeks passed, she had come to understand more and more the preciousness of his supplies and the measured use of each package and sack he allotted himself.

When the mutton stew, such as it was, was bubbling merrily, she moved to the edge of the camp and squinted into the near darkness. Sassy stood picketed to the same spot Tyler had placed her that morning. The horse's presence did nothing to relieve her concern. She eyed the rifle then stared back into the night. If Tyler hurt himself or had a run-in with an animal, she would never be able to rescue him in time. Maybe he'd left the rifle thinking she would feel safer, just in case the gang did trace their path up the mountain and found their campsite.

Renee moved back to the ring of fire. She rubbed her upper arms to ward off the chill, amazed how the warmth of day could fade so absolutely into coldness. Nudging the coffee closer to the fire, she readied a mug. When the brew boiled, she poured the thick, dark liquid and took a cautious sip. Bitter. Very bitter. But it was hot and she was cold. She'd get used to it.

Chapter 21

Tyler ran his hand over his hair and down his neck, massaging the knot of tension at the base of his skull. Renee's words mocked him. If the Loust Gang had somehow tracked him and was on its way, he was risking Renee. But there was far more at stake. Only Rich knew Tyler's other secret. The one that could get them all killed.

Tyler chided himself for being foolish enough to think the gang would stay over in the Dakota Black Hills and not come looking for him. If they trekked this far away from their usual home base, there was no reason to delude himself that they were here for anything else except finding him. Renee had been a casualty of their search, nothing more. He should have moved on like he'd planned from the beginning. But Rich had become a good friend and had needed someone to herd in the mountains. The offer to buy into half the sheep had been appealing as well as the prómise of seclusion.

After all Rich had done for him, Tyler couldn't let him down now that he had experience with the sheep.

Tyler chuckled dryly, thinking back to the lessons of that first month taking the sheep up the mountain to summer pasture. He'd treated the animals roughly, using the dog more frequently to bunch the woolies tight whenever he got tired of them wandering too far. He'd even tried to force them through dense brush on a narrow trail, angered when they scattered every which way to avoid the tangle of undergrowth.

And he'd reaped guilt for his mistreatment when Rich met him a month later in the summer range at the top of the mountains. The man's expert eye surveyed the herd and his sole comment, "They've lost a lot of weight," filled Tyler with shame and the certainty that Rich knew what he'd been doing. When they rode down to check on the sheep, the animals scattered from Tyler's presence. Again, he felt Rich's knowing eye on him.

"Sheep should feel comforted by your presence, not threatened."

Yet even after that, Rich had been patient. His parting gift had been the Bible and a request to "start with the twenty-third Psalm."

Each word of the book had challenged Tyler's attitude toward the sheep in his care. Nose flies had given him the opportunity to work closely with the animals, applying the ointment that gave them relief. He'd used the time with the animals to put into practice the gentle manner of the shepherd in Psalm 23.

The small book had taught him something about kindness and mercy and stirred in him a longing for someone to offer the same to him. Rich had, and when Tyler had tried to thank the man, Rich's response had been, "Thank the Lord, son."

Sometimes when Tyler gazed out at the burst of colors in the sunset or witnessed the breathtaking beauty of hidden meadows on the mountain range, he knew there had to be a God. Rich would have agreed with him on the matter. "He waits for us all," would be his response, though Tyler didn't quite know what it all meant. Now, with the worry that Marv might be hunting him, he wondered if God would protect him if he prayed and asked.

It seemed so odd to pray. Weak. Yet Rich wasn't weak and Tyler knew the man prayed, and often. And what about protecting Renee? If the gang lurked in the territory searching for him, he risked her safety by not getting her away as soon as possible. Why should he expect her to stick her neck out for him? Because he'd grown used to having her nearby? Because he enjoyed those moments when he had someone to talk to? And she was beautiful, like Anna. But not like Anna at all.

Teddy returned to his side as Tyler set the last trap. He climbed to the lookout again to gauge the mood of the herd, pleased to see in the waning light that they were restful and calm. He watched the newborn lamb toddle toward its mother. Reprimand bloomed in his mind as he likened the lamb to Renee. His expectations, and the similarity of their willful ways, pushed him to demand too much from her too soon. Just as the lamb must learn and grow, he had to let her. He was not her shepherd, God was.

Tyler lowered his head and drank in the cooling night air. He loved the richness of nighttime in the mountains but something had changed. What once he found soothing now brought a twist of restlessness. Maybe he would tell Rich it was time for him to move on. If God protected him from the gang, he could take the herd back in the fall and travel west, maybe to California. With the decision bright in his mind, Tyler headed toward camp. He hoped Renee would be asleep, that she wouldn't take him up on the idea of leaving. He quickened his pace, anxious to see if the strong-minded woman had already stripped him of provisions and started Sassy down the mountain.

Sassy sent Tyler a nicker of greeting as he drew closer to camp. He scratched the horse's neck. Relief flooded him when he saw Renee's huddled form sitting by the fire, a book spread in her lap, a curtain of dark hair preventing him from seeing her profile. But she was there.

He left the horse and strode up to the fire, holding his hands near the heat, waiting for that moment when she would see him. She didn't move, a sniff the only suggestion of life.

"It's cold out there," he said, trying to open a conversation.

She raised her head then, eyes red, streaks of wetness leaving tracks on her cheeks.

Fear stabbed and he wondered if she was hurt. He scanned her from head to toe and saw nothing amiss. "What happened?"

Renee shook her head and swiped a tendril of hair from her cheek. "I'm sorry."

Whatever he had expected, it wasn't an apology. He opened his mouth to respond.

"You think I'm selfish."

He held his tongue, unsure where she was going with this.

❧

Renee stared down at the book in her lap and scratched Teddy's head as he lay beside her. Through fresh tears she could see the blur of words. "I helped myself to something to read. It got too quiet." She lifted her head and saw his slight nod.

"I'm glad you didn't start out in the dark," he offered.

"It came out all wrong," she blurted. She hesitated and stilled her thoughts to think through what she wanted to say. "I know you wouldn't keep me up here if you thought it was dangerous—"

"Which is why I suggested you leave, because it could get that way if they find me."

"But you also thought I was thinking about myself too much."

He didn't answer but turned his head away from her, his shoulders almost a physical wall. "I can see in you what I myself used to be."

His words slid over her, a promising ointment to the open wound of her guilt. "My foolishness got Thomas killed."

"He might not be dead, Renee." Tyler faced her and removed his hat. "Did you see his body?"

"No."

"If they shot him, they didn't let him get real close before they did it. He might have just got himself scraped by a bullet. Enough to give him some pain and knock him out. If they had you on their hands, they probably didn't pay attention to what happened to him."

Hope sprang up in her. She pressed her lips together and blinked back tears of relief. Who better to know these things than Tyler? Like it or not, he would understand the inside workings of a gang, their weak points and strengths. She drew in a shaky breath. "What do you know about God?"

Tyler hunkered down. "Know He's here, even now. I see Him everywhere. All the time. In the beauty of the mountains. In the timidness of the sheep, His creation, and what we are to Him if we follow His ways. I didn't see it at first, mind you, but I expect Rich knew I would eventually. You can't help but acknowledge there's a God when you're up here."

She'd seen it, too. It was as if God Himself was reflected in the heights of the Big Horn Mountains. The trees. The grassy patches. Even the wild animals. Fierceness contrasted against wild beauty. Her eyes slid over Tyler. Here was a man who had been fierce and unruly at one time and had grown to become someone different. She wondered if he was aware of the change in himself.

Tyler sat back and stretched his legs out, the position he inevitably took while sitting at the fire. "I'm no preacher." His soft voice crawled across the distance that separated them. "But I know I didn't like who I was. Guess I knew that even when I was an outlaw."

"Did you ever shoot anyone?"

"Never had a need to. Most saw you coming and figured whatever they had on 'em wasn't worth their life."

"They've shot people recently. Lots of people."

He scratched the side of his cheek, the fire flickering red highlights in his tousled brown hair. "They got greedier. More aggressive. With all the patrols out here, it's getting harder to pull a job." He lifted his head. "Your pa must be missing you."

The sudden shift in conversation jarred her less than the idea of her pa missing her. Could he miss her? "Thomas meant everything to him."

Tyler picked up a stick and began breaking it into small pieces. "I think you've convinced yourself of that. It's the burr under your saddle."

Hot denial rose in her throat then sank down to the pit of her stomach like a rock.

"He must have loved your ma pretty powerful."

"Then why doesn't he hate Thomas? She died giving birth to him."

He chuckled. "Don't guess he looks like her. Or walks like her. Can't you see how it could twist a knife in a man's gut when there's a constant reminder of what he's lost?"

Warm wetness rolled down her cheek and landed salty on her lips and tongue. "I just wanted it to be like it was before she died."

Tyler turned his eyes to the darkness beyond. "Death always changes things."

Chapter 22

Silence followed his last statement. He drew his attention back to Renee. Tears rolled down her cheeks, and the sight stirred an ache in him to cradle her close. Yet he had no right. No reason. But the desire burned in his chest and took him back to that one time he had held her. She'd been light in his arms. A soft warmth that left him bereft when they parted.

Over the last weeks, she had come to be a part of his routine, an essential part of camp life. He'd never felt so close to someone since Anna. Yet Renee had her own problems to resolve. Someone so young shouldn't be saddled with someone like him. He had nothing to offer, and life on the mountains herding sheep, running from his past, was no life at all.

He exhaled sharply and threw the stick aside, the pieces scattering. He jammed a hand onto the ground and pushed to his feet. "I'm going to. . ." He paused. She raised her head to look at him, and something hard lodged in his throat at the vulnerability in her eyes. "Check on Sassy."

She nodded and scrubbed a hand over her face as she leaned forward. Her hair slipped around her shoulder, dark and rich. She reached for a spoon and stirred whatever it was in the pot. As if feeling his stare, she glanced up. Heat rose up his neck at having been caught.

"Tyler?"

He cleared his throat and pulled his hat lower over his eyes. "Yeah?"

"What was that book you wanted me to read?"

The image of the little lamb rose in his mind, transforming into a mane of dark hair, a pert nose, and. . . His cheeks puffed out on an exhale. He really needed to get a grip.

"Read?" He groped for the context of her question. The book. . . She was asking about the passage he had suggested she read. Maybe the Bible would provide her the same comfort it had given him. He certainly had nothing better to offer. "Psalms. Twenty-three. It's about a shepherd."

She nodded and got to her feet, light as a feather. Pushing aside the flap of the saddlebag, she found the small volume. She shot him a smile and made herself comfortable, using his bedroll as a brace against the rocks at her back. Her hands brushed over the delicate pages, turning them one by one.

Tyler realized she would have no idea where to find Psalms. He crossed to where she sat and crouched, lifting the book from her lap and turning the pages back from Malachi to the worn pages of Psalms. "Here." He pointed.

Her finger grazed the edges of the pages, yellowed by his fingers and the passage of time. "You read these often."

"I do. It's. . .comforting."

She raised her face, her nose inches from his, her gray eyes solemn and pleading. "Will you read it to me?"

He stopped breathing, wondering what her skin would feel like beneath his fingers. Her expression shifted, the corners of her eyes crinkling with amusement. He lowered himself to the ground and pulled the Bible onto his lap. "Guess I could do that."

He forced his mind to ignore the woman next to him and fixate on the image of the little lamb. "'The Lord is my Shepherd,'" he began. The Lord was Renee's Shepherd as well. It was up to him to show her that.

❧

Renee listened to Tyler's voice, the words, and the message. When he finished the chapter, he cleared his throat, hand resting on the open book. She admired his long fingers. There was strength in his hands. Tenderness for the sheep in his care, yet toughness, too, called upon when he had to set traps or take burrs from their wool or give gentle discipline to a straying sheep. "You're a shepherd, what does it mean to you?"

He stared out into the night. She watched his face, set in profile against the firelight. Funny how she couldn't imagine that face twisted into a cruel sneer or his words and actions rough and threatening, in keeping with the reputation of an outlaw.

"I try and supply the sheep with all that they need. I believe God is that way. He might not give us what we want, but He fills our needs, knowing what's best. But just like Punky, we can think we know better sometimes."

She grinned and wondered if he thought her a Punky. The wayward ewe could definitely be a problem, just as she had caused herself a heap of trouble.

Tyler continued, telling her of his scouting trip in the early spring before bringing the sheep into the mountains, when he assessed the places along the trail and removed overgrown shrubs. He often spent time damming a shallow stream to make a deep pool for the sheep to drink from en route to summer pasture, or clearing meadows of poisonous plants. "There's a lot of work that goes into caring for the sheep ahead of time. God's like that. He plans things out, knowing what we're in for and smoothing the way. Sometimes we think it's so hard or the way too tough, but He's there."

When silence fell between them, Renee placed her hand on his arm. She felt him tense, and when their eyes met, she caught the change in his expression. Saw him swallow. "You're a good teacher," she observed.

He acknowledged her comment with a slight nod. His gaze swept over her face, his eyes lingered on her lips, and then he jerked away as if stung by her presence. With a quick movement, he slapped the Bible shut and pushed to his feet. "Best go check on Sassy."

"Yes, Tyler." She smiled up at him, sure now that she'd seen something more than friendship in his eyes, and it gripped her with a desire for something more. "You better go check on the horse."

She watched the vague outline of him as he gave Sassy grain and fiddled with the picket line. Tyler had wanted to kiss her. The thought, at least, had entered his mind; she was sure of it. How was it a former outlaw, a man who lived a wild, criminal life, could shy from her like a newborn lamb? His gaze had held her captive, too, for that long second when she understood the depth of respect and emotion his presence churned in her. The awakening both thrilled and scared her. She'd seen what he had become, his commitment to the sheep, the way he had forcibly redirected his life away from the irresponsible and dishonest tendencies of an outlaw.

Renee closed her eyes and curled into a ball, resting her forehead on her arms. If she tried, she could make him love her. Then, maybe, she'd finally feel safe.

Chapter 23

Tyler stroked the horse's flank, and Sassy bent her neck and dug her nose against his side. When he didn't respond to the playful overture, the horse nibbled at his sleeve. But Tyler was in no mood for games. He'd almost kissed Renee. If she'd moved an inch in his direction, he might have, and that would have been disastrous.

Reading to her, he had hoped she might be coming to understand the importance of her actions to those around her. That bad choices often clung like a burr. Tyler sighed. Rich Morgan had probably held many of the same thoughts about him when he'd visited the sheep camp that first month.

He could love her. Maybe he already did love her, but it was too dangerous to love when Marv might be a step away, biding his time. Marv had a powerful motivation, and Renee knew nothing about it. It was better for her to go home. He needed a plan to get her away from here.

Tyler pushed at Sassy's nose, and the horse nudged back. He leaned into Sassy and wished for the solace of the fire and his Bible. Renee's presence seemed more threat than comfort now. Exhaustion punched him in the gut, and he moved, his limbs heavy, toward camp. Renee watched him in silence, yet he felt the weight of her expectation. He picked up a plate and drew in a breath before heading toward the fire and the pot of stew. Ladling some onto his plate, he took his seat a safe distance away and tried to ignore her presence altogether.

His whispered prayer for the food became a desperate plea for help. Spooning in his first bite, he rolled the broth and meat around on his tongue. Not bad. Her cooking had improved over the last week.

"How'd I do?"

The simple question held a note of vulnerability. In answer, he dipped his spoon for another bite. "Real good."

"Did you love Anna?"

He frowned down at his plate, the bowl of his spoon sinking into the broth of the stew. Love Anna? Such a tough subject to talk about, and he was so tired. "Didn't get the chance to love her."

"But you cared for her."

"I did," he conceded, wary, weighing his words. "She was a good woman." *I could have loved her.* If given time and under different circumstances, he would have married her.

He spooned another bite into his mouth, then another, and then decided he'd had enough. Rising, he met Renee as she jumped up to claim his plate.

"I'll take care of these," she assured.

Tyler nodded, grateful to be done for the day.

❧

Renee lay awake for a long time thinking about what he'd read to her from Psalms. She watched as the flames danced and twisted, high and hot, and then lowered as they licked through the supply of wood. She didn't want to think about Tyler or Anna or her father or Thomas.

Her decision to run off and drag Thomas along to look for a gang of outlaws seemed such an immature thing now. In hindsight. Still, she had learned from her mistake. Whether Thomas lived or not, and she wholeheartedly hoped Thomas was safe just as Tyler suggested, she would give more thought to her actions.

Should she have been more responsible? Sure.

Could she change? Of course. Tyler had.

Did she want to change?

She bit her lip hard as tears burned again at the back of her eyes. It wasn't a matter of her wanting to change; it was more a matter of her needing to change. The Bible spoke of change. Bits of memory, chats she'd had with her mother, scratched the surface of her mind. She did her best to capture and bring them into focus, but the memories were dull and she had been young. Perhaps reading the Bible more would show her what her mother had understood.

God? She breathed the word. *All I know is. . .*

She didn't know what to say and felt foolish pretending to talk to something she couldn't see. But Tyler had said He was everywhere. Didn't that mean He was here now? In the dying fire? The night that gripped her in its blackness? *All I know is I need this change. I need You, I think, but I don't know how. Help me understand.*

❧

Morning light stretched its dome of brilliance across the sky. Renee yawned and braced herself up on an elbow. The fire flared hot again, but Tyler was not there. She stumbled from the blankets, taking the time to roll everything into a tight bundle to keep out critters or, she shuddered, snakes.

She moved around the camp, combing tangles from her hair and then twisting it into a knot to keep it out of her face. It didn't look like Tyler had even taken the time to eat breakfast. Taking the bucket to the creek, she bent to draw water. Her hair tumbled down and touched the surface of the water, floating on top for a minute before sinking into a sodden mass. She snapped the strands back over her shoulder and tucked stray strands behind her ear.

Turning, bucket in hand, she saw Sassy moving toward her, Tyler astride, a baby lamb across the saddle. She could tell from the way Tyler moved in the saddle and the stiff expression on his face that something terrible had happened. When he caught sight of her moving toward him, Tyler stopped the horse.

"Cat got into the sheep last night. Killed three ewes and this lamb."

His voice did not betray emotion, only a resignation that told her this type of thing had happened before. "Are you going after it?" she asked.

He shook his head. "No. Probably a young cat being taught to hunt by its mama."

She could see the blood along the lamb's head and the canvas-wrapped package behind the saddle then realized something horrible. "You skinned it?"

"I'll coat the bum lamb to see if the mother will adopt it." Tyler nudged Sassy into motion. He got to camp ahead of her. By the time she reached the perimeter, he was astride the horse and headed back out.

"Can I go with you?"

Chapter 24

Tyler debated with himself over his answer. To have her so close. . . He gritted his teeth. He could use the help, and he needed to treat the sheep for scab. Messy work.

"You could treat them for me while I take care of the dead."

His answer was her solemn nod. "I don't mind."

Unable to come up with anything that might discourage her, Tyler turned Sassy sideways, kicked his boot from the stirrup, and offered his hand. She set the bucket of water on a narrow ledge about four feet off the ground, covered it with a towel, and rushed back to him.

His roughened palm scraped against her softer one as he aided her ascent. She settled herself behind him in the saddle, her hands resting along his waist. He took a deep breath of the cool morning air. He had to keep his head. She was just a girl whom he had rescued. A pretty girl. A selfish girl who might have gotten her brother killed. Not his type.

Where the trail narrowed, he slowed Sassy and allowed her to pick her way along at her own pace. Renee's hands gripped his shirt tighter until he feared she might rend the material. "Sassy's a mountain horse. She knows these trails."

"Is that your—" Sassy slipped and cut off what she was saying. When the horse regained its footing he could feel her grip weaken. "Was that your way of offering comfort?"

He grinned at the irony. "I suppose it was."

They rode in silence until Sassy cleared the last of the rocks and carried them into the meadow. The sheep were spread out on rolling hills, while the craggy peak of another mountain showed its balding head. Snow capped the mountain and the sun beat down on the green grass of the long, narrow valley that put the white dots of sheep in contrast.

"It's even more beautiful from here," she whispered.

Tyler didn't respond but led Sassy through the hundreds of sheep toward a craggy spot that backed to thick woods with heavy underbrush. Blood smeared along some of the rocks where he'd found the dead ewes and the lamb. He searched among the stretch of sheep in front of him and listened for the telltale sounds he knew the bum lamb would make, unable to find its mother and denied by other ewes the chance to nurse.

Teddy panted into view and lay down beside Sassy.

"Good boy, Teddy," Renee called to the little dog.

Tyler dismounted and gave Teddy an absentminded scratch as he surveyed the sheep, listening for the orphan lamb's cry.

"What do I need to do?" Renee asked as she slipped to the ground unaided. "You know I'll help."

Thick shame rose and made him clench his teeth. Hadn't he just tried to discount her character? Yet she had helped before. Many times over the last couple of weeks they had worked side by side among the herd. His load caring for the sheep and cooking had been lightened because of her presence. He had a responsibility to at least be fair in his assessment of her abilities. "There's a bum—" He pursed his lips and waited.

"A lazy sheep?"

He hid the grin. "No, a motherless lamb. A bum. He'll be looking for some supper. You'll hear him."

Tyler watched as Renee processed the information he'd just relayed. With a slight nod and a determined tilt of her chin, Renee waded into the herd of sheep. He absorbed the animals' reaction to her presence. Her lithe body bent over the head of one particularly friendly sheep that trailed her a few feet. She spoke to it, though he couldn't hear what she said. A spring lamb tottered over then leaped away when Renee laughed. Her hair spread around her shoulders, and even as he watched, as if she knew his eyes were upon her, she reached up, gathered it into a long tail, and wrapped it into a loose knot.

An ache stabbed through him, and Tyler turned from the scene, glad he hadn't been caught watching her. It would send her the wrong message. As soon as he got through the day, he would get her down off the mountain and back home, away from Marv and the threat of the gang coming for him. But after the damage the cat inflicted on the herd, he needed her help one more day. Tyler flipped open the saddlebag and withdrew a jar of salve. "Renee!"

She looked up, her hair sliding a bit, her face bright with happiness. "He's so cute!" She laughed and pointed to the lamb who nibbled at her knee.

"There's work to do." His gruff tone was not lost on her, and the joy slid from her face.

He held up the jar and pointed. "I need you to smear this on their faces while you're looking for the lamb."

She hurried to him and took the large jar without a word, turning to go when he heard the plaintive wail of the bum. He led Sassy forward as Renee began working over the sheep. A dirty job. Smelly, too, though she didn't complain.

When he found the lamb, working its head from under the protesting underside of a ewe, he gathered the baby close. At least the lamb had received the first few weeks of nutrition from its mama. Working as quickly as he could, Tyler fit the skin of the dead lamb over the live one then began looking for the mother of the dead baby. It took him an hour to locate the right ewe, standing off by herself, engorged and restless. He set the baby down beside her and the lamb immediately scampered to her. Twisting her head, the ewe nudged the baby and smelled along its side. The lamb tucked up underneath the ewe and began nursing as the mother sniffed the baby's backside.

Come on, mama. Tyler cheered the two on as the sniffing and nursing continued. At last the mother stopped and seemed to relax. Tension drained from Tyler's shoulders.

❧

Renee worked until the muscles in her back bunched so hard she could no longer bend over and had to kneel, which made her knees sore. Tyler returned to camp twice to replenish the salve. He brought back cold bacon and pancakes, and she devoured them like a starving dog. Teddy stayed near her, hoping for a scrap and relishing the strip she tossed him.

"We're on the last group," he announced. He smiled down at her, and she saw the exhaustion in every line of his face. His eyes, especially, showed a deep weariness that his grin belied.

"What's so funny?"

"You should see yourself."

Somehow, she didn't quite care what she looked like at that moment. He didn't look much better, and they both smelled faintly of the tar used in the salve.

His smile bled away. "I'm proud of you," he whispered. The simple praise swirled in her head. "You've worked hard." His tone held wonder, as if he was seeing something for the first time, mesmerized by what he witnessed.

Her tongue wouldn't form words. She saw his hand come up and felt the gentle stroke of his finger against her cheek as he swiped a tendril of hair back from her face. His gaze fell to her lips and Renee recognized his struggle. She kept still, her resolve to get him to love her crushed beneath the heel of something else. She already loved him. This man. A fragile love, perhaps, for what did she really know about such things? But it felt right. It felt good and secure. Something she wanted to revel in and cherish, not bend to her will and force upon him—that wouldn't be love anyway, would it?

He withdrew his hand, his gaze surrendering hers. He stepped back and turned to look at the sky, and everything Renee had felt seconds before became vulnerable as doubts snaked their way through her heart.

Chapter 25

Tyler had wanted so much to kiss her. To smooth away the splotch of salve clinging to her cheek and enjoy the feel of her soft lips against his. His will had nearly crumbled when he yielded to the desire to graze the hair back from her cheek. Touching her. Drinking in the devotion he saw in her eyes. She had worked so hard, the words of praise had come easily to him. He had kept a close eye on her as he moved among the animals, noting the moment when she had stopped stooping to administer the salve and begun getting down on one knee. He knew all too well the strain of muscles after a long day of working among the sheep.

The difference in her work ethic and the ease with which she accepted the long arduous chores endeared her to him and broke whatever preconceived notion he had of her being a selfish brat. She had grown in the time she'd been with the herd. Just as caring for that first herd had grown and matured him.

"Got somewhere I'd like to show you. Tomorrow, after the sheep are settled, I'll take you there."

"Sure." She nodded and took a step away, her eyes drifting toward the last group of animals.

His eyes followed the line of her silhouette, captured by the wild tousle of her hair and how warm sunlight brought out glints of red in the strands. She'd knotted it over and over through the day. Now, Tyler doffed his hat and yanked at the pigging string tied there. "Here, it'll keep your hair off your face."

An automatic reaction, her hands reached for the strands loosened by the constant kneeling and stooping. "It has been a trial today."

"It's beautiful." He swallowed, wishing he hadn't said what he thought out loud.

She took the string from him and bent double. She combed through the dark mass then straightened. Gathering it close in one hand, she tied the string around the ponytail. "That's so much better."

"Should have thought of it sooner."

She picked up the jar of salve and moved out into the last group of sheep. To his right, Tyler caught sight of the jacketed lamb, happy in his newfound mother and nursing, his little tail flapping back and forth in joy. Tyler understood completely.

❧

When Tyler didn't move on, Renee risked another glance at him. He made quite the picture among the sea of white sheep. The pasture, dotted with lush patches of grass, and the mountain rising strong and lonely behind Tyler, seemed to echo her opinion of the man himself.

She was grateful to have her hair out of the way and couldn't quite deny the pleasure his comment brought. Whatever Tyler was, he was not a man given to soft words.

Moving among the last of the group, Teddy at her side, Renee lifted her head when she caught a strange humming in the air. She glanced around to see what it might be or where it might be coming from, and that's when she realized it was Tyler. Singing. His voice, rich and buttery soft. Teddy moved off toward Tyler, slow and easy. The sheep, too, were close to Tyler, some of them lying down.

As he worked his way into another verse of "Clementine," Renee let the music flow over her. Even the sheep she tended seemed lulled by the sound of his voice. Many began to lie down, freed from anxiety by the sound and presence of the man they most trusted. Just like the Shepherd in Psalm 23. The sheep had everything to be content, and what they didn't know they needed was being supplied before they knew of the need. Like the application of the salve. Tyler saw the need before it became a problem, smoothing the way for the timid, helpless creatures.

Tears blurred Renee's vision as she knelt to apply the tar mixture to the head of a ewe. With Tyler's song soft in her ears, she knew she needed salve, too, of a different sort. She bit her lip, chest heaving. *Lord, I've made such a mess. Forgive me.*

She scratched the ewe's face where the wool did not grow then rubbed at the tears that trickled down her face. *Let me be like this sheep.*

Renee continued to apply the salve to the heads of sheep, meditating on their behavior, on the differences in their personalities. Perhaps she was most like Punky and, like Tyler, God would need to be patient with her. But hadn't He already been patient? Even through the disaster of seeking out the Loust Gang, God had brought her here. Now she would return to her father a different person and to Thomas—*God, please let him be alive*—a different sister.

Tyler called out to her on the other side of the group. Pulled out of her reverie, she realized she had subconsciously been hearing a sharper, distressed baaing for some time. Tyler motioned to her. The sheep divided in front of her, alerted by her faster pace. One of the pregnant ewes lay down in the pasture, obviously straining to give birth. Tyler stood off a distance from her and motioned for Renee to come to his side.

"Nice voice."

He ducked his head and jabbed a thumb over his shoulder. "Got something even better. Thought you'd like to see this one, too."

The ewe lay a ways off from the herd, seemingly in great pain. Renee winced with every stretch of the ewe's neck and plaintive cry. "Is it hurt?"

"It won't be long now," Tyler whispered. "She's given birth before."

As if that explained away the obvious pain the ewe suffered now. Still, Renee couldn't be upset with Tyler; he'd seen the event thousands of times. With each passing minute, the ewe's stress raised. The baby finally made an appearance, but things seemed to stall halfway through. Panicked by the sight of the baby's ears twitching yet still clear of the mother, she turned to Tyler. "Shouldn't you do something?"

He grinned down at her. "She's doing fine. Just watch."

True enough, another few seconds and the ewe jumped up, the rest of the baby slipping to the ground. The baby shook its head. The mother stood for a minute then turned and began to lick her newborn.

"At least she didn't give birth in the middle of a winter storm like she did last time."

Renee couldn't take her eyes off the baby. It wiggled but lay in place as its mama licked over the wet coat.

"She'll lick the baby dry. It helps the lamb not chill."

She didn't know what to say, how to explain the tidal wave of emotions that flooded her at the beautiful picture of mother and child. A picture she hadn't appreciated at the first birth she'd witnessed. It awoke the ache for her own mother and magnified the pain of losing her after Thomas's birth.

"Why don't you stay and keep an eye on them? I'll finish up," Tyler offered.

If she responded, she couldn't remember, but he left her alone to watch the miracle. Every time the baby tried to stand, Renee's heart swelled with pride. When the baby flopped over, a surge of despair tightened her chest. The irony of witnessing this new birth just when she had repented, was not lost on her. It warmed her and she smiled her thanks to God for allowing her to see what He himself had seen when she asked for forgiveness. The wonder of new birth, though, she grimaced, spiritual rebirth wasn't quite so messy. Except when you considered the burden and dirt that sin and her own willfulness had placed on her soul. Tyler rode up on Sassy just as the baby gained its feet and began nursing in earnest.

"Let's get back and get something to eat."

A bubble of satisfaction lifted her on its wings as they traveled to camp. She lay her forehead against Tyler's back, too exhausted to sit up. Every movement of the horse made her eyes heavier with sleep until Sassy began the climb up the sharp hill to camp.

"Got some eggs hidden away for a night such as this."

Eggs. The idea of food didn't even appeal, though she was sure her body had burned through the pancakes and bacon long ago. Tyler touched her leg, and she roused from her drowsy state long enough to make the slide to the ground.

Her boot caught in the stirrup, jarring her fully awake. Tyler's hands were there, steadying her as he worked the boot free.

"You're about to collapse," he said.

"Sorry. It just hit me all of the sudden."

"No need to be."

They led Sassy up the steep incline and into camp. Tyler picketed the horse on a new patch of grass while Renee gathered some sticks for the fire. Hot coals still glowed. She knelt to blow on the coals, and pain shot up from her bruised knee. At least she had learned how to build a good fire while being with Tyler. Thomas always teased her about her lack of fire-making ability, grousing every time he had to relight the one in the ancient cookstove because she let it go out.

Renee sat back from the flickering flames, gripped by a longing to see her father and a swell of panic that Thomas might indeed be dead. She closed her eyes, needing to know one way or the other for her own peace of mind.

"Hey."

She opened her eyes to see Tyler in front of her. Concern etched a narrow furrow between his brows. "Hey," she drawled.

He chuckled. "Thought you'd fallen asleep sitting up."

"Just thinking."

"About the lamb? Thomas? Home?"

She gasped. "How did you know?"

He raised his hand and touched her cheek, and she felt the wetness smear against her skin. "Tears were my first clue."

She blinked and swiped at the place his finger had just touched. "I'm just tired."

"Not wanting to go down to the cabin?"

"Maybe tomorrow night."

"What about frostbite?"

She frowned, catching the mischievous twinkle in his eyes. "I see you didn't get your tent put up."

He shrugged. "Maybe tomorrow. I'll throw out another blanket for you."

Unrolling her bundle she made short work of getting comfortable, smothering a yawn with one hand.

"Not hungry?"

"Too tired."

"Then roll in for the night. I'm gonna fill up on an egg and that bacon." He got to his feet. "I'll cook you up a big breakfast in the morning. Speaking of. . ." An insufferable grin split his face. "You're not gonna be wanting to move much in the morning. Everything'll hurt."

Chapter 26

Everything did hurt, too. Renee wondered if it was just her imagination, but even her face seemed sore. The sun blasted down from the east. Her muddled mind blinked wide awake as it registered it to be nine o'clock or later.

"Eight thirty, to be exact," she heard Tyler confirm.

When she moved to jerk upright, she groaned and released a long, most unladylike grunt.

"Walking is the best medicine for the soreness."

"Aren't you sore?" She tilted her head his way, noting his casual position. "How long have you been awake?"

"Been up before dawn. Someone had to check on the ewe and the bum," he said, eyes twinkling.

She stretched her arms out one at a time. "And the baby?"

"Right as rain. Need a hand up?"

Renee scowled. "If you can do it, so can I."

"We'll be doing a lot of walking."

"I can't wait," she drawled.

"Good." He swung to his feet in one easy motion, looking not at all like a man suffering from sore muscles. When he towered over her and reached his hand down, she raised hers to meet his.

Humor lurked behind his grin. "I'll take it nice and easy."

And he did, too, raising her just enough to allow her to get her feet underneath. When she stood full height, he gave her a wink.

❧

Tyler had thought about this moment all morning. As exhausted as he'd been the night before, he'd lain awake watching through the flames as Renee slept. He suspected she hadn't even removed her boots or done the nightly ritual of braiding her hair that he'd observed many times. Maybe women didn't do that if their hair was already pulled back. How would he know?

He smiled at the top of her head as she stamped one foot, then the other, wincing each time, her hand firmly tucked in his. When she worked the stiffness from her legs, it took sheer willpower for him not to pull her close. He satisfied himself with a wink and served up the fresh corn cake he'd made. He handed her the plate. "You work on that while I get you some eggs and a nice slice of mutton."

She ate standing, a smart choice in his mind since getting down would cause even more pain. He lowered the hunk of mutton down from the tree, unwrapped it, and sliced a chunk for their supper as well as some for Renee's breakfast and a piece for Teddy.

Tyler rewrapped the meat and pulled on the rope to raise it high into the thick bough of the evergreen, one of the last firs at this altitude before the balding peak of the mountain cooled too much for growth. He wanted this day with her, to show her the one place he loved most on the mountain. Then they would begin the ride down together. He could return to the mountain in peace to handle whatever the Loust Gang had in store for him. But facing the mountain range alone held no joy for him. Not after tasting life in camp with Renee.

He jerked the pan from the fire, irritated that Renee had wiggled under his skin so easily. He slapped the meat into the skillet, gratified, somehow, by the fierce sizzle and the immediate cloud of smoke that rose up. He stabbed at the hunk with his fork and flung it over, jamming the pan just outside the fire to continue cooking. Stomping back to the pack, he dug deep into a thick canvas cushioned with a blanket. The eggs stayed cool here but they were probably at the end of their freshness, so he might as well cook them.

When he glanced over at Renee, she was licking her fingers. The flash of a smile curving her lips caused him physical pain. He jerked the pan off the heat and took another stab at the mutton. It was almost done. With a quick motion, he cracked the egg into the pan and tilted it so it wouldn't bleed over to the meat. He poked at it a bit and let it bubble.

"Something wrong?" Renee's question took him off guard.

"Be ready soon, just hang tight."

"No. I meant you. Did something happen to make you. . .grouchy?"

He pursed his lips and motioned for her to bring him a plate. Forking the mutton steak onto the plate, he flipped the egg in the skillet with a flick of his wrist.

He could hear the grin in her voice. "You've stomped and slung and slapped ever since fetching that meat."

Had he? "Didn't mean to."

"It's all right. I just wondered if it was something I'd done."

Tyler didn't know how to respond. No. It hadn't been her fault, but neither had he realized that he'd been crashing around camp like a pawing bull. Truth tickled at his brain. He stared at her and tried to imagine being without her. He gritted his teeth and turned away. He was a fool not to have taken her straight down the mountain. He didn't need another day of torturing himself with her presence while reconciling himself to what would soon become the reality of her absence. But he had promised. He slipped the egg from the skillet, set the pan aside, and spun on his heel. "I'm going to gather Sassy. When you're done, come on over and we'll ride."

❧

Renee watched Tyler go. Every bite of the mutton and egg brought a delicious treat to her tongue as she watched him adjust the cinch of the saddle. Maybe it was the mountain air or perhaps the fact she hadn't eaten in so long, aside from the corn cake, but everything Tyler made tasted good. His behavior, though. . . That posed a puzzle, to be sure.

When she finished, she dabbled some water over the plate. As she swirled the liquid around, she tried to grasp Tyler's change in mood. It didn't make sense. She dried the plate and fork and turned, bouncing right off Tyler's chest. She gasped.

His hands clasped her arms to steady her. "Was just coming to fetch the rifle."

She felt the strength of his fingers dig into her upper arms for the second it took her to regain her balance. "I didn't hear you."

Tyler nodded down at her, his gaze trailing from her hair to her eyes. He dropped his hands and leaned past to pull the gun from where it rested behind the water pail. Opening the chamber, he checked the load.

"We're not hunting anything, are we?"

"Never go anywhere without checking your gun."

She considered that. "I'd rather not go if you're hunting that cat."

Tyler lowered the rifle. "We're hunting, but not animals. This is just for protection."

Chapter 27

Tyler insisted Renee ride while he walked. He enjoyed meandering through the wooded areas, retracing the path they'd taken that last day to summer pasture. As much as he thought he knew the Big Horns, something always surprised him. Teddy usually came along, but he'd left the dog with the herd, lying in the sunshine atop the ledge.

"Aren't you getting tired of walking?" Renee asked about half an hour from camp.

"Was just thinking how much I enjoy exploring. Walking's the best way to do that."

"You should have left Sassy behind."

He'd considered it. Walking would loosen up some of those muscles Renee strained, but he didn't want her to push past the limits of her strength. "Might think differently on the return trip. Uphill," he teased.

"Well, then, stop."

Renee's command took him by surprise, but he pulled on Sassy's bridle and Renee slid to the ground beside him, clinging to the saddle for support a minute longer than usual.

He couldn't help but grin.

"I'll thank you to wipe that smile off your face."

He slapped the ends of the reins against his thigh and laughed, aware of the glint of sunlight on her dark tresses. "Who says I'm smiling?"

She raised up her right leg and shook it, rubbing her hands along the knee.

"Does it feel swollen?"

Turning toward him, she grimaced as she put weight on it. "No, just stiff and sore. I don't think riding was helping it, or anything else for that matter."

Sunbeams streamed down on them, and he debated telling her of his plan to get her home. The words wouldn't come, though, and when Renee raised her face to the sunlight, exposing the creamy column of her throat, he vowed to simply enjoy the day.

"Oh!" she gasped. "It's beautiful."

He followed her gaze to the sky where an eagle dipped down toward the mountain peak. Funny how he'd stopped noticing the birds and stopped hearing the sounds of the mountains, except where they presented the possibility of danger to the herd. One sound in particular he listened for now. He could just make it out. A low roar that seemed more a hum at this distance.

Renee tilted her head. "There's something else. Something strange."

"That's where we're headed." He gave Sassy's bridle a tug and moved forward. Renee matched his strides. They ducked through dense woods, and he held the brush apart for her to lead Sassy through a narrow, choked trail.

On the other side of the natural sound barrier, Renee cocked her head to one side. A smile split her face. "A stream?"

"Something like that, but more." He was having fun with this. More fun that he'd ever thought possible.

Renee frowned and skipped over a fallen log then grimaced as she rubbed her knee. "We're almost there; might as well just tell me."

"Hard for you to be patient, isn't it?"

"I've never liked the surprise side of surprises, but I do love them after I know what they are."

Tyler roared his laughter.

He sobered when Renee slapped Sassy's rump so hard the horse set off at a good clip, burning the reins across his palms and out of his grasp. Stunned by the suddenness of the horse's action, Tyler stared in amazement after the departing animal. Sassy didn't go far before wheeling and gazing at him as if he'd lost his mind.

And it was Renee's turn to laugh. At him. Tyler threw back his head and let loose a piercing whistle. Sassy arched her head, trumpeted a whinny, and trotted back. His hands smarted from the sting of the reins slipping through his hands, but he wouldn't let Renee know that. Let her have her fun.

"I'm sorry," she said, coming to stand beside Sassy, stroking the horse's neck and nose.

"Don't I get an apology?" he asked.

"Sure." She threw a smirk over her shoulder. "Do you want your ears scratched, too?"

Tyler had never seen her quite so lighthearted, and he wondered if telling her of his plans for the next day would fill her with excitement or despair. "We're almost to the place now *if* I can gain your cooperation."

"Don't laugh at me," she warned, though her eyes danced with mischief.

❧

Renee followed Tyler and Sassy, the splash of a nearby stream growing louder, to almost a roaring sound that both puzzled and delighted her. When they went through yet another copse of trees, her breath caught at the sight. Ahead of them, a hundred-foot waterfall crashed down into a pool. Gossamer mist rose where the water struck the surface of the pool. The meadow surrounding, dotted with wildflowers, gave way to more rocky barrenness as it sloped upward toward the mountain peak. It was a beautiful spot. Perfect. Tranquil.

"Great gathering place for all manner of predators," Tyler offered.

"I was just telling myself how perfect it seems. How did you find it?"

"Actually, I brought you here to look for Indian artifacts. Makes sense they'd congregate at places where there was water. You can find arrowheads and pots, scrapers." He shrugged. "It's fun."

"Do you ever use this for sheep?"

"We did until two years ago. Lightning hit a tree, and it burned things up before rain put it out." He lifted his arm to point to the far right of the meadow. A lone, blackened tree stood sentinel to the waterfall. "We figured to give it a few seasons to recover before we brought the sheep back."

Tyler loved these mountains. If they were more to each other, she could imagine that he would share many spots like this. A hawk shrieked overhead and dove down to a thick patch of grass. As the bird lifted into the air, a struggling body could be seen in its claws. Renee marveled at the bird's power and speed, and its ability to perceive its prey from such a distance, then descend and capture with the time it took to exhale. She wanted to lie down in the grass or bathe in the waterfall and feel the water on her head. She wondered if it would bruise her with its force or make her fall over.

She turned to Tyler to ask and caught him staring. His gaze held no apology. Her breath caught at the intensity of his eyes. Hazel, more green than brown. Beautiful eyes, really.

"Are you ready?"

The question hung between them, and she couldn't decide if he was referring to the hunt for artifacts, or something else entirely. He didn't flinch, and the blood hammered hard through her veins.

"The camptender should have been here by now."

Her shoulders tightened. His expression didn't match his words, nor the flat tone, almost devoid of feeling. She opened her mouth to respond.

"Might be time for us to head down the mountain and get you back to your pa."

"I thought you couldn't leave the sheep."

"Wouldn't be the best, but sometimes we don't have a choice. Your pa needs to know you're alive. If Thomas didn't make it. . ."

What Tyler said was true, she knew. Yet why now? She'd resigned herself to having to wait, so why was he suddenly so comfortable leaving the sheep? Granted, they were in summer pasture and no longer moving along the dangerous trails. Too, the camptender was late arriving, something she hadn't much thought about, and supplies were low. Tyler must know he had to go down to restock soon or he'd have to hunt food. His diet would dwindle significantly. And then there was the threat of the gang seeking him out.

"You were right. It's too dangerous to have you here. I knew it then and I know it now."

Her throat tightened and her breath choked. "Tyler—" The flatness of his words, the certainty with which he made the announcement. . . Didn't he feel anything? Had she been mistaken? "Is it that easy for you?"

Chapter 28

Her question seared hot pain of accusation through his chest. In the limpid pools of her eyes, he saw desperation and hurt. If he said yes she would think him a cad and he would be a liar. But saying no opened up emotions that would make things so much harder.

"Things like this are never easy, Renee. But sometimes we have to do what we have to do to protect others."

"And you're just realizing this *now*? You've kept me here all this time. . . ," she sputtered, anger building. "I don't need your protection, Tyler Sperry. Do you hear me?" She folded her arms across her chest, her lower lip trembling. "I can take care of myself."

Both the words and her expression snagged him deep inside. Renee Dover, ever the rebel. You could cover the self-centeredness, but it didn't go away so easily. But what if the basis for that seeming self-centeredness was hurt? Over her father's perceived rejection and the loss of her mother. . . Didn't it then become something like self-preservation? The need to protect oneself from further hurt.

Sassy nickered softly and turned her head. Tyler reached to stroke the animal's side, not bothering to curb his words now. "Just like you did with the gang? I wonder if Thomas would agree."

Her mouth opened then closed tight, lips a thin line. She retreated a step, arms tight across her chest. "What about Anna, Tyler? You think I need that kind of protection? That you can offer it?"

Behind her the waterfall crashed into the pool, its thunder matching the pounding in his temples. From the recesses of his mind he heard Dirk's gun going off. Saw Anna's body jerk with the impact of the lead and sag into his arms, dead before he got her to the floor.

Renee's focus shifted over his shoulder, her lips parting. A second before he turned, he made out the jangle of harness, the creak of wheels. Sassy's whinny made him reach for the rifle as he turned. It slid from the scabbard with ease as he braced himself for whatever threat lurked behind him. "Get on Sassy and ride!" he growled at Renee.

He went to one knee as a wagon jostled into view. His breath came easier when Rich Morgan raised his hand from the driver's seat. Tyler eased his finger on the trigger until he realized a man sat next to Rich. A gun in his hand. Aimed at Rich.

Marv.

He pivoted on his knees and pushed to his feet to see Renee struggling into the saddle as she tried to turn Sassy around. Raising his hand, he slapped the horse's rump just as a bullet rang out, kicking dirt at Sassy's right flank. The horse reared, spilling Renee to the ground. He fell to his knee as he jerked back toward Marv and the oncoming wagon. Others joined the wagon, coming up from behind on horseback, rifles raised. Marv stood up in the wagon and swung to the ground as Rich brought it to a halt.

"Cover him, Lance," Marv ordered, venom in his voice. Lance guided his horse to the side where Rich sat and dug his gun into Rich's side.

Marv's hard eyes never left him. "It's been a long time, Sperry. We have to thank this gentleman for leading us to you. Dirk heard of a sheepherder in the mountains. Sounded a lot like our good friend. It took us awhile, but then this gentleman's ranch hand let us know he was on the way up to see you. Simple, you see?"

Tyler didn't dare take his eyes off the man. Renee slid beside him. "Get behind me," he commanded in a raw whisper, hating it. All the protection he had to offer Renee, stripped from him in seconds.

"Lay that rifle aside now, Tyler. Nice and easy-like. Rand!" Marv barked. The potbellied man rode up to him. "Appears like Sperry has a friend of yours. Think you can manage to keep her from getting away this time?"

Rand's eyes narrowed to points, a laughable tough-guy expression for the little man. "Won't let her get away this time, boss."

So they recognized Renee. He felt her fist his shirt, and a mangled sob shot a dart of hot air against his back where she leaned, trembling, against him. He had no choice. Every man of them held a gun or rifle.

"I like this," Marv crowed with a twisted smile. "Two hostages to make sure you do exactly what we want."

"It's a long way down the mountain, Marv."

The man threw back his head. "Sure it is. We'll let you walk it. The girl can ride with the old man. And then. . ."—Marv nodded—"then, my boy, you can show us where that money is you stole."

❧

Rigid with cold, Renee slumped against Rich Morgan on the driver's seat, grateful for the human contact. It had taken two days to get to this point. Miserable, long days of clawing through narrow paths and staring down the barrel of Rand's gun every time she made a move. When the trail widened, Rand made her ride with him in the bed of the wagon behind Rich and Marv.

When Rand ordered her to sit beside Rich on the driver's seat instead of the bed of the wagon, she had welcomed the company, even under the circumstances. Whether Rich had given away Tyler or not, she didn't know, but she'd observed the man over the days and nights. His quiet demeanor, the strange twinkle in his eyes on the rare occasion their paths crossed. None of it made sense, and if she seldom saw Rich, she almost never saw Tyler except from a distance.

Marv rode Rand's horse and Rand rode in the bed, his ever-present gun a sharp reminder of the precariousness of the situation. But Rich's solid presence comforted.

It was Tyler she was most concerned for. They kept him walking the whole trip, hands bound with ropes, the ends held by Lance and Dirk, who rode on either side. Every time Tyler fell, he was cruelly jerked to his feet. When they broke for camp, they offered food to her and Rich. Tyler, from what she could see, got very little if anything.

Rich's shoulder felt solid and reassuring beneath her head. She didn't know if they would let them talk but she had to try.

"You making it?" Rich's question caught her by surprise. She waited for the poke of Rand's gun or his terse command for silence, but it didn't come. Emboldened, Renee answered.

"It's cold." Funny how she had so much to say, yet all she could get out were those two words.

"It's the fear talking," Rich offered as he guided the team along the rock path.

They jolted along in silence before she could form another question. "Tyler?"

"He's tough."

She closed her eyes, her throat a burning ache. He didn't look tough. She dared not turn around in hopes of catching a glimpse of him. Rand would surely bark a threat and wave the gun in her face. But the nightly stops showed her how much the walking had worn on Tyler. It pained her to see the slump of his shoulders and the constant rotation of guards who woke him as soon as he nodded off.

Oh how she wanted to believe he was tough enough to endure. She wanted so much to talk to him. Touch him. Tell him. . . She gulped and bit down on the wave of tears.

"You can't imagine my surprise when I saw him up here with a girl. Do you know these men?"

She sniffed and sat up a little, losing herself in the explanation. Her rescue and the subsequent weeks she'd spent with Tyler, it all tumbled out. She told him of Thomas, their search for the gang, and her rescue, all in a whispered voice that Rand either didn't hear or ignored.

"Tate took sick right before he was to leave, which is why I'm here. Didn't know about these varmints following me, though, or their talk with Tate. Blindsided both of us, they did."

She held her breath. His explanation seemed reasonable. She wanted to believe the man hadn't betrayed Tyler. "He told me a lot about you."

She felt the rich rumble of near-silent laughter roll through Rich's chest. "I'm sure he did."

"Good things."

"Tyler tell you about his first month with the sheep?"

Had he?

"Had those sheep so scared of him. They weren't feeding well and were dropping weight. He had a lot of anger in him then."

Anger. Tyler?

"You know about Anna?"

She nodded against his shoulder.

Rich shifted in the seat, and she looked up to see his expression of surprise. "Reckon he must love you, then."

She didn't know how he drew that conclusion from the fact that Tyler had told her about Anna.

"Hurts don't heal easy-like. He was pretty bad off when I found him. Almost dead. . ."

It was her turn to listen. Rich told her of those first days of Tyler's recovery, when Rich didn't know if Tyler would live or die. "When I knew he'd live, I thought he'd die from the hurt and the hatred he carried."

"The sheep," she breathed.

"What's that?" Rich asked above the din of rattles and creaks.

"The sheep. Tyler said the sheep taught him so much. Psalm 23."

Rich's silent laughter vibrated through him again, and for the first time since their capture, Renee smiled. It wasn't hard to see why Tyler held such respect for the man.

They didn't stop until after dark since the trail was broader. When they finally stopped, the blanket of night smothered everything. Rand kept close to her and Rich until Marv and Lolly came out of the dark and motioned for her to move.

"Lolly'll take care of the team tonight." Marv pointed with his gun. "I want the two of you over here." She and Rich followed him to a spot where Dirk and Lance were busy building a fire. Marv motioned them to a spot on the ground and held the gun on them until Lolly returned with rope to bind their wrists in back of them and take over guard duty. The campfire lit the area enough so she could see Dirk and Lance, but there was no sign of Tyler or Rand.

By her best estimate, they had another day on the trail. She longed for a glimpse of Tyler. She felt a nudge from Rich the same moment there was a grunt off to their right, and Tyler fell to his knees within the circle of firelight. Marv loomed out of the darkness behind Tyler and stabbed a knee into Tyler's back. Marv's fingers grasped Tyler's hair and pulled, arching him backward. Tyler grunted in pain. Renee's heart slammed in panic. "No!" She struggled to get to her feet but Lolly shoved her down again.

"Stay put," Rich cautioned her.

"I can't—"

"Shut up!" Lolly exploded. He raised his hand in threat.

"Hitting a woman is a good reason to die," Rich growled at the man.

Lolly spit a laugh and lowered his hand. "Coming from a man with his hands tied behind his back, that's a real threat."

Rich kicked out hard and fast. His foot slammed into the back of Lolly's knees and sent him sprawling, the gun flying from his hand.

Marv released Tyler. Unsupported, Tyler slapped hard against the ground. Marv scooped up Lolly's gun, his face slashed with rage. He lifted the gun and brought it down on Lolly's head.

Rich grunted low in his throat. Renee cringed back, shuddering breaths taking tears to the surface. She pressed her eyes into her knees. Afraid of the rage she'd just witnessed, of the harm that Marv threatened upon them all.

"Now listen here, old man," Marv growled. "You think you're so smart. Don't think I won't hesitate to put a bullet through you. Got it?"

Renee strained for Rich's response, not daring to look up or even move.

"Good. Then we understand each other."

His footsteps retreated and she raised her head, afraid Marv would return to torment Tyler who still lay sprawled on the ground.

"Not so smart," she heard Rich whisper. A little grin played at the corners of his mouth when he caught her glance. "He knocked out the man who was guarding us."

She looked back at Tyler, holding her breath as Marv hovered over his inert figure.

"He'll leave him alone," Rich predicted. "Marv needs him alive."

Renee studied the man, comprehension dawning. "You did that on purpose, didn't you?"

Rich's smile held no humor. "He's like a son to me."

Chapter 29

Tell me about the money," Renee asked when the camp quieted.

Rich nodded. "He told you about Anna, so you know she was killed by that bullet."

"He never mentioned money."

"I suppose he didn't. It was his insurance, and his revenge for Anna. Marv got hit in the heist, along with Lance, so instead of changing their plans, they went to the same meeting place they'd agreed on when they trusted Tyler. He followed under cover of darkness. Found the money and was hauling it off on Sassy when one of 'em woke up. Tyler took two bullets before Sassy got enough distance between him and the man firing. Must have rode for a couple days like that.

"I was out riding fence when I saw a lone horse at the edge of my property. Sassy never left Tyler even though she was bleeding from her right shoulder. Took some tending to get her back together." He sighed heavily. "Don't know how Tyler got there, but he must have been awake and riding hard for at least a couple days to get up from the Basin." Rich went quiet, and Renee thought he was done talking when he started again.

"Near lost him. If it weren't for Jesse, one of my ranch hands whose daddy'd been a doc, Tyler wouldn't have pulled through."

"The money?"

"Yeah." He chuckled low in his throat. "It was obvious to me right off that the bags tied over the saddle were full of money. Hadn't heard of a robbery, but decided it best to let him tell his story. Hid them in the barn to keep them away from my ranch hands and prevent unwanted questions.

"It took near a month for me to get the whole story from him. The gunshots messed him up and his memory was spotty, but he was messed up on the inside even more. That kind of healing takes time and patience in a man like Tyler."

A man like Tyler. An outlaw, Rich meant. "But he did heal," Renee breathed. "I never would have guessed him capable of doing. . .well, the things that outlaws do."

"That's the beauty of it all."

Rich's words lingered. She thought she understood. It was the change in Tyler, the inside healing to which Rich referred. "What about the money? He stole it from them."

She felt Rich shift next to her. He rolled his shoulders. "His intention was always to give it back to the town."

"Then why hasn't he before now?"

Rich pursed his lips. "You'll have to ask him that."

❧

Sweat poured down Tyler's face. His arms ached. Tendons unused to stretching pulled hard against bone as he forced his hips backward through the circle of his arms. If he could just get his bound wrists in front of him. His shoulders screamed for mercy as he wiggled backward, jaw clenched, his breaths measured lest he gasp too loud and awaken one of the men nearby.

When his hips cleared the circle of his arms, he rested. Beads of sweat burned his eyes and he shrugged the stream away, ignoring the searing pain in his arms. It had to be done. He had to get Renee out of here. Rich, too. They kept Sassy with the other horses during the night and Marv had ridden her a few times, knowing a quality animal when he saw it. Sassy's long-legged gait had appealed to Marv even when they worked together. Now that they were close enough to the end of the trail, it was the perfect time to free Rich and Renee. They could ride Sassy off the mountain and summon help. Tyler had no doubt that Marv would get the location of the money out of him then shoot him. Dying didn't scare him, but if he had to watch another woman die for his mistakes, or even Rich. . .

Lord, please. I can't let this happen. Please don't let it happen.

❧

Renee detected movement beside her. In a heightened state of semi-consciousness, she realized the shifting and sawing sound had been going on for some time. It was still dark. She'd fallen asleep stretched out on the ground. Her arms and shoulders, even her neck, ached from the pressure of having her wrists tied behind her back.

Through the darkness, she saw Rich. He still sat upright, and the sound was coming from him. She bit down hard on saying his name. Noise wouldn't be wise until she knew Marv hadn't sent back a guard. Judging by the snores coming from behind the glowing coals of the campfire, she guessed Dirk and Lance still slept. No sign of Marv or Lolly, or even Rand, and that made her cautious.

A low grunt beside her brought her attention back to Rich. Moonlight was scarce, and they were closer to the tree line than the dying campfire. She squinted into the darkness, able to make out his form but nothing else. She saw him move then scoot closer until his face was near to hers. She leaned in toward him before it dawned on her that his arms were free. "Find Marv, Rand, Lolly. Dirk and Lance at the fire. Move quiet. Get their guns." She felt tugging at her wrists and his heavy fingers working at the knots. "Hands are numb," he apologized. "I'll bring Tyler. Wait by the horses."

Chapter 30

Renee's nerves stretched to the breaking point. She moved with great care through the dark, expecting any minute to step on a stick or roll a rock that would bring one of the gang stabbing a gun into her side. She tried to keep an eye on Rich and the direction he took, but she couldn't see him.

She wished Rich had told her how fast she needed to move, or how long he thought it would take him. She concentrated on finding Marv, Lolly, and Rand first, since Dirk and Lance slept almost in plain sight. Movement at the dying fire caught her eye. She stilled and crouched.

It was Rich. His body passing in front of the glowing embers had been what alerted her. She hoped he found Tyler. That Tyler was able to walk. That Rand or Lolly or Marv weren't guarding him, keeping him awake as they had since capturing him. She bit her lip hard. No time for tears, she forced herself to move and concentrate on her task.

A still, dark form lay on the ground. She leaned over the man. Lolly. If any of them would sleep heavily, he would. With narrowed eyes she tried to make out the form of a gun. Tried to remember what she'd seen him carry over the last few days. A gun, not a rifle, she decided. When her hand touched the coldness of the barrel, a thrill shimmied through her. She pulled air into her lungs through her mouth and eased the weapon away from the still form. With delicate fingers, she picked it up and placed it in her waistband. She crept farther around the perimeter where she found another dark form, this one just outside the light of the fire where Dirk and Lance lay. She would have to work fast.

Her only assurance as she worked to find the man's gun was the heaviness of his breathing and, if she wasn't mistaken, the smell of alcohol. This man's rifle lay next to him. His arms almost hugged the weapon. Fighting for time, she left him and moved to Dirk and Lance, trying to keep low to the ground. A gun lay on top of its holster, along with a rifle, both in easy reach of Dirk's hands.

She faded into the darkness at the perimeter, searching for a stick. A long, thin, sturdy stick that wouldn't snap under the weight of the holsters. The rifle she could carry. She hurried back to the fire, startled when Dirk mumbled and rolled over, almost on top of the gun.

❧

Tyler saw the movement in the dark. His mind, muddled with lack of sleep, couldn't grasp who it was. He resigned himself to getting caught. His bound hands lay in his lap, arms numb from the effort he'd put them through, wrists chafed raw from the war to break the bond by sheer brawn.

The dark form knelt beside him. "Where's Marv?"

Through the haze of exhaustion, he recognized that voice. Blood flowed freely into his cold, numb hands as the bonds at his wrists were loosened. Rich was free, giving them a chance to escape. *Renee?* He wanted to ask the question but refrained, his mind alive with new hope.

"Come on, son," Rich whispered against his ear. "Go get Sassy and a horse for Renee. Be alert. Marv."

Tyler struggled to his feet. His legs ached with the effort, but he moved. Rich faded away, his warning about Marv heavy in Tyler's mind. That Rich had already assessed all the men and their whereabouts didn't surprise him. Tyler slipped away as quietly as he could, alert for any sign of the one wild card in the deck. He tried to reason out where Marv would have gone.

Marv had always been a restless sleeper. Never one for more than two or three hours before he started prowling. Tyler remembered waking to find him whittling by the fire or working on a bottle of whiskey. He never drank enough to get drunk, but he did drink enough to make him meaner.

Tyler noted the dull glow around the campfire and slipped farther into the darkness. His eyes shifted back to the fire, and he realized something was moving. A slender figure. It could only be one person. On cat feet he inched closer, incredulous as he watched Renee lift a gun and slip it into her waistband. She turned her back on the man and dropped to her knees in the dirt. Tyler could just make out her wielding a stick, digging in the dirt. What was she doing? He inched closer then saw the figure behind her move a little, releasing a gut-ripping snore.

To her credit, she didn't startle. She just stabbed harder at the dirt. What could be so important? He wanted to yell at her to run. He gained the circle of dim light when she glanced up. Her mouth gaped open for a gasp or a scream, he wasn't sure which, but she caught herself and relaxed, recognizing him. He saw the depression in the ground she'd been digging at with the stick. A gun. She was trying to dig out under a gun to pull it free from underneath one of the men. Her progress had taken her about halfway.

The man to her back moved again. Tyler swung forward now, fast, but careful not to kick dust. He lunged for the gun in her waistband just as the man at her back shot upright. Pivoting on the ball of his foot, Tyler brought the butt of the gun down hard and Lance slumped back, unconscious.

❧

Renee scooped the freed gun from the ground. Tyler gave her a shove that propelled her into the darkness. Heart thundering, she shot a look back over her shoulder. Tyler stood there, gun aimed at Dirk. Dirk didn't move, probably in too deep a sleep to have heard the grunt of his comrade as he took Tyler's blow.

When Tyler turned to follow, relief crashed through Renee. She tried to keep herself from running, but anxiousness to be out of the camp, now that her deed was done, pushed her pace. Rich loomed in the darkness. His hands shot up to still her momentum as he slipped Sassy's reins into her palm. He held his hand out for her as she bounded into the saddle.

Tyler broke through. Renee kicked her foot free of the stirrup and held Sassy steady as Tyler mounted behind her. Rich started out on the sturdy paint he'd chosen. They rode as fast as they dared in the darkness, alert for movement behind them. Renee's tension mounted until she realized Rich, of all people, would know these trails best. Tyler, too. She could trust them.

When the sun broke over the horizon, she saw it. Having been on the southwestern side of the mountain in summer pasture, it was the first real sunrise she'd seen for a while. She drank in the colors, warm in the natural embrace of Tyler's arms.

She noted the way Rich kept his eyes to the ground. At times he would stop and let them ride ahead. Renee didn't understand but neither did she ask, afraid to know the answer.

"You might as well try and get some sleep." Tyler's voice sent a shiver through her. She sat up straighter, embarrassed to realize just how much she had slumped against his chest.

"I'm not tired."

His chuckle lit fire in her cheeks. "Couldn't have proved it by me." His arms snuggled against hers as he adjusted the reins from one hand to another. He breathed against her ear. "Rest, Renee."

She sat upright, refusing to give in, wanting to touch and heal the raw, bloody wounds around Tyler's wrists, but the rocking of the horse and the warmth emanating between them lulled her. As she drifted off, she thought she felt a slight pressure against the top of her head. *Must be dreaming.*

Chapter 31

They weren't far from Rich's ranch now. Sassy had kept up well with the hurried pace. Tyler frowned. And hadn't the long-legged frame of the horse been part of the reason he'd bought her to begin with? An outlaw needed the fastest horse he could find.

Rich worried him though. The man knew something Tyler didn't, judging by the way he kept stopping to search for tracks and signs.

They were breaking free of the mountain now. A stream ran near the base. He would let Sassy drink her fill before the flat-out run to Rich's ranch. Once there he could take the money and make the long trip down to Cheyenne. He should have done it a long time ago.

Renee shifted against his chest. She felt so right in his arms, light and beautiful. Her hair tickled his chin, and he breathed in the pure pleasure of knowing that she was safe. He pulled her closer and kissed the top of her head as he had done numerous times.

Rich rode the paint out of the tree line. Though they hadn't spoken since leaving the camp, they were far enough away now to risk it. Besides, the outlaws didn't have any of their weapons to come chasing them down.

"It's Marv," Rich started.

The words stirred Renee to the edge of wakefulness. Tyler tightened his arms to make sure she didn't fall should she forget she was on horseback. But he processed the threat Rich's words implied.

"The ranch?"

Rich nodded. "He's planning a double cross."

"He doesn't know where it is, and neither do any of your hands."

"True, but he has a huge time advantage. After everyone bedded down, he left. Probably four, five hours ago."

"What about the rest? Wouldn't they get suspicious?"

"Nothing they can do about it now anyway. Not without their guns." Rich stroked his chin. "He clubbed Lolly for some minor infraction, which left us without a guard. I'm wondering if that was part of his plan."

"Trying to slow them down. Or us."

"Hoping there are more dead than alive when it's all over."

Renee sat up straight in the saddle. "Who are you talking about?"

Rich answered. "Marv was missing when we escaped."

❧

She should have known. Tyler and Rich said little else until they got to the stream to let the horses rest and drink water. Tyler dropped the reins and dismounted first. "Would you like some help?"

His eyes shone bright, but dark crescents lent credence to his true state. "You need to sleep."

"Sheep and outlaws don't keep strict hours. I'll be fine."

Renee swung her leg over the horse's neck and slid down to the ground. She thought Tyler would step away. But he didn't. When she looked up, his face was so close she felt his breath. He reached out his hand to touch her hair. She felt a tug and realized he was releasing the string that held her hair back.

He pulled a strand around her shoulder and her heart became a wild, twisting thing. She stayed still as he looped a strand around his finger then let it go. His hand climbed to her cheek and his eyes raised to hers. "When we get closer to Rich's ranch, I want you to take Sassy and go. Your father needs you, and you need to know about Thomas."

It was true. She knew it. She needed to end the agony that she was sure, now, plagued her father over her whereabouts. And she would tell him of her part in Thomas's death, and beg his forgiveness. If things didn't work out with her father. . ."I'll come back. Maybe Rich will hire me to work sheep, too."

"Renee." She could see what it cost him to say her name. "Listen to me." His hand fell away, and she witnessed his struggle in the pain of his eyes, the twist of his mouth. "I need you to—"

"To what?"

"You need to find yourself a good man. One who'll tame that wild spirit and take good care of you. Do you understand?"

"I'm coming back."

He chuckled, a dry sound that held no mirth.

"I will, Tyler. I can't stay away forever. I can't find someone else." She reached out to touch him. The beat of his heart, the warmth of his skin solidified her decision. "You're the only one for me."

In the second it took for her words to sink into his mind, she knew he would not touch her. He would not commit himself when he felt himself unworthy or incapable of doing so because of his past. The knowledge freed her, and she rose on her toes to press her lips against his.

❧

Tyler did his best to remain cool to the feel of her hands against his chest. Even as she rose on her toes and he steadied her with his hands, he determined not to give in to the flood of emotion building. He would put her away from him and know he had done what was best for her. He could send her back to what she knew before the Loust Gang. Hope that she would find someone to love her.

Her lips shifted against his and he felt her hands fist the material of his shirt, pulling him closer. And when he finally closed his eyes amid the pressure of her lips and realized what he held in his arms, and the good-bye the kiss symbolized, he could hold back no longer. And he didn't want to.

Chapter 32

"We became good friends."

Rich Morgan's chuckle rankled Tyler more than the moment when the man interrupted their kiss to tell Tyler there was something he needed to see. "That's sure how I kiss my friends."

Tyler scowled.

"Look, I can see why you'd be a bear after an old man pulled you away from that beautiful young woman, but we don't have much time."

"We were saying good-bye."

"Uh-huh."

"What's that supposed to mean?"

"It means, son, that you're a goner. Done." Rich Morgan's smile reached from ear to ear. "You talked children yet? I need more help around the ranch. Start 'em young and they'll have all the experience they need by the time they're in their early teens."

Tyler knew the man. Knew his good humor would plow through any bad situation. He also knew there was a solidness to Rich that pulled no punches and took no prisoners. Sure, he'd gotten carried away in the kiss. But it had been good-bye. Renee knew that. He knew it. It was settled.

He snapped a glance over his shoulder to the topic of their conversation. She stood beside Sassy, combing through her hair with her fingers. Watching *him*.

"Friends are a good thing," Rich jibed.

He scowled over at the man. "What did you want me to see?"

"If you think you can be civil, I'll tell you."

Tyler hauled in a breath. "Sorry."

"She's got you in knots whether you want to admit it or not. Don't think I've been around for sixty years to all the sudden come up lame. You love her. Why can't it be that simple?"

"Is this what you brought me out to talk about?"

"Someone needed to. And after seeing that kiss, I thought it might be time. She loves you."

"Did she tell you that, 'cuz she's never mentioned it to me."

"Doesn't have to be words, my boy. Remember, while Marv, Lance, and Dirk had you bound up, me and the little lady were spending some time together. Didn't take long for me to see the way her pendulum swung when it came to you."

Tyler lifted his face to the sky and rubbed the back of his neck. His muscles still held the ache of his bondage. Renee was right. He was exhausted. Troubled, too, by her, by Rich's words, by his reluctance to let her go. "I told her to take Sassy and ride away."

"Why?"

Tyler jerked his hat from his head and shot the man a glance. "I would think it would be obvious."

"Are we talking about Anna now?"

"About all of it. I was an outlaw, Rich. Who's going to believe that I've changed? What's to say I won't swing for the crimes I did? Is that what I give her? She's young—"

"So are you, son."

"She'll find someone else."

"What about you?"

"If I swing it won't matter, and if they do let me go, then I deserve to be alone."

Rich's dark eyes stared hard at him, into his gut, until Tyler felt like the man was reading his soul.

"You wanted to tell me something," Tyler prompted.

"If I die, you get the ranch."

Tyler groped at the bald statement. What it meant. All that Rich was offering him. "If you die?"

"Marv's going to take someone out. Might as well be me. I just wanted you to know that, to give my son something to live on."

He flinched. He knew Rich didn't have family. Had known it since the time he could remember things about the robbery. "Me?"

"You've an honest heart. It's what I saw. You couldn't do that robbery because it went against what was in your heart. I want a man like that working for me. I'd like to think my son would have been like you, had he lived."

Tyler swallowed. *Had he lived...* "You won't die."

Rich's sober expression immediately melted. "Good. Then I'd like at least five grandchildren."

Tyler shook his head. "It's my fight, Rich. I've made my decision. I want you to take that paint and get Renee out of here. I'll go in alone."

"You think you're the boss?"

"Rich..."

"I'll fork my own broncs, son. If this man wants you, then he's got to go through me first."

Tyler slapped his hat back on his head. "We'll see about that."

❧

Renee's eyes burned with unshed tears. She sniffed and held tighter to the material of Rich's shirt.

"Never thought he could be so stubborn," Rich said.

Renee had to agree. Tyler rode tall in the saddle, his suggestion she ride double with Rich more a command. Rich accepted the idea without a word, though Renee could tell he didn't like it. Whether because he didn't want to ride double with her or something else, she had no way of knowing.

"He wants me to leave before we get to the ranch. Take you away with me," Rich explained. He grinned at her over his shoulder. "Not a bad idea if I was thirty-five years younger."

His good-naturedness warmed the spots of her heart that had so longed for a father's attention. "How can we do that? Marv could kill him."

"Don't worry, little lady; I've got a plan."

Tyler wheeled Sassy when Rich's ranch house came into view. His eyes grazed hers before settling on Rich's. "This is as far as we go," he said.

Renee's chest tightened. Before Rich could bring the paint to a halt, she grasped his shoulders, leaned forward, and swung her leg over the rump of the horse. She stumbled but caught herself.

She held Tyler's attention now. Hard, cold eyes masked the warm gaze of the man she knew and loved. He was preparing himself, putting on his outlaw face. She wanted none of it, not after the kiss they shared. His touch had shown her his heart, and she wasn't going to leave until he knew where she stood on matters.

His eyes raked over her, hard, like diamonds. She touched his leg. "Get down off that horse and tell me good-bye, Tyler Sperry, *then* I'll leave."

Chapter 33

Foiled. By a slip of a woman with dark hair and eyes that flashed such an enticing mix of fire and old-fashioned stubbornness. Tyler stabbed a glance at Rich. The man's raised eyebrows emphasized the quirk of his lips. He should have known the older man wasn't going to do a thing to help him out. Renee already had Rich on her side of the argument. At least she hadn't bucked him altogether and demanded to stay.

He could refuse her request and stay put astride Sassy, but her hand on his leg and the memory of their last kiss eroded his resolve to have the thing with Marv done as soon as possible. With Rich and Renee out of harm's way, he would be free to live or die, without threat of watching yet another person he loved die for his transgressions. He met Renee's gaze, knowing the folly of doing such a thing while trying to deny himself. One last kiss. If he lived, he'd hope she would stay away; if he died, it would be his last, perhaps his only, completely happy moment.

Tyler dismounted. He clung to the saddle for a second, warring with himself, until he felt her fingers against his back.

"Tyler?"

He turned and reached for her, wanting to be done with this thing. He was in over his head the moment she curled into him and he felt her lips on his cheek, his nose. He tasted the salt of her tears and followed the path with his lips.

"Don't send me away."

He closed his eyes, breathing deeply of her hair, captured by the scent of her. "Your love will ruin me."

Her hands framed his face. "You'll be stronger for it."

"Not facing Marv."

"What if he kills you?"

Her tears flowed freely now. For him. "Then you'll be strong. You'll find someone else."

"I don't want someone else. I love you, Tyler."

"I can't put you in harm's way. Marv would kill you if he could. Please, Renee..."

She rose on her toes and kissed his lips. A quick, light kiss that twisted his insides. She moved as if to pull away. He licked his lips, coldness gripping him. If he never saw her again...

He pulled her to him, kissing her like he wished he'd done from the first. When he raised his head, he buried his face in her hair. Her shoulders trembled, and he tightened his embrace. "Renee..."

She pulled away, fresh tears darkening her eyes and bleeding twin trails down her cheeks. When her fingers rose to his face, he felt the wetness of his tears being brushed away. He clasped her hand and kissed the palm. He took a step back, closing her fingers around the kiss. "I love you."

He turned his back and dragged himself into the saddle, leaving her standing there, her hand fisted against her cheek. Rich would take care of her now. Without a backward glance, Tyler kicked Sassy into a gallop.

❧

Marv would be careful, Tyler knew. He would make sure he knew the lay of the land and how many ranch hands were working the place before he rode in. Rich's hands lived in a bunkhouse a good distance from the main house. This time of year there were two, and unless Rich had given orders for them to keep watch on the house, their duties would keep them away from the main house.

Marv would have free rein of the place and, Tyler hoped, would leave the hands alone. If they caught him doing something, Marv would shoot them, no questions asked. Tyler circled behind the main house and decided to ride up on the bunkhouse first. If Jesse and Tate saw him, they wouldn't be overly alarmed and give him away. They were loyal men, both having worked at Rich's Rocking M for years.

Tyler calculated that Marv had made himself comfortable in the main house by now, tearing things apart in his desperate search. His disadvantage would be his greed. If Marv had waited to get the information from Tyler, he would have saved himself time. The man's impatience seemed out of character. That he left the rest of the gang to fend for themselves, too, was unlike the calculating methods Tyler knew Marv to possess and utilize.

Could it be that the heat was becoming too much for the main man of the Loust Gang? Marv was smart, but he was getting older. At fifty-five most men didn't want to be on the run. Age would cause his action and reaction time to slow. And the serenity of a nice, warm fire in a place of his own, far away from threat of capture, might be just the thing Marv sought. He'd probably hoped Tyler would break quickly and when he didn't, Marv had come up with this alternate plan.

The low, flat roof of the bunkhouse came into view. Tyler surveyed the ground for evidence of a horse, or a man on foot. When he finally arrived at the bunkhouse, he found no sign of Tate or Jesse. Their gear indicated their presence, but they were either far out in the fields, shot, working, or tied up somewhere. Satisfied that they would not be victims in a shootout between him and Marv, some of the tension melted from his shoulders.

It took Tyler two hours to make a sweep of the bunkhouse, corral, and other outbuildings before he satisfied himself that the hands were out working and not in danger. They would be returning for supper, and judging by the angle of the sun, Tyler knew he had about four hours to find and deal with Marv.

Chapter 34

Supports held stalwart beneath the sagging overhang of Rich's front porch. Tyler studied the roofline then the windows of the ranch house. Smaller than some he'd seen, the place had provided a warm haven for him the fall and winter of his recovery. It had become home to him. Even in the days on summer pasture, he looked forward to returning for the winter months. To sitting with Rich and talking about growing the herd or debating the merits of raising sheep versus cattle.

Tyler cut off the flow of memories. If he didn't pay attention, he would lose his edge. Marv would recognize a moment of weakness and take advantage of it, and it didn't take long for a bullet to kill.

He entered the house with the Navy revolver Renee had lifted from Lolly, clearing the corners, stabbing glances in the places a man could hide. The kitchen was a mess of cooking utensils, pots, and plates scattered across the floor. Cupboard doors hung open, emptied of their contents. Ash and soot from the fireplace settled a black mess all over the floor, showing boot prints leading to the room next door but disappearing as the soot wore off the sole of the shoe. Marv would be the only one with reason enough to tear everything apart. The outlaw must be angrier than a bronc not to have found the money. The damage to the house became more immense as Tyler swept through the back rooms. Floorboards had been pried up in places. Walls sported holes where Marv must have thought a hollow space hid a secret.

Tyler's tension mounted. The last place he wanted to check was the spot where the money was hidden. If Marv had given up and lay in wait, watching, he would expect that to be the first place Tyler would go.

On stiff legs, Tyler left the ranch house, scanning the area in front of him. When he reached the barn, he hesitated. Something moved inside, scratching along the front wall of the building. Tyler drew air into his lungs and swung the door open just enough to slip inside. His eyes, adjusted to the light outside, rendered him blind in the dim interior. He held the Navy loose but ready. He sank to a crouch as soon as he cleared the door and swung in the direction of the sound. A shot whizzed over his head.

Tyler took aim and fired. Marv grunted and rolled along the ground. Tyler scrambled, ducking behind the half wall of a stall, leveling his other gun on the bale of hay behind which Marv had taken cover.

"You thought they'd kill us all," Tyler taunted the outlaw. "They won't come riding in to save you now, Marv. Not after you crossed them."

Silence greeted his words, but Tyler knew Marv's methods. The man would reload, his mind skipping ahead to escape routes. Always analyzing. Always one step ahead.

"I'm dying, Tyler. Don't matter none to me what you do."

Dying. Such a cold word. Even colder because of the life Marv had chosen for himself. But was it a ploy? A statement meant to distract? Then why was he here? After the money?

"You near ruined us over that girl. Dirk got ya, though, didn't he?"

Bait. Marv was trying to get him angry, distract him enough to shoot wild or do something dumb and make himself a target. But he held the trump card. "I'm the only one who knows where that money is."

"Not the only one, son. Rich told me where to look." Marv's dry chuckle grated against Tyler's ears. "Men will do most anything when there's a gun pointed at their head."

Acid stirred in Tyler's gut, yet he was hesitant. Rich wouldn't betray him.

"Seems I'm not the only one who knows how to double-cross."

Tyler closed his mind. Marv was playing him. He knew it. Had witnessed the man do it countless times to get his way. Tyler steadied his grip and aimed the gun at the spot where Marv hid. "Are you sweating yet, Marv?"

"I just want to ride out of here, Tyler. You let me go and I won't put a bounty on your head. That money can buy even a dead man some loyalty."

"Not if the rest of the gang catches you first."

Tyler forced himself to think. If Marv had the money, what was he doing in the barn? There were no horses inside and Sassy was back at the bunkhouse. It didn't make sense, so it must be a pack of lies.

"Let me go, Tyler."

"Where's your horse?"

"Behind the barn."

Twisted with indecision, Tyler licked his dry lips. "Throw your guns over here. Both of them. Then you stand up, slow-like. I'll be drawing a bead on you the whole time."

Tyler heard the guns slide across the dirt floor and raised his head enough to confirm. "Now get up and head out the doors."

Marv got to his feet, his eyes cold, haughty. Tyler ignored the man's smirk and motioned with the gun for Marv to precede him. When they emerged, Marv started toward the back of the barn. Tyler wrestled within himself. He'd come so far, protected the money for so long. He couldn't let Marv ride off with it if what he'd said was true. There was only one way to be sure.

"You put your hands against the wall of the barn. Turn around and I'll cut you down."

When Marv did as he was asked, Tyler sidestepped to the well. Rich had built a shelter over the hole and a platform around it. With his gun on Marv, he used his other hand to reach under the roof. He felt the small latch, grunting as he twisted his arm to feel in the cavity there for the two sacks. Tyler's stomach soured. Empty.

Rich *had* betrayed him.

Marv dived to the side and skidded in the dirt.

Tyler's moment of indecision made him too slow, and his bullet went wild. Marv popped up just outside the barn door. He wrestled with the door. Tyler aimed and fired. The bullet spit dirt beside Marv's hip. Marv slid inside the darkness of the barn. Tyler sprinted to the barn door and stood beside the opening. He couldn't see but neither could Marv, and he knew exactly where Marv was headed. Tyler sprang through the air, arms wide, in the direction of Marv's guns. He caught the man, toppling him to the ground. He grabbed Marv's right hand as they rolled in the dirt. Marv launched a wild punch with his free hand that choked the breath from Tyler.

A strong patch of sunlight swept over the place where they struggled.

"Let him go, Tyler," Rich Morgan's voice rent the air.

Marv took advantage of Tyler's distraction and landed a kick to his kneecap. Marv leveled his gun at Rich just as Tyler struck out and connected with the side of his face. Two guns sounded as one. Marv staggered, clutched at his leg where blood spurted through his now-empty hands. Rich lay still in the barn door.

Tyler lunged for the outlaw, kicking away the gun. Marv dodged him and sprinted for the doorway, out into the open. Tyler panted for air, his lungs cramping, as he gave chase. He skidded around the corner, but Marv already had the horse in a gallop.

Tyler closed his eyes, the reality of Marv leaving with the money a fresh punch to his stomach. With slow steps, he retraced his path and dropped to his knees in the dirt beside Rich. The bullet had caught the man high in the shoulder. He sucked air with every breath, pained over the betrayal. "You double-crossed me!"

Rich's eyes peeled open and a grin split his face. "Is he gone?"

Tyler bunched his fist in Rich's shirt, yanking him to a sitting position. "You double-crossed me!"

Rich grimaced, his hand hot iron around Tyler's wrist. "What are you talking about? I almost got myself killed to help you. Where's Marv?"

"Rode out," he spat. "With the money."

Rich shoved Tyler and pressed a hand to his bloody shoulder. Tyler didn't move to help him. "No he didn't. I've got the money."

Tyler frowned. "He said you told him where it was. I checked. It's gone."

"Like I said, I've got the money." Rich struggled to stand, sending Tyler a scathing look. "If you'll help an old man to his feet, I'll show you."

Tyler was numb. Even as Rich led the way into the ranch house, as his gaze came to rest on Renee's slender form at the cookstove, he felt oddly hollow. She barreled into him and he embraced her absently, as if watching a mirror image of himself making the motion.

"Is he dead?" she asked against his shirt.

"Rode off." His lips felt stiff. "With the money."

Over Renee's shoulder, he watched as Rich wadded a piece of linen and placed it over the wound at his shoulder. "Don't mind me; I'm just bleeding to death." He leaned forward and hefted a sack with his good arm, slapping it on the table, the thud and jingle belying the weight and contents of the bag. "There's one." He bent double again, and when he straightened another bag joined the first. "Told you he didn't get the money. He must have fed you that line hoping you'd get nervous and show him where it was hid."

Tyler gulped, choked by the truth that stared him in the face. He knew Marv's ways. Why had he ever doubted Rich?

Renee filled in the blanks. "Rich circled around the back of the barn and we got the money first thing. He knew Marv would eventually find it or trick you into showing where it was."

"But I got to thinking"—Rich continued, sinking into a chair—"that you might need some help, so we kept an eye out. Waited for hours out back here, watching as Marv made mincemeat of the house. When you came in later then headed for the barn, we were watching."

Tyler pulled Renee closer. "If you hadn't come back I probably would be dead."

"Which is the very reason why I wasn't going to leave you here by yourself." Rich lifted the linen from his shoulder and blanched.

Tyler released Renee and went to the man, straddling a bench. He ripped open the shirt and scanned the wound. "I'll have to get that ball out."

Rich made a face and swayed. "Would like that right well, so long as you can do it with me sitting down."

Tyler didn't bother to tell the man he was already sitting. He took Rich's good arm and got him vertical. "Let's get you in bed; then I'll get to work." He glanced at Renee, already stuffing wood into the cookstove to encourage a fire. "Hot water, as soon as we can get it."

Rich leaned hard on him, and a new worry crawled up Tyler's spine. "I'll send Tate to get the doc."

"I'll be all right. I'm a tough nut to crack."

Tyler guided Rich to the edge of the bed and helped get him settled.

"Upping the ante on you, son."

Tyler's concern burgeoned at the disconnected muttering. "Try to rest."

Rich gripped Tyler's arm. Tyler turned back and caught the distinctive twinkle in Rich's dark eyes. "I'm not daft; I mean it. I'm upping the ante on you."

"What are you talking about?"

"Six instead of five." Rich fell back on the mattress with a deep sigh.

"Six what?"

"Grandchildren. By my reckoning, taking this bullet for you's worth one more."

Chaper 35

Tyler's boot hit the bottom step of the ranch house porch when the door swung inward to reveal a healthy, robust Rich Morgan.

"The prodigal has returned!"

"And the lame can walk again!"

Rich's face twisted into a scowl. "Wasn't quite that bad. Tate bugged Doc to stop by again last week, and I told him to stay away or I'd shoot him. I'm not a cast sheep and the buzzards aren't circling me."

Tyler embraced the man, glad to feel the fitness of his frame and see him on his feet. "So Jesse and Tate were good nurses while I was gone."

Rich shouldered past him, dipped water into the coffeepot, threw in some grounds, and put it on to boil. "Not nearly as pretty as Renee, though their cooking might be a mite better."

Tyler slumped into a chair, relieved to have the long trip behind him and to see Rich in good spirits and stronger. "I won't tell her." He longed to ask if Rich had heard from her but didn't. She'd wanted so much to get home after finding out Rich was going to survive. They'd ridden together, Renee on Sassy, he on a bay mare, until reaching territory Renee recognized. Their good-bye had been rushed when one of her father's hands spotted them and rode out to accompany her home. She'd started throwing a thousand questions at the man as they trotted off. But she'd remembered Tyler long enough to gallop back and share a quick kiss and peel off a promise of, "I'll come back" before galloping away with the hand.

The time had come for him to get back down to Cheyenne with the money anyway. Fear of returning to the site of the robbery had left him lame long enough. So he'd kept riding, knowing the long days ahead would be lonely but would also give him time to think. Rich's last words to him offered a measure of comfort. "They give you a hard time, you let me know and I'll get Tate to bring me down stretched out in a wagon to set them straight."

Tyler stretched his legs out under the table. "Jesse got the sheep off the mountain, I see."

"Said Teddy was right where you left him. Guess he'd found his share of rabbits, picking his teeth with their bones when Jesse got there. Sheep hadn't strayed nearly as far as they would have if Teddy hadn't been with them."

Though Rich hadn't come right out and asked, Tyler knew the man waited for his report. "They were glad to have the money."

"Why, sure."

"In the end, they let me go. Said it was a fair trade, if not way too late."

"And Anna?"

Tyler jerked his head toward Rich. "Anna?"

"Did you put her to rest while you were there?"

Riding into Cheyenne again had been a trip back in time. Tyler had visited the store out of necessity, but also a perverse need to face all that his dishonesty had set into motion. He'd asked the sheriff about Anna's parents, but they'd left town and he didn't know where they'd gone.

"Best thing you can do for yourself is move on."

Tyler knew that to be true; the emotions and disgust over what he'd done didn't grip him as hard as they used to. The sheriff had summed it up best as he rode with Tyler to the outskirts of Cheyenne. "You'll always live within the grip of regret, but don't let it rule your life."

"All we have to do is wait for Renee to return." Rich's words tugged Tyler back to the present, the smell of coffee as comforting as the crackle of the fire. Yet he felt unsettled. Something was missing.

Tyler gulped the brew Rich placed in front of him, realizing he had no taste for it at all. The brevity of Renee's good-bye rolled through him, accusing, suggestive in its very brevity. He scooted out of the chair and rose to his feet. "She might meet someone else. It might be for the best anyway." He spun and headed for the door. He'd lose himself in work around the ranch, but he didn't want to hear Rich's voice on the matter. The man retained high hopes for the two of them, and Tyler didn't know if he hated the disappointment of Renee not returning more for Rich or for himself.

❧

Renee wondered if Tyler had returned to the Rocking M or if he was still in Cheyenne. She eschewed the ribbon of color marking the sunset, her gaze stroking the horizon to the northeast. How many times had she regretted the swiftness of her good-bye kiss, sure she would see Tyler within a month or two, the past laid to rest, Thomas alive and well, and her relationship with her father repaired?

How wrong she had been.

"Renee?"

She turned, her father's tall, slender figure a shadow in the doorway. "I'm here."

"It's a beautiful night."

"Yes."

Knot Dover sagged into one of the rockers on the porch. "He's done better since you got back. You know that, don't you? I think the worry over you was hindering his recovery."

She gripped the porch railing tighter, swallowed hard.

"Keller is working with him on getting the strength back into the leg."

Yes, she knew that. Keller, a man her pa had found in town and hired to work with Thomas, had a way with injuries such as the one her brother had sustained. "He should be back East getting an education as a doctor."

"We've talked about it. He's surely more a doctor than most of the ones over in Cheyenne."

From the corral, Sassy spotted her and whinnied. Renee pushed away from the railing and shuffled to the animal, scratching her ears and rubbing her sides. She didn't know her father had followed her until he spoke again. "Time you took her home."

She combed her fingers through Sassy's mane, already slick from the daily attention she gave the horse. Touching Sassy took away the sadness of being away from Tyler. "I can't leave Thomas."

"Sure you can." Knot Dover put his foot up on the lowest rail of the corral gate. "Thomas is a big boy. He'll regain the use of his leg, you watch and see, but there's someone up at that Rocking M, isn't there? Greg said you were with someone the day he found you riding in. Must be the sheep man you talk of so much. He's more to you than a shepherd by my guess."

"I don't think I could be happy knowing Thomas—"

"No." Knot's voice snapped the syllable whip-like then softened. "You're not going to sacrifice your happiness for guilt. Thomas wouldn't want it." He stripped off his hat and swiped his forehead with a kerchief. "It took losing you and Thomas to see that was what I was doing. I was afraid to be near you, to let myself be happy because it seemed like your ma's death required me to be miserable. I won't let you do that." His gray eyes, so much like her own, were dark with determination. "You plan on riding on out tomorrow. You say your good-byes to Thomas, and I'll tell Greg and Dale to go out with you. We'll be needing to get some things together for you that you'll be wanting over there, since I'm guessing you'll be staying." His smile reached his eyes. "Your mama would want that, and this way I'll know how to find you."

Chapter 36

Renee crested the hill that overlooked the Rocking M. She glanced back at Greg and Dale and raised her hand to let them know all was well. They turned their horses toward home. She traced their path until they were dots on the horizon, using the time to gather herself, her thoughts. She'd not heard from Tyler since the day they'd said good-bye. She hoped he was home, that all had gone well for him in Cheyenne, and that Rich's recovery was complete.

The chill of winter was beginning to bite. She shivered beneath her heavy coat. Drawing the reins into her hands, she gave Sassy her head. As she neared the ranch house, she thought she saw Rich on the porch. He disappeared inside and another man emerged, a familiar profile her heart recognized instantly. Her tears smeared against her face, chilly paths of ice in the cold air of Sassy's gallop. She slowed the horse to a lope as they approached. Tyler swung down from the porch and hurried to her side, touching her leg, a question in his hazel eyes.

"I came home," she said as she slid from the saddle. Tension ebbed from his face as he gathered her into his embrace. She breathed the smell of him and felt the pressure of his lips against her hair.

"I was afraid—"

She raised her face and touched his lips, his cheek. "You had nothing to fear. Didn't your heart tell you that? Besides, it'll be spring again in a few more months, and I wanted to hear the sheepherder's song."

His arms tightened, and when his lips touched hers, she felt the thrill of his silent promise.

"Well, well..."

Renee heard the throaty groan Tyler gave as he broke off the kiss and turned toward Rich. "Can't you leave us alone for two minutes?"

"Sure I can." Rich's smile was unrepentant to Renee's eye. "Just wanting to make sure you're properly chaperoned and all." Rich turned toward the corral. "Tate!" Renee saw a disheveled young man striding from the direction of the barn. "Why don't you hitch up the wagon. We're needing to make a trip into town for a preacher."

Tyler slanted a crooked smile down at her. "I think he just asked you to marry me."

"We'll be back before sunset if you two will hurry," Rich urged. The man turned and headed back inside. "I'll be back in a minute."

Renee rose on tiptoe. "Should I tell *him* yes, or you?"

He stroked the length of her hair, twining a tendril around his finger. She watched as the lock retained the shape and bounced gently against her shoulder. His fingers grazed her jaw, her cheek. She raised her face to meet his kiss. "Tell *me*."

She raised her hands to his shoulders, clasping her hands behind his neck as his lips hovered inches from hers. "Yes," she breathed.

The Cattle Baron's Daughter

Dedication

To the heroes of the West, who stood their ground and believed in the dream of home, land, family, and peace.

Chapter 1

1889

The jingle of spurs punctuated his every footfall. Ryan Laxalt knew almost no one in Buffalo, Wyoming, though he knew his name would spark controversy and trouble. A man stepped from the stagecoach office and spat on the ground. When he raised his head and saw Ryan he nodded and swiped a hand across his lips. "If'n you're here to pick up someone, settle in. The stage should be here shortly. Name's Ronald P. Coltrain."

"Looking for information," Ryan said.

Ronald's eyes narrowed, and his gaze swept Ryan from head to foot. "You the law?"

"No."

"Then I ain't got nothing worth saying."

Ryan kept his hands loose at his sides, where his tied-down guns showed much about the manner of man he'd become in his long absence from Buffalo. "You might wish you'd talked."

Ronald licked his lips. "Stage is coming in. I've got work to do."

With a nod, Ryan swung away and retraced his steps. He should have expected as much. Few men wanted to snitch on another.

He leaned against a post support and squinted up and down Main Street. Strange, this street. What person would lay out a town's main road with a bend in it so you couldn't see straight from one end to the other unless you stood in the middle? His mother and father had chosen Johnson County as a place to settle and raise cattle. The town of Buffalo had come along later. Ryan remembered little of the actual town, though his travels had brought him to the Big Horn region once or twice. He'd left to make his own way as a foolish teen. He shook his head and used the heel of his boot to scratch the calf of his other leg. Back then he'd thought he had better methods of earning money, bigger dreams than working hard all day as his father had. Now, remorse at his arrogance stabbed guilt into his gut. The world had made quick work of shattering his idealistic thoughts.

Ronald popped his head out of the stage office and froze in place. He tilted his head as if listening. At first Ryan heard nothing; then the rattle of traces and the snap of a whip accompanied the distant rumble of horse hooves. He waited and watched as the driver brought the rig to a stop. A plume of dust lifted and spread, encompassing the coach. The driver sprang from the seat as if it were on fire then relaxed against the boot and rolled a smoke as the stage door swung outward. A tall form moved from the shadows of the interior and filled the narrow door. The man turned sideways to accommodate the width of his shoulders. By Ryan's eye, the man was an easterner. Fancy dress, a vest—rumpled but not looking too much like a man who'd come a far piece in the torturous interior of a hot stagecoach. He supposed the stranger would be a handsome man by a woman's standards, though to Ryan's way of thinking, he was far more fastidious than any man should be.

Behind him a door slapped into its frame, and a rounded woman wearing a dirty apron hurried by him. Other townspeople gathered, too, excited at the prospect of someone new coming to town, and probably even more curious because the man was so well dressed.

Ryan recognized only one face, and age had laid crags and sprouted more than a few gray hairs on the head of Papa Don, owner of the store. Most of the rest were too young for him to recall their faces.

The fancy man smacked dust from the legs of his trousers and turned to the coach, oblivious to the small band of people gathering or the dog sniffing at the wheels of the stage.

Ryan straightened. He had more to do than stand around and ogle the newcomer. But when the man at the stage held out his hand to someone inside, and pale, feminine fingers tucked into his, Ryan's curiosity got the best of him. A slender woman in a dress of Montana-sky blue descended from the stage, and her crop of red curls fluttered in the light breeze. He thought he caught the scent of flowers but crushed the absurd idea when he considered the distance separating him from the stage. The young woman's expression showed relief as she spoke to the man at her side. Her husband, no doubt. If for no other reason, he had to respect that the man had hitched up with a woman of such beauty.

Ryan turned from the spectacle of the arrivals just as the stocky woman who had passed him minutes before embraced the willowy figure of the younger woman. A long-ago dream burst to the forefront of his desires. He'd wanted a wife once, before his choices had made marrying dangerous. His gaze landed on the young woman again, still caught in the embrace of the elder woman. Her eyes were closed, and a smile brought radiance to her face. When she opened her eyes, she stared straight at Ryan from over the woman's shoulder. She offered a friendly, open smile that neither committed nor encouraged—exactly what he would expect of a married woman. Yet the smile was a punch in the gut, a reminder of what he could have had.

❧

Olivia heard the murmur of Phoebe's voice, even the upward hitch at the end of the string of words that indicated a question, but she couldn't concentrate. The man's eyes bore into hers. He seemed angry, though she didn't understand why. He was a stranger to her. Not a surprise, considering she'd been away from Buffalo for going on ten years. When the man spun on his heel, she traced his path along Main Street with her eyes.

She felt a touch on her elbow, and she pulled back from Phoebe's embrace to see a look of concern on her worn but pleasant face. "I asked if you were feeling well."

"Oh." She patted her hair—a mass of ringlets her aunt's maid had insisted on before she left Kansas. "I'm fine. Just tired."

"No doubt, dear. It's hard to sleep on those rocking conveyances of misery." Phoebe patted her arm. "You stop by Landry's, and we'll serve you up something warm before you make the trek out to your pa's ranch."

Olivia hesitated. She'd been so excited to see her father, yet he was nowhere in sight. "Won't it be too much to feed another mouth at this time of day?"

"Between getting the cattle in, branded, and ready for the drive"—Phoebe shook her head, her reddish-brown hair sweeping her shoulders—"the hands don't come in much during the day in the spring."

Even in her letters, Phoebe Wagner was a chatty woman. Olivia remembered very little of her as a nine-year-old, before her father had sent her east to boarding school, but she'd always looked forward to Phoebe's letters. If only she could say the same about letters from her father. After the first four, he'd never written again, and Phoebe became her only tie to the place she called home.

"Gather that pigheaded pa of yours and get him to bring you to supper sometime if you don't want to stay now. I know you must be excited to see the ranch." Phoebe patted Olivia's cheek, her hand warm and rough. "I'd love to continue this visit, but I have to run. Landry's not often nice enough to let me walk out on a whim, whether or not business is slow. Good thing the stage arrives after lunch." She touched Olivia's hair "Who would have thought that pale Irish skin and wild red hair would yield such a beauty? Best wear a hat out in this sun though, or those freckles will get worse. And I'll expect a full report on your companion"—she darted a look at the man traveling with Olivia—"as soon as you're settled." And with that, Phoebe wheeled and marched back up Main.

Olivia felt an uncomfortable flare of heat in her neck and turned her head just enough to make sure Tom Mahone had not heard Phoebe's last remark. Her lungs expanded, and she drew an easy breath when she saw him speaking with an older man, who turned and spat into the dust. Olivia grimaced and averted her face, his low chuckle letting her know he'd seen her look of disgust. She hoped the majority of the town had better manners. The stories she'd heard back east about the West made Olivia wonder if she should have heeded her aunt's admonition. *"Westerners are a rough lot"* had become Aunt Fawn's much repeated warning.

Tom Mahone stepped to her side and offered his arm. "I've arranged with the stage driver to load your trunk into a rented wagon. We'll head out to your father's ranch after we eat. Apparently the Occidental is the best place, though Landry's is closer."

Olivia blinked and stared at his arm. "I'd like to head out as soon as possible. It's been ten years, Mr. Mahone. I'm sure you understand my eagerness to be home again."

Tom had picked up the stage in Kansas, and rather than keep her silence, she'd welcomed the easy chatter that had flowed between them. She'd never thought to ask him where he was going, surely not Buffalo. "Don't you need to get back on the stage before it leaves?"

Tom tilted his head and pursed his lips. "I believe Buffalo will suit my purposes just fine. Spinner tells me there's a bigger town close by, and those mountains are something to look at."

Olivia already felt pricks of perspiration. "Spinner?"

"The stage driver." Tom's eyes were sober upon her. "So you won't have supper with me?"

"I'm sure you understand." In the bright sunshine, she saw what the relative darkness of the coach had masked, a two-inch white scar beneath Tom's right eye. It took the edge off his fastidious dress and pale skin. Perhaps the man knew more about life outside an office than she had previously thought.

Without another word, Tom tilted his head to indicate the approaching wagon and helped her up when it rattled to a stop. The driver grunted at her, the same man she'd seen Tom speaking to moments ago. "Good afternoon, ma'am." His grin revealed yellowed teeth. She steeled herself not to react to the disagreeable sight. "I'm Ronald Coltrain."

As the horses pulled the conveyance down the main street, Olivia felt the rise of anticipation. A sudden urge to slip the pins from her hair and twirl in the sunlight captured her fancy, but she only straightened her skirts and folded her hands in her lap.

Dust rose into her nostrils as a rider galloped his horse past. Olivia blinked at the rather shabby wooden buildings, a far cry for those of the east. As the wagon continued, she glimpsed a man entering Landry's Restaurant. Dark hair, lithe frame, familiar to her. . . Her heart squeezed in her chest when she caught the man's gaze, and then the wagon rolled past, and she was on her way home.

Chapter 2

Ryan pushed the wide-brimmed hat down on his head to protect himself from the pulsing waves of heat. He had almost decided to take his noon meal in the Occidental's restaurant, but had changed his mind when he found the dining room empty. Landry's restaurant held a handful of patrons. Besides, the rounded woman he'd seen hugging the new arrival might offer up some information on the town. Waitresses tended to glean the latest news from the patrons they served. As he prepared to enter Landry's, the rattle of a wagon made him turn. The curly-headed beauty rode next to Ronald Coltrain. For an instant, their eyes met, until the wagon passed on down the road and he was left with the image of red curls and amber eyes, packaged in a fancy dress of the latest style. Not his type even if she hadn't been married.

He took a table farthest from the door, his back against the wall. The air smelled of the deep flavors of roasted meat but also held a tinge of sweetness. A man with a towel tucked into the waistband of his trousers headed his way, giving off an air of boredom. Probably the type roped into the restaurant business by his wife, who was no doubt tucked back in the kitchen slaving away over steaming pots of the daily special.

"What's smelling good to you tonight, stranger?"

Ryan flicked his gaze over the other people, gauging their reaction to a stranger in their midst. Nobody seemed to show any interest. "Meat. Potatoes. Is that cherry pie I smell?"

"Dried apple."

Ah, he should have known. Cinnamon was the sweet undertone hanging in the air. "I'll have a large slice."

"Name's Robert Landry. If you need anything else, just holler."

"Much obliged." Ryan tilted his head, purposely withholding his name. Landry didn't appear concerned by the omission. He spun on his heel and stopped at a table to inquire after two men. Ryan decided by their dress that they were either ranchers or drifters hoping to get hired for the roundup and drive. And considering they acted as if the food in front of them was their first in days, he guessed they must be drifters.

He considered the handful of others in the restaurant and wondered where the stocky woman was. He had half a mind to saunter toward the kitchen area to see if he could catch a glimpse of her, but he had to be cautious. The problem was not so much in getting information on what had happened to his father, but in trusting those who talked to him to tell the truth. He couldn't hide his identity, not in a small town, but for these first few hours, he wanted to remain nameless and gather as much information as he could on his father's murder.

Landry reappeared with a hot cup of coffee and the pie. He set it down in front of Ryan with a gentleness that belied his size. "You looking for someone, mister?"

"Who's askin'?" he said, careful to measure his movements so he wouldn't appear startled by the question.

"You're not familiar. Reckoned maybe I could help you along the trail a little faster."

Ryan relaxed in his chair and gave himself time to sip the hot brew before he answered. "Looking for work. Thought there might be some to be had around here."

"You're late into the season. Most have hired out for the roundups. Could still ride out and see. Some of the bigger spreads might need a hand."

"What's the biggest you got?"

"Rocking S is plenty big, but so's the XR."

Ryan felt tension biting at the nape of his neck. He took a bite of the pie. The cinnamon mixed with the tang of apples was sweet on his tongue. "The Rocking S. That Sattler land?"

Landry turned and started back to the kitchen, not seeming the least affected by his question. A good thing, Ryan reasoned.

"Yup. That's the one," Landry said.

Ryan allowed himself a small smile, congratulating himself on his first victory. He could try to ask more of the man but doubted Landry would be willing or able to sit still long enough. "Is there a woman that works here?"

"Phoebe?" Landry stopped and turned, brow raised to punctuate the question.

"Red-brown hair?"

"That's her. She had to take plates of food over to the jail. I'll tell her you asked after her."

Ryan took the last bite and sipped his coffee. "No need." He would seek her out later.

❧

Olivia's pulse jumped as they rounded the low hill shielding the entrance to the Rocking S. Despite the clear blue skies, a warm wind traced fingers down her bare neck and sent the curls tickling against her ears. She swiped an errant strand from her eyes and blinked. Her father would know, as Phoebe had, that she was arriving. Her happiness flickered. Of course he wouldn't be standing by the gate, nor the stage, waiting for her. He was a busy man, and she had chosen one of the most hectic times of the year to come home.

"Your father must be beside himself with excitement." Tom's voice was low, his smile beguiling.

"It's been a long time. Everything has changed."

"He will be amazed at the woman you've become."

Olivia refused to look his direction. His kind words bordered on flirtatious, and what had begun innocently enough as two people stuck in the same stagecoach now seemed to hold a trace of something else entirely.

Tom leaned forward and touched her hand. "Would you allow me to come calling? Perhaps we could take supper in town together. Soon." He emphasized the last word.

Olivia's lips parted, but her tongue felt paralyzed. "Perhaps," she finally said. She turned her attention to the corral. The outbuildings looked in fine repair. The curious eyes of men, both on foot and horseback, stared her way.

The wagon stopped rolling, and Olivia rose to her feet almost as soon as the wheels stilled. Without waiting for Tom, she gathered her skirts as close as she dared and hopped to the ground. She heard Tom clear his throat. The driver chortled. "Beat us to it, she did."

She didn't wait to hear more and rushed to the main house, knowing full well she had the attention of every male on the ranch. Her automatic response was to knock, but she laughed and shoved the door inward. "Daddy? Daddy, I'm home!"

An old cowhand raised watery hazel eyes from the wide-plank dining table where he sat. A dusty younger man sat across the table. "There something I can help you with, miss?"

Years fell away as the voice washed over Olivia. "Roper?"

The wiry old Rocking S hand squinted at her and rasped his hand against a covering of mostly gray whiskers. "Livy?"

"Li'l Livy, I believe you called me."

In slow motion, Roper unfolded from the chair, face bright with recognition. "Why, circle the wagons and call me an Indian. You're all grown up!"

"Where's my father?"

The younger man scratched his chair back and rolled to his feet. "Best get back to work, Roper." The man's gingham-blue eyes latched on to her, cold as the lake ice she skated on back east.

"You don't know who this is. This here's Olivia Sattler," Roper offered. "Boss's daughter."

Cold blue eyes snapped to her face then skimmed the length of her. Her skin crawled. "I'm Skinny Bonnet."

"I wanted to see my father." Her flat words were meant to send a warning.

Skinny fingered the edges of his vest. "I'll get him for you. Went down south of the property."

Without another word, he left. Roper remained where he was. "He's the foreman. Has a way of nettling people."

"You speak from experience?"

Roper shrugged. "Not everyone likes him. I'd better git before he starts in on me."

Within seconds Roper was back, her trunk across his back. Heat flared in her cheeks when she recalled its weight and saw the frailty of the man who labored to carry it. "In your room, miss?"

"Yes, please, and thank you so much."

"No problem."

A weight settled on Olivia's shoulders as Roper left and the quietness of the empty house surrounded her. The sharpness of her mother's death penetrated deeper than it had in the years since she'd left. No wonder her father and aunt had decided it best for her to leave Wyoming. She stood at the kitchen table, the same one she remembered from her childhood, and traced the grain of the boards, worn by time and the presence of many hands on its surface. Though neat, the kitchen seemed hollow. Lifeless. And Olivia felt the pang of loneliness so familiar to her at boarding school. Even in the midst of her circle of friends, she'd felt alone when the girls talked of their families and friends, bragging about their privileges and current gossip.

Olivia touched the seat where her mother had presided over the table and felt the coldness of the wood. Sorrow reached down deep into that part of her heart that acknowledged her mother's absence and yanked hard. She would make sure to find her mother's grave, near a shining pond and a tree with arching limbs. It was all she remembered.

With effort she turned her thoughts to taking charge of tasks her mother would have done. Cooking seemed the most obvious. Crossing to the pantry, she assessed the staples along the shelves. Bread would be the perfect beginning, so she lifted down a half-empty sack of flour. Upon straightening, she noticed her mother's apron hanging from a nail beside the shelves. For as long as she could remember, it had been the place Lillian Sattler hung her apron every night after supper. Olivia let the flour sack slide from her grasp and reached a trembling hand to the hard evidence of a presence long gone.

Her eyes closed as she held the delicate white apron against her cheek. Its various smears and smudges and the smell of home and family rolled Olivia back ten years to those times she stood on a stool and watched her mother knead bread or make pies. Even those times her mother shared her favorite peppermints. A rare treat indeed! She tried to bring her mother's face into tighter focus. A face much like her own. She could see her mother's smile as she laughed at one of

Olivia's young inanities and smell the fresh peppermint that clung to her when Lily Sattler knelt to hug her close.

Enmeshed in her thoughts, Olivia didn't hear the creak of the front door or the soft steps that drew nearer. A hand clamped her shoulder as her name was spoken. She jerked and turned, hand at her throat. Her father's face greeted her, and she sank into his outstretched arms. Tears burned her eyes and demanded release.

"Welcome home, daughter."

She had no words. Between the surprise of his approach and the reality of his presence after so many years, she could think of nothing to say.

He held her away from him, his smile wide but stiff. As if he'd had little reason to smile for a long time. Craggy wrinkles appeared around his eyes and mouth. His face seemed leaner, darker, more leathery than she remembered. His hair was grayer and thinner.

"You stole my breath," he said. "I thought I was watching your mother."

"Oh Daddy!" She nestled close to him again, releasing the tears that filled her eyes and blurred his image. With her mother's apron in her hands, it was almost like the three of them together again.

"Imagine my surprise to find a beautiful young woman in place of the little girl I sent off so long ago."

"You could have visited. Or sent for me. Or. . ." Olivia bit her lip and her father pulled back, his hands holding her shoulders.

"And I'm sorry for that. Phoebe told me to visit. I meant to. . . . It just never seemed the right time to leave."

For ten years? She turned from him, hiding the sheen of tears burning for release. "I'm going to make bread and a cake. Butter cake, your favorite."

His gaze fell to the apron in her hands. "Just like your mother."

She heard the wobble in his voice and turned in time to see his hand wipe at his cheek. She went to him and hugged him hard. He propped his chin on the top of her head. He must feel as she did. Like her mother's ghost had somehow entered the kitchen and orchestrated the tugs of grief from those she loved.

At last her father released her. "I won't have you cooking tonight. Marty will do those honors, butter cake and all. We'll eat that cake up, and you can retire for the evening. Stages aren't big on comfort, and you must be exhausted."

He crossed to the front door, flashed a grin that didn't quite reach his eyes, and was gone. Probably off to raise the alarm to his men that a lady would be present at chuck. Funny how she'd forgotten that her father was not a man of many words. Where she had expected a flowing conversation of news as they played catch-up, she'd received much less.

Her aunt Fawn had tried to warn her about being the only woman among men.

With a sigh, Olivia hooked the apron back on the nail and realized the room had grown dim. Outside the large window, clouds were rolling in. She raised the chimney on a lantern in the center of the table and lit the wick. A welcome splash of light pushed the shadows back as a draft of cold air swept around her ankles.

Chapter 3

"I'm going into town tomorrow, Ryan." Josephine Laxalt stood a full head shorter than her son, but Ryan knew what a determined woman looked like when he saw the tilt of his mother's chin and the gleam in her eyes. "You won't change my mind."

"Father would want me to care for you."

"I, who have cared for others all my life"—Josephine's finger wagged—"need no one to care for me. I will work in town."

Ryan hunkered down in his space at the table and wished he hadn't eaten in town so he could do his mother's greens and ham the honor it deserved. He knew she measured how much he ate—had done so ever since he was a boy. Something about making sure he grew straight and strong. He smiled at the memory of her frowning when he'd reach for a sweet before his plate was clear of the last crumb.

"There are things I can do on the ranch to help you," she said, "but it was Martin's dream, not mine. I want to be with people again, son. You take the ranch. Fulfill your father's dream."

He debated telling his mother that he had reached his decision and would take his father's place—his rightful place—as owner of the Lazy L. Perhaps she wouldn't feel the need to ply him with sumptuous feasts or cry out her grief on his shoulder night after night. He knew her grief was partly due to the fear that she would lose him again to the life he had built away from her.

"You must find a nice young woman. Having warmth in your life will settle you. Make you happier."

He squirmed in his seat, feeling very much like a quivering lizard in the hand of a small boy. Twenty-six years old and still a child in his mother's eyes. Yet no anger burned through him at the thought. His mother had worked hard all her life. She was generous and kind, loving and stern. But there was something else at stake, and Ryan struggled to understand his mother's blindness to the obvious.

"He was killed, Mama."

Her hands stilled then knotted together and rested on the edge of the table. She stared at her plate.

"You know it's true," he said. "It's what brought me home and what I must do to—"

"It is not your fight." His mother's voice was a harsh whisper—as fierce as he'd ever heard it. "Your father believed things could be made right peaceably."

"And that attitude got him killed."

His mother's head came up. Her dark eyes were placid yet determined. "Because you do not understand, just as your father did not understand."

He pressed his lips together. "What is it I don't understand?"

"That these men do not want peace. They want war."

"Then I'll give them war."

"By doing so, you would leave me alone. You think you can hold back the force that is against us, but it is too great. There are too many of them." Her hand chopped the air. "It is not your fight."

"If I'm to be a rancher, I must try."

She gasped. "You will run the ranch then?"

"Yes. I'll have Bobby hire more men to help ready for the drive."

"They will fight you even in the roundup. Claiming unbranded cattle as their right, no matter whose property the animal is on."

He absorbed her words. "I won't let them."

"You will become their enemy."

"Father's way did not work. Let me try my own methods."

His mother bowed her head. "Yours will not work either."

"I'll use caution."

Her slim shoulders rose and fell on a sigh. "I will cook for you and keep the house, but I will work in town, too."

His mother stood to her feet and gathered her plate. Black hair curled in tendrils around her face, softening the lines bracketing her eyes.

"Who did it, Mama? Tell me."

Her spine stiffened. Without replying, she plunged the dirty dish into a bucket and swirled it around. "I will not speculate. It is dangerous. What is done is done." A lone tear slipped down her cheek. She smeared it away with a wet hand. "Your father is gone and cannot return to us."

❧

If Olivia thought home meant pleasant days spent in lengthy conversation with her devoted father, she'd been out in the Wyoming sun too long. Jay Sattler never sat longer than necessary to eat before he rose, kissed her cheek, and was out the door.

It had been three days since Olivia's arrival on the stage. In those days she had cleaned every corner of the ranch house and cooked all the meals except that first one. Any attempts to open a real conversation usually fell flat after a few monosyllabic answers from her father. She wanted more than anything to sit down and cry, and she knew just the person whose shoulder she wanted to saturate.

In her room she contemplated her gowns—fussy styles and materials that would never hold up out here. She wanted something that gave her the freedom to ride. Thinking of her mother's clothes, she wandered into the room her parents used to share. The pegs on the wall held nothing more than a pair of her father's trousers. She chided herself. It made sense that her father would have packed or given away her mother's clothes.

Olivia crossed to her own room and debated over the gowns again. She had one brown day dress that had very little adornment, though the style was in keeping with the use of a bustle. Olivia had made the decision to leave all her bustles with her aunt, trying to travel as lightly as possible. Aunt Fawn had put up a fuss, lecturing her about "proper dress" and "stylish women of fine education," but Olivia had been adamant, mollifying her aunt by suggesting she could order one once she arrived in Buffalo. Her aunt's glower had given voice to her doubts, but Olivia had remained firm, and the bustles had stayed in Aunt Fawn's care.

Olivia hugged herself, delighted to be free of the constraints of fashion. Huge bustles, restrictive corsets. . .

Aunt Fawn would swoon.

She yanked the lid off a hatbox and pulled out her top hat. A must for any riding costume back east. With a grin of delight, Olivia stuffed the hat back into the box. She'd be trading a top hat for a wide-brimmed western one as soon as she could. Her day seemed to take on a life of its own. She changed into the brown gown, frowning at the added length going bustleless added in the back and sides, but fingering the silky material and appreciating the expense that had gone into it. Funny how she'd never considered her mother's simple styles compared to Aunt Fawn's lust for the latest fashion, not to mention her insistence that Olivia dress accordingly.

Now she would be free of all that, and it felt good. Right, somehow. Though Aunt Fawn had made her feel welcome, there was always an underlying coldness. Or maybe oblivion was a better word. Aunt Fawn didn't know there was a world beyond her own, making her incapable of understanding Olivia's confusion when she compared her mother to Jay Sattler's older sister. Fawn's stiff smile never failed to show her displeasure when the subject of her brother's ranch operation came up, and Olivia realized she'd always resented that silent disapproval.

No matter. She was here now, and despite what her father thought she should do to occupy her time, Olivia had no intention of spending her days twiddling her fingers. She could keep the housework up without problem, but she intended to find a job. In Buffalo. As soon as possible.

Chapter 4

"You could work at the saloon as a barmaid."

Olivia gasped at her friend's straight-faced suggestion. "Phoebe Wagner!"

"You'd get a fistful of tips."

Before Olivia could sputter her utter disbelief, she saw the mischievous spark in her friend's dark eyes. "How terrible of you."

Phoebe spat a laugh as she set a cup of coffee in front of her friend and took the seat opposite. "Thought that might take the starch out of you."

"Am I that bad?"

"When you got off that stagecoach, I thought the queen had come west."

Olivia studied the rim of her cup and the chip in the handle. The words settled over her more like an observation than a rebuke. "It's a change."

"Got that right. But you're here now, and you'll adjust. Your mama was a kindhearted woman, and underneath all that starch your aunt rubbed on ya, you'll be one of us in no time."

"Tell me about her."

Phoebe tugged at a wild bright red curl and shrugged. "What's to tell? She was a good woman. She gave me a chance when I needed it and taught me what my drunken pa never could."

Olivia sipped the bitter, hot brew, made a face that drew a laugh from Phoebe, and plunked her cup back down. "When did Daddy let you go?"

"After you left."

Olivia studied her friend's small apartment over the rim of the coffee cup. There wasn't much to look at. Phoebe lived simply. Olivia had never known ostentation until she'd lived with Aunt Fawn, and then she'd accepted it as a new normal. Her father's home reflected the same simplicity as Phoebe's. Self-conscious now, Olivia frowned at her gown.

Phoebe laughed. "We'll get you over to the dressmaker. She can make you some sensible clothing. No use wearing those draperies in this heat."

"It's the latest style."

"Latest style or not, it's best put away for visits to Aunt Fawn." Phoebe drained the last of her coffee. "I need to get myself back downstairs or Landry will have my hide."

"Is he hiring?"

"Sure he is." Phoebe glanced over her shoulder. "But your schooling is best put to use doing something else. You said you enjoyed writing. Why not ask Jon at the paper if you can work as a journalist?"

"A journalist?"

"Why not? Didn't you work for that fancy Philly paper for a time?"

"I wrote a couple of articles that the *Inquirer* bought." She lowered her voice. "Mostly on fashion, but only because Aunt Fawn drilled me on the latest trends. It was dreadfully boring."

"Really now?" Phoebe's smile was bright. Too bright. "I promise you won't miss the bustles, bows, stays, and braces once you've done without them."

Fancy frippery and fine footwear were all the things embraced back in Philly. She tilted her head and thought on it a bit. "But I look forward to fitting in and being a western girl again."

"You always were a bit of a tomboy."

"Yes, I suppose I was. Maybe that's why Aunt Fawn was so determined to dress me to her liking."

"And now"—Phoebe opened the door—"I've got to get downstairs. Let me know what you find over at the paper."

Left to herself, Olivia found the small, one-story building with BUFFALO BULLETIN written on a board and mounted above the door. The smell of ink and oil made her nose twitch. A lone man was bent over a tray, shuffling through tiny, ink-stained blocks. He didn't acknowledge her presence, and despite three desks tucked into a corner of the room hinting at other employees, no one else came forward.

"Good morning, sir."

She frowned when he didn't respond. For all intents and purposes, the man didn't look old. He certainly wasn't old enough to have hearing problems.

"Good morning?" She tried again.

The man's hands paused. He squinted at the tray, wiped his forehead with the back of his hand, and continued his search for another letter. Olivia cleared her throat for a third try, determined to make sure her voice projected this time, when the door opened behind her.

"Miss Sattler. What a pleasure."

The wheat-brown hair, longer on the collar, and his trim mustache and pale skin were a welcome sight. "Mr. Mahone."

Tom Mahone took her hand in his and squeezed, delight making dimples in his cheeks. Olivia didn't miss the light of admiration in his eyes. "How is Marv treating you?"

She followed Tom Mahone's gaze to the back of the man sifting through the small blocks of wood. His voice dropped. "Marv is shy. Especially around women. He's a good worker though."

Worker?

Tom stepped back and spread his arms. "The paper is mine now."

Marv turned from his work to glance wide-eyed at his employer. His eyes grazed across Olivia. His hand hit a container, and letters spilled to the floor. Olivia watched as the man stooped to pick up the pieces. When she moved to help, Tom touched her elbow.

"Marv can clean it up. I'm much more interested in hearing about the reason for this delightful visit. Perhaps it is too much to hope that you were coming to see me?"

"I don't know how I could be when I didn't know you owned the paper." Indeed, even Phoebe, the woman whose finger was on the pulse of Buffalo, had still thought the paper was owned by another.

"Jon was ready for retirement." Tom turned, unable to see the moment when Marv again raised his head, stabbing his employer with his eyes. When he caught Olivia watching him, he returned to his scramble for the pieces.

"I need a reporter. Didn't you tell me on the way over that you did some work for the *Philadelphia Inquirer*?"

Olivia flinched. "Why, yes. . ."

"There now. A woman like you must be bored sitting on a ranch all day. Take up a pencil, and let's get to reporting. I've already picked up the latest on the flood that occurred in Johnstown."

In the coach, Tom had seemed like such a laid-back gentleman, but his manner now seemed brusque, cocky. Olivia frowned, trying to sort her feelings and still follow the conversation. Something about Johnstown. "Pennsylvania?"

Tom dragged a chair from behind the desk and offered it to her. "Please."

She gathered the yards of her skirt in one hand and slipped into the chair, suddenly aware of her ill-fitting gown. "You were saying about Johnstown?"

"Flooded. Looking at almost ten thousand dead."

She had heard of the town, especially the elaborate hunting and fishing club, whose membership was a source of great envy for her aunt Fawn. But what Tom was saying didn't make sense.

"The dam burst and sent a geyser of water down the hillside. Terrible, simply terrible." He perched on the edge of the desk and waved a hand in dismissal. "What I really want to know is if you'll take the job."

She held up her hand. "Tom, slow down."

He braced his knuckles against his knee and leaned forward. Devilment emanated from his eyes and the twist of his mouth. Even the scar on his cheek seemed to pucker into a half-moon grin. "I'll pay you exactly what I would pay a man—an offer you won't find in most men-only small towns. How can you refuse?"

Chapter 5

Streams of morning light played off Josephine Laxalt's hair. Every angle of her body and face spoke of her stubborn determination to get a job in town. They'd spent breakfast discussing—no, *arguing* would be the better word—over the wisdom and necessity of such a move. Ryan didn't want to think about it anymore. His mother's mind was made up, and his ability to sway her was nonexistent. The only man who could change his mother's mind was dead, and he was even beginning to question his father's success rate.

His mother swayed on the wagon seat, her right hand clenched along the edge to secure her position. He groaned in frustration. Women! Or maybe that should be *mothers*!

When did she get to be so stubborn? He relaxed his hands on the reins. He'd always wondered where his own stubbornness came from. The thought helped to snuff his irritation. "Where do you want to go exactly?"

They rode along for a minute in utter silence. When Ryan stole a sideways glance at his mother, he witnessed the softening. She now stared at her lap then lifted her dark eyes to his.

"Phoebe might help me find a job. Stop right there in front of the sign that says LANDRY'S."

He didn't bother to tell her he knew the place. When he brought the wagon to a halt, he set the brake and hurried to the other side of the wagon, half-expecting his mother to vault to the ground. She didn't. Instead, she beamed a beautiful, charming smile at him. And because of that warm charisma, he could see why his father had run into trouble being angry at his mother.

"You're a charmer."

She placed her hand along his cheek, her grin fading. "And you, my son, are as well. Flash that beautiful smile at some young woman, and she will be yours forever. You've a good heart." Tears puddled in her eyes. She turned away and dabbed at her eyes.

Ryan brushed his fingers through his hair. He felt weighted with weariness. A cowboy rode by, his horse's hooves kicking up a cloud of dust. He moved to his horse's head and scratched along the animal's cheek, debating his next step and the wrath of his mother's disapproval if he stirred the debate over her working in town.

Across the street, the door to the *Buffalo Bulletin* yanked open. Through the dissipating dust, he could see heavy brown fabric and recognized the auburn beauty he'd seen at the stage office days ago. She moved as if in a trance. Ryan flinched as she began to step into the street. A team of oxen pulling a wagon barreled down the center of Main. The driver stood and yelled. The woman didn't appear to hear. When she stepped out into the path of the wagon, Ryan sprinted across the street. His boots plowed dust as his right arm hooked her waist. Her eyes widened, and a little scream wrenched from her lips. He drove her backward, lifting her off her feet. Trace chains rattled, and the curses of the driver rained down on them as the wagon bolted past.

Ryan spread his left hand at her back to help her keep her balance as she recovered. She blinked at him, dazed.

"My pardon, ma'am. Those oxen were moving fast."

"No. I—"

Up close he could see the spray of freckles across her nose. It gave her the look of an imp, albeit a beautiful one. Her light auburn hair tickled the slender column of her neck. Ryan swallowed and straightened, and when their eyes met, the jump in his pulse forced him to draw air into his suddenly starved lungs.

"I'm afraid. . ." She gave a little laugh and glanced down. He realized his arm still curved around her waist. Her husband would take offense if she didn't.

Ryan jerked his hand back as a crushing wave of retribution washed over him. He turned away. "Be careful crossing the street."

A lilt of laughter caught him midstride, and the silken brush of her hand at his elbow coaxed him to turn and face her. "I will be more careful, kind sir. And thank you. I fear my mind was far away. Do you. . . ? Might I know your name?"

Too late Ryan remembered to remove his hat. She must think him a dolt. He certainly felt like one. "Laxalt. Ryan Laxalt."

"Thank you, Mr. Laxalt. As my first article for the *Buffalo Bulletin*, I shall write on the danger of not watching where one is going while crossing a busy street."

He caught the twinkle of mirth in her gaze, but a withering self-rebuke tightened his stomach. "Leave my name out of it unless you want blood on your hands." A look of dismay slashed her features, and he turned on his heel and stalked off. Anger welled at his harsh tone. All she had done was tease, but the gentle jab of fun had hit him square. To have his presence announced in such a public manner would surely bring the wrath of his father's murderer down on his head before he could do his own investigation.

❧

Olivia watched Ryan leave, her spirit stale after his harsh words. His dress pegged him as a cowboy. She didn't intend on wasting another second thinking of his gray eyes and dark hair. That he'd saved her was one thing, but his hard dismissal was, well, rude. Beyond rude. Reprehensible. Aunt Fawn would sniff and *tsk-tsk* and encourage her to move along.

But Olivia watched him go against her will. His ground-eating stride exposed his eagerness to be away from her as much as the level of his anger. *Blood on her hands?* She'd done nothing wrong. *And, no, Mr. Laxalt, I won't write an article about you, unless it is to eschew rude manners and name you as an example.* That would require the use of his name though.

With a sigh, she picked up her skirts and gave a yank to the heavy material. Nothing to clear a mind like the idea of a new dress. She glanced up and down Main and was relieved to see a store two doors down from where she stood. She would begin there.

Even as she stepped toward the store, she felt compelled to glance over her shoulder. No sign of Ryan Laxalt. The slightest tug of disappointment nagged. Her foot caught in the folds of material, and she tripped. She grabbed at a post that sliced a splinter into her palm. Tears collected at the burn of the injury. It had wedged deep into her skin. And it was long. She rubbed the area around the splinter with her free hand and kicked at the excess material pooled around her feet. Feeling much like a horse pulling a wagon, she let the unwieldy material drag through the dust on the road. She was determined to be done with all her fancy gowns once and for all.

Pushing inside the store, she paused to inhale the familiar scents of wood, leather, and spices. It was a smell like no other—and one that settled her, cloaking her in familiarity. A short, balding man set aside the paper hiding his face and greeted her with a smile.

"I heard you'd come home to Wyoming, little Livy Sattler." His friendly face creased into wrinkles that hadn't been quite so deep ten years ago. Still, Olivia would never forget Papa Don.

Looking into that kind face stripped away the years, and she was suddenly the small child at her mother's side ordering a stick of candy in a shy voice and hiding her face in her mother's skirts. A knot formed in her throat.

Papa Don stopped at his candy display and, eyes twinkling, plunged his hand into the peppermint jar. He held out the sweet to her as he closed the distance between them. Tears threatened when she closed her hand around the candy. Papa's face blurred beneath the onslaught of her tears, and she felt him press a kerchief into her hand.

"It's the memories, isn't it, child?" His soothing voice rolled over her as she sniffed. Aunt Fawn would have been mortified at her public display, but she didn't care. This wasn't Philadelphia. "When I lost my dear Ellen five years back, it was so hard to come back to the store."

She sniffed and did her best to push back the emotion. "I'm so sorry. I don't know what came over me. I just. . . . The smell seemed so familiar and—"

"No need to explain. I guess a woman has a right to some tears."

How could she have forgotten Papa Don's kindness? He'd always had the utmost patience while she looked over the candy selection. His wife had been a rosy-cheeked woman with a quick laugh and pleasant voice, good for a pat on the head or compliment. In that little-girl place of her heart, she'd wished they were her grandmother and grandfather, because her real ones were so very far away.

"Mama Ellen. . ." She paused to consider how easily the familiar title slipped from her tongue.

"Took sick and never could shake it."

She held out her hands to the older man, and he took them. "I have such fond memories of her."

"She always had a soft spot for you, Miss Livy. Now"—he squeezed her hands and let go then extended his arms out to take in the goods surrounding them—"what can Papa Don do for you?"

"I need some dresses made. Is there anyone in town who could make them, or could I order some?"

A draft of hot air rushed and swirled around them, announcing someone's entrance. Papa Don lifted his head and waved. "I'll be with you in a moment, Mrs. Laxalt."

Olivia caught the image of a dark-haired woman who was shorter than her by a foot. She saw the woman's nod and heard her soft, accented "Thank you, Papa Don." Olivia wasn't sure what it was about the woman's voice that drew her, but she watched as the woman made her way to a corner of the store that held fabric, thread, and other sundries.

When she turned back to Papa Don, the sun seemed to rise in his smile. He, too, followed the departing back of his patron. He jerked his head in Mrs. Laxalt's direction and said, "That's the woman for you. Sews a streak from what I hear." His voice dropped even lower. "Probably could use some extra money right now, being she just lost her husband. Came in earlier asking if I'd advertise for her in the window. I told her she could make use of the new sewing machine I got in." He winked. "Best advertisement for merchandise I could hope for."

A new widow. Olivia's heart ached for the woman. To have loved and lost. . . And she didn't appear to be that old. Early fifties.

"If you want, I can ask her," Papa Don offered.

"Timing is everything, and God's timing is perfect," her mother's voice whispered through her head. It had been part of a Bible lesson long forgotten, but stirred now because it fit the circumstances. Olivia shook her head. "It'll give me a chance to introduce myself."

Without waiting to hear whatever response was forming on Papa Don's lips, Olivia crossed to the dark-haired woman rubbing at the splinter tip.

"Would you happen to have a needle to get a splinter out?" The woman's smile pinched to concern, and her gentle touch and soothing words as she worked to dislodge the splinter was the balm Olivia's heart needed.

Upon closer inspection, she could see better the simplicity of the woman's dress and the strands that had escaped the brush. More white than black threaded through her shiny hair, albeit more heavily on the right temple than on the left. Her eyes flashed with bright alertness yet held a softness that promised long hugs and tables heavy with the favorite dishes of her loved ones. Beautiful eyes. Soulful and loving.

Chapter 6

Ryan knew a man's chances of picking up local information revolved around the saloon, the livery, and the store. He began at the livery, hoping he would not have to enter the saloon at all, out of respect for his mother's reputation among the townsfolk. But should the need arise, he would have little choice. His worries found relief when he saw a boy working a shoe onto a horse.

"Your pa around?"

"No sir."

"He own this place?"

"Yes sir." The boy let go of the horse's leg and straightened, wiping a thin line of sweat from his brow. "He leaves me in charge most days. You needin' a horse?"

"No. Not today anyhow. I was just wondering if you knew anything about the shooting that took place here a couple weeks ago."

The boy's light gray eyes grew wary. "You the law?"

Ryan spit a laugh he didn't feel. "Just curious to know what people are saying about who did it. Name's Ryan."

"Lance Daniels." The boy set aside his mallet and stuck out his hand. He gave Ryan's arm quite the workout. Whatever the boy was, he wasn't weak. His slim build covered lean muscle. "Most 'round here think Laxalt got what was coming to him. Stealing cattle's a hanging offense."

Hot denial came to his tongue. Ryan clenched his jaw. Best to let the boy talk.

"Skinny found Sattler cattle in with Laxalt's." The boy shrugged. "Seems clear that Laxalt was jealous of the big ranchers and decided they could spare a few head to fatten his herd."

"Who's Skinny?"

"Sattler's foreman."

"That's a strong accusation."

"Sattler, Bowman, and Michaels are pretty much the law 'round here."

"Nobody thought to investigate the accusation?"

Lance leaned against a stall door and shrugged. "Why would he lie?"

Ryan touched the brim of his hat. "Good question." He pivoted, and a trace of dust rose around his feet. "I'll be sure to use your services when I'm in town. Horse could use some new shoes."

"Bring him over, mister. We'll take care of him."

His business concluded, Ryan crossed to Landry's. The woman who seated him was the same one he'd seen hugging on the beauty he'd held in his arms earlier.

Better not to dwell on the way she had felt against him. He had done what any man would have done in his place, but she was not his to think about.

"Sit anywhere." The woman motioned. "Name's Phoebe."

Ryan scanned the few people in the restaurant and saw no sign of his mother. Phoebe set a lemonade in front of him and hovered at his elbow as he studied the two choices scribbled on a piece of slate at the back of the dining room.

"I'll have the chicken."

She was coarse of face and round, but her smile was bright and her expression open and honest. She looked to Ryan's eye like a woman quite capable of caring for herself. That his mother would be friends with such a woman shouldn't surprise him.

After replaying the boy's heavy accusation and considering the general restlessness he'd read about since arriving, Ryan thought he might understand his mother's concern. If the townsfolk thought his father guilty, proving otherwise would be hard work. The experience he had in such matters would come in handy. And there was no excuse for a man accused of rustling getting a bullet in the back. A man had a right to face his accuser. He didn't plan on resting until he found the person who'd killed his father. His muscles suddenly burned with the need to move, and he wished he hadn't ordered. Phoebe appeared with his food and set it down.

"My mother. She was coming to talk to you."

Phoebe's eyes widened. "Your mother?"

"She was going to ask you about"—he swallowed—"about finding a job in town."

Phoebe remained still, palm flat on the table, brows lowered. "Josephine Laxalt?"

He hesitated. "Yes." He shook off the chagrin. It was time to let it be known he was home.

"Haven't seen her today." Her eyes shifted to the windows at his back, and her smile appeared, triumphant and playful. "But I think I just found her. She's with Olivia right there."

Ryan twisted on his seat to follow the woman's finger then stood to get a better view. His mother stood with her back to him, talking to the woman he'd rescued not even an hour before.

"She's a pretty one, isn't she? You've not met her yet?"

"We've met," he managed to say. When his mother and Olivia turned and headed for Landry's, a blast of nerves assaulted him. He put a hand down to steady himself, and warmth oozed over it, soft and squishy. He closed his eyes in horror over what he'd just done and inhaled as a titter of laughter squeaked from Phoebe.

"Here you go."

He opened his eyes to see the square of cloth Phoebe held out to him. Her face was red and her eyes much too bright. She hicupped on a giggle as he withdrew his hand from the mashed potatoes and accepted the cloth. With quick wipes, he rid his palm and fingers of the mess.

Phoebe greeted the women as they drew closer.

"Ryan, what are you doing here?"

"Finished my business early. I thought you said you'd be here." He didn't even try to keep the accusation from his voice.

His mother stiffened. "I am not the child, son."

"Forgive me, Mama, but there's much to worry about when I know we have enemies."

His mother gave him a tight smile then turned to indicate the woman at her side. "I want you to meet my new employer, Miss Olivia."

Ryan's head whipped upward, and the woman his mother pressed forward gave him an awkward smile. "I believe we've met."

"You crossed the road without looking." He tried to inject humor into his voice.

"Thank you for caring." Her words were mild, but her eyes flashed.

He dragged in a breath. She had whiskey eyes, though he was sure she would hate that description. Her eyelashes swept down over cheeks splashed pink from sun, exertion, or natural color—he didn't know which. Ryan stood to his feet, more aware of her than he wanted to be.

"Let's sit down and eat," his mother said. When he caught her eye, a twinkle sparked in those familiar brown depths. One of those amused looks she shot him every time he'd let loose with a lie as a child. Why, then, was he surprised when his mother sat across from him, leaving Olivia the spot beside him as the only choice. "Ryan, would you help. . ."

"Why is there a. . . ?" He followed Olivia's eyes as she took the seat he held for her and realized evidence of his sloppiness—soiled napkin and palm print in the potatoes—lay for all to see. And laugh at. "Perhaps you should watch where you place your hand, Mr. Laxalt."

❧

Too late Olivia felt the heat of a blush as she realized how that comment might sound. She pointed at the potatoes to emphasize what she referred to. Ryan Laxalt's eyes shone. Whether with mischief or guarded amusement, she couldn't quite tell, but at least he didn't offer a leering look.

Shoving back the offending plate, he resumed his seat. Despite his earlier terseness, she noted that he was able to admit his wrongs. Well, at least to his mother. His earlier flash of anger stuck in her mind like a burr.

"Miss Olivia asked me to sew some dresses for her," Mrs. Laxalt said. "She needs proper clothes for the West."

"Especially this heat."

Ryan's eyes rolled over her, touching what he could see of the gown. When his eyes raised to hers, a stab of awareness tilted her world off balance. It had to be his eyes. Curious eyes. Pale yet not pale at all. His dark hair curled at the ends but was longer than she'd seen most men wear.

"Papa Don said he would allow me to set up shop in that back corner of the store where he keeps his materials. I can work there and be out of your way, son. Others might even ask me to sew."

"If that is what you wish, Mother."

The hard clench of his jaw contradicted his easy statement. Olivia wondered at his reluctance. Was his displeasure aimed at her working in general? Or maybe at Josephine working for Papa Don or even herself?

"You are God's blessing to me this day, Miss Olivia," Josephine said.

Phoebe chose that moment to materialize with tall glasses of lemonade. "It'll clear the dust from your throat. Imagine my surprise to see your son, all grown up, worrying over his mother's whereabouts."

Josephine favored Phoebe with a smile and reached to pat Ryan's hand. "He is a good boy to worry over his mama. I was to come to you and ask for work, but this young woman has asked me to sew for her."

Phoebe's smile seemed to sag.

"All will be well, Phoebe," Josephine soothed.

Not understanding Josephine's words to Phoebe—almost a reassurance of sorts—Olivia looked to Ryan. His silver eyes flashed, and his dark brows lowered like clouds heavy with storm.

Josephine seemed eager to smooth the moment, and before Olivia could form a question that might clear the fog, she smiled. "I'll be in town tomorrow to begin. Will you be able to come in and be measured?"

"I have work to do on the ranch." Ryan formed the words on stiff lips.

Josephine's hand reached to pat his shoulder. "I can get into town by myself. No use you thinking you have to escort me in and out."

"Doesn't the Laxalt ranch border ours?" Olivia asked. "I could come by and pick you up in the mornings until we're done settling on materials and. . ."

Phoebe's panicked eyes flashed to Ryan then Josephine, and beside her, Olivia felt the stiffening of Ryan's posture. The storm in his eyes broke, and his lips formed a thin line.

Josephine reached to squeeze her son's hand where it white-knuckled his glass of lemonade.

"You're a Sattler?" He spit the words.

Olivia flinched and leaned away from him, singed by the heat of his question. "Jay Sattler is my father."

Chapter 7

"You knew, Mama." Ryan tried his best to contain his rage and confusion as he guided the wagon along the road out of town. He stared at the horse's ears because he could not look at his mother. "I'm trying to understand."

"I met her in the store, and she needed clothes. I need work."

"Not this. No. I can take care of you. The ranch will support us as it always supported you and Father."

"It is not your decision, and I don't want you to get involved."

He rolled his head on his shoulders to relieve the rising tension biting into his neck. "Sattler killed Papa. That does involve me."

"You do not know for certain."

He couldn't believe his mother's stubbornness on the issue. It should have been clear to her why he had to wedge himself into the situation. What kind of son would he be if he heard the news of his father's death and didn't return home to care for his mother?

Josephine's lips compressed.

"He was accused of rustling cattle. That's stealing."

"And you think your father would do such a thing?"

"No. Of course not. But that's why I need to clear his name of this accusation. To find out who killed him and why the accusation was made in the first place. Until then, I ask that you not be seen with Olivia Sattler."

"Because she's a Sattler?" His mother's expression grew dark with disapproval.

"And you're a Laxalt."

She drew herself erect. "I would hope by now that you realize the sins of one don't reflect on anyone but the person doing the sin. Olivia Sattler just arrived in town yesterday after years spent in Philadelphia."

"I know that." At least he knew that she'd just arrived in town.

"Then you must understand that her role in anything involving us is only in your head."

He stiffened at that and slapped the reins against the horse's rump.

"Stop punishing the horse," his mother bit out. Her hand clasped the side of the seat as the wagon lurched forward.

Chastened, Ryan pulled gently on the reins. The horse slowed. "If I don't do this, Mama, I would never forgive myself. He was my—"

"Would he want you to ride the trail of revenge?"

"Would he, or is it your wish that I avoid the trail?"

"Then it is revenge you want."

"Justice."

His mother released a heavy breath, and her voice was low and terse. "They will kill you, Ryan. I can't bear to lose you, too."

On impulse he hauled back on the reins and set the hand brake. "You've refused to tell me anything. Tell me now. Convince me there is no need for me to find the truth." He bit the inside of his cheek and his eyes scanned over the blue horizon that framed his mother's small form.

When her dark head dipped and he heard a sniffle, Ryan clamped his eyes shut. Nothing could diminish him to a bumbling, penitent blob of boyhood like seeing his mother cry. Dutifully he yanked the kerchief form his back pocket and pressed it against the back of his mother's hand.

"Mama. . ."

"If something were to happen to you, my heart would break completely."

He didn't understand. He had been away from home for years. He could have died several times over, and she wouldn't have known for weeks, maybe even months or years. But now, because he was nearby, she suddenly feared him dying? Maybe he did understand her point. He shook his head. No, not really.

"Do you know what it would be like to have not only my husband but my son murdered as well?"

His spine went rigid. His jaw hardened. "So he was murdered."

Her mouth flew open. "Yes. No. Ryan, listen to me. You must not do this thing that you think you need to do. They will hunt you down as they have others—"

"Others?" If her tears had made him indecisive, the idea that Sattler made victims of others steeled his resolve. Without saying a word, he released the brake and set the wagon into motion. Rays of sunshine waned, weakened by impending evening, and a cooling breeze sifted over his neck and face. His mother remained quiet, chin lifted high, but the quiver of her lips told him her tears were just below the surface of her composure.

"I only want peace."

He released a heavy sigh, his words soft. "Sometimes, Mama, you cannot have peace until you have waged a war."

❧

Olivia pressed the hat down on her head and tilted it to observe the effect in the mirror. Saucy, but the look was too overconfident for her. Plus she wasn't in Philadelphia. She doubted very seriously that Wyoming women would have need for a small hat angled to effect. Besides, if the sun was any indicator, those wide-brimmed hats she'd seen on so many since arriving would serve better to keep her fragile skin from breaking out in sun-induced freckles. Tucking the hat back into the box, she heard her father's boots on the front porch. Her heart sank at his arrival. At the discussion she would have to have with him. She placed the hatbox on her bed and smoothed the front of her bustleless gown. Tomorrow morning and the promise of sensible clothes could not come soon enough.

Olivia took one more look at herself in the mirror and frowned. She hoped Ryan Laxalt's dark attitude toward her would not demand his mother break the agreement for those dresses. Josephine's sadness had been palpable after Olivia had spoken her father's name. Ryan had left the table without so much as a "good day." But the worst part had been the conversation with Phoebe that had followed.

As she had watched Josephine meet up with her son outside the restaurant, his face a mask of controlled rage, Olivia had demanded that Phoebe explain why the sound of her father's name had brought such a reaction.

Phoebe had twisted her hands together in abject misery. "It's a long story."

"Without my dinner companions, I have plenty of time for conversation."

Scanning the dining room with a hopeful look, as if a patron might enter at any second and rescue her from the conversation, Phoebe grimaced and sank to the vacated chair. "It's an old problem."

"Old? As in something that has happened since I left?"

The transformation in Phoebe startled Olivia. Her friend's face went pale, and she slumped somewhat. "Your father is not well liked around here, Livy."

Not. Well. Liked. A troubling thought perhaps, but something Olivia felt could be shrugged off—if not for Phoebe's reaction. That alone spelled trouble of the worst kind. "There is no need to shield me from things, Phoebe. I am not a child."

Phoebe had cupped her hands around the lemonade. She flicked off beads of condensation, and the drops scattered and fell to the floor. Phoebe smoothed the dew from another side of the mug and rubbed her hands together, never once meeting Olivia's gaze. She waited, calculating that for Phoebe to show such reluctance to broach the subject, the news must not be good. Somehow Olivia was not surprised. Hadn't her father been distant? As if circumstances tied him in knots. Nothing like the jovial, lighthearted man she remembered. Or was that the ideology of a young child biased toward her daddy?

"There's a silent war taking place."

Olivia remained still as Phoebe hesitated. "The big ranchers seem intent on creating problems for the small ranchers. I think the attitude is that all land belongs to the big ranches, and that the little ranchers and farmers should yield their land, their cattle—everything. A small rancher south of here was found murdered about three months ago. Sheriff said he had news the man was a rustler."

"They murder rustlers?"

"Normally hang them."

Olivia shuddered. "How terrible." But what does it have to do with my father and the Laxalts?"

"Couple weeks ago there was a shooting. Martin Laxalt was found dead, shot through the heart."

Another murder? Olivia felt the blood drain from her face. Ryan Laxalt was thinking her father was responsible for the shooting that had killed his father? "Ryan's father rustled cattle?"

Phoebe shrugged. "Depends on who you ask."

Something squeezed her throat and shallowed her breathing. Phoebe rose to her feet, but Olivia sucked in a great breath of air and motioned her friend down. "It's impossible. Tell me it's impossible. My father could never do such a terrible deed."

Phoebe reached out and squeezed her hand. "We're not saying your father pulled the trigger, but he might have had a hand in. . ."

Disbelief raged through Olivia. That her father could be so accused was unthinkable. "I thought you were our friend."

"I am your friend, Livy. But your father has changed over the years."

Weighted by the insinuation, Olivia bolted from her seat, unable to hear more. Phoebe hadn't tried to stop her.

The trip home had been long, but Olivia had used it to do some serious thinking. There was only one way to clear her father's name, and her new job at the paper might be useful in allowing her to dig around and ask questions without raising suspicion. Her father had to be innocent, because the opposite was too unbearable to consider.

Chapter 8

Ryan waited in the wagon to take his mother to town. His mother wasn't happy with him, and he knew it. Not only had he turned a deaf ear to her talk of getting herself into town, but when she'd laid eyes on the rifle he clamped beneath his arm, Ryan had realized his error.

"You cannot do this." She grasped his forearm.

Josephine Laxalt's eyes held horror and pain, and Ryan felt remorse in every sinew and muscle. She didn't understand, and no matter how hard he tried, she never would. But he should have thought better of hauling along the rifle and inadvertently showing his intentions. He did the only thing he could do. He equivocated. "I'm riding the fence after dropping you in town. I might need the protection. And if anyone troubles us. . ."

He knew by the sidelong glance his mother gave that she saw right through his words.

"Whoever killed Father might just think it best to finish off you and me. It's our land they want, Mama, and we stand in their way." He placed his hand on her shoulder. "Please, let me handle this."

They rode to town in silence as the sun stretched higher in the sky and the cool breeze of night yielded to waves of familiar heat. Few people stirred in town this early, and those who did either affected oblivion at his presence or raised a hand in greeting. He wondered if the silent message his presence at the Lazy L sent was even now being stewed over by those who thought his father their enemy. Ryan hoped so.

"Wait for me," his mother said as they pulled up to the store. "I will make sure Papa Don is ready for me before you leave."

Minutes stretched, and Ryan grew restless, even fearful for his mother. He'd just lifted his foot to beat a path to the door when his mother popped out, Olivia Sattler at her heels. The red-haired woman laughed at something. Her pale skin a complement to the delighted flash of her whiskey eyes. Ryan glanced away, unnerved by the way his heart slammed at the sound of her laughter. Or was it her presence beside his mother? Sattler versus Laxalt.

His mother's dark eyes sought his. For a moment, she said nothing. Olivia busied herself with settling a sign in one corner of Papa Don's store window. "Miss Olivia and I will be fine. We will get much work done, and she will return me to the ranch this evening."

"I'll come get you."

Josephine's chin came up. "There is too much work to do on the ranch. You will listen to your mother in this."

His anger came hot, but he would not argue. Not here, in hearing distance of the Sattler woman. When he lifted his gaze, her eyes were on him. His mother took a step closer to Olivia and smiled at her as if they'd been friends forever. Confused by his mother's rejection, Ryan lifted the reins to back the horse up when he heard Olivia's words. "I'm so sorry."

He stilled, jaw clenched. Silence roared in his ears. He turned. She stood by the wagon, sunlight glinting against her face. The apology was for him alone. She took a step forward, eyes pleading. "I know I can't bring your father back, but you must believe I have no knowledge of. . .anything of my father's dealings. He's—"

Her voice broke, and she averted her face, the crisp outline of her jaw showing her struggle for composure. "It's like he's a stranger to me."

Her words hit him worse than a bullet to his gut. Not because of any feelings of sympathy toward her, but because the truth of her words twisted too deep. His mother didn't realize what a stranger he was to her. The few letters he had sent home had been truthful accountings of the type of work he'd found himself engaged in after those first wandering years. And then the offer had come to make real money.

"I want to find the truth," she said. "Tell me what you know, and maybe we can piece things together."

More words. These were soaked with sincerity. Her very presence twisted his insides and made him want to believe. Ryan withdrew from her gaze and focused on the window at her back—and at the small sign she had just placed there. JOSEPHINE LAXALT, DRESSMAKER. INQUIRE WITHIN.

Ryan tightened his fists and turned away. "Sometimes it's better for a man to ride alone."

❧

Josephine's dark eyes were on Olivia as soon as she entered the store. She didn't ask what had transpired between them, but Olivia could see the question in her eyes. Troubled more than she liked by Ryan's parting words, Olivia knew the man meant to do something. Soon. Revenge seemed such a harsh thing, but convinced as he was that her father had had something to do with the death of Martin Laxalt, or even that Jay Sattler was the one who pulled the trigger. . . .

"If you want to choose between these colors"—Josephine wrestled the bolts of chambray onto the section of counter Papa Don had allotted her—"we'll be done with all this."

Olivia reached out and cupped her hand over the older woman's. Josephine's dark eyes snapped to hers.

"He's hunting my father, isn't he?" She held the woman's gaze, waiting for the least flicker of guilty knowledge.

Josephine's shoulders slumped. "He is a good boy, but he cannot accept what is beyond his control."

"And what is that?"

The older woman tried to withdraw her hand. "We are friends. I—"

"If my father has done something wrong. . . If he is guilty of this thing, this murder, I must know." She swallowed. Disbelief raged in her mind. Her father would never shoot another man. Ryan Laxalt was crazy.

Josephine's shoulders quivered. "I do not know what your father has done. I know my husband is dead. Shot by a man who remains faceless. How can I accuse him of a deed that I did not see?"

"Your son seeks the truth."

Josephine's eyes closed. "He is full of anger. But anger makes you blind."

"You don't want to find out who killed your husband?"

Something cold and fearful tightened Mrs. Laxalt's features. "I fear the finding will get him killed."

Olivia digested those words. "I can't believe that my father would kill anyone."

"It is often hard to believe the worst of those we love."

"Your son—was he not with your husband when all this happened?"

"He returned after his papa was killed. Ryan has been away these past years. He left before your mama took sick."

Hard as she tried, she could not remember Ryan Laxalt as a boy. Not from socials or church or any other town events. But her world had been narrow as a child, and she expected there was much she had been oblivious to.

"He was a Texas Ranger for many years," Josephine said. Olivia did not miss the small smile of pride Josephine allowed herself. "Brought down many bad men."

Olivia recalled her uncle talking about Texas Rangers, Indians, and the outlaws they brought down. He'd been fascinated with all things West, and Olivia had often thought that if he'd had his druthers, he'd leave Aunt Fawn, move from Philadelphia to the West, and never look back.

She didn't know whether the fact was directed at her as a warning or as a passing comment meant to showcase a mother's pride in her son. Whatever the reason, Josephine said nothing more. She bent her head to the task of cutting yardage, her hands whisking wrinkles from the fabric as she cut.

Chapter 9

Directly after her fitting, Olivia went to the newspaper and tried to engage Marv in a conversation on the whereabouts of Tom Mahone. Maybe he had picked up news of the Laxalt murder and the underlying tension in the territory.

Marv's world seemed focused around placing paper onto an easel of sorts. Olivia watched the man in silence, mesmerized by the machine itself, if not the man's focus on his work. Marv glanced up at her before taking down two sticks with a thick blackened pad at one end. She saw why the brown end was stained when Marv moved to a tray and daubed a bit of stiff black ink on the ends. With movements sure and fast, he worked the paste between the ends of the sticks until it was smoother; then he patted it onto a tray of letters. He lowered the easel with the paper onto the tray and shoved it beneath a large, heavy-looking section. He pulled a handle once, then again, and rolled the platform back out. When he peeled the easel section back from the tray of letters, Olivia gasped at the wonder of seeing the process to make a printed paper.

As many times as she had read the papers in Philly or enjoyed the books, she had never seen the process. "How wonderful!"

Marv lifted the paper from the easel and held it carefully, brows knit.

Olivia slipped over to see the paper he held. "Will you show me how to do that?"

For the first time, Marv looked right at her, his hazel eyes were sharp, even hard. "Not for a woman. It's messy work and hard."

"I could help put the paper in the easel thing—"

Marv turned away and stepped toward a rack with other papers spread across it. Frustrated with the man's terseness, she was tempted to turn and leave, but she worked here now, and she might as well get used to Marv's silence—and he might as well get used to her presence.

A little desk in the corner suited her purposes for the present, but without Tom's guidance, how would she know what to write about? She went to the pages hanging along a drying rack. Dozens and dozens. They all seemed the same, but deep into the rows, she found a page that wasn't. The paper was dry, and the date was from a month ago. The editor was listed as Jon Pembroke. She read the articles, little tidbits of town news, but it was the column on page two that bit deeply into her heart. Her father's name appeared then disappeared beneath a layer of other names. Names she remembered from childhood. They were referred to as barons on the pages before her, and the writer was linking them to the death of a man. Bolder than the rest of the article was the notice right below it, posted by her father and spouting a warning that rustling from the big ranches would not be tolerated and would be dealt with swiftly.

Marv was suddenly there beside her, his hand on her arm. "I'll take that, miss. Mr. Mahone wouldn't want you to have seen this."

She whirled on him. "Why?"

"It's Jon's words. They didn't quite see eye to eye on things."

"Jon?"

"The old editor. Loved this paper and working for the town."

"He's—he's. . .dead?"

Marv shrugged, but he wouldn't look at her. "Left town real fast. Mr. Mahone's the editor now."

"What do you know about this?" She pointed to the article on the second page. "About this murder."

"Sheriff Bradley never arrested anyone. Said there was evidence only that George had rustled from Bowman's ranch, discovered during the roundup."

"Did you know the man?"

"The sheriff?" Marv grimaced. "Not much of the law in that man, if you get my meaning."

"I meant the man accused of rustling."

"Knew George real well. Good man. Trying hard to make a living. It's not right—" He stared down at his feet. She waited for him to finish.

"I've said too much."

"But it's not right for a man to steal another man's cattle, right?"

Marv held her gaze, eyes pinpricks. He held out his hand for the paper. "No. Now if you'll just let me have that. . ."

Olivia surrendered the sheet. Marv's dialogue was the most he'd ever said to her. His barely constrained anger was evident even in the way he walked, each step more a stomp. It didn't seem like a good time to introduce herself so he would stop calling her "miss" either, but being faced with more evidence that her father, and some of the big ranchers, were not held in high esteem added to her already troubled mind.

Olivia wandered out onto the street before she formulated what she could do, if anything, with the information. Where was Tom Mahone in all this, and were George's murder and the Martin Laxalt "rustling" charges related somehow? Landry's was busy when she stepped inside, but Phoebe took one look at her face and motioned her through the dining room to the kitchen. Her friend's hand on her shoulder directed her to a chair. Cold lemonade was pressed into her hand. She sipped at the drink, watching the owner's blurred movements as he expertly cooked and filled orders. His nod in her direction was the only acknowledgment of her presence.

Olivia processed the article again. The realization that her father's warning might have led to George's and Laxalt's deaths was sickening. Her mother would have been appalled and, had she lived, never would have allowed her husband to go to such lengths to protect his interests.

"You look pale as the moon."

Olivia blinked and raised her head. Phoebe's wan smile gave her courage. "I just read an old paper from a month ago about a man's death. George was his name. But there was something else, too. My father had penned a warning against those bent on rustling." She tried to formulate the question that rose in her mind about the whole thing—the simmering anger of Marv and the sudden departure of the old editor coupled with the deaths of two men.

Phoebe glanced over her shoulder. "I'll be back for the lunch crowd, Mr. Landry."

Her friend motioned her to follow. Olivia got to her feet and followed Phoebe up the back steps to her apartment. She made herself comfortable in the same chair she'd sat in on her previous visit, and her eyes searched the face of the woman in front of her—the angle of Phoebe's shoulders, the lines beside her eyes. Olivia's fingertips went cold. With a mixture of dread and acceptance, she realized that the emotion on Phoebe's face could only be identified as anger. And she thought she knew whom the anger was directed at.

❧

Ryan knelt beside the gate. Traces of the crime were long gone, but he'd still returned to the spot where Bobby Flagg, foreman of the Laxalt ranch, had discovered the body of his father. Because of his worry over his mother and attempts to keep a firm hand on the roundup—no, he admitted, because of his anger at the deed—he'd allowed himself to believe his father a victim. Now, touching the very dirt that he imagined held vestiges of his father's spilled blood, Ryan wondered if it was possible that his father had rustled cattle. That had been the accusation. Laxalt head counts had been up in spite of the hard winter of 1886–87 and the drought of the previous summer. Bobby had assured him that his father had worked hard to bring water in from the low-lying, spring-fed pond at the far end of the Lazy L.

Ryan's spine stiffened. The gate where he stood was about half a mile from that pond. Thirsty Sattler cattle could have smelled the water and bunched against the fencing, doing damage in their desperation for a drink. He swung into the saddle and debated. He could look at the fencing around the pond or he could talk to Bobby.

It took him an hour to find the foreman, but when he slid from the saddle,

Bobby was there with a ready grin on his ruddy face.

"Cody and Ty are working ten head from the brush down there. Got their hands full."

Sweat streaks showed on the man's face. He helped it along by smearing the back of his leather-clad hand across his forehead, leaving a dark stripe of dirt.

"Looking like we can head out in a few more days."

Ryan nodded slowly, pondering Bobby's words. "Sounds good," he said, "I wanted to ask you something about that pond. Place where you found—" He squinted into the sun and swallowed over the bulge of emotion wedged in his throat.

"Pond was a major player summer of '86. Only place that had any water at all. That it was on Laxalt property nettled everyone. Sattler and Bowman both tried to claim it was theirs before that summer, but they got downright nasty about it when the drought hit. Let their cows push against the fence and break through. Me and Martin finally realized we'd always have to maintain a hard patrol on that section."

"Was he patrolling when he got shot?"

"No. Not that far away from the pond. Ty was over there that night. Said he heard a shot but thought it was one of Sattler's men shooting a critter of some sort. They'd been doing it throughout the day."

Bobby shifted in the saddle. "Me and the men went into town the other night for a drink and to look over the crowd for hands to hire. Heard some talk about you."

Ryan gave a stiff nod. "Expected as much. Whatever's said, just don't let my mama hear." Josephine Laxalt would prefer to think of her son as honorable.

Bobby inclined his head. "I was hoping it might help tame Sattler and Bowman some."

Ryan doubted it, and he already knew what Bobby's opinion of the big ranchers was; they'd discussed it as soon as Ryan had arrived on the ranch. Everything congealed into a ball of frustration, tight and hard, deep in his stomach. He gripped the reins and funneled his rage into action. "Need an extra hand?" He was already turning the mustang toward the hollow where his men struggled to bunch the cows.

"Sure, boss. Can always use an extra hand."

Chapter 10

I'll be leaving town shortly. Starting up a little ranch of my own over by Bowman's. He's already given me trouble."

Olivia tried to process all that Phoebe was saying. Her friend would be leaving Buffalo. To start her own ranch. Alone?

Phoebe's eyes took on a glint. "I'm partnering with Jacob Isley. He's got himself a little house out there already. It was my idea to use his land for cattle. He's wanting to farm it, but I convinced him otherwise."

"You're marrying him?"

Phoebe pursed her lips. "I'm not the marrying sort. At least not yet. Might settle down someday. But that piece of land is big enough to hold us both, and there's an outbuilding where Jacob's already set up his things."

Olivia opened her mouth.

Phoebe crossed to her, and the anger came back into her expression. "Bowman's not playing nice. He's already threatened Jacob. Your father was out there with him one day, trying to convince Jake to take the buyout he was offering. A generous sum, but we aren't aiming to sell and move just because someone was getting too big for their britches and thinking we should."

"You said my father wasn't a nice man."

Phoebe plucked at the material of her skirt. "They've gotten clannish. Going around small ranches and making all kinds of accusations."

"But. . .why?"

Phoebe didn't respond. She crossed to a table and began yanking pins from her hair. It fell around her shoulders in a stream that she brushed with long, languid strokes. Olivia met her eyes in the mirror, begging her friend for an answer.

"It might be best"—Phoebe twisted her hair and inserted a pin—"if you use that reporting job to do some serious reporting."

Olivia couldn't grasp what Phoebe meant.

Her friend sighed and set the brush aside, facing her. "Tom Mahone is on their side and was hired to skew public opinion against small ranchers. Maybe he thinks by hiring you, you'll report what he wants you to."

"Why would he think that? He doesn't know me." Indeed, their talk had been superficial at best during the journey west.

"He knows you're a Sattler."

❧

Ryan leaned against the mustang's heaving side and uncinched the saddle then rubbed along the place where the cinch strap had lain. The horse's hard run had done him good—made him feel alive in a way he hadn't since coming to Buffalo, or since finding out his father was dead. No, murdered. He needed to remember that.

Bobby, Ty, and Cody had retired for the evening, joking about how to prepare the fat rabbit Ty had shot into the dust on their ride back from the west field. The men were dusty and tired but in good spirits and confident of the fact that the really hard work was almost done.

Ryan wanted to join them. They shared laughs as they built a small fire to roast the rabbit on, and he felt the pull to shed the yoke of responsibility and eat with them rather than endure the too-polite conversation, or even the pervasive disagreements, eating with his mother would offer.

The rattle of a distant wagon brought him alert. The men, too, heard it and turned to scan the horizon. Bobby's steps took him a few paces into the clearing where he could get a better view of the approaching people. Ryan interpreted the hard look Bobby sent his way. His foreman feared his father's murderer might be coming back.

He crossed to the man. "Not in a wagon. They'd be on horseback." He knew who was in the wagon and sought to further reassure Bobby. "My mother insisted on riding back here with that Sattler woman."

Bobby's shoulders relaxed, and he let out a low whistle. "Heard she was back. She was just a sprout when she left. Took her mama's death real hard." The man shrugged and turned away. "Not sure how to feel about having her here."

Ryan didn't miss the irony of his mother riding with a Sattler, and neither did the men. Wasn't that the whole reason he'd cautioned her against whatever friendship she was developing with Olivia? "I'll make sure this is the last time she feels welcome here."

Bobby stopped, his broad back a barrier. "Whatever your mama wants is okay with me." He turned his face in profile, and his words drifted over his shoulder. "Olivia Sattler is a pretty one, but she's a Sattler just the same."

Chapter 11

Ryan was at his mother's side as soon as Olivia brought the wagon to a halt. He reached up to help his mother down, not oblivious to the smile on her face that wilted as soon as she saw him. He hated to think his mother might actually be enjoying Olivia Sattler's company while dreading his.

"Now go help Olivia down."

"No need." He let the words sink in, and waited for Olivia's whiskey eyes to meet his. "She won't be staying."

"I invited her for supper, Ryan."

He clenched his jaw tight, disgusted. His mother's hand touched his elbow and squeezed hard against his biceps. He never would have thought she possessed such strength in her hands.

"You can eat with the men tonight."

It was her own brand of rejection. A standoff of wills. She would not back down from befriending Olivia, and he would not back down from insisting she was the enemy. What played out in Olivia's expression caught him square in the chest. She lowered her eyes and picked up the reins. Her left hand drifted to release the hand brake she had just set. Every line of her body seemed cowed with disappointment. Just once she glanced his way, and he saw the sheen in her eyes. His mother's hand left his elbow as Olivia lifted the reins.

"I'll eat with the men," he said, and spun on his heel, away from the conflicting emotions stirred by these two women. Factions that should be at war with each other but insisted on pulling a blanket of peace over a crime. He would not do that. Could not. And hadn't he wanted to eat with the men anyhow?

❧

A shift in the planes of Josephine's face flickered disappointment then resolve as she stared after her departing son. Olivia reset the brake, unsure what to say or how to think. Words seemed such a waste in the face of this conflict. She could see why Ryan would be angry and why his anger would extend to her, but she also felt regretful that he would keep her at arm's length without giving her a chance.

Throughout the simple meal, Josephine absorbed all that Olivia shared on fashion trends and city life. But it was hard to miss the plaintive glances the woman sent toward the front door as darkness descended. He was all she had in the world, and Olivia felt responsible for the grief her presence brought to their relationship.

Between clearing the table and wiping the last fork dry, Olivia made up her mind. "I'd like to go talk to Mr. Laxalt."

Josephine flinched. "My son, you mean."

"Yes."

"He will not talk to you."

"He might listen to what I have to say."

"What can you say to lessen the pain, Olivia?"

Olivia squeezed the towel she held. The baldness of the question surprised her. "Perhaps I can convince him that I am not his enemy."

"You bear the name Sattler."

She sighed. "Yes, I know. But you don't seem to hold that against me."

"I know your hands are clean of my husband's blood."

"Then I'll talk to him." She passed the towel to the woman, determined to bridge the gap between mother and son.

"Remember that our workers also see that you are first a Sattler, second a woman."

Hand on the door, Olivia's smile was tight. "But I am also your friend."

Chapter 12

Firelight flickered against the rough wall of the barn. Olivia's heart pounded, and her neck muscles were tight with worry. She changed directions, not wishing for her looming shadow to announce her presence. She would do this her way. She skirted the barn and came up the other side, directly in front of the house where the ranch hands bedded. Voices rose and fell with laughter. Words overlapped as the men tried to top each other with whatever wild stories they told. Horses seemed to be the subject from what she could comprehend.

She lingered at the corner of the building, telling herself she was not spying on the men. She wanted only to be prepared. One peek let her know the positions of the men around the fire. Ryan leaned back on an elbow, ankles crossed. Across the fire were two other cowhands, both sitting on wooden stumps. Empty plates were stacked at their feet, evidence that they had finished eating.

Ordering her thoughts, Olivia lifted her foot to step into the open but was stopped suddenly by the unmistakable click of a cocked hammer and a gravel voice at her back. "Never shot a lady before."

She spun, and a hand pushed her against the rough poles of the building, pinning her. Pale eyes burned into hers. The stranger's face was half in shadow, and firelight danced along the other side. She shuddered hard, for the man's face gave the impression of a demon come to life.

"Any reason for a woman to be poking around here, Mr. Laxalt?"

His overloud voice hurt her ears. She twisted to get free of his grip on her wrist. The looming figure of Ryan Laxalt appeared, and then the other two men came into view.

"My mother's guest, Ty. Let her go."

Ty seemed reluctant to obey, and his lips twisted in a sneer. "Your mother's guests always take to spying on people?"

Ryan didn't answer, but he nodded at the man beside him. "Bobby."

The larger man of the three seemed to interpret that message and motioned the other two men back toward the fire.

Olivia felt pinned beneath Ryan's dark eyes as she rubbed the place Ty had gripped. Prickles of fear and relief dueled for first place along her spine. "I wanted to talk. . . ." She stared at her feet and knotted her hands in the material of her skirts.

"Ty is keeping watch."

She raised a hand and rubbed the soreness of her wrist. She would have a bruise.

"He does a great job."

His eyes flicked downward. "I'm sorry if he hurt you. Men are sometimes rougher than they realize, especially when threatened."

Her breath halted. When she searched his face, the darkness hid his emotion. But his choice of words—was he excusing himself? "I'm no threat."

"You're a Sattler."

"You can't think I'd have anything to do with your father's death. I just got here."

Ryan hesitated and stared into the darkness. A shot of wind ignited the fire, stripping the shadows from his eyes long enough for her to see the wariness.

She tried again. "Did you agree with everything your father ever did?"

❧

Ryan said nothing. The answer was universal. Children never agreed 100 percent with their parents. He understood her point and admitted it to be a valid one.

"The accusation is that your father stole from mine." Her voice cut the silence. "Shouldn't we worry more about getting to the truth of the matter than standing here accusing each other based on loyalty? Neither of us was here when it happened."

"I do not condemn you for your father's mistakes."

She shifted and both hands worked along her upper arms as if warding off a chill. "Is that why you growl at me? Disapprove of your mother befriending me? Because I'm a stranger to Buffalo, and this is a display of western hospitality?"

Her questions plucked at that place down deep that remembered a man's responsibility of gentleness and respect toward a woman. Things were different in eastern cities, he knew. Especially among higher-class individuals. The proper male-female roles more defined. He'd hated his visit to New York, which had showed not only the lowest of the lowest class of people, but the highest of the high. The chasm between the two classes had sickened him. He did not wish to see the big ranchers crush the small. That event would make citizens of the West too much like those in the East. Yet his duty was clear. Miss Sattler deserved at least to be heard."My apologies. My father and I did not agree on much, as I'm sure you and your father do not see eye to eye."

"My father is not the man I remember, Ryan."

Hearing his name fall from her lips in soft tones provoked a frown. Impatient, he jerked around and motioned. "Let's walk." He had no desire for his men to overhear whatever she had come to say.

Beyond the building and out of reach of the light of the fire, the moon guided his path toward the corral. He didn't turn to see if she followed, almost hoping that she did not.

"I want to help."

Her voice flowed over him, silent and entreating. He wondered if he could love her, and the suddenness of the thought rocked him off balance. He clung to the fencing surrounding the corral and lifted a booted foot to the bottom rung. His forearms scraped against the wood. The mustang came to him and nibbled at his sleeve, and still he could not answer her.

"Tom Mahone hired me to write for the *Buffalo Bulletin*."

Every part of his body felt the warmth of her presence as she appeared beside him. Her hand on his arm was placating, and he knew her eyes would be beseeching him to relent. "Tom Mahone is on their side from what I've been told."

Her breath whispered out on a sigh. "I. . .I need to know the whole story of your father's death."

"I'm sure your father would not approve of you teaming up with the enemy."

"You are not that, Ryan."

His throat closed at the gentleness of her statement "We're definitely not on the same side."

"Only because you have chosen what side you think I'm on, never considering that I am a mature woman with thoughts and opinions of my own. I am not afraid to align myself against my father, but. . ."

When she did not continue, he finally turned his head to her. A small smile played on her lips, though she wasn't watching him but rather stroking the mustang's side. He wondered why she felt so compelled to befriend his mother, or his mother to befriend her. It didn't make sense to him. He could not deny his curiosity. "But?"

She tilted her face up, the soft moonlight limning along her jaw and sparkling in her eyes.

"I want to print the truth. Not as my father sees it or even as you see it, but as things truly are. Both sides of the story. Maybe it will help one side better understand the other."

"I don't think Tom Mahone will like that too much."

She lifted her shoulders and sank her fingers into the mustang's mane. "I'll cross that bridge when I come to it."

Despite himself, he had to admire her spirit. He could even understand what it was his mother saw in the woman: a trait indefinable but indomitable. "So we are to work together?"

The question hung between them as she twisted a chunk of the mustang's mane around her index finger. She pushed away from the railing and brushed her hands together, her gaze meeting his. "I think that means we must first be friends. Don't you agree?"

Chapter 13

His eyes ran over her hair, auburn in the darkness. There was a straightforwardness about her that he liked, and his instinct rejected the possibility that her offer of friendship might be a trap. Nevertheless, he would be careful.

"I learned this afternoon that Phoebe was leaving Landry's. She's moving out to a ranch beside Bowman's."

"Jacob Bowman," he said.

She nodded. "I remember him from a long time ago. He was a sourpuss."

"Still is."

"Have you always lived here? I mean, before you left."

He thought back to his restless feelings as a young man. He'd worked the ranch beside his father, and his mother taught him reading and arithmetic late at night. Not until he was ten did he realize a world existed beyond the Laxalt ranch.

"I left when I was fifteen."

"I don't remember you."

"You wouldn't."

The material of her dress rustled, and he glanced at her. The tenderness in her expression caught his breath. "Tell me about your father."

He closed his eyes and swallowed, ordering his thoughts. "He was a hard worker."

"I can see that in your mother."

Of course she could. They had both poured so much of themselves into the ranch. Building it beyond their expectations and sacrificing so much in the process. Why was he only now able to see that? He'd chafed through his teens at the thought of hard work and sweaty palms, rope burns and trail dust. He'd hated it, and he'd taken that hate out on his father more than once. His father's impatience with him had erupted during a violent storm. Thunder and lightning had slashed the sky and rocked the world as driving rain pounded their bodies. They'd had to ride out into the pasture after Ryan's confession that he hadn't shut the gate. The young cattle might have spooked at the sound of the storm and run off a cliff.

He'd been so angry that night. So disgusted with having to go back out in the weather. Who cared about the cows? Didn't his father ever think of anything other than the animals?

Ryan remembered those burning thoughts that proved his immaturity. Even now he experienced a wave of bile at his foolishness. His father had had a right to be angry with him and his attitudes. But there was no use dwelling on it now, for he could turn back the hands of time no more than he could take back the bullet that stole his father's life.

"What about you?" he asked, wanting nothing more than to trounce the grief balling in his gut.

"My mother died, and my father thought it best that my aunt Fawn raise me. So I was bundled back east."

"How old were you?"

"Nine, but she'd been sick for months. It was harder right at the end. Daddy wouldn't let me in to see her."

What could he say to that? To have your mother die at such a young age must have been devastating.

"I remember praying to God every night to heal her. . . ."

"Did you get mad when He didn't?"

Her eyes flicked to his. "Why, no. Of course not. I knew He had other plans for me."

"You accepted it"—he snapped his fingers—"just like that?"

Her shoulders rose on an inhale, and he could almost feel the grip of emotion that brought a glassy sheen to her eyes. He reviewed the question, angst bunching the muscles in his neck. He needed to know the answer for himself. For all his mother's talk of the Lord, of peace that passed understanding, he'd never felt it for himself. Never understood it or experienced it as his mother had—and now as Olivia claimed.

"I missed her, yes, but in my nine-year-old mind, my mother had taught me that God knew far more than we did about our future. She'd taught me to lean on Him when I didn't understand something. And—" Her voice faltered. She pressed a hand to her lips. "I knew that Mama would be in heaven and I would see her again."

"You make it sound so simple."

"It is simple. As a child. It's the grown-up ideas and experiences that muddy the water of faith."

He massaged his forehead and felt the cold sweat along his brow. God had been little more than a nuisance to him for so many years. Now the cold deeds of his hired-gun days scorched a trail against his conscience. *You've never done anything to regret.*

"Your mother is so proud of you being a Ranger."

He could not look at her. "I've not been a good man." A mild description, to be sure. But he could not bare his heart to her. To God, but not to her. Some sins cut to the bone.

"I guess this conversation means we're friends." She flashed a smile.

She'd taken him by surprise. Her candor, her kindness. Even glimpsing the light of her faith had warmed the cold places of his heart. She stirred his curiosity, and he could not deny the help she would be in getting at the truth behind his father's death. For the first time, he was willing to dig deeper than his assumption that Jay Sattler had fired the gun.

❧

Olivia walked back to the wagon alone. Ryan had stayed behind at the corral. She thought she understood. Decision made, he needed to put distance between them, and though Olivia would be the first to admit she had little experience with men, she thought Ryan Laxalt might be fearful of working with her. His reluctance didn't make sense, though, and she shook her head as she released the brake and got the wagon rolling toward home.

Home. The word taunted.

Talking of her mother had felt natural and good, but calling the Sattler ranch house home left her cold and lonely. When she pulled up to the hill overlooking her father's house, her heart froze in dread. To enter those empty walls and pretend conversation with a man who mumbled answers and seldom smiled. . . If not for the need to be on horseback instead of in the wagon to do it, she would shoot off into the vastness surrounding the house and disappear. The idea did tempt though. But her father would expect her to be there and probably even now wondered what was keeping her so late. She wondered if her mother had ever felt such a disconnect—like her presence was merely a warm body in the house to her husband rather than a person with wants and needs, emotions, and a heart to share.

It shouldn't be like this.

As Olivia sat in the dark and stared at the house, her throat thickened and burned. Every bit of her rebelled against the idea of going into that loveless home to spend time with a man who barely knew she existed and didn't seem to care whether she was here or back in Philadelphia.

The horse dipped its head and curved its neck to look back, ears pricked. She heard the approach of a horse and rider and stiffened in the seat, but the sound stopped suddenly. Olivia gasped and darted a glance over her shoulder, trying to pinpoint the movement. A dark shadow moved closer. "Miss Olivia?"

Though he whispered, she recognized the deep voice as that of her new friend. She could make out the sweeping breadth of his shoulders and the glint of his dark hair in the pale moonlight.

"Is all well?" Ryan's whispered question reflected the concern in his face.

She saw his eyes dart between the house and the outbuildings. She couldn't help but feel touched by his presence. "I was just going in."

"You were still for too long. I thought you might be ill."

"You followed me?"

His teeth shone in the silver light. "I did. Riding this late at night is dangerous, even for a man. My mother would never have forgiven me if I hadn't made sure you were safe."

"Oh."

"Now that I know you are well, I'll be going before. . ."

He did not need to finish. They both understood the risk. He drew the reins up, bringing his horse's head around to turn the animal in a tight circle.

A swell of loneliness, maybe even pity, rose. If only she could go home with him and bask in the friendship she'd found with his mother. They could cook and talk and. . . "Ryan, wait." He stopped the horse and wheeled the animal broadside.

What could she say? He would not understand, and she wasn't sure she wanted him to. Her mind raced for an excuse to cover the impulsive words on the tip of her tongue. "Tomorrow. Maybe we should. . . I mean, could you show me around? I'd like to meet people, learn the names of some of our neighbors. We could meet in town and ride out to neighboring ranches. Someone knows something about your father's death."

She couldn't quite see all the details of his expression, but she thought she heard a smile in his tone. "It will help you with your article writing."

The front door of the ranch house opened. "Olivia?"

Ryan raised his hand and dug his heels into his horse's sides. The animal lunged forward, gained its footing, and settled into a gallop.

She set the wagon into motion. Her father waited until she pulled the horse to a stop. His hand touched her elbow and aided her descent. "Sorry I'm late."

"Was somebody with you?"

"A neighbor, making sure I got safely home."

If her father suspected anything amiss, he didn't question. "Been waiting supper for you. Got some leftover beans on the stove and a biscuit. You get on inside; I'll put the horse up."

Olivia raised on her toes and kissed his cheek. "I missed you, too, Father." Before he could form a response, she hustled past him and into the house.

Chapter 14

The sun beamed down unmercifully. Ryan's mother had insisted he take an extra hat for Olivia to wear when they went out for their ride. He now wished he'd never said a word about Olivia's request. His mother treated it like the official announcement that they were courting. Even as he dropped her off at the general store that morning, she'd trilled and chattered and moved with such a light step and quickness that he knew her hopes were soaring. Probably itching to knit baby booties.

He did his best to ignore all her mama-flapping ways, but when she eyed his head critically then asked him to bend down, her attempt to smooth down his cowlick right in front of the general store for all to see was the last straw.

"Never could tame that patch of hair," she groused.

He stuffed back his embarrassment, hoping the red-hot heat on his neck wouldn't climb higher. Ryan did his best to remain stone-faced, imagining the stares of a thousand townspeople spearing into his back and smothering grins of laughter. Bad enough he had to bring his mother into town, but for her to make a spectacle of him as if he still wore short pants and suspenders. . .

He adjusted the hat on his head lower over his eyes and hauled himself into the wagon. He left the conveyance at the livery and paid for the use of a dun. The Wyoming sunshine beat down hot on his shoulders, but the breeze against his face from the forward momentum of the dun eased the sweats. He and Olivia had never discussed what time to do the tour, cut off as they'd been by her father's appearance. As he made his way down Main Street, he figured he'd duck into Landry's and the newspaper office to see if Olivia was in town.

Landry's came up first.

Phoebe greeted him with an index finger pointing at an empty table in the corner and a nod of the head. The woman had her hands full in what was either a late-breakfast rush or an early lunch. No, too early for lunch he decided as he slid into the chair. At least from the table he had a clear view of the street and the comings and goings of people. Should Olivia pass, he could meet up with her and put a time on their planned ride.

Phoebe brought him water and dashed away when he held his hand up to indicate he wanted nothing else. When the crowd had dwindled somewhat, she slumped into the chair across from him. "I'll be so glad to be out of this place."

"Don't let Robert hear you."

She snorted. "He'll have someone to take my place before the door shuts behind me." Phoebe plucked at her apron and drew in a deep breath.

"You're leaving?" He recalled Olivia saying something about it.

"Got a place outside of town. By Bowman's. Me and Jacob Isley are hooking up to run it."

Ryan nodded. Jacob Isley wasn't a man he remembered, but he could see Phoebe hitching up with a rancher. "You know much about what's going on 'round these parts?"

"You mean the shooting of your father." It wasn't a question, and the way her eyes hardened told him she knew quite a bit on the subject. She tugged a rag from the pocket of her apron.

"Seems Sattler is getting too big for his britches."

"He's sure not the affectionate type. Olivia's hurting something awful. He's turned cold since his wife's. . ." She clamped her mouth tight and gave a little shake of her head. "But I guess that affects Olivia more than it does you."

If Olivia was hurting over something, Phoebe was right, it wasn't any of his business. "Olivia and I are supposed to ride around the town. She wants to meet her neighbors."

Phoebe had been rubbing a chunk of hardened yolk off the table when her head jerked up. "You and Olivia?" Her brow knit. "Riding around where?"

"Is something wrong with that? You thinking we might need a chaperone?"

Phoebe returned to the yolk, alternately scraping at the sunny patch with her nail and rubbing over it with a damp cloth. "Could arouse some talk, but I don't expect talk will worry Olivia. Or you for that matter."

"Got a mind to ride around myself. Check out Sattler's property more thoroughly, especially that section that butts up to our ranch."

Phoebe tugged at the lobe of her right ear. Her tongue darted out over her lips, and she would not meet his eyes. "Just be careful. Keep Olivia safe."

She didn't give him a chance to ask for an explanation before she scraped the chair backward and hurried toward the kitchen. Conversation over.

❧

When Olivia emerged from the general store garbed in her first new piece of western clothing, a riding skirt, she felt like she had finally shed her city-girl ways. It felt good. As soon as she opened the door to the *Bulletin*, Marv's gaze caught hers then lowered to the floor. At least now he would look at her. Tom rose from the desk at the back of the room and motioned her forward. His smile stretched from ear to ear. Hair pulled back taut and wet with a generous amount of hair oil, Tom Mahone looked every inch a charming personality, except for the dark shadow of his eyes and the scar on his right cheek.

"Mr. Mahone."

"Olivia. I've been meaning to speak with you. How are you coming on your first article? It's due Friday, as I'm sure Marv has told you."

Tom's eyes slid to Marv, and she didn't miss the way the older man responded with slack-jawed amazement.

She bided her time forming a response. Thick tension buzzed in the room. "I haven't been in very often," she said, eyes on Marv. Did she imagine the release of tension in his thin shoulders?

"I see." Tom leaned forward, the squeak of his chair loud in the room. "I don't tolerate lateness, Olivia, and I won't accept just anything to run in this newspaper."

His smile was fashioned to take the sting from his words, she was sure, but his message came through loud and clear. If she did not write what suited his tastes, her articles would not be run, and she could be fired. He leaned forward, and she braced herself.

"Have you thought any more about having dinner with me?"

Olivia lunged upward, disgusted by the man's taciturn personality. Though she'd never met the editor of the Philadelphia newspaper, there had been no such pressure to report styles according to the fashion editor's taste. And that was the difference she realized. This wasn't the city where several editors headed different sections of the newspaper. The *Buffalo Bulletin* was run by one man, and she must not forget that. Attractive though he might be, she did not approve of the way he shifted and twisted to fit his own purpose.

She started for the door, calling over her shoulder. "I bid you a good day, Mr. Mahone. I'll have my article on your desk Thursday." There. Take that.

"Miss Sattler." She could tell by the squeak of his chair that he was on his feet. Next thing would be a protest from him, something calculated to smooth matters over. She didn't stop to listen.

Chapter 15

Ryan called himself every kind of fool for sitting around doing nothing while waiting on a woman. The dun stood three-legged at the hitching post, dozing in the heat of the afternoon sun. He was paying good money for the horse, and here he sat. Doing nothing. Waiting on a woman who might or might not show up in town just because she asked to ride with him. His brain was becoming as brittle as a cow pie in the sun.

Phoebe checked on him one more time, probably hoping he would just leave. With the beginnings of lunch, the crowds would explode, and she would need his table. He would check the paper's office. Decision made, Ryan flicked a coin onto the table and stretched to his feet. Dust hung in the air outside the restaurant, residue of the passage of a fast-moving wagon down Main. He unhitched the dun, who seemed uninterested in anything other than staying right where he was.

He glanced once more at the office of the *Buffalo Bulletin*. A slender form ducked from the newspaper office. Soft strawberry hair, a delicate complexion. . . His heart beat harder at the sight of her, and he kicked the dun into motion.

"Been looking for you." He wished the words back as soon as they left his mouth. He sounded like some pathetic sop. Leaning forward, he rested his hands on the pommel and finally noticed the thin line of her lips and the dangerous flash pulsing from her eyes. Though she stopped, she acted as if she hadn't heard a word he'd said.

"Something wrong, Miss Sattler?"

Her skirt skimmed along the road, and her feet left a small trail of smoky dust with every step that drew her closer to him. "I can't wait to get out of this town and get some work done on my first article."

He covered his grin as she scurried up into her wagon and backed the horse up. He enjoyed seeing her rankled. He bet Tom Mahone was just now realizing what a spirited filly he'd employed. But how she figured on exploring rough terrain in a wagon was beyond him.

"I'll drop the wagon off and get a horse. Daddy left a list of some things to pick up," she said. Her words came out like an explosion of buckshot. "I'll meet you at your place."

Whatever emotion had her in its grip, it sure wasn't the joy of riding with him that he'd hoped to elicit. Still. . . "Sounds good to me." He turned the dun as she struggled to back the horse.

"Harder to learn a wagon than a saddle," he said as he dismounted. He put a toe on the step up and hesitated. She grinned, put the reins down, and slid over to make room for him.

"Lesson number one. Make sure you put even pressure on the reins. The horse'll know how to back up, but he needs some time."

❧

She took in his words and ways, studying how he handled the reins as he backed the wagon far enough away that she would be able to turn out onto the main road. Without another word, he handed the reins to her and jumped down. He lifted his head, and one side of his mouth curled upward. "You look nice. Just like you never left Buffalo."

"Your mother's doing. She's going to make a name for herself in this town."

"Not all her doing." And this time she saw the appreciation in his eyes. He lifted his brows and winked, and she felt her blood warm at the attention.

"You, sir, are a flirt."

Ryan didn't respond. He was too busy settling himself in the saddle. He motioned her forward and allowed the dun to fall into step alongside the wagon, far enough back that she would have to turn to see him.

Back at the Sattler's Stable, it took some time to find a hand available to saddle a bay mare that looked gentle. The hand worked slow enough that she could follow his moves as he settled a blanket on the horse's back then threw the saddle on and put a belt around its belly that reminded her of a corset. As he gave her a hand up, she was grateful that her father didn't appear to ask where she was headed.

Ryan was waiting at the place where the Rocking S touched Laxalt property. His back was to her, and he held the reins of his horse loose in one hand. She studied his silhouette until the beat of her horse's hooves alerted him to her presence and he turned.

"Are you ready, cowboy?"

When his gaze met hers, a smile creased the corners. It softened the hardness in his face.

"You should smile more often. It makes you look younger, gentler."

"Since when is a man supposed to look gentle?" He turned and fiddled with something behind the saddle then held out a battered hat to her. "It'll keep the sun off your face."

She accepted the hat, chagrined that he might have noticed her freckles. The hat was big on her head and slid down over her eyes until she angled it back. "Don't most mothers want their sons to grow up to be kind and loving?"

He ran his knuckles along his cheek, and she followed the motion. "You've got me there, though too much of that can smother a man."

"Guess that's why God gives us a father and a mother. We learn different qualities from each."

The horses picked their way down a rock-strewn path that emptied into a grassy plain. A stream rushed through on its way to the horizon. They stopped their horses, dismounted, and let them drink. The quietness of the rangeland was comfortable, almost sacred. It seemed a shame to break it, but she had to ask the question uppermost in her mind.

In slow, measured moves, he helped her get back into the saddle then did the same. "Why do you think my father killed yours?"

He lifted his hat and pushed a hand through his hair. His lips formed a frown. "Some wire was cut." He moved the dun ahead of her bay. "I've no doubt my father saw that. My best guess is he confronted your father and came out on the short end of the stick."

"Couldn't it have been anyone? One of Daddy's ranch hands?"

"They work for him."

"Guilt by association?"

❧

The edge in her voice showed what conclusion she was jumping to. Funny how after such a short time knowing her he could envision the clouds coming over her face. A beautiful face. Beautiful hair. She was dainty, and he wondered if she would feel fragile in his arms. . . .

Crushing his wayward thoughts, Ryan slowed the dun until Olivia came even with him. Sure enough, her expression was severe, and she looked just like a woman ready to bawl. Ryan adjusted himself in the saddle and cleared his throat. "Didn't we just settle this yesterday? Friends, I think, was the final offer."

"Good." She angled her face away from him and tilted the broad brim of her hat to further obscure her face. "But sometimes we're going to have to ask each other hard questions. We should be ready for that." She rested her hand against the pommel. "It could have been one of Daddy's ranch hands who took it upon himself to handle things."

Ryan wanted to protest but could not. Hadn't he just come to the same conclusion?

"Evidence is gonna be scarce," he said. "There's been too much rain, and too much time has passed."

"Then we'll have to rely on people."

Rankled by her logic even as he was forced to acknowledge the soundness of it, Ryan stuck his hat back on his head. "Bobby saw the wires cut—"

"Who's Bobby?"

"My foreman."

"He saw the wires being cut, or he saw the cut wire? One indicates he saw the deed done, the other that he saw only the evidence."

Ryan closed his eyes, already lost in the labyrinth of her reasoning, no matter how sound it was.

"Our problem, Ryan, is we need facts. Someone knows who pulled the trigger. It's figuring out who knows what or who saw the deed done—that's the trick." She tossed him a look, all vestiges of vulnerability gone. This was the face of a woman with a task that needed done. "Before we go to the obvious people for help, let's ride north of here."

"That would be Hector Maiden's property."

"Big rancher or small?"

"A farmer mostly. A few head from what I've heard."

She nodded. "It's a place to start."

He'd lived a good portion of his life being directed by the whim of a man's belief in his own version of the truth. It had been a shot at a man who later turned out to be innocent that turned his stomach. An innocent man laboring under an accusation, only to be found innocent long after his body had grown stiff and cold.

She kicked her horse into motion. Left with little choice, Ryan got the dun moving, feeling his lead in this fight slipping through his fingers. Worse, it didn't bother him near as much as it should. Her lithe body seemed to take to the gait of the horse easily. No sir, it wasn't near so hard to follow her lead as he'd thought it might be.

Chapter 16

They've shuffled their big boots all over my farm trying to stir up trouble."

Olivia nodded over the cup of coffee Hector Maiden had supplied. She'd let the farmer know right off who she was, that she wrote for the *Buffalo Bulletin*, and that she wanted to know the truth.

Hector obliged her, even though his coffee was weak and the slice of corn bread he offered looked like he'd had to scrape off the mold before putting it on a plate for her. Ryan sat across from her. He glanced at the corn bread then back at her, one eyebrow raised. He'd no doubt seen her reaction to the corn bread.

Hector sat at the head of the table, fingers drumming the surface with one hand, stroking the length of his bushy, yellowed beard with the other. "Don't own much, but what I have is mine." He made a fist and slammed it down on the table. "I don't aim to give it over to them just because Bowman thinks his cows might need a nibble of my corn."

Olivia nodded in agreement. "What about Martin Laxalt? You heard about—"

"Martin was a good man. Helped me get up the fence in the back for some cows. Reckon on starting to build a herd. That'll stir a rattler's nest with Bowman." Hector barked a laugh that showed his teeth—or lack of them.

She snatched a glance at Ryan. She realized in the noise of Hector's diatribe just how quiet Ryan was by nature. A listener, her aunt would call him. Hurt lines traced a path between his brows, and she knew the mention of his father had twisted a fist in his grief.

"Do you know about the shooting?" Olivia asked.

Hector continued to chomp on his mustache. "Know what I heard. Sattler did the deed. Accused Martin of rustling his cattle. Two met out by that fence, and Sattler took the opportunity to pull the trigger. Reckon he thinks it's just a matter of time before Martin's widow packs up and leaves."

"They have a son," she said.

Hector bobbed his head. "Knew him when he was a lad. Left when he was a tadpole. Hotheaded. Grieved Martin something awful. Who knows? Might marry his widow myself. She's some kind of cook, and we could put our land together. That'd give Bowman and Sattler heart trouble for sure."

Olivia glanced at Ryan. His mouth was set in a firm line.

"Mr. Maiden"—Olivia pointed to Ryan—"this is Ryan Laxalt, Martin's son."

Ryan shot her a perturbed look.

"Well, why didn't you say so, son? Guess my marrying plans will have to wait then." Hector bellowed another laugh before his voice quieted a notch. "Sorry about your pa."

Olivia nipped the point off the corn bread and steeled herself against the dryness of the morsel and the thought of eating mold. It was all the man had to offer, and she wouldn't turn her nose up at it for anything.

She stabbed at the corn bread again and scattered the dry piece to make it look like she'd eaten more than she really had. A quick glance at Hector assured her he wasn't taking notice. But Ryan's eyes darted away the second she glanced his direction. He'd been watching her. The most minute tilt of his lips said it all.

Mischief stirred in her head, and she set her fork aside. "I don't think I can eat another bite." All eyes came to her. Giving Ryan her brightest smile, she slid the plate across the table to him. "Finish this up for me, won't you?"

❧

Olivia breathed in the night air as she waited for Ryan to appear from behind Hector's cabin. She grinned up at the moon. Her horse shifted its weight, and she ran her fingers beneath its mane and scratched. When she finally heard the outhouse door moan a low creak and Ryan's boots rustling through the dry grass, she made sure to busy herself looking for something to help her into the saddle. The porch would have to do.

"I guess you're mighty proud of yourself."

She started at his nearness. Arching a brow, she clapped on the hat he'd let her borrow. It hadn't settled onto her head for more than a second before he whisked it off. She turned to face him. "Hey!"

He held it high over his head with one hand and put a finger to his lips with the other. "Unless you want Hector to talk all night, you'd better not let him know we're still out here. Besides"—he lowered the hat, his smile wide—"it's getting dark. There's no need for you to wear this."

He nested her hat inside his and tied them behind the saddle before mounting the dun.

"I suppose we can leave now." She couldn't resist the jab.

"Worst corn bread I've ever eaten."

"At least you were polite."

She led her horse over toward the porch and started around its head when she felt Ryan beside her.

"Need a hand?"

"I'll use the porch."

His arm snaked out around her waist, and she was yanked back against him. His hand clamped down across her mouth, and his voice was a hard whisper against her ear. "Someone's out there."

Her heart slammed. His hand fell, but she could feel his tension. He left her in a rush, and she rocked on her feet for want of the support his body had offered. He went into a low crouch and moved forward a fraction. The night air moved in around her. She shivered.

Chapter 17

Ryan heard the noise again and settled his hand against the butt of his gun. Something was going on. He heard Hector's few calves moving and the sheep bleating, but he could see nothing.

He ducked around the back corner of the house where he could get a better view and still be in shadow. Glass shattered nearby, and a muffled curse rent the air as the barrel of a shotgun slipped through a back window.

Hector.

"Whoever's out there better get."

Flat against the house, Ryan knew Hector couldn't see him. He sidestepped until he could grab the barrel of the gun. "It's me," he whispered. "Ryan Laxalt. Someone's stirring your cows."

Hector's eyes were bleary, and his hair exploded from his head. "What you still doing here?"

Ryan put a finger to his lips and jabbed his head toward the door, indicating the man should come outside. He glanced behind him and retraced his steps to the corner of the house. Olivia stood there, his rifle in her hands. Seeing her preparation pleased him.

"I thought you might need my help. Was that Hector?"

"He's coming out. Let's get back to the horses and take a ride."

With Hector leading the way, they followed a worn path along the front section of his land where the new fence had been put up. The calves had calmed. His sheep were quiet.

Olivia had been silent the entire time. On occasion he would pull the dun in closer to her to gauge how she was doing. Her expression was always alert and intense. "It could have been a wild animal," she said. A thought that had already occurred to him.

Darkness was blanketing the hills when they finally left Hector's farm. Olivia came abreast the dun and smirked at him. "At least he didn't ask why we didn't leave right away."

"Or offer any more corn bread."

He liked the sound of her laughter, muffled as it was in light of the situation, and the way her hair flowed over her shoulders and down her back as she vented her mirth. He couldn't help but grin, and it felt freeing somehow. He'd become too serious. Perhaps too single-minded.

"Thinking about your father?"

Ryan sat up a little straighter.

"I think about my mother all the time. More now than when I was in Philly. I guess being here makes it more real. I can feel her here." She gave a little laugh and shrugged. "I'm sure I sound silly."

"No. You were sent away. It makes sense that coming back would stir everything up. Maybe you didn't have time to grieve. And now, God—" He paused. How long had it been since he'd directly referred to the heavenly Father? "God brought you back here for a reason," he finished, not even sure where such an idea had come from or if he even believed it. Olivia did. All he knew was the squeeze of his conscience made the weight of his past deeds unbearable. It seemed too easy a thing to shift the load to God and be done with it. Too easy for a man who collected money to murder. But only once. He gasped for breath as he saw the face of the man, twisted in pain.

Ryan looked over at Olivia, trying to forget. Centering his focus on her eased his guilt. Maybe God had a hand in bringing Olivia home to Buffalo. And maybe, just maybe, it was so that their paths could cross.

❧

Olivia decided she liked Ryan without a hat. It made him seem less tough, more little boy. She wondered if he would get embarrassed if she gave voice to that thought or if he'd think her plain crazy. He might even get offended or angry.

In many ways, Ryan was a mixture of man and boy. Hector's observation about Ryan as a boy had revealed a crack in his tough-guy facade. Funny how she'd never figured him as someone quick of temper. Quiet, yes. Even brooding. But angry?

"God brought you back here, too," she suggested to his silhouette. His jaw worked for a few seconds before he met her gaze and nodded.

"I wish I'd come back sooner."

"You can't bring back your father, Ryan. He's gone."

It was there in an instant, the flash of temper. For all her conclusions about him, she could see that Hector had been correct. Yet there was something else, too, and she recognized it because it mirrored what she felt. Grief.

"My mother needs me."

"She's always needed you." Even in the short time she had known Josephine, Olivia saw her innate kindness and devotion to others. Now focused on her son. "I'm sure it hurt her terribly when you left. She's proud of you. You should have seen her smile when she told me you were a Texas Ranger for four years."

His quietness said a lot about him, whether he realized it or not. Olivia decided that Ryan's temper might have been quick once, but maturity had helped him learn to turn the anger inward in quiet reflection.

"Yeah, well, it wasn't quite like that."

She blinked up at him, confused.

"I worked for a Ranger once. Mentioned it in a letter. They hired me to track a man wanted in Texas and Oklahoma." His chest heaved. "I found him."

"You took him back to Texas?"

"Naw, he got wind that someone was on his heels. Makes a fella twitchy. He pulled lead on me, and I plugged him."

"But. . ."

"Purely self-defense." His gaze was searching. "You're surprised."

She said, "I mean, how did your mother think you were a. . . ?"

He raised a shoulder. "Guess she read in the letter what she wanted to read. I worked for them for a few years doing odd jobs."

She mulled what he'd revealed about himself, surprised at his past. Shooting a man seemed such a brutal thing. Savage. When she sneaked a glance at his profile, she wondered how such blatant violence could thrive and what its presence meant for the future of the West. But shooting in self-defense—that had to be honorable and right.

They rode in silence except for the creak of the saddle, the plod of the horses' hooves, and the distant howl of a coyote. When they got to the gates of her father's ranch, she slid to the ground, hoping the walk would stretch her muscles and relieve some of the ache she knew she'd feel in the morning. She slipped the reins over her horse's head and turned toward Ryan.

He smiled. "We didn't get very far."

"No, we didn't. If it hadn't been for Hector's corn bread. . ."

He shrugged. "What can I say? I was trying to be considerate and help a lady out."

She burst into laughter. "Your mother told me you had a soft heart under all the 'crust,' as she put it."

He swung his long leg over the back of his horse and dismounted. "Then I shouldn't disappoint. I'll walk with you to the house."

"I don't know. My father. . ."

"He'll never see me."

She wanted to say no, especially after the earlier incident. "It's not necessary."

He made a face and put a hand over his stomach. "Neither was the corn bread, but I did it anyway."

She shook her head and gave up trying to dissuade him. He came near and held out his hand for the horse's reins. She surrendered them to his warm palm, more aware than she wanted to be of his height, the broadness of his shoulders, and the shadow across his face that hid his gray eyes.

"We should do this again."

He hesitated, and in that second her heart cantered with expectation and the longing to spend more time with this man. To know his heart as she had discovered the heart of his mother.

His tone came out hard. "Based on what Hector told us, you could be right. Others know another side of my father's shooting."

She released a heavy sigh. His father's murder. He still believed that her father had pulled the trigger. The only reason Ryan wanted to spend time with her was because she'd offered to help him get to the truth. She must not allow herself to think his motives might extend to anything more.

Chapter 18

Ryan felt himself drawn as if by an undertow toward Olivia Sattler. When her fingers had grazed his, he'd been distracted by the silver light across her cheek. She would fit into his arms quite nicely.

Madness. All of it. He had scrambled to set his mind on the right track, throwing out some blather about Hector and the possibility that she might be right to assume others could help them find the truth. Of course she was right. He'd become more convinced of that as he'd listened to Hector talk, but he couldn't help but consider how disappointed she must feel to know that despite Hector's help, the truth of his words still pointed a finger at her father.

He could not deny the thunder of his heart as his fingers caressed hers or the churn of softer emotions her closeness brought to the surface.

He led her horse, his mind clearing now that he wasn't distracted by the sight of her. An animal hadn't scared Hector's sheep; he was sure of it. "I'll spend the morning over at Hector's. That way I can satisfy myself by knowing whether it was animal or man out there tonight."

"Ryan." She stopped him with a hand on his arm, but she wasn't looking at him, and her body was tense.

A man stepped from the shadow of the barn. "Miss Sattler."

"Skinny, you startled me."

The foreman nodded his response and almost yanked the reins from Ryan's hands. The horse jerked back. "Heard you were in town, Laxalt."

Olivia's voice wobbled with uncertainty. "He was just seeing me home."

Skinny's hard, pale eyes raked him. "I'm sure Mr. Sattler will thank you for seeing his girl home. Now get out of here."

"I'm here for Olivia. Not for you."

"And I told you to get."

Olivia filled his vision as she wedged herself between them. "Leave Mr. Laxalt to me, Skinny."

Skinny ran a hand over his bare scalp. His hard frown turned his face mean. Without a word, he led the animal away, steel in his eyes. The man had too much sand to let Olivia have the last word on the matter.

Ryan clamped a hand on her shoulder, spinning her to face him. "Don't ever do that again." His words came out hard. Much harder than he'd intended.

"I think I just saved your hide, and you have the nerve to tell me 'Don't ever do that again.' What? Should I let him blow your head off next time?"

"He couldn't draw; he had the horse's reins in his right hand."

"You could just say thank you."

It had escalated far beyond what he'd intended. "Thank you." He clipped the words, sinking beneath the weight of them and the hurt and anger his rebuke had generated.

She shook his hand from her shoulder and walked away. Ryan felt a coldness at the loss of her presence and a deep shame. He knew she'd meant well, but a man didn't need a woman to fight his battles for him.

❧

Seething over Ryan's insolence, Olivia found great satisfaction in slamming the door behind her, even as late as it was.

"Where have you been?"

She turned, searching through the darkness of the kitchen in front of her for the source of that voice. Her father moved, a shadow in the darkness. A light flared, and then the chimney of a lamp was lowered. Her father's face came into view.

"I was over at Hector Maiden's."

"Alone?"

"No."

"Tom told me he hired you to write for his paper."

The shift in subject caught Olivia off guard. If he knew, what did he expect from her? Confirmation seemed absurd. Surely he wouldn't demand she quit, stay home, and be a good little ranch girl.

Olivia crossed the room and sat down across from him. His gaze probed hers, questioning. She felt much like the schoolgirl in front of the class, asked a question that she did not know the answer to.

"I'm sure you'll do a good job. I've some ideas for a few stories."

So this is how it was to be. She lifted her chin. "As do I."

"I told Tom you would do a good job."

She filled her lungs with air and did her best to bite back the surge of anger and the tears that stung. "I've been here for weeks, and our first real conversation isn't anything about how glad you are that I'm home. It's just about me doing a good job working in town?"

"Reputation is everything."

"It's nothing if you're not human."

Jay squinted his cocoa-colored eyes, a mirror of her own. His mouth drew into a hard line. "That's no way to talk to your father."

"Is that what you are to me? A father?"

"Don't forget who paid for you to be with your aunt all those years."

"It wasn't my choice to go to Philadelphia in the first place. It was your choice,

Father. The choice you made for me."

"You were happy."

"I was lonely."

"You adjusted."

Words dissolved on her tongue. She stood to her feet, trying to compose herself before the dam of her emotion burst. "I miss the days when you were a father and not a stranger. But it's been a long time. Perhaps too long."

As soon as she was out of the circle of light, she picked up her pace until she reached the sanctity of her room. There, in the darkness relieved by a ray of moonlight, Olivia sat on the edge of her bed and covered her face. Hot tears squeezed from her eyes in spite of the defiant fists that balled to hold them back. But the dam of her will did not hold. Pulling her knees to her chest, she rocked, wishing for nothing more than a loving hand or a tender touch.

Oh Mama.

Chapter 19

Ryan tied the dun to the back of the wagon and waited at the side for his mother to appear. When she did, her smile beamed brighter than the light from seven oil lamps. She wanted details of his time with Olivia, so he knew she'd forgive him for spending the morning with Hector Maiden and taking her to town late.

"So you must tell me when you are going out next."

He groaned and thought about how Olivia had stalked away from him the previous evening. "I don't know. Probably not for a long time."

She touched her hand to his as she tamed her skirts with the other and hiked herself into the wagon. "You were a gentleman, I hope."

Ryan took his time rounding the wagon. He might as well continue to answer the endless string of questions. If he grew silent, she would only dig deeper, prying open his shell much as he'd seen a sailor do to a clam once. The image made things bearable somehow, and his mother's stream of speculation and advice over the few miles into town made one thing clear to him: she wanted grandchildren. Lots of them. And she loved him. Love, to her, translated to a life spent with someone. Only there was one problem, and he told her about it as soon as he'd helped her down into the street in front of the general store. "We're not in love, Mama."

She stopped, turned, and smiled. It was the grin of a woman sure of herself. "You will be, son. She's a beautiful woman."

"I thought you wanted me to marry for love, not for beauty."

"Ah"—she shook her finger at him—"see? You are admitting that you have noticed how pretty she is. You see, I was talking about her inner beauty. You, on the other hand, are the one who notices her outward beauty."

He didn't respond. He should have known better in the first place. His mother could twist things around until his mind felt frayed like a used rope. He felt as if he'd scaled the Big Horns by the time he'd returned the dun to the livery and started back toward the ranch. And all because a little scrap of a woman knew him better than he knew himself. He wondered if all mothers had a way of turning their children inside out.

Bobby wanted him to go over the books. A task he welcomed. He wanted to learn more about the holdings of the Lazy L and forget about women.

He slapped the reins against the horse's rump to hurry her along. He needed to give more attention to the ranch. At the Y in the road, the right branch led to

Sattler's spread, the left to Laxalt land. He stopped the wagon and considered Olivia and their hasty parting. Phoebe's words that she thought Olivia might be hurting over her father's inattention stirred his mind.

Ryan blew out a breath and adjusted his hat more firmly on his head before setting the horse into motion at a good clip. A mile ambled by when he spotted a dust cloud in the distance and paused the wagon to squint. The rider was coming fast, the horse and rider a dark blur.

His hands tightened on the reins as the rider became identifiable. When Bobby Flagg stopped, his apple cheeks were red from exertion.

"Headed to get the sheriff." His breath came in pants. "Found cut fence on that piece between our property and Hector's. Went to talk to Hector Maiden." Bobby hunched forward over the saddle.

"Easy, man."

Bobby shook his head. "Hector is beat up. Not quite conscious."

"Who's with him?"

"Cody. Ty was taking care of the fence."

"You get on to town. I'll get over to Hector's. Ask Phoebe if she can bring Mama home tonight."

❧

Olivia's body sagged in the saddle. What had started as a glorious morning was quickly becoming a savage beast of heat. She fanned the material of her blouse and slid to the ground of Main Street. Tom Mahone was not in the office, and Marv sat at a desk. His long, thin face showed displeasure.

"Good morning."

"I had nothing to do with it," Marv said.

Olivia understood at once what the man referred to—the conversation with Tom the previous day and the veiled suggestion that Marv had told her about the article's due date.

"He says things like he told me to do them, but he didn't. I had no way of knowing anything about a due date. I just keep the machinery running around here. If he keeps pushing me, I just might quit. Shoulda left with Jon."

"I have my article right here." She slipped the papers from a leather clutch and unfolded them. Though the article spoke only of her impressions of Wyoming as a city girl coming west, it was a start. She had wanted to write about Hector Maiden's revelations but changed her mind at the last minute. She preferred to gather more facts.

Or maybe it was the dark frown on her father's face that burned in her imagination whenever she tried to put Hector's observations on paper.

"They don't want your opinions, Miss Sattler. They want someone who'll write what they want to print."

"I see that, Marv."

"Your daddy. . ."

She waited for him to continue, but he only pressed his lips together and returned his attention to a piece of metal sitting on the desk.

"Do you think he killed Martin Laxalt?"

Marv's look was hard for a second before his gaze fell to the desk again. "Martin was a good friend. Didn't deserve what happened to him. George neither." His gnarled hands skimmed the metal pieces in front of him. "There'll be others, too."

Coldness crawled along her spine. She didn't know Marv. Wasn't sure if the crusty old man could be trusted or even if her fears were something she should talk about. She'd heard so many people express negatives about her father, but she wanted to believe he was the man she remembered. Yet so many little things stirred her fears and concerns to the contrary. Marv's face was drawn into lines of concentration as he worked over the part he held. And she didn't know if she wanted to dig any deeper.

Chapter 20

The general store promised relief from the heat and companionship in the form of Josephine Laxalt. The Singer sewing machine whirred and sputtered in the corner of the store, and Olivia noticed a woman hovering at Josephine's elbow. It appeared that they were discussing the sewing machine's wonders.

"Ah, Miss Olivia," Papa Don greeted her as he waved good-bye to a departing customer. "Is today the day you receive the rest of the clothes Mrs. Laxalt has been sewing for you?" He wagged his finger as he shook his head. "I tell you, that machine is never silent when she is here."

"Good for business, I'm sure."

Papa's eyes sparkled. "Very good. Sold two of the new-fangled things since Mrs. Laxalt has set up shop in the corner." He leaned on the counter and cupped his face in one hand. "What can I do for you today?"

She lifted her gaze to the shelves filled with jars of candy and seeds and hesitated. "I'd like some. . .peppermints."

Papa Don straightened and lifted down the jar of candy. "How many?"

"I. . ." Her throat closed. Here was a man who'd known her all those years ago. More importantly, he knew her father and mother. She could still hear Mother's voice ordering the sweet. "A nickel's worth."

"Ah, you're your mother's daughter." He turned and scooped peppermints from the canister. "Your pa always ordered extra sugar for your mama to make fruit pies and cakes. Still does. Guess his cook has a sweet tooth, too."

Anxiousness rose up in her, and she blurted the words. "He doesn't talk about her."

The man's expression folded into sadness. "I suspect he has a lot on his mind."

Emotion burned along Olivia's throat. "What does he have on his mind, Papa Don? What has changed my father so much?"

Peppermints slid from the scoop into the little bag. With careful precision, Papa Don creased the top. "That'll be a nickel."

Olivia hesitated, the nickel clutched in her hand. She was confident that his hesitation, the same hesitation she'd seen in Marv, stemmed from a knowledge of something dark. "Please, Papa Don. I must know. Something is very wrong, and you know about it."

"Give your papa some time, Livy. Sometimes men need time."

Time? "This isn't about my mother's death. He's not a grieving man anymore."

"Maybe you coming home brings it all back." But there was a lack of conviction behind the words.

The door of the general store swung inward with force and bounced off the wall. "Don!"

Papa Don's gaze snapped to the visitor. Bobby Flagg stood there, his hat in his hands.

"Beg your pardon, ma'am."

"What is it, Bobby?" The storekeeper's gaze flicked to her then back to the foreman. His voice was a whisper. "Something's happened?"

"Found Hector Maiden. He's beat up pretty bad."

"No!"

The voice came from behind them. Josephine Laxalt came into view, her dark hair a direct contrast to the paleness of her skin. Her eyes went to Papa Don. "You see? They are dangerous. If we continue to resist, they will hurt us all."

Bobby Flagg pivoted and jammed his hat back on his head before he was through the door. Olivia had only a minute to make her decision. Her gaze went from Josephine's pale face to Papa Don's tense jawline and sober eyes.

"Tell me, Papa Don." Her words sliced the tense air between her and the older man. "Please stop hiding the truth from me."

❧

The doctor arrived at the Maiden property just as Ryan stepped from Hector's house. He raised his hand to the gray-whiskered man with a large paunch and impossibly skinny legs. Only the presence of the clutch bag proved the man's occupation.

"Bobby's on his way in. He told me Hector's been laid low."

Ryan nodded and motioned the man into the house, not missing the frankly curious gaze the doctor speared at him.

"Name's Doc Herald. You must be Laxalt's boy. Heard you were in town."

Ryan's answer was to swing the door to Hector's room wide.

Doc Herald stepped inside and set his bag at the foot of Hector's bed. Ryan retreated a step.

"Could need some help. You've done a good job cleaning the wounds, but I'd like to roll him over and take a look."

"There's some gashes that need stitches," Ryan said from the doorway.

Doc Herald ran his fingers over the buckle of his leather bag. His gaze flicked over Ryan. "No need to be offish, I'm not one of the bad guys."

Ryan stilled. That was a strange choice of words.

"Your father was a good man. Didn't deserve what he got."

"What did he get, Doc? A bullet in the back?" It hadn't occurred to him until that moment how natural it would be for the doctor to have taken care of his father's body.

"I didn't see the deed done, son. They brought his body into town."

"They?"

"Your daddy's men. Your men now, I guess."

It lined up with what he'd been told by Bobby, except the part about his body being taken to the doctor.

"Was nothing I could have done," he said. His eyes narrowed as he tried to thread the needle in his hand. "Shot in the back. Went clean through the heart."

A wave of sickness welled in his stomach. He forced himself to relax and allow the tension to drain away. "Got any thoughts on who did it?"

Doc Herald lifted Hector's eyelid and picked up the threaded needle. "I've heard a lot of rumors. It's a serious charge to lay at anyone's feet."

"Seems to me the same name keeps coming up."

"Sattler? Yeah. But I wouldn't go poking a stick at that rattler. You might get a bullet in your back, too."

Was the doctor trying to warn him off? "They're picking the fight."

Herald's needle dipped into the gaping wound along Hector's cheek. "I'm not sure there's any defense."

Ryan turned away and pulled the door closed, unable to endure the conversation another minute.

"Hey!"

The door whipped inward, and the doctor stood there. His eyes flicked to the room beyond Ryan's shoulder. "Listen to me. Your father's dead because he tried to stop them," he whispered. "I'm not for anyone in this thing, but I don't want to be burying any more good men either. You want to win this, you'll have to band together. I've told them all that for months, and I think they're finally listening."

"Who worked Hector over?"

Doc Herald glanced back at his patient. His brows lowered. "My guess is Hector overstepped himself."

"We heard something last night when I was over here talking to him. Came out this morning to check on it. We didn't find anything."

"They're watching everyone. Probably saw you and decided to pick a fight."

"Framing me?"

"That'd be my guess."

"Sattler." Ryan hissed the word.

"Bowman and Michaels." The doctor's nostrils flared. "It's not just one of them, son. It's all of them together that's making things so tough."

Bobby Flagg walked in the house, sweat-streaked and dirty from the ride. But it was the slender, redheaded form that slipped by Bobby who stiffened Ryan's spine and made him feel like he was plunging off a cliff.

Chapter 21

Couldn't get her to stay in town, boss." Bobby shrugged.

Olivia's head jerked around, and she plunged a hand to her hip. "It's not like I was asking permission. If I want to come and see Mr. Maiden, I'll come and see him."

"Check on Cody and Ty," Ryan said to Bobby. "I'll be down there as soon as I finish up with Miss Sattler."

Olivia sauntered closer, stopping two feet in front of him. She was covered with a thin layer of Wyoming dust, and her nose had a fresh sprinkle of freckles on a deep pink background.

"You've got sunburn." As soon as the words escaped, he wanted to groan in exasperation.

She rubbed at her nose and winced. "I didn't have a hat."

Staring down into her upturned face sent his senses reeling. What was this woman doing to him? She was pretty. Check. She was spunky. Check. She was maddening. Check. She was a Sattler. The enemy's daughter!

He spit his words. "We need to talk, Olivia."

"How is he?"

"He'll recover." She seemed so concerned. "They beat him pretty good, but nothing's broken that I could see."

"They?"

"I was with him this morning. All was fine that we could see."

Every word his mind formed jammed up in his throat. Watching her, those eyes. . . His heart squeezed in his chest. "I need to ride down to Ty and Cody. Find out if they've discovered any reason behind the attack on Hector." He was a fool. A coward in the face of a slip of a woman who balled him up inside so tight he had trouble drawing breath.

"I'll ride with you."

He gulped. "It's probably a better idea for you to—"

"We can talk."

Talk. Sure, he could do that. He'd listen while her lips moved and her eyes blinked and that little nose continued to get redder. He lifted his hand, intending to touch the tip of that sunburned nose, but he caught himself, embarrassed at the pull of impulse. "You can't continue to ride in this heat."

Her smile was a slow upward curve of pink lips that were at once teasing and amused. "You'll let me borrow yours, you being the kindhearted sort."

Ryan called himself every kind of idiot for letting Olivia Sattler get under his skin. The sight of her astride her horse with his hat flopping down around her ears took too much of his energy away from the problem of Hector Maiden's assault. He should never have allowed her to ride with him. He should have demanded that she stay behind and boil water, or do something, for Dr. Herald.

He slowed his horse to allow himself more time to survey the surroundings. He needed to look at the fencing and the crops for signs of intruders or stray prints, but everything around him faded away as he fell under the spell of watching her.

She twisted in the saddle and jabbed her index finger into the brim of his too-large hat to tilt it away from her eyes.

Those eyes. . .

"Something wrong back there?"

Ryan shifted in the saddle and raised his head as if he'd been searching the ground the whole time. "Everything looks fine."

"Does it?"

He glanced at her and caught the look she gave him and, again, that amused smile. He cleared his throat. "Cody and Ty probably have a lot to report." He leaned forward and squinted at the ground, looking for footprints, dung, marks of passage, anything that would mean he wouldn't have to look at her. To his dismay, he could feel the heat of a blush on the back of his neck.

"I think you're cute, too."

Her words snapped him upright. She appeared innocent sitting astride her horse. But that smile was back, and now she was laughing.

"I—" He cleared his throat to loosen the words wedged there.

"Right." She faced forward, the words falling over her shoulder. "You keep looking for sign. I'll ride ahead."

And with that, Olivia Sattler poked her horse in the sides with her boots and left him stewing in the Wyoming sun—and suffocating in the cloud of dust kicked up by her horse's hooves.

❧

Olivia knew she shouldn't have goaded Ryan. Her comment had embarrassed him. She never would have guessed the deeply tanned cowboy with the dark hair and silver eyes was capable of blushing so nicely. In Philly the good-looking men had often been full of themselves. Even those with lower social standing were stodgy in manner—humility was never a part of their makeup. She realized now how distasteful that world had been. It was part of the reason she'd grown so restless to leave and come west. And now here she was, galloping on a horse in the middle of a pasture so wide, beneath a sky so blue, that she felt free and settled. This was home.

Or it would be home if not for the cloud over her head.

Her joy deflated. Papa Don and Josephine Laxalt knew something. It seemed everyone knew something except her, but she'd had little time to beg the merchant for the full story. Riding to see Hector had taken primary concern.

She slowed her horse until Ryan caught up. He reined in the short-legged mustang that put her at eye level with him.

His expression seemed guarded. Tough. And she wanted so much to reach out and touch his arm and try to make sense of the emotions his presence stirred in her. But it wasn't the time, and he must think her terribly bold for what she'd said. Aunt Fawn would have had the apoplexy.

Her nose tingled, and she touched the tender spot. She'd known exactly what he'd wanted to do when he'd lifted his hand earlier, and the very idea had tripped the beat of her heart. But he had pulled back at the last minute, and she wondered if she'd repulsed him somehow. Maybe she was too forward or too—

"Are you feeling all right?"

She put a hand to her neck, mulling the question. The answer was a resounding no, but saying as much would bring more questions. "I saw your mother today. This morning, to be exact."

"Oh no."

His reaction stopped her cold. "Oh no?"

"She told you she's knitting booties?"

"Why. . .no. Baby booties?"

Ryan averted his face, but this time, this close, the stain of red on his neck was very noticeable.

"Is she making them for someone?"

"Forget I said anything." He closed his eyes and exhaled sharply. "Go on."

She leaned forward to stroke the horse's neck, her words coming fast. "Papa Don knows something about my father. There's more to all this than we're seeing, Ryan. I'm convinced of it. Marv said Tom Mahone wants me to write what he wants me to write. My father even suggested a few subjects for me to use for my articles. Then Papa Don seemed strange when I started talking about my father. And then Bobby came in, and your mother started warning Papa Don that someone was going to get hurt. They know something, but no one wants to tell the whole story."

She blinked at the wetness that had gathered in her eyes. She hadn't meant to cry. It seemed such a silly thing to do. Olivia swiped at the tears and gasped at the friction of her hand on the tender, sunburned skin. She felt a warm bundle against the back of her hand and realized Ryan was offering his kerchief. She blotted the wetness and choked on a garbled sob.

"I don't know why I'm crying."

"Because you're hurt and confused. That would be my best guess."

She nodded at his assessment. When she faced him, his hat slid forward. He breached the distance between them and tilted it back on her head. His eyes smiled into hers. "Now could you say that all again a little slower?"

Chapter 22

Ryan listened to Olivia and tried his best to connect the dots. He wondered if she realized how much her heart showed in her face. Even the hurt when she talked of her father's remoteness.

He told Olivia what Dr. Herald had suggested. The similarities seemed too much to dismiss easily. "It's like everyone is watching the bully, but no one wants to help."

"Because they're afraid," Olivia said. Her voice was flat, resigned.

Ryan drew his mustang closer to the bay and reached across to touch the back of her hand. There was nothing he could offer in the way of comfort. Not until they knew more. "Let's go see what my men have found."

She nodded, and he withdrew, taking the reins and setting the pace. When Bobby came into view, the sheriff was with him. His small eyes were on Ryan as he drew closer. Ryan instantly disliked the man.

"Laxalt. Heard Martin's son had come back." He offered his hand. "Sheriff Bradley."

Ryan shook his hand and kept his expression neutral. He turned as Olivia stopped her horse and slid to the ground unaided.

"Who's this?" The sheriff jabbed a thumb Olivia's direction.

"Olivia Sattler."

"Sattler's girl?"

"It's not Sattler's boy." Ryan regretted the poke as soon as it left his mouth. No reason to rile the man. Bobby laughed and slapped his leg.

"Still the smart-mouthed kid I remember."

Ryan couldn't recall the man. He wondered if the sheriff's memory was faulty or if he'd just given ear to the rumors about his character based on the past and formed his own opinion.

"What have you found, Sheriff?" Ryan pressed.

"Your man here says he found the fence cut and was going to talk to Hector about it. Being that this section of the fence borders your property, it means you'd better put that smart mouth to doing some explaining."

Ryan had asked for that. He noted the myriad of hoofprints in the dust and weighed what he was seeing against what he wasn't seeing. "Aren't all our cattle bunched up for the drive, Bobby?"

"Just a few in this pasture. No more or less than last check."

Ryan turned his attention to the sheriff and raised his brows. "Why would I cut my own fence?"

"You tell me. Throw off suspicion. Hector have something you want? Maybe you're taking up where your daddy left off."

Bobby exploded. "That's a lie!"

Ryan raised his palm to soothe the foreman. "I can see where you're taking this, Sheriff. This isn't an investigation at all. You're acting as judge and jury."

"Makes perfect sense to me. You cut the fence then went to see Hector and did a little fist work on him. He's not a young man, which means you'd have the advantage. Your foreman already said you were out here this morning."

"You should look for someone with bruises on their face," Olivia said. "Ryan doesn't have a mark on him."

"On his face, Miss Sattler. Doesn't mean there aren't marks elsewhere, unless you. . ."

A hard edge of indignation propelled Ryan forward. He gripped the man's shirt and pulled him to his toes. "That was uncalled for, Sheriff. Miss Sattler is a lady, not that you would recognize one."

He felt Olivia's hand on his arm. "Ryan, let him go."

"Not until he apologizes."

The sheriff's face went red. Bobby moved up behind the sheriff. "I think the boss is right. No reason to insult the lady. Seems you're the one with the smart mouth."

Sheriff Bradley's eyes shifted to Olivia. "You have my apology."

"Louder," Ryan growled.

"You have my apology, Miss Sattler."

Ryan let go and took a broad step back. "Why don't you get on up to the cabin, Bradley? Sheriff's no good if he can't get the whole story before throwing insults and lynching an innocent man."

Bradley's scowl was ugly. "I'm telling you like I see it."

"Then maybe you'd better open those little eyes of yours and take a closer look. One based on fact. Hector and I talked last night and heard a commotion among his cows. We were investigating this morning to make sure all was well."

"Why did he need your help doing that?"

"He didn't. I came because I wanted to see for myself if he had found anything. You can't blame me for being cautious since my father was murdered."

"Murdered," Bradley spit. "That's your word."

"That's all the word you need."

❧

The tense group moved toward Hector Maiden's house. They met Ty and Cody on the way back, and Bobby fell back with them. Olivia heard them whispering. No doubt Bobby was filling his men in on what had happened.

She rode close to Ryan, catching glimpses of him. She was worried that he might get caught in the middle of the mess.

"What if he's not awake?"

Ryan's chest lifted, and his breath exploded on the exhale. "Sheriff has his way, he'll probably hang me."

Olivia gripped the reins tighter in her right hand. "That's not funny."

"Wasn't trying to be funny."

"What if Hector can't remember anything?"

"Then I'm in big trouble unless we can figure out who did it. I don't think our sheriff is going to be much help."

"He doesn't know that you did it."

Ryan's eyes went over her, and a lazy grin broke the solemnity of his expression. "You don't know that I didn't."

She wanted to protest his statement, but a valid doubt niggled at her. She didn't know. Or did she. . . "In my heart, I know you didn't."

Ryan took a kerchief from his pocket, rolled it, and tied it around his neck. "Appreciate that, Livy."

Chapter 23

Hector woke up as the afternoon faded to evening and a chill rent the heat of the day. Ryan sat at his bedside, opposite Sheriff Bradley. He'd sent the hands back to the Lazy L and had tried to get Olivia to head home, but she'd given him a stubborn look, complete with hands on hips and sunburned nose tilted to the ceiling. He'd retreated.

Hector's bedroom was still redolent with the smell of the pork Olivia had fried up for supper when the man first showed signs of waking. Hector's grimace of pain became a groan.

Sheriff Bradley got to his feet and leaned over him. "Hector? You hear me?"

Hector's head moved back and forth against the thin pillow beneath his head.

Ryan went to the doorway, his footsteps alerting Olivia. "Hector needs a drink."

She nodded, and he returned in time to hear the sheriff's question.

"Who did this, Hector? We're needing to know."

"Take it easy," Ryan warned. "Let him get his head about him. Miss Sattler's getting a drink."

"I'm the sheriff." The older man scowled. "We're doing this my way, Laxalt. I'm not having any hired gun tell me how to do my work. Don't have any respect for a lawman who turns dark horse." He leaned forward as Hector's eyelids fluttered. "Hector?"

So he knew. Tension throbbed behind his eyes. He'd thought his reputation as a Ranger might help him; he should have known turning hired gun would erase all the good.

Ryan thought he heard a door shut. Feminine voices drifted to him. Ryan retraced his steps. He was surprised to see Phoebe huddled with Olivia. Phoebe saw him and waved him over.

"I came out here to warn you, Ryan. Sheriff Bradley is one of them." Phoebe's lips pursed as if she'd tasted something sour. "I had hoped you would leave town quick, but you haven't, and we all agree it's not fair for you to take up this fight alone, ignorant of the depth of the threat you're facing." She glanced between them. "Both of you."

Ryan digested the information. He felt the light weight of Olivia's hand on his arm.

"You're talking about Papa Don and Mrs. Laxalt?" Olivia asked.

Phoebe's eyes flashed. "There's more of us. Many more. We're all trying to band together, but they've got too much money and too many of the major players on their side."

"Sattler?" Ryan asked.

"Bowman and Michaels. All three of them." Phoebe nodded.

The weight of Olivia's hand shifted as she tightened her hold and swayed toward him. Her face was pale and pinched with stress.

Ryan drew her up against his side. She molded into him. Phoebe placed a hand on her friend's shoulder. "I'm sorry. I was so excited to have you come back, but not to this. I had hoped your presence might. . ." Phoebe glanced away, clearly distressed.

"Who else is involved?" Olivia asked.

"Doc's on our side," Ryan said.

She tilted her face to his. "He told you that?"

"Just about. But he was vague."

Phoebe nodded. "We're a cautious bunch for a reason." She faced Olivia. "Tom Mahone is their puppet. He'll say anything they want him to say."

Olivia's face turned into his shoulder, her words muffled. "Why didn't you tell me that when I told you I was going to work for him?"

❧

Olivia jerked back from Ryan, the fire of temper consuming her weakness. "I thought you were my friend."

Phoebe didn't meet her eyes. "How do you tell the daughter of the territory's biggest rancher that he's leading a band of killers? I tried to hint to you, thinking maybe you would go to him and have a talk. That having you home would soften him up some."

"He doesn't have time to talk. Not about things that don't matter to him."

"I used to work for your daddy, back when he was a loving father. But. . .people change. And I've watched him change over the years. It's as if the absence of your mother's gentle influence opened the floodgates to vileness."

Olivia shuddered with suppressed rage. "Did he kill Ryan's father?"

"There's no way to prove anything." Phoebe brushed at her riding skirt. "They work like that. No witnesses. No warning. Their men do a lot of the dirty work, especially Skinny. It's rumored that he's a hired gun from up north."

Questions sprang to her mind, but Olivia clamped down on the urge to ask them when Sheriff Bradley's raised voice hollered from the bedroom. "I know you're out there, Laxalt. Hector's saying some mighty interesting things about that temper of yours. Says you're good with your fists, too."

Ryan's inhale whispered in the silence. Olivia touched his shoulder, fearful of his reaction. "He's baiting you. Go back to town with Phoebe. I'll tell him you left. Send your mother over or Papa Don or Marv"—Olivia turned to Phoebe for help—"anyone who you know is on our side."

At first she thought her pleadings had fallen on deaf ears. She felt the knot of Ryan's muscles beneath her hand, and his dark eyes gleamed with anger then faded to frustration. Tension melted from his body.

"Ryan, listen to me. You can't go in there alone."

"She's right, Mr. Laxalt," Phoebe whispered. "Bradley will do whatever it takes to protect the big bosses. Even shoot you in cold blood."

His eyes rested on Olivia. "My men can keep the sheriff company and be witness to what Hector really says. I'd rather have you with me."

Chapter 24

Ryan hated leaving, even knowing that Bobby, Cody, and Ty would do everything they could to keep Hector safe from the sheriff. His horse kept pace with Phoebe's long-legged pinto and Olivia's bay. On the edge of Maiden's land, another rider moved out from behind a low hill and sat in their path. Ryan tensed, and his hand went to the scabbard that held his Marlin rifle. Phoebe glanced over at him and shook her head then waved at the man in their path. The stranger waved back.

Phoebe brought her horse up next to the man. Her mouth was moving before her horse had come to a full stop. "Ryan's men are with Hector."

Ryan worked his horse's pace down to a walk and pulled up between the man and Olivia, keeping his side to the stranger and his hand near the leather sheath that held the gun. Just in case.

"You must be Martin's son." The man nodded. "I imagine your presence has put some knots in Bowman's plans. Heard you were a Ranger."

Ryan shrugged, feeling no need to explain beyond that for now. "Something like that."

Phoebe turned to Olivia. Twin spots of color bloomed on her cheeks. "Jacob and I changed our minds. We're going to get married." She laughed.

"Bowman's not too happy since the arrangement will give us more land," Jacob added, sharing a smile with Phoebe. "But we don't aim to make things easy."

Ryan tried to take in all the information that was being dumped on him, setting up the people who were the main players and those who were merely the puppets. Olivia didn't appear to be listening. Her eyes were on the ground as she unconsciously rubbed her horse's neck.

"Did the sheriff make a scene?" Jacob asked Phoebe.

She nodded over at Ryan. "Tried to pin the whole thing on him."

Ryan had a question of his own. "How did you know about Hector?"

"Word travels fast in a small town, Laxalt. Phoebe works at Landry's, so she can keep her ears sharp for rumors and accusations that Bowman, Sattler, or Michaels might be trying to churn up. It's how they've worked for years. Accuse the little man. Dispense with him and take over his property."

"How're they doing it? Setting up the scene? All those hoofprints. . ."

Jacob and Phoebe shared a look. Jacob shrugged. "Your pa was a good man. He saw what the big ranchers were trying to do, and he got vocal about it. Tried to figure out how they did it, too, but with the sheriff playing favorites, it's not like they need much more than a few hoofprints and a cut fence."

Phoebe guided her horse around his and over to Olivia. The two talked in low tones.

Jacob continued, "Him, Jon, and George tried to start their own paper arguing against the high price to register brands and the portable cabins the big ranchers are using to claim more property. George never had a chance. And there were threats against Jon. Anyone who stands in their way."

"George was killed?"

"An easy target because he was far out and a widower. No witnesses. Same as Hector." Jacob glanced toward the women and lowered his voice. "I know Phoebe's been awful worried about Miss Sattler."

With all that had been revealed, Ryan knew Olivia must feel very much caught in the middle. Without her father, she had no family.

"Phoebe," Jacob called. "Let's get on into town. I think it's a good time to bring them into the circle. Papa Don has gotten everyone together."

Ryan tugged on the reins and fell back with Olivia. He wanted so much to reach out to her. He couldn't guess what she must be feeling and thinking. Though she had suspected her father's underhanded ways, to have them confirmed must be a terrible, heartbreaking shock.

He brought the mustang close to her mare and pulled his hat from her head. "Guess you don't need this now that the sun's not so high."

She barely raised her eyes.

"Livy?"

Her chin jerked up, and he saw her emotions contained in the sheen hazing her eyes.

"Maybe things aren't quite as bad as you think."

She averted her face, and he could see the moisture skid a streak down her cheek. "It's worse."

He reached out and touched the back of the hand that rested on her leg. "Does that mean you regret coming back? Even if it means you wouldn't have met a gentleman like myself?"

His try at humor fell short. She sniffed and pulled her hand away to wipe at her eyes. "I guess I just need some time."

He let it go, acknowledging his bad timing in delivering such a line. He was content to ride in silence beside her and used the time to form the questions he still wanted to ask of Phoebe and Jacob. To his surprise, they skirted Main Street and came up behind the Occidental and the other buildings before dismounting at Landry's. An outbuilding shielded them from any curious eyes that might be looking out of second-story windows. A man—or was it a boy? Ryan couldn't tell in the darkness—claimed each of the horses and led them into the shelter.

Olivia was at his side, hugging herself. "It might be better if I didn't go inside," she whispered. "I'm the enemy."

He clasped her hand in his and rubbed along her cold fingers with the pad of his thumb. "I won't go in without you. Whoever's in there must know you've been gone for so long there would be no way you could be a part of anything."

"You didn't."

"Because I've come to know you. They will, too, but you've got to give them that chance."

She cocked a brow. "You speaking from experience?"

He lifted his hand to her cheek. "Yes."

Her smile was fragile. "I'm afraid."

Ryan lifted his head to see Jacob entering the back door of the restaurant. Phoebe stood outside a moment longer, her face turned toward them.

"You're with me and Phoebe," he said. "There's no reason to be afraid."

Almost against her will, her right foot took a step forward. Ryan's hand on her arm urged her along, and before she knew it, she was in the back room of Landry's second floor living space staring open-mouthed at the familiar faces surrounding her.

Chapter 25

It's not going to stop. When the governor repealed the Maverick Law, things really heated up."

"Maverick Law?" Olivia snapped the question. Her hand hovered over some papers. Ryan smiled. She was following his urging and taking notes of all that was being said about Bowman and Michaels, though he did notice that the Sattler name hadn't come up once. He could only attribute it to the group's deference to Olivia.

"Unbranded cattle become the property of the Wyoming Stock Growers Association," Papa Don explained. Based on what Olivia had overheard earlier, the storekeeper's presence hadn't been a surprise. Neither, for that matter, had Marv's. But Ryan's mother's presence, along with a half dozen men from small ranches on the other side of Hector Maiden's and west of town, had surprised him.

"It's to their benefit?"

"Yeah." Marv nodded. "We banded together to get it repealed. Wrote a dozen letters. Your daddy made the trip to talk to the governor himself."

"It's why he got shot." His mother spit the words then covered her face. Phoebe put her arm around the woman, and things grew quiet. Across from them, Ryan swallowed hard, feeling the weight of his father's sacrifice.

Marv cut through the silence. "Latest issue of the paper will feature Miss Sattler's article front page." He gave her an apologetic look. "Mahone's showboating the fact that a Sattler works for him."

"Did he try and run any more lies about us small ranchers?" a man Ryan had never seen before asked.

"Not much this issue," Marv acknowledged.

"It's their word against ours. You still sending those articles out to the papers in Sheridan and Casper?"

Marv nodded. "If anything happens, there'll be more than just us knowing our side." He stole a look at Olivia. "I didn't know what side you were on at first, but since you're here. . ." The man hesitated. "If you want to help us out and write about the injustices going on, I'll put them in the little paper me and his pa"—he bent a thumb at Ryan—"got started before them murderers killed him."

Olivia's gaze went to Ryan's.

He inclined his head to let her know the news did not surprise him.

"It's the principle of the thing. We have to get others to understand and fight." Landry finally cut through the silence. "They're doing their best to take land that doesn't belong to them. It's what George's death got 'em—and the burning of Tandry's cabin east of Bowman's range. Hector getting beat up wasn't a random act; it's a warning."

"Of what?" Ryan asked.

Landry swiped beads of sweat from his forehead with a meaty fist. "Hector filed for a brand. Cost was high, but he had to do it. If the brand isn't recognized. . .it's trouble. They rejected his petition, which makes anything carrying his brand illegal."

"Let me guess," Ryan spoke up. "They have their hand in the board that decides these things."

A man with a medium build and bright red hair spoke up. "They can deliver fines and take the cattle, undoing the years it's taken a man to build his herd, not to mention wiping him out financially."

"That gives them a reason to beat him up, too. But why bother him? His herd of calves isn't even that large."

"They'll say he stole those calves. Beat him up to make a point with the rest of us—that they're winning." The red-headed man leaned an elbow on his knee. "They know you're around?"

"Yes," Ryan said.

"Then you can expect trouble."

"Sheriff's already fingering me for doing the deed."

Murmurs went up around the room.

"I left my men there."

"Expect more trouble when your men start the drive, and you're all alone."

"It's like I've said for months," Doc Herald's voice squeaked out, "if we don't band together, they'll crush us. One by one. This seems to indicate Hector is the new target."

Doc continued. "I'm sure he still wants the Laxalts. If he can put the blame from Hector's beating on young Laxalt here, then he's killing two birds—"

Josephine moaned and covered her face. Phoebe hugged the woman close.

"He's already trying to do just that. Which is why I left my men with him."

"I agree with Doc," the redhead said. "We've used every excuse for why we can't stand together. I know we're all pressed for time and money, but it's our only chance. I don't want another man's blood on my hands when there's something I can do to help. We need to set up a guard or patrol at Hector's until he can get back on his feet. He'll have to hire some help."

Conversation flowed around him, yet Ryan didn't hear a word of what was said. Instead, his mind was filled with Olivia. The sight of her. The scent of her hair for that brief moment he'd held her against his side outside Hector's cabin. Her delicate freckles and the humor that lit her eyes and confounded him. As if she felt his gaze, she faced him. A deep well of sadness etched her expression.

Ryan couldn't look away. She was beautiful on the outside, sure, but her spirit captured his interest—her ability to stand for right even though it was her father in the wrong. She'd been a friend to his mother, and his mother obviously loved her already.

Across the space her eyes probed his for an answer to a question he didn't quite comprehend. She raised her hand to her hair, and his gaze followed the movement. Her finger caught a strand and twirled it around her index finger in a nervous gesture. He breathed air into his lungs and wondered at the pull she had on him and what it could mean. She lowered her hand, and the strand of hair bounced into place beside her cheek. A brave smile curved her lips, reaching out to encompass him.

And then he knew what had happened, what had shifted within him, and understood the feelings her presence stirred.

Ryan Laxalt had a clear vision of what it all meant—he was a doomed man.

❧

Olivia was jostled and lost sight of Ryan as the crowd shifted around her. Phoebe leaned close. "The meeting's over." Her friend's voice held a distinctive smirk. "Not that you noticed."

Pulled back to the present, Olivia felt the heat rush into her cheeks. "I got distracted."

Phoebe patted her shoulder. "Of course you did."

Jacob stood in front of Phoebe, and her friend smiled and placed her hand in his. The sight of Phoebe taking Jacob's hand brought a swell of sadness. They wouldn't see each other as much. Her world would become even lonelier. "Phoebe"—she tugged on the back of her friend's riding skirt—"will we see each other?"

"I'll be around. We can still visit."

Phoebe pulled her into a hug. A question rose in Olivia's mind that she had long wanted to ask of her friend. "Where's my mother buried?"

Phoebe flinched. "You. . .don't remember?"

"I remember a big tree and a mound of dirt beneath it. Daddy didn't let me stay there long."

Her friend's mouth opened then closed. "The tree. . . Your mother is. . .under the tree." Olivia didn't understand what she was seeing in Phoebe's expression. It wasn't a difficult question, or shouldn't have been. Her thoughts beat a warning tattoo.

Olivia felt a presence at her back and a hand against her elbow. She half turned toward Ryan, trying to make sense of Phoebe's struggle and the stab of fear it brought.

Jacob slipped a hand around Phoebe's waist, and the action seemed to give her strength and settle her panic. "Ask your father," Phoebe said. "He'll know."

Chapter 26

The red-haired man's name was Pete, and he told Ryan not to worry about Sheriff Bradley. "We'll be keeping an eye on Hector. Bradley talks big, mostly because he knows he's riding the big horse."

"You mean Bowman?" Ryan asked.

Pete spit into the tall grass and cleared his throat. "Bowman, Michaels, Sattler. Whoever waves the money at him. Pardon me, ma'am. Meant no disrespect."

Ryan sought and found Olivia's hand buried in the folds of her riding skirt. She gave Pete a vague smile before Ryan helped her into the wagon next to his mother. Both women were quiet, but Olivia's paleness had him most worried. He tied her horse behind the wagon his mother had brought into town. Olivia set the pace. Pete caught up to him astride his own horse.

"Heading your way. I'm west of town. It'll give us a few minutes to talk."

Ryan let the wagon move ahead to give them privacy to talk. "Did you set up guard for Hector?"

Pete tilted his head. "Didn't you hear us do that? My night's tomorrow."

He pursed his lips. "Guess my mind wandered."

"Your night's Monday." Pete scratched his chest and bobbed his head. "They'll probably target Isley next."

Ryan was incredulous. "Phoebe?"

"Yeah." Pete spit again. "Bowman wants Isley's land pretty bad. And the fact Jacob's marrying Phoebe and adding her proved-up section to his means there'll be trouble."

"Jacob's on guard?"

The red-haired man shrugged. "Sure. It's become a way of life."

He noticed for the first time the guns Pete was wearing. "You pack all the time?"

Pete nodded. "Good idea with so many snakes crawling around, if you get my drift."

A vague path shot off the main trail ahead. It would be the route Pete would take. Ryan berated himself for not paying closer attention during the meeting. He should have asked more questions.

"Reckon if you worked with the Rangers, it means you're a fair shot."

"Fair," Ryan said.

"We'll be glad for your help. Your daddy was a good man."

Hearing the words ripped open the grief again. It seared along his muscles and set his nerves to tingling. His father was a hero. Ryan was a killer. The burden of that bent him up on the inside. But there was no use wasting energy on his past right now. All he could do was take up the cause his father had championed and step into the empty boots his death had left behind. Maybe there would be some redemption in that.

❧

Olivia could hear the whispered words of the men behind them. She wondered what they would talk about out of their earshot, and then thought it probably better if she didn't know.

"This is good," Josephine said. "Ryan getting to know these people will help protect him. I am sorry though, for you, my dear."

Olivia squeezed her eyes shut. "Me, too."

"Your father is not kind?"

"He is. . .distant."

The woman leaned close to her and planted a kiss on her cheek. "You are a good young woman. I would be pleased if you would let me remain your friend."

"I need all the friends I can get."

"This is good. Ryan will be your friend, too."

"He is, yes." Ryan's mention of baby booties slipped through her head and pulled a smile from her.

"I worry about him."

"He's smart. He'll be careful."

Josephine's eyes snapped to her. "Yes. Maybe now. Maybe for you."

Olivia's palms dampened, and she wiped them down her skirt. "I don't know about that. My father wouldn't be pleased to know we are friends." Did her feelings for Ryan and her friendship with Josephine put them at greater risk?

"This is nonsense. Your father is his own man, making his own decisions. Ryan sees that. I see that. I will not allow any man to dictate who I can and cannot befriend."

"Thank you, Josephine." The wagon rattled on. Olivia noted no other sounds of conversation from behind her. Pete must have taken the turnoff toward home. She wondered if Ryan could now hear their conversation.

"Will posting guards work, do you think?"

Before Olivia could form an opinion, Josephine answered her own question.

"We cannot know what works until something is first tried. I would give up the ranch if it meant keeping my son safe."

"What does he want?"

"To fight, as his father fought."

"You mean for the ranch?"

"Yes."

Olivia pulled on the reins to slow the team along a rocky section of the dirt road. In all her grief, she'd forgotten Josephine's. "I am sorry about your husband."

"My husband's death brought my son home. That is enough."

It must have been terrible for Josephine, those weeks before Ryan returned. To be alone and never know whether she would see her son again. In some ways, Olivia could understand all too well what the woman was feeling.

"Ryan is the type of man who could not live with himself if he did not try to find the man who killed his father."

"But then what?" Josephine's voice went high with strain. "When he finds that man, will he also kill to gain revenge? The beginning of blood spilt forms a long line of death."

She tried not to imagine Ryan holding a gun to her father's head. Pulling the trigger because their investigation led him back to Jay Sattler as his father's murderer. Olivia tasted Josephine's fear.

"The only hope for my son is to gain the attention of the law or walk away and leave this thing alone."

"But you were at the meeting tonight. Doesn't that mean you believe in what they are doing?"

"I want to help, but I do not agree that they should seek out trouble. Band together and try and find peace, yes."

Olivia saw it clearly then. Josephine blamed her husband for getting himself killed. While she could understand the woman's logic, she also could see Ryan's and the rest of the group's need to protect themselves against the pinch of the larger ranchers.

"He is a careful man. Not the angry young man who left here all those years ago."

Josephine gave a little grunt "I see he has told you much."

No, she wanted to say. She really didn't know much of the man Ryan had been, but she was learning the man he had become. And she wanted to learn more. Much more.

The wagon picked up speed on the smoother stretch of road. Sattler range was coming up. Olivia wondered if Skinny would be on watch, reporting to her father who his daughter was with.

"You can drop me at the edge of the property gate." Olivia pointed. "I'll walk."

"Yes. This would be for the best."

Olivia hoped Ryan wouldn't take it into his head to follow her to the door again.

❧

When Olivia stopped the wagon at the edge of Sattler property, he straightened in the saddle. Olivia stepped to the ground and came to untie the bay. He saw her intent and gave the mustang a jab to catch up before she could get in the saddle and fade into the darkness.

"See your mother home, Ryan." Her voice shot out to him as she lifted the reins over the horse's head. "She's tired."

"My mother would be the first to chastise me for letting you walk in the dark alone."

"Ryan." She moved close to him and reached out to touch his leg. He could hear the pleading in her voice. It drew him. Soothed him. Without thought, he slipped to the ground, the saddle creaking beneath his weight. He faced her in the dark, the new moon wreathing her face. She had been so pale earlier. Stressed, no doubt, by the day's events.

"I'll ride beside you." He cupped his hands. The moonlight dimmed as the sphere slipped behind a cloud.

"I'm a liability, Ryan, don't you see that? I'm not fitting into my father's plans. If they see you, it gives them a reason to shoot first. If they see you with me, then it's an even better deal, because my father's rid of me."

He straightened. "It takes a cold man to kill his own daughter."

"He wouldn't have to be the one to pull the trigger."

"I don't believe he would order your death, Olivia. It's. . .inhuman. You're letting your emotions run wild."

He heard her sharp intake of breath as she hugged herself. He wished the moon would appear so he could see her face better, but it lurked behind the dark clouds that threatened rain but never followed through on the promise.

Ryan didn't know what to say. Her fear chilled him. She was just as vulnerable to her father's rejection as Phoebe had thought. He only wished her friend was here now to offer her female counsel. An idea skittered through his head.

"Come home with us."

He heard her gasp.

"My mother is there," he said, trying to deflect any immoral suggestion. "She can chaperone. I'll sleep in the bunkhouse." The silence embarrassed him.

"I would like that very much."

He heard a whisper of movement and saw the blur of her, like fog in the night. Her hands touched his shoulders, and he could feel the warmth of her close to his chest, her breath warm against his chin, then the softness of her lips on his cheek.

His heart raced, and he put out a hand to steady her. His fingers had only skimmed her waist when she stepped back into the darkness. His head spun with the quickness of her action and left him with a longing to feel her close to him again.

"You're sweet, Ryan. Let's see what your mother thinks first."

Chapter 27

Ryan could have told Olivia that his mother would exude happiness and light at the thought of having another woman around. What he didn't expect was the way the two chattered and laughed far into the night, as if all the cares of the evening held no weight. It was late. Late enough that he lifted the bundle of blankets and clothes he had gathered earlier and left the two sitting at the kitchen table. Olivia was listening intently to his mother's memories of her as a child. And of her mother.

He was eager to hear what Hector had said to his men about his assault. Surely with witnesses to the contrary, Sheriff Bradley would be forced to back off his accusation.

Bobby, Cody, and Ty were sound asleep, along with three other men who lined the rows in different positions of repose. Ty's snores vibrated the bedframe he'd crashed on, while Cody slept like a dead man, still and quiet. The grunts and coughs coming from the men hired for the drive brought back all the days he'd spent on the trail, gulping dust as he helped move cattle. He'd spent those wandering days realizing the painful reality that living means working, and that Martin Laxalt was a man who had only sought to bring his young son to understand and embrace the truth of it.

He stretched out on the last of the two unoccupied bunks and laced his fingers behind his head. When he'd first come to Buffalo, he'd thought he would avenge his father's death and move on, but now there was Olivia. He closed his eyes to bring the vision of her face into full focus. He could see the flash of her eyes and felt again the feathery brush of her lips against his cheek. He raised his hand to touch the spot and smiled into the darkness; then he closed his eyes and fell into a deep sleep.

❧

Olivia hadn't heard Ryan leave. She'd been unable to hide her disappointment at finding his bedroll gone from the space beside the front door. She would see him in the morning, she was sure, and the nighttime chat with Josephine had sharpened so many memories dulled by the passage of time. Exhaustion pulled at her, and she made the move to stand, smiling at the woman across from her. "I guess I'm more tired than I thought."

"Tomorrow is a good day for rest. A picnic. I baked bread this morning and can make bacon sandwiches."

"Picnic?"

"Of course. Saturday should not be all work."

"Where will we go?"

"To see Hector and take him bread, then out to the pasture beyond the hill. It is beautiful there." Josephine arched her back and stretched her arms. "The morning will be busy. We must cook for the hands. They leave on the cattle drive on Sunday. Monday at the latest."

She thought that might mean Ryan would be leaving as well. Her insides ached at the thought of yet another friend leaving. Her mother had always taught her that she was never alone. That God was always nearby. Even Aunt Fawn, in her own way, had sought to soothe her homesickness with promises of God's presence. It had brought her peace then; it could as well now. She smiled and covered Josephine's hand with her own.

"You can stay as long as you'd like, Olivia. You are welcome here." Josephine hesitated as wetness veiled her eyes. "I have always wanted a daughter, and you are like a daughter to me."

Olivia couldn't deny the draw of Josephine's words. Already God had answered the prayer of her heart.

Chapter 28

Ryan spent the morning with Bobby shoeing the extra horses. It was hot work that had them both soaked with sweat. When Ryan lowered the last hoof to the ground and stretched his aching back, Bobby swept him over to the chuckwagon for another check on progress. Bedrolls were already loaded, and the cook, Welt Ribbin, was stacking sacks of flour and beans. To Ryan's eye, Welt Ribbin looked older and more shriveled than a man of forty-nine should. Bobby must have seen his hesitation.

"Got him cheap."

"Hope it doesn't mean he's a terrible cook." Drives were hard enough without having to endure undercooked beans and burned bacon.

"Already tried him out. Makes the best biscuits I ever had."

Welt waggled his fingers, indicating Ryan should pass him another sack of beans. "I'll get 'em fed up and happy. Sleep like babies, they will."

Ryan raised the sack to the bed, and Welt dragged it over and stacked it.

"If'n you're done with me, I'll head over to the house and see if the womenfolk need some help. Teach them how to make some of my famous biscuits." Welt grinned and leaned so close Ryan could smell his fetid breath. "Not many women can make a good biscuit."

Amused at the man's audacity, Ryan kept his mouth shut. Soon enough Welt would figure out that Josephine Laxalt would rather be dragged by a horse through town than have a man in her kitchen. And especially a man who thought he could cook better than her.

"Should I have warned him?" he asked as they watched Welt waddle toward the house.

"Naw, your mama will have fun putting him in his place." Bobby lifted his hat and swiped at the sweat on his forehead. A frown mark folded a deep crease between his brows. "The men got to talking last night. . ."

Ryan leaned against the side of the wagon. "About?"

"Seems Cody and Ty are thinking one of us should stay. Help you guard the place."

"I can handle it."

Bobby gave a stiff nod. "Wasn't thinking you couldn't. Might keep the wolves at bay if they thought you and your mother weren't vulnerable."

Ryan stretched upright, his sore muscles protesting. "Like I said, I can handle it."

"As stubborn as your father."

He pushed off the wagon and lifted his nose. The acrid smell of burned hide filled the air.

"Almost done with the trail brand. Looked over Almanzo's herd yesterday. It's smaller than ours, but he's adding four men to the drive."

"More help will be a welcome thing for all involved."

"Ken's over at Hector's," Bobby said as he scattered the hot coals of the shoeing fire. "I'm headed over to relieve him."

"Ken?"

"One of the hires. Snagged him yesterday from a bar. Guess he was too scruffy for the big ranchers to notice."

"Is gathering hands always a problem?"

"Not until the big ranches got to hiring away our regulars. More money."

"Ken done a drive before?"

"Yeah. Up from Texas to Kansas."

"What brought him all the way out here and put him in a bar?"

"Drinking to forget, he says. Lost his woman giving birth to their son."

"The boy?"

Bobby shook his head.

"I want a clean trail, Bobby."

"I will, boss. No booze." The foreman stared hard over Ryan's shoulder, his jaw working. "I'm thinking the man needs a friend more than anything else."

Ryan could see where his father would have taken to the kindhearted foreman. That the man had a good eye for men also helped make him a good boss. A quality his father would have seen right away, just as his father seemed to see all the qualities a man was capable of, even if he never produced them. "Guess every man needs someone at some point."

"Sure, boss." Bobby lifted his hat and fanned the smoke. "That little Sattler gal wouldn't be such a bad friend."

Ryan glanced at his foreman, searching for any sign that Bobby meant disrespect. He saw only honesty in the man's weathered face, but he didn't want to answer the unspoken question and changed the subject. "Sheriff Bradley give you a hard time?"

Bobby shrugged. "Hector was talking just fine right before Ken got there. Never said one word about you beating him up, but he couldn't remember much either. That lump on his head might be the reason for that."

So the sheriff had been bluffing. No surprise. Ryan ground his teeth together, vexed by the dishonesty of a man who'd taken an oath to be upright in his dealings.

"The herd is smaller this year."

Ryan knew what that meant. "We'll pay the men what we owe and make do."

"Sounds like you might be planning to stay on permanent."

"What do you think Cody and Ty would say to that?"

Bobby's grin was huge. "They'd welcome it. We all would. Sattler would pick off the cattle one by one if he had to." The foreman shifted his weight and plucked the hat from his head as Cody and Ty came in from the corral. "Cook must not have gotten the boot from your mama's kitchen. He's waving at us to come eat."

They entered with the rest of the hands, bareheaded and polite in the company of the two women. Ryan noticed more than one curious glance at Olivia. She seemed oblivious to them all as she wore a path between the cookstove and the table, passing Josephine in the rush. Welt set a platter of biscuits on the table and took his seat at the end nearest to the kitchen.

"Your mama didn't like it too well, but I whipped up some biscuits and convinced her."

What Welt didn't see was the rolling of Josephine's eyes and the secret smile she shared with Olivia.

Ryan heaped a biscuit with jam and let the conversation flow around him. He offered a word here and there to keep things going, but his sole interest was in the woman folding squares of cloth on the other side of the kitchen. Her hair hung loose on her shoulders in soft waves that made his palms itch with the need to touch them. She turned, and he dropped his gaze. The last thing he needed was for her to get the wrong idea about his attention.

When Olivia refilled mugs of coffee, he found himself watching her all over again. He was mesmerized by the tiny smile she flicked at Welt as he passed her an empty platter. Then she was near Ryan's end of the table offering a refill on coffee. He nodded and held his cup. Her skirts rustled, and he did his best to ignore the sight of her slender hand holding the coffeepot. He fastened his eyes on Bobby and spouted some inane conversation he hoped made some sense. If Bobby noticed anything amiss, he didn't show it. Only when she returned to the cookstove was he able to draw an easy breath.

Bobby leaned forward and asked a question that made no sense to him. Something about pink bunnies and cancan skirts? But he trusted his foreman had asked a sensible question and it was only his hearing that couldn't make out the right words. He nodded at Bobby in answer.

Bobby reared back in his chair and barked a laugh.

Ryan scowled. The foreman leaned forward, and this time Ryan paid close attention.

"I thought she might have you distracted. I asked if you wanted to dress the horses in cancan skirts." He shook his head. "She's got you tied up tighter than a roped calf."

Bobby's tan face creased into a grin. Before he could form a proper retaliation, the foreman scooted his chair back and addressed the hands. "Let's get going, boys. We've got a long day before pulling out tomorrow." He ran a hand over his neck as he returned his attention to Ryan. "I'll take care of things, boss."

❧

Ryan sat rooted to his spot as the men filed out of the kitchen. Maybe he'd change his mind and go out on the drive. But his mother tied his hands. He couldn't leave her, and when his gaze landed on Olivia, all thought of leaving became distasteful.

Olivia stacked plates, and he rose to take them from her. Her smile made his mouth go dry. His mother appeared, holding out a sack tied with hemp in one hand. She placed it on the table in front of Olivia. "Here you go."

"What's this?"

His mother's smile encompassed both him and Olivia, and those dark eyes shone with mischief. "A picnic lunch."

Olivia sputtered. "But I thought. . ."

Josephine half turned toward her. "I never said the picnic was for you and me."

Olivia blinked up at him.

Ryan didn't know what to say, but the idea of spending the day with Olivia. . . There was only one correct answer. "Thank you."

Chapter 29

"Your mother is quite the plotter," Olivia said. She tipped her chin toward the sunshine. It felt good to see her so at ease, but he knew Jay Sattler would not take kindly to his daughter lodging at the Laxalts'. He didn't know how she would react to the question, but it begged to be asked. "What about your father? He needs to know where you are."

Olivia scratched her cheek and touched the tip of her nose where he saw that the skin had begun to peel. "I'm going to move into town. Live in Phoebe's old apartment and work for Robert."

"Quitting the paper already?"

Her look was scathing. "You know Tom wouldn't print anything I wrote unless it was what he deemed acceptable. I'd rather write for Marv."

"He can't pay you."

"And I wouldn't want him to. It's my way of making up for whatever wrongs—"

"Don't do it to spite your father."

She sighed. "No. Your mother said the same thing, and I'm not."

"Are you going to tell him?"

"I will. Today. Later. I just want to think about it and make sure it's the right thing to do. To pray."

To pray. Ryan squinted into the morning sunshine. Maybe it was time for him to give God a chance. It would feel good to embrace something bigger than himself. And yet it was more than that, too. He'd heard enough from his mother to know her opinion on doing what was right when faced with choices. His most regretful choice had been condemning an innocent man before knowing the full truth. A mistake he determined with God's help not to make again.

His gut clenched as the familiar weight of guilt shifted against his conscience. He'd been wrong. Wrong to kill. Wrong to condemn without hearing both sides. It would be easy to excuse his behavior as shooting in self-defense, and he had, but he had also been determined to bring the man in to jail and collect his money whether the man was dead or alive.

The weight of his sin pressed harder. If only he could have a second chance. But he couldn't. He could only learn to be fair and patient. He squeezed his eyes shut. *I'm so sorry.* His throat thickened. *Help me be the man You want me to be. Fair. Honest. Hardworking.*

❧

Olivia followed Ryan through narrow cuts and wide pastures. They rode for an hour by her best guess toward the Big Horns. It didn't seem to her that he was following any certain path but just meandering. She wanted to ask, but he seemed so deep in his thoughts.

Her own problems swirled thicker than the dust coating every stitch of her clothing. In the deep recesses of her mind, something Phoebe had said the previous evening bothered her, but the more she tried to focus on it, the further it slipped away. She wondered if Ryan had picked up on anything.

"Ryan?"

He reined his horse in closer, all attention on her. "Need to stop? It sure is hot."

She set aside her question and let him think that was going to be her request. Besides, a rest would be good. Her hips ached from being in the saddle for so long. "I guess I need to do more riding."

"There's a stream up ahead. We'll stop there." His grin put a sparkle in his eyes that pulled her in. The angles of his face gave him a tough appearance, but his smile melted away the hard edges, and she could see more of the little-boy mischievousness that his mother had probably had her fill of when he was young. "It's the far corner of your father's property."

"I don't remember this part." That wasn't saying much, since her father's ranch was bigger than her nine-year-old body ever could have hoped to explore. But now, on horseback, she wanted to see it all.

East of them, the sun glinted off water. Nudges of the past came forward. She pointed. "Let's go there."

When they stopped in the shade and she knelt to drink, the need for rain became even more apparent. Tree branches arched over a very shallow pool, familiar somehow.

"It's not the best quality, but it's wet," Ryan said. He led the horses closer so they could drink. "I should have warned you to drink your fill before we left."

"I wish you would have."

The horses didn't hesitate to suck up the water.

She pulled off her hat and fanned herself. Ryan knelt at the edge of the water. His broad back hid his actions from her view, but when he faced her and held out his damp kerchief, she accepted it without hesitation.

"Press it to your neck. Like this."

He took it from her hand and refolded it into a long rectangle. "Now lay it across the back of your neck."

She lifted her hair with one hand and placed the cool rag along the hot skin. Ryan plucked the string from his hat and held it out. "As much as I love to see your hair down, better use this to tie it up. You'll be cooler."

Feeling like a child, she reached out to take the thin piece of leather. Aware that he was watching her, she lifted her hair, gathered it together, and looped the leather tie around her curls. She felt his eyes on her and marveled at how easily they had come to know each other. Things had changed between them since those first days, and she welcomed it. But even as she felt drawn to Ryan and thought he felt drawn to her, she worried what danger their relationship presented to him and his mother.

"We should eat. I'll need to check in with Bobby."

"I thought Bobby said he would take care of things."

Ryan glanced at her as he lifted the sack of food from his saddlebags. He fussed with the hemp, not looking at her. She allowed herself a little smile. Ryan Laxalt, she realized, was shy. If living in the city had taught her anything, it was socialization. Still, she should have seen that his quiet nature would align itself with shyness.

Olivia took a step closer. "Need help with that, cowpoke?"

He raised his eyes to hers and held it out. "Can't seem to get my fingers around that knot."

When her hand brushed against the bag, he withdrew as if touching her meant spreading cholera. "Ryan?"

He looked like a man trying hard not to show fear. "I'll get the blanket."

"Wait a minute."

He stopped and faced her.

"Don't you think it's time?"

A bead of sweat trickled down his cheek as she took another step closer. "For what?"

"To kiss me."

Chapter 30

She held out her hand to him. An offer. An invitation that he would be a fool to ignore. "Shouldn't we. . .I mean. . . Don't couples court first?"

"I'm open to that idea, too."

Ryan relaxed as laughter bubbled in his chest. She was so honest. She'd seen right through his excuse of eating so they could get back. He didn't want to go back, truth be told, but neither was he sure what to do with the feelings being near her stirred. He felt unsure of himself; having never been a ladies' man put him at a disadvantage. What did he have to talk about other than the ranch and his mother and the Wyoming heat?

He would be nothing like the men back east. Suave and mannerly in their crisp jackets with their fancy pocket watches and perfectly barbered hair.

"Ryan?" She took a step closer, and he felt choked by her nearness.

"Did you have a lot of admirers back east?"

Her brow knit. "You mean, did I have a beau?"

He gulped air and nodded.

"No. Though Aunt Fawn sure tried. The men were always worried about calling cards and proper dress." She made a face. "It's one of the reasons why I wanted to come back, though I didn't quite understand that until I was able to put away the fancy dresses and expensive hats."

"You don't miss it?"

"Ryan Laxalt." Humor glinted in her gaze. "What are you so worried about? That I have someone waiting for me back east?"

"No. More that you might not."

She shook her head. "I don't understand."

"If you did, that would end everything. But because you don't. . ." He reached out to cup her cheek, and she nestled her face against his hand. Though the light of her spirit beckoned him, the reality of who she was made him hesitate. He could not broach the subject in his heart without lancing the fester of another worry. "I want to do this right, Livy. No secrets."

Her smile dimmed. "Secrets?"

"Not mine, but the one we would have to keep from your father."

She pulled back. "We'll tell him, then."

"Do you know the wrath we might suffer as a result? I have to think of my mother's safety, of our ranch."

Olivia presented her back to him.

"I'm sorry. It's as much a problem for me as it is for you." He wanted to continue that statement. To speak the truth he'd known to be true in his heart since that night at the meeting, but the words died before crossing his lips. Not here. Not in the shadow of her father's disapproval.

"Ryan. . ."

There was a tremor in her voice, but when she faced him, she raised a hand to point, a new alertness in her expression. "That tree. It's the one I remember. This pond. . .Daddy tied the horses up here, and we walked over to my mother's grave."

He lifted his eyes in the direction she pointed. A large bur oak stood, it's massive branches each as big around as a sack of flour.

"Are you sure?"

"Yes," she breathed, a new excitement in her voice.

He took the lunch from her and tied it to the back of the mustang's saddle then gave her a hand up. They moved in unspoken agreement toward the spot. As they neared, the green crown appeared to rise out of the ground to show off its thick trunk. Yet Ryan saw no sign of a grave marker.

"Oaks are pretty common to this area." He tried to smooth over the obvious. "It could have been—"

"No. It was this one, Ryan. This tree—I'm sure of it. I remember the pond, the slow walk up here from the water, and the mountains framing the background."

He scanned the area farther out and glimpsed something through a thick copse of trees. "There's a cabin over there. If anyone's there, they might be able to tell you if there's a grave nearby." Ryan doubted it. A memory from when she was nine years old would be more than a little hazy. Surely. On the other hand, if she was at the grave of her mother, wouldn't it have made an indelible impression?

To him the cabin didn't look very old. Nothing moved, but there was a curious mix of spring flowers blooming in the front. A rose grew in wild abandon at the corner of the house. Greenery would have withered by now in the drought, yet the rose's green leaves made Ryan cautious. Someone had watered the rose—daily, by the looks of it. The flowers in the front were healthier closer to the bush, recipients of the runoff, no doubt.

Olivia galloped her mare to the place and slipped to the ground before he could caution her. She ran to the front door and pounded her small fist against the wood.

Ryan scanned the cabin and thought he saw the slightest movement at a tiny window. He left the horse to cross to Olivia as she pounded again. A scuffling sound came from within and then a scream.

Chapter 31

Olivia's fingers curled around Ryan's arm. The horror of that high-pitched scream jolted through her body. When the door suddenly swung open, a pale-faced woman glared at her then over her shoulder at Ryan.

"What do you want?" She turned to look behind her, shifting her body as if to block the view. "Mr. Sattler send you here with the food?"

"I'm sorry." Olivia's voice snagged the woman's attention away from Ryan. The matron stared, eyes narrowed. A slow dawning of understanding twisted her expression a second before she slammed the door.

Olivia turned away, shaken and confused.

"Livy?"

Ryan placed his hand on her shoulder.

From inside the cabin they could hear the woman's raised voice calling out to someone. Nothing made sense, not the woman's reception or her reaction or. . .

Olivia caught movement out of the corner of her eye at the same time Ryan's hand on her shoulder gripped harder. She turned to see a woman standing there. Her curly hair, gray at the temples, was smoothed back and held by two combs. And her face. . .

"Olivia." Ryan breathed her name.

The woman giggled, arms wrapped around herself. "I sneak out the back door sometimes. Agnes never remembers to lock it." She tilted her head in a childish way. "Are you my little girl?"

❧

Ryan held on to Olivia's shoulder, bracing her up. The resemblance between the two women had struck him at once, and the sickening truth presented itself the moment the woman asked that question.

Olivia half turned to him, and he pulled her back against him, sharing his strength with her. Agnes flung open the front door and gasped when she saw the childlike woman.

"Lily, you shouldn't be out here bothering these people."

Olivia seemed to come alive and broke free of his grasp. "Mama?"

Agnes moved to block Olivia's advance. "Listen, child." Her voice became softer, placating. "Listen to me. It's not what you think. Go home. Talk to your father. Please."

"I want to talk to my mother."

"I can't let you do that." Agnes raised her voice; her tone was firm. "Go inside now, Lily." She spoke over her shoulder. "You're not safe out here."

Ryan curled his arm around Olivia's waist and pulled her away from the woman. With one last backward glance at them, Agnes followed Lily inside.

Olivia seemed dazed. No tears. No hysterics. Nothing. He turned her toward him. "Olivia?"

"Mama." Her little-girl voice rocked his spirit.

He ran his hand over her springy curls. He was afraid to speak for fear of making the situation worse with what he could only speculate. He held her close; his hand cupped the back of her head, and her face was buried against his shoulder. Ryan rocked her as they stood, wishing he could absorb the emotions pummeling her mind and heart.

❧

Shock waves pulsed along Olivia's nerves. She felt on fire with disbelief. The enormity of all she'd just experienced. Her mother. . .

Alive.

Olivia closed her eyes. Ryan's arms were protective and warm when she felt so cold and hollow. Phoebe's stricken look as Olivia had asked about her mother's grave burst into her mind and crumbled her emotions further. Phoebe had known. She was sure of it. Bile burned in Olivia's throat. How many others knew? One after another the questions rolled through her mind.

"Livy. . ."

Ryan's rough whisper was filled with concern.

"You're shaking. Are you cold?"

She nodded against his shirt, and he massaged her arms, trying to bring warmth into her skin. She felt cocooned in a white haze where no thought penetrated and nothing mattered. She felt herself lifted, carried, and she was going to shut her eyes against the bright light. . .the sun? But the light persisted. Only the wall of warmth at her back seemed real. Then she blinked and understood that she was on the mustang. Ryan was behind her with his arm securing her in place, and they were galloping. Trees blurred by, and the heat beat down on her bare head. Ryan shifted behind her, and the heat lessened.

He stopped, and she watched uncomprehendingly as he knelt and lifted something. Then he was beside her again, and she felt the saddle shift as he mounted behind her. His rough fingers plucked at the neck of her dress, and a coolness lay there that brought out the shivers all the more.

"Lean against me, Livy. I'll get you home."

Home.

The word echoed strangely through her mind, disjointed, not a part of her or who she was. She pitched forward on a sob, but his strong arm kept her from falling.

"Livy." His voice broke, a pleading whisper against her ear, and then nothing.

Chapter 32

Olivia's mother ran to her, arms outstretched. Lillian Sattler whispered cheerfully against her nine-year-old ear. The sun shone down on their shoulders as Lily embraced her daughter and filled her in on the trip into town. Her words were a blur in Livy's mind, but her mother's skirt scratched against her cheek, and her hand was warm as she cradled Livy's face for a kiss then pulled out a small sack of peppermints.

Olivia's velvet slumber became the backdrop against which other long-forgotten scenes flashed. Smells. Her mother's golden bread slathered with jam. Lily's white apron. Tiny stitches that marked the passage of her mother's needle along the seams of Livy's favorite green dress. And underscoring all of it, the smell of peppermint. . . .

"Olivia?"

She opened her eyes, fully expecting to see her mother, but the scent dissipated and the face had dark eyebrows and hair. Kind eyes and gentle hands. She recalled the rasp of a voice against her ear, of warm arms lifting her, but not this woman's voice or arms. It was a man's. . . .

"Mrs. Laxalt." She breathed the word. "Ryan?" She closed her eyes, trying to piece it all together. Her mother's voice but not her mother at all. It had been the voice of a childlike waif; only the face was that of her mother.

Josephine lifted a cool cloth to Olivia's forehead. "Stay quiet. Sleep. Ryan went for the doctor. I've never seen him more worried than he was over you."

"Mama?"

Josephine went still, staring down at her in a strange way. "I'm not your mother." Her soft hand stroked Olivia's cheek. "Though I would dearly enjoy the privilege."

Olivia felt the stream of wetness streak her cheek. She was unable to find the words to clarify the miscommunication, and she wasn't sure she had the energy anyway. Josephine's words were enough, like a warm blanket on a cold winter night. She would wait for Ryan to return. She stiffened in fear.

"What is it, child?"

"Ryan's coming back, isn't he?"

"Yes, my baby. He'll bring the doctor."

Fear exploded in her chest, and she turned her head aside. A sob escaped, followed by another. Josephine leaned in close and slipped her arms around Livy's shoulders. She lifted her to a sitting position, where Olivia let her tears fall in a daze of hurt and confusion.

"I'm here, Livy. I'm here."

Her throat throbbed with the fierceness of her crying and the rawness of wounds ripped open by a dose of harsh reality.

❧

Every beat of the mustang's hooves was synchronized with the pounding of Ryan's heart. He had felt Olivia's despair and seen the evidence of her confusion as he'd rushed her to the only place he could think to take her—back to his mother. He knew his mother's love for Olivia would be a succor.

Anger burned like a hot coal in his gut. Jay Sattler had known his wife was alive. He'd sent Olivia off thinking her mother dead. Cold reasoning nudged at him with the truth. If Livy's mother had fallen into a stupor of unconsciousness and woken with her mind weakened, perhaps Jay had meant only to spare his daughter the distress. That he had shipped Olivia east made perfect sense in light of the truth, but it didn't excuse the man from not telling his grown daughter upon her return. Did he truly think she would never find out? She at least deserved to know the truth as an adult and be given the chance to deal with it in her own way.

His thoughts shifted back and forth as he rode, oblivious to the scenery. Only the beating of the horse's hooves and the need to get back to Olivia seemed real. He wanted to hold her close, feel her breath against his cheek, stare into those whiskey eyes, and know for himself she would endure the shock. They would face it together. He would bring in Jay Sattler and demand that the man talk to his daughter and help her understand why he had done what he had.

In the heat of the day, Buffalo was a lazy town. Ryan didn't see anyone. When he found the doctor's office empty, he went first to the Occidental across the street, then to Landry's, hoping to find the man at lunch. Robert Landry himself was waiting on the two patrons present in the dining room.

"What can I get for you, Laxalt?"

"Looking for the doctor."

Robert's meaty fist swiped along his shirtfront. "He's out." The man's eyes slid toward the back of the room then fastened on Ryan again. "Got that bridle you were asking for out in the barn if you want to look at it. Not giving it to you cheap though."

Ryan opened his mouth to protest then caught the meaning of Robert's words and actions. He sidestepped the man. "I'll take a look at it."

Together they went through the back door and out into the shack behind the restaurant. Robert shut the door as Ryan struck a match and lit a lantern.

"Heard this morning that Bowman found some of his stock gone. He's accusing Jacob and Phoebe of rustling his cattle. Apparently Jacob went after Bowman and took some lead for it. Doc's over there now."

"They find evidence?"

"Sheriff Bradley doesn't need evidence. You know that. He just needs the big boys to line his pocket with money."

"How'd you hear?"

"Pete came in for the doc." He ran his hands down his aproned waist. "You got an emergency?"

Ryan squeezed his eyes shut and rubbed at the space between his eyebrows where all his tension seemed to be settling. "Went out for a ride this morning. Found a cabin back in the woods on Sattler's property. Olivia wanted—"

"You were out riding with Olivia?"

"She asked Phoebe about her mother's grave."

Robert's nostrils flared, and he spit an oath.

"You know then?"

"Everyone knows."

"Then why didn't anyone have the guts to tell her? Do you know what it did to her to stumble upon her mother living out in the middle of nowhere, guarded like a criminal?"

Robert's hand clamped down on his shoulder. "You've got to understand. Sattler's in control. It's his secret, and the whole town knows about it. If one of us told it and he found out, do you think for a minute he wouldn't take out his revenge?"

"Isn't he doing that anyway?"

The big man's hand fell away, and his expression went bland. "Yeah. I guess he is." His words were soft. "Agnes is a good woman. She's paid well to guard Lily."

"You seen her lately?"

"Lily?" He shook his head. "No. Never. One of Sattler's men picks up supplies to take out there."

Ryan's mind tracked Robert's words closely. The inflection changed when he talked about Agnes. "You know Agnes pretty well?"

Robert's eyes snapped to his. "About once a month she comes to town for supper."

"Doesn't anyone question that? Who she is? Why they never see her."

Again Landry shook his head, his expression pained. "No. She's my wife."

Chapter 33

Robert Landry shared everything then. The reason he was both indebted to Sattler and appalled by what the land barons were doing to the little men. "I thought I'd have to close the restaurant, but Sattler offered to help me out. We went way back, so I didn't think a thing about it. But he confided that Lily had become too much for Phoebe, and he needed someone else. He asked Agnes if she would do it, and she agreed. The money was good. It helped us stay open when the Occidental would have put us out of business."

"That's it? You're content never to see your wife? No one wonders where she is or what she's doing?"

"Rumor was she was going a couple towns over to help her invalid mother. Jay must have started it. How could we dispute that without backing ourselves into a corner? But eventually people figured things out."

"How about Olivia?" Tendrils of temper made him curl his fingers into fists. "What about the little girl who was sent away thinking her mother was dead?"

Robert's brows lowered. "You think I haven't thought of that? But what's the alternative? She finds out her mother is crazy?"

"Well, she found out anyway." Ryan spit the words.

"If anyone can help her through this, you can, Laxalt."

A dust devil swirled down Main Street then petered out as Ryan directed his horse away from Landry's. Everyone in town, even those at the meeting last night, wallowed in their fear of Bowman, Michaels, and Sattler. Despite the agreement that they needed to take more action and the effort to protect Hector as he healed, it wasn't going to be enough. Ryan felt sure of that now.

As much as he wanted to head back to Olivia, he couldn't. In spite of the secret Phoebe had kept from Olivia, the woman had been a friend. He didn't agree with the way she'd handled things, but neither did he agree with Robert, and there was no changing any of it now. What he could do was counter the sheriff's casual disregard for upholding justice, and he would have to do it alone.

Following Robert's directions, Ryan headed out of town the same way he'd come in, at a fast gallop. If Jacob Isley was laid low by a bullet, he would head out there to check on the situation, let the doctor know of Olivia's need, and help Phoebe keep Sheriff Bradley in line.

The face of his father loomed in Ryan's mind, and he thought Martin Laxalt just might be smiling.

❧

Olivia woke with a start. Josephine's hand stilled her and smoothed her hair back.

"What time is it?" she mumbled, noting the shadowed light in the window.

"It's getting on suppertime. Are you hungry, child?"

All Olivia could think of were the bacon sandwiches that never got eaten, of Agnes standing in the doorway then slamming the door in their faces, and of her mother's frail silhouette and her singsong voice.

"My mother is alive."

Josephine's dark eyes glittered. "Ryan said something about you finding your mother. Do you want to talk about it?"

"Where's Ryan?"

Josephine stood up from her chair and stared out the window. "I don't know. He should have been back by now. He was pretty upset, and I suspect a lot of his anger is focused on your father."

She understood at once what Josephine feared. That her son would try and take on her father and end up getting shot.

"He loves you, you know." Josephine turned, a small smile on her lips. "I've never seen him like this."

Olivia didn't know what to say, so she said nothing. He was late returning, and Josephine's fears were becoming hers. She pulled herself to a sitting position, and energy flowed into her limbs. If nothing else, she needed to make good on her promise to tell her father of her intentions to move into town and work at Landry's, but what she wanted more than anything was the whole story about her mother. To know why he had chosen to keep her mother's life a secret. Had her mental state embarrassed him? She could not leave her mother alone, not now that she knew the truth.

She shifted and swung her legs to the floor. Josephine pulled the chair away from the bed.

"Are you sure you're feeling better?"

"I need to go to my father." Josephine's hand guided her to her feet. "Did you know my mother was alive?"

Ryan's mother shook her head. "I knew only what you were led to believe, that she had been sick and died."

Satisfied, Olivia smoothed her skirt, frowning at the wrinkles. "If Ryan returns with the doctor, tell him I'll be back, but please, please don't tell him where I went. Not yet."

"He will know."

It was true. She had already told him earlier that she had plans to talk to her father. After finding her mother, it would be the most logical conclusion to explain her absence.

Olivia put her hands on Josephine's elbows and squeezed. "Then if he's bent on coming after me, make sure he has a gun."

Chapter 34

Doc Herald shook his head as he came out of Jacob Isley's room, mad through and through, if Ryan was any judge of the man's expression.

"Who shot him?"

Doc Herald slumped into a chair and crossed his arms. "Never could get a straight answer out of anyone. Phoebe says it was the sheriff. I believe her more than the others put together. Bunch of lowdown snakes, if you want my opinion on the matter."

Ryan scratched his cheek. "Where is she?"

"Sheriff has her down at the place where he found the so-called evidence."

He pushed away from the table he'd been leaning on. "I'm headed there then."

"Be ready for anything, Laxalt. They're getting bolder."

"Because we haven't been shoving back hard enough."

Doc's eyes lit with amusement. "Do some shoving then."

"It's about time, I think."

With his hand on the door, Ryan turned. "You know anything about Lily Sattler's condition?"

Guilt spread over the doctor's face, and he dropped his gaze. "She was a sick woman."

"She's alive, Doc, and you know it. You the one who treated her?"

The doctor sat up. "Sattler knew something wasn't quite right. She'd had a fever that raged for days. Terrible. I did all I could to get it to come down, but... Then she slipped into unconsciousness. When she finally came around, she wasn't the same."

"Her mind went."

Doc nodded. "Jay took it hard. Mighty hard. He justified telling Olivia her mother was dead because it was true, to a point."

Ryan's grip tightened on the smooth wood beneath the pads of his fingers. "Olivia found out today. We found the cabin back in the woods."

"Oh my—"

"It was like it shattered something inside her. I rode into town to get you."

Doc was shaking his head. "Where is she?"

"I left her with my mother."

"Best place for her. She's strong. For any girl to take a stand against her own father, that's saying a lot." Doc scooted around in the chair and stood. "I've done about all I can for Jacob. Might be a good idea for me to go with you down there."

Ryan appreciated the man's offer. "Come on then." He turned toward the mustang and pulled his Marlin rifle from the saddle. "You might need this."

❧

The sun had begun to sink when Olivia reached her father's house, bathing the yard and house in a rosy glow. No one came out to question her arrival or ask about her absence. The hands must have still been out on the range. She lifted her booted foot and took the last step to the front door of the home she'd been raised in. Her father had to have had a reason for what he did, muddled though it might have been by the grief he'd surely felt over her mother's sickness. Olivia inhaled deeply and raised her hand to knock. The pressure of her fist unlatched the door, and it swung inward with a low moan. But no one was holding the door.

The bare wooden floor creaked, and she jerked back. She stood still, straining to hear movement, and hugged herself against the chill of her stretched-tight nerves. Pulled by memories, she went to the section of the pantry where her mother's apron hung. Tears burned her eyes as she stroked the familiar material. She'd come for answers, yet maybe she'd been wrong. If her father would not answer her questions, the woman with her mother would surely know something.

She took the apron down off the peg and went out to the front porch where she settled into an old rocker. She would give her father some time before she went to Agnes. If he wouldn't answer her questions, she would at least confront him about his dealings with the other cattle barons. She should have done so long ago. If Ryan arrived, she would do her best to bring the three of them together and work peace into the relationship, and maybe, just maybe, her father could learn to accept Ryan.

And Ryan. He wanted to do things the right way and tell her father of their plans to court. She would honor that, and if her father didn't open up to her on the matters weighing on her mind, then she would move forward with her plans to live and work in town. And if Ryan Laxalt was part of that future—she smiled—then she would welcome his love and companionship.

The sun set over the dry land, leaving a vast expanse of pale sky fading to dark gray in its wake. She knew it wouldn't be long before her father came home. She gathered the apron close. She would wait; she had time.

Chapter 35

Sheriff Bradley struck an authoritative pose as Ryan and Doc Herald drew rein on their horses. All around the man and his companion, a bedraggled Skinny Bonnet, were hoofprints. Sharp edges of cut wire winked at Ryan as he swung down. Phoebe sat on a rock not far from the area in question.

"What do you want, Laxalt?"

Things would not go well, Ryan knew, but he was determined to keep things civil until he could take a closer look at the ground. Doc stood silently a little behind him.

"Since Jacob can't look at the evidence himself, Doc and I decided we'd be his eyes and ears."

"This is evidence. You can't come closer."

Phoebe stood and blinked as if dazed. She lurched forward then broke toward them. Doc Herald took a step in her direction and reached to steady her when she stumbled. "You should be at the house with Jacob," the doctor told the woman.

"I had to come. He wouldn't believe me." She shook her head, and her eyes welled with tears. "It's not fair. Jacob didn't even do anything." Her gaze swung to Ryan, and he felt the weight of duty being placed squarely on his shoulders.

His gaze went to Skinny's dusty boots then the dark scowl on the foreman's face. "That evidence you want to protect so much. . . Seems to me Sattler's man has already been allowed the privilege to examine it."

"I'm working for Bowman on this." Skinny sneered. "I'm an investigator."

"I think it's time we hire ourselves an investigator who doesn't have a stake in the big ranches."

Bradley's expression tightened. "I don't like the sound of what you're saying."

"And I don't like a sheriff who can't give a man a fair shake at defending himself before he starts shooting."

"Seems we're even then."

The sheriff's smile was cold, and Ryan understood how the man would think such a thing. "I learned from my mistake, Bradley. That's the difference between us. It's why I didn't kill Sattler right off."

"You sure didn't give Stephens a chance. You collected your money though, didn't you?"

"And I took it back when I discovered the truth."

"That doesn't make Stephens alive again. It just means you're a hotheaded killer."

There would be no convincing the sheriff of anything. "You would understand that last part better than most."

Bradley's lips twisted. "Jacob had it coming."

Phoebe took a step forward, eyes blazing. "That's not true—" Ryan held out his hand to block her momentum and halt her protest. She blinked at him, confused.

"Trust me," he whispered.

She gave a reluctant nod. Ryan swung his attention to the foreman then to the sheriff, who had positioned himself between Ryan and the area in question. Skinny Bonnet hadn't moved a muscle. Strange behavior for a man so bent on action. Stranger still that the man hadn't offered more than the sneering reprimand.

"Watch that Bonnet," Doc Herald said close to Ryan's ear. "He's poison."

"That's why I gave you the rifle."

Doc blanched and glanced at the weapon in his hands. "Should have told you, I'm not one for shootin'."

"Hard times call for hard decisions, Doc. If you can't do it, hand it off to Phoebe. She'd be delighted to put some holes in the sheriff's hide about now."

Ryan took a deliberate step forward then another. The sheriff flinched and glanced over his shoulder at Skinny. Ryan ignored both men and skimmed along the dusty, hoofprint-laden ground. "How many head?"

"Thirty," the sheriff bit out.

"Doesn't look like prints enough for that many."

"You callin' me a liar, Laxalt?"

"No." Ryan let the word settle. His eyes flicked to Skinny. "I'm calling Bonnet a liar."

Bonnet's angular jaw tightened. His faded eyes were pale as a rattler. His hand hovered over his gun, and Ryan held his breath. He was sure the man's stillness, his lack of appetite for violence, had less to do with the rifle in Doc Herald's hand and more to do with the boots on his feet.

It was simple, really, Ryan knew. And it heralded back to a case he'd worked for the Rangers to expose a group of rustlers. "Not going to draw, Bonnet? Most men would shoot me dead for such a thing. Especially those with a quick temper."

Skinny opened his mouth and spewed a stream of vileness.

Ryan let himself smile. "My mother would make sure you spent a day and night locked in the outhouse for such talk."

"Wait till it's just you and me, Laxalt. Just you and me on a hot day, and I'll be watching the buzzards pick your eyes out."

"So why don't you move over here, and we'll settle it. These good people can be our witnesses."

Out of the corner of his eye, Ryan caught the sheriff pivoting toward him. He turned to meet the blow and used his forearm to deflect the punch. It was the bark of the Marlin that stilled the sheriff. His slit eyes rounded with wonder and shock. He staggered back and clutched his midsection.

"You're not hit, Bradley. Doc couldn't hit the side of a barn." Ryan swiped the sweat from his upper lip and kicked the sheriff's gun along the ground and toward Phoebe. "But don't take a swing at a man when he holds all the cards."

Bradley sputtered and straightened. "I don't know what you're talking about."

"Sure you do. That's the reason why you tried to crack me along the head." Ryan knelt in the dirt and measured the length of the hoofprints, following their path with his eyes. Behind him he heard Phoebe's sharp intake of breath and knew she, too, understood where he was going with his words.

"Looks to me like Mr. Bonnet is rooted to the spot." He stood and rubbed his jaw. "For good reason, too. Doc, why don't you hand that rifle to Phoebe and take Skinny's guns."

Skinny's face twisted. His hand flashed downward, but the rifle barked again, and the shot twisted Skinny backward and to the left. He didn't move.

Sheriff Bradley grunted and glared. His face ashen.

"Now." Phoebe's voice cracked like a shot. "I suggest you stay right where you are, Sheriff. At least until Ryan's had himself a chance to check out the bottoms of Mr. Bonnet's boots."

❧

Jay Sattler moved from the shadow of the night and into the fingers of light flickering from the lantern Olivia had lit. His beard shaded his jaw and hid his mouth, but his eyes, vacant, hurt, told a tale of despair. He had transformed into an old man as soon as Olivia had invited him to the porch and told him she had found her mother.

"It didn't have to be this way, Daddy." Her heart squeezed tighter with each word.

He stared out into the night. "Were you with Laxalt last night?"

"Is that all you care about?"

"It's enough." His voice came heavy. "You think I want my daughter taking up with a Laxalt?"

"You mean 'the enemy,' don't you? But he's your enemy, not mine. I have no ties to this land, remember? You made sure of that when you sent me east."

"I didn't want you to know. . . ." He cracked his knuckles, and Olivia saw his struggle. "It all came out wrong."

"You told me she was dead and watched me grieve."

He jerked toward her. "It was better that way. Don't you see? You would have rather had a mother who was crazy?"

"Yes."

"You wouldn't have, Livy. Believe me. You say that now that you're an adult, but as a nine-year-old, it would have shattered you."

She couldn't say anything. He had made the decision for her all those years ago, and what was done was done. "You were ashamed of her?"

Her father didn't answer for long minutes. The night breeze swept through, hot and dry, perfuming the air with the scent of dust and cattle dung—a smell Olivia would always associate with this moment.

Her father lowered his chin to his chest, and she heard his sharp intake of breath. The sound should have softened her, but she could think of nothing but her mother stuck in that cabin, of her nine-year-old grief, and most of all, of the man she had known as her father who had turned into a stranger with decayed morals.

"I wanted her to be well. Can you understand that? I thought that getting her away to a new place would help. Be less stressful on her mind and help her to heal. But it never helped. Nothing helped." His chest rose. "All I wanted was my family."

"Then why did you send me away?"

"Your mother. . .everything. . .it was too much. I couldn't think." He clamped his hands onto the railing. "What do I know about raising a girl? It was too much, and then Fawn offered."

"She knew?" Olivia felt a new wave of anger. This one directed at her aunt.

"No, of course not. She wanted to take you and give you the training you needed to be a lady, and I thought it was what your mother would have wanted."

"You know it wasn't. I would have been happier here. All the time I was in Philadelphia I felt like an outsider, and you never wrote."

"What was there for me to say, Olivia? Could you have handled the truth? Did you want to know what it felt like to—" He collected himself and squeezed his eyes shut, fingers pressed against the lids. Her own throat burned with the honest answers to his questions.

"It was ripping me apart inside. And I knew"—his hands fell to his side, and his eyes were red with trace emotion—"I knew I had to protect you from the pain of the reality. She doesn't know who I am. Didn't remember you or me or. . .anyone here. She thinks I'm just some nice man who delivers supplies and likes to listen to her talk." His chest heaved.

Olivia stood. The coldness she'd felt for her father was melting.

"I touch her, and she screams. Like I'm a stranger, a madman come to torment her or hurt her." He choked, and his voice was thick as his breath caught.

Her mother's change was killing her father, had been killing him for all the years she'd been gone. If nothing else, it was still clear that he cared for her, needed her to be whole. But Lily was unable to do so. The knowledge tore at Olivia and stirred her sympathy to new heights.

"Was it the fever?" she asked.

Jay shrugged. "Doc says it happens sometimes. The body recovers, but the mind gets stuck in the past." His lips pursed, and he stared up at the moon. "Lily loves to talk about her childhood. She has vivid memories of her parents and her dog." He closed his eyes, and his fists clenched.

"When I heard you were coming back, I didn't know what to do. It was so much easier to let things stay as they were."

Chapter 36

Olivia hugged herself. She wasn't quite willing to move to her father. Too many unanswered questions needed explanations.

"I've heard rumors."

Jay glanced at her. "It was what I feared, that others would tell you before I could find the courage to do so."

"No," she corrected, gathering her courage. Olivia was anxious that the shift in subject would shut down the line of communication. "No Daddy. I meant rumors about Martin Laxalt. About cattle rustling and. . .and. . ."

His mouth hardened.

"I wanted so much for it all not to be true, but the more I see, the more I hear. . ."

"It's that Laxalt boy. He's putting things in your head."

That her father could harden so fast to what she had to say was a mental punch.

"His father is dead, Daddy. I think he has a right to know what happened."

"Simple. Martin was rustling my cattle."

"Who told you that?"

Jay glared at her then stared off into the night. Her heart sank at the implication of the silence. But the fact that he stayed on the porch at all gave her hope.

"Daddy, please."

"Skinny's in charge of the men. One of them saw the cut fence and the hoofprints. What's this young man to you, Livy?"

"I love him."

Jay's eyes drilled into her. "I didn't pull the trigger if that's what you want to know. Laxalt got testy about the whole thing and pulled a gun. Skinny shot him out of self-defense." His shoulders slumped, and he hooked a boot around the bottom rail of the fence.

"Doc says he was shot in the back."

"Then he's lying!"

"Or your foreman is."

A minute passed in silence; then her father's mouth firmed. "You love him?"

"Ryan's a good man."

Jay laughed, a humorless sound. "My daughter loves the son of a thief."

His eyes cut to hers.

"He's not a thief, Daddy. Martin Laxalt was trying to get some of the restrictions lifted on brands. He's a hero to many."

"How do you know that? Been listening to them, haven't you? Small ranchers who invade our territory and steal our land."

"What happened to you thinking of them as neighbors? Men with the same hopes and dreams as you once had."

Jay stiffened. "I guess we all know where those hopes and dreams got me."

It was a bitter statement. Olivia glimpsed the hard shell her father surrounded himself with rather than dealing with painful things. "I have dreams, Daddy. Do you want to hear them?"

Jay Sattler's boots echoed along the porch to the front door. "Are you coming in for the night, or are you headed over to Laxalt's again?"

The accusation in his eyes made her head spin. She averted her face, pained by the rejection.

❧

Ryan shut his eyes for a moment and swayed in the saddle. He stretched, feeling the weariness of the mustang as it cantered toward home. Doc Herald followed close on his heels.

"You staying awake, Laxalt?"

Ryan suppressed a groan. "Don't want to be. But, yeah, I am."

"What you did back there. . ."

He didn't want to talk about it. Doc had tried numerous times to express his awe at the discovery of Skinny Bonnet's boots and the odd but effective wedge of wood with the hoofprint in relief on the soles.

"When I finally understood the direction of your thoughts, it was amazing."

Ryan shrugged. "Bonnet got sloppy. He wasn't measuring off his steps to resemble a cow's stride."

"And you got that all because he kept so still?"

Doc was unfamiliar with anything related to cows. Still, everyone had their gifts. He remained quiet as the horses went down a hill, their hooves churning dust. They were almost to the turnoff to Sattler ranch. He was tempted to take the route and roust Sattler from sleep to tell him of Skinny Bonnet's and Sheriff Bradley's fall from grace. Only his concern for Olivia kept him heading west toward home. Doc said something else, but it was lost as Ryan increased pressure on the mustang's sides and the animal put distance between them.

In mere hours, Bobby would be rousting the men, and they would start the drive. Ryan allowed himself a small grin. Without Skinny on the loose and the sheriff to back up every bad deed, perhaps small ranchers would have a greater chance at the next roundup. But that was a year away.

Ryan slid to the ground in front of the house and leaned against the mustang for a minute to collect himself. With heavy limbs, he released the saddle's cinch and lifted it from the mustang's back, returning for the saddle blanket and bridle.

A slap to the rump, and the horse gladly trotted into the corral. Doc pulled in at that point. He was blissfully silent as he tied his horse out front.

Ryan motioned for the man to follow, noting the light beaming through the panes of glass before he opened the door. His mother sat at the table, as he knew she would, but he didn't expect the lines of worry around her mouth or the words that she spoke.

"She's not here, Ryan. She went to her daddy's and hasn't come back."

His head fell back, and he released a heavy sigh.

"Looks like my services aren't needed after all," Doc murmured, and clutched his black bag. "I told you your mama's care was the best thing for her. Now I'm headed back to get some sleep." He turned at the door. "You've got yourself quite a son, Mrs. Laxalt. A chip off the old block."

❧

"You're exhausted," his mother said. "She is a smart woman, son. She will not dare ride through the night alone."

Ryan paced along the wood floor, grateful his mother did not probe for details about the doctor's pronouncement. But she was wrong about one thing. Olivia. There had been too many times when she'd tried to ride out alone at night, determined to get wherever she was going. And he knew something his mother didn't. If news got to Sattler of Skinny Bonnet's death and the sheriff's fall at his hand, Sattler would retaliate. Kill his cattle. Stage a rustling during the drive. Play his trump card and forbid Olivia from seeing him. Even now he could have formulated a plan to exact revenge.

"Drink this."

His mother pulled on his arm and directed him to the table. She pointed at a cup of coffee.

"You are just like your father, debating a problem when there is no solution to be had."

Torn by indecision, Ryan sipped at the brew. His mind was rocking with images of Olivia on horseback at night, falling to the ground—as delirious and unfocused as she'd been after seeing her mother.

His mother's hand weighted his shoulder. "Ryan. . ."

He pushed back the chair and lunged to his feet. Her hand slid away. "I'm going after her. There's too much at stake. It could mean losing everything."

"The cattle?"

Ryan half turned toward his mother. "The cattle are the least of my worries."

Chapter 37

Tears stung Olivia's eyes as she held the apron close to her cheek. Sleep would not come, and every one of Ryan's warnings about riding alone at night kept her in place. She turned over on her bed and considered undressing and slipping between the covers, but the sound of hoofbeats coming fast stopped her.

She knelt at the window. Footsteps from the direction of her father's room told her he had heard the commotion as well. Her heart pounded in fear. If it was Ryan, what would her father's reaction be? Or Ryan's? She could see him being angry over what her father had done to her mother. Angry for her sake. She stood and strained to see through the darkness. It wasn't Ryan. She sagged against the wall in relief.

"What is it?" Jay Sattler's voice broke through the night sounds.

"Trouble." She heard the stranger's hiss. "Skinny was shot and killed. Laxalt—"

"Hush," Jay shot out. "Come inside."

She wanted to follow the conversation but knew that her father would retreat to his office for that very reason. Ryan was involved. Her heart sank at the notion that he might be hurt or followed, that even now her father could plot a way to bring Ryan to heel for whatever trouble he had caused.

Olivia plucked the apron up off the bed. She smoothed her hand over the material and mouthed a prayer, grasping for a thought that would make what she should do clear to her. *Lord, what now? What can I do?*

Ryan would not kill unless he was threatened. He was that sort of man. His father had been honorable. But she also knew his temper could rage hot. A specter of doubt inserted itself into her mind.

The inactivity would drive her mad. She bounced to her feet and stuffed the apron beneath her unsullied pillow. A tap on the glass froze her in place, and a face appeared at the window. Dark hair and silver eyes.

Ryan.

She gasped with a hand to her throat, at once afraid and relieved.

He put a finger to his lips and motioned her outside. She knelt inside by the open window. Their faces were inches apart. "I can't."

"Is your father holding you?"

"No. But I'm afraid for you. For Hector and—"

He jerked his head toward the hitching post. "Whose horse?"

"I don't know."

Ryan seemed to consider that. "Something happened tonight. Sheriff Bradley's going to get taken in by the marshal. Skinny Bonnet was the one staging the ground to look like cows had been rustled at Jacob's ranch."

"Jacob? You mean Phoebe's Jacob?"

"It happened tonight. Earlier. Jacob was shot, and that was where the doc was. Olivia?"Ryan's hand touched hers, and she started at the feel of his fingers against her. Her eyes snapped to his.

"What are you afraid of?" The tears came then. Ryan brushed them from her cheeks. "Come outside."

She sat on the sill and twisted. He pulled her through the window and supported her until she could get her feet under her. When he turned her in his arms, she saw in his eyes not a reflection of her own desires but the love and devotion he'd yet to put into words.

She framed his face, needing to hear the words locked deep inside him. They would dispel her doubts and remove the tarnish her father's veiled accusation had placed on her decision to stay at the Laxalts'.

He drew a breath, and his chest swelled. He held her close and searched her face, her eyes. His exhale washed over her.

"Ryan. . ."

"I love you, Olivia."

"We've got to get out of here."

"No."

"What if he comes after you?"

"Listen to me. Things are much different now. Your father no longer has the sheriff to back him, and Skinny was their hired gun." His hand stroked down her arm. "I have to face your father, Livy. For us."

She knew he was right. As much as she wanted to escape and be done, they would never live in peace until this thing between the Sattlers and Laxalts was finished. And Jay Sattler held the key.

❧

He'd wanted to kiss away the trails marking her cheeks. But he could not bring himself to ply her with stolen kisses on the front porch of her father's house, considering the ill will between their families.

He stroked her hair, unable to find words to express his hesitation so that she would understand. Or maybe she did understand. "You need to go back inside and get some sleep."

She nodded against his chest. "We talked. Him and me. About my mother. I understand now, but. . ."

Her head sank down as the last word tumbled from her lips. He absorbed the silence, giving her the time she needed. He gauged the vague sound of voices coming through the window that allowed them the time for a stolen moment. When her silence stretched longer than he could endure, he lifted her face.

"Tell me."

"I tried to help him see that what he was doing was wrong. What he was allowing. Your father. . .everything."

He traced the curve of her ear with his finger. His father's face bloomed in his mind along with the words of his favorite phrase, and he heard himself repeating it. "A wise man once told me that what you can't work out, you can pray out."

Her hands tightened on his arms. "Do you believe that?"

A deep sadness rose in him. "I didn't, but I'm beginning to."

As if on cue, the heavy thud of boots on the wood floor beat out a warning. She pulled away, balancing on the window sill and twisting through the opening. He turned away and rounded the corner where the angle of the house, even with the moon shining down, kept his cowhand in shadow.

He raised his hand as Cody shook his head to indicate he had seen or heard nothing new since their arrival. Ryan jerked his head and went to the corner of the house, glancing around to watch as a single man exited, gathered the reins of his horse, and turned the animal. The dim profile wasn't one Ryan recognized, but he had an idea by the flashes of silver on the bridle and saddle that it might be Bowman or Michaels, and he wished mightily he could have heard what was said in the impromptu meeting.

Cody sidled up beside him, brow raised. Ryan nodded. As Ryan rushed to his horse, he knew his hand would settle in for the night, just as they'd planned. Someone needed to keep an eye on Sattler, and Ryan's command, above all else, had been for Cody to protect Olivia if she needed it.

Chapter 38

Ryan worked through the night alongside Bobby. There was a fever pitch of activity so the drive could get a head start if there was going to be trouble.

"Take 'em out of here, Bobby." He gave the signal to his foreman. Bobby raised the handkerchief around his nose and mouth, and the other men followed suit. It was the official sign for the hands to start moving the cattle. The indignant moos almost drowned out his words as the ground vibrated beneath the onslaught of hooves.

"Things will go well," his mother said. A cloud of dust rose into a dense ball as the cattle bunched together and picked up speed. "God knows we have had much to handle."

Ryan didn't respond. His mother's words echoed through his mind more as a prayer. The early start would give Bobby extra time to make six miles before resting and finishing with another seven or eight for the day.

"It's time for me to face Sattler."

"What about Olivia?"

The question stirred his doubts. She'd obviously been distressed at her father's refusal to change his ways, though seemingly touched by Sattler's explanation of Lily. Finding the strength to stand against her father would be a hard test of her loyalty and love. Surely she knew that if Jay Sattler could not be turned, her association with Ryan—or any of the small ranchers—would mean a rift in the father-daughter relationship.

In the wake of her emotions, his declaration of love had seemed the right thing to do. He would not take the words back. He just hoped he hadn't been premature, that the light in her eyes would not fade under the test to come.

❧

Her father's back seemed an indomitable wall as he sat sipping coffee from his favorite tin mug. Olivia tied on her mother's apron, prepared to stand her ground against her father's preconceived notions of how Lily should be cared for. She fingered the edge of the apron, drawing strength from the familiar item.

"I see you stayed last night."

She firmed her lips as his statement flared through her. "You've grown suspicious of your daughter's morals?" She strained to keep her tone light, matter-of-fact instead of challenging. "Isn't the hope I would develop good morals part of the reason you sent me to Aunt Fawn and that fancy school?"

Jay sighed into his coffee cup. "One thing you have learned is the art of debate.

Your mother could fashion a rebuke with a soft word, but it always came through loud and clear."

Vestiges of the broken emotions he'd shown the previous night showed in the faraway look in his eyes and the sad turn of his lips.

Olivia sat across the table from him—the same place her mother had occupied all those years ago. "I want mother to live with me." She kept her eyes on the table, wading out deeper into the pool of her desires. "Being out there all alone. . . I think it might be good to have her around people again."

"Olivia. . ."

"It's important to me to try and help her as much as I can, Daddy. Don't you see that? Did I tell you what she asked me as soon as she saw me? She asked if I was her little girl. She recognized me." Not until she felt the tickle on her cheek did she realize she was crying. She swept back the moisture and met her father's eyes, letting him see her determination.

"And what does your Mr. Laxalt think of that?"

His mention of Ryan made her cautious. "He's not 'mine.'"

"Weren't you defending him?" His tone was accusatory. "Trying to make peace between our families so you could marry him?"

Olivia clasped her hands in her lap. "Josephine Laxalt has become my friend—"

"You want me to believe you're doing it for his mother?"

"Let me finish, Daddy."

Jay opened his mouth then lifted his mug and took a long pull.

She took a deep breath and continued. "They're all my friends—"

The mug slammed down, making her jump. "Do you know what your friends did last night, Livy? They murdered an innocent man."

"Innocent in whose eyes?"

Her father's eyes narrowed. "What do you know of all this?"

"Enough to know there is another side to the story."

He stroked a hand down his beard and cracked the knuckles on his right hand. "Whose side am I hearing? Laxalt's? Did he come visit you last night right here under my roof?"

Olivia rose to her feet. She was shaking with fury. "There was a time when I had a father who was caring and kind and loving. Who would hear a man out before he condemned him. Whose heart was bigger than his ranch and who delighted in the idea of having and being a good neighbor. What happened to that man, because he doesn't live here anymore. If you know where he is, Daddy"—the sob rose in her throat and burst out—"if you know where he is, let me know. I'd love to talk and laugh with him again." She plucked at the knots of the apron and swept it from her body as she rushed across the room.

"Livy! Livy, come back here—"

She didn't stop until she got to the corral where a hand saw her running. She smeared the tears away. "Please, saddle up the mare."

"Yes ma'am, Miss Sattler."

Olivia glanced over her shoulder, waiting, almost hoping, that her father would appear, beckon her back, and wrap her in his arms. But the door didn't open, and she was soon riding into the early-morning wind.

Chapter 39

The sun was high in the sky when Ryan wiped his neck with the kerchief and adjusted his hat. It had taken all morning to break the pretty little mare, and his mind had begun to wander from the task, a dangerous thing when on the back of a bucking horse. He opened the gate and gave the mare a slap on the rump to send her off into the pasture to graze.

No sign of Olivia. No sign of Sattler, and he wondered after Cody, too. The man must be hungry by now, and he hadn't given specific instructions to the hand other than to watch over Olivia and report on strange activity among Sattler and his men.

His mother appeared on the porch and raised her hand. He thought she was shading her eyes until she extended her arm. A lone rider was coming from the direction of Buffalo and Sattler's ranch. The silhouette didn't match that of Olivia, nor did the dark horse seem familiar. Whoever it was must know they were giving him plenty of time to collect his guns, and that meant the person came without ill intentions.

"It's Jay Sattler." His mother's voice sounded breathless. Her dark eyes filled with worry.

"Go inside. Leave this to me."

"I'll go inside, but that rifle will be keeping me company."

Ryan put his arm around his mother, amused by her spirit. "You do that." He leaned to pick up a stick, took out his knife, and relaxed on the step.

When Jay Sattler brought his horse to a stop right in front of the step where Ryan sat whittling on a stick, he angled his hat to get a better view of the man. "Good afternoon, neighbor. Light and sit."

If Jay wanted trouble, nothing in his body language gave hint of it. "Olivia went off this morning. Thought she might be here."

"Haven't seen her."

Ryan rose to his feet as Jay advanced. "She's all I've got, Laxalt. And you. . .you've turned her against me."

"You come to talk or to accuse? Because if it's the latter, I've got my own accusation to level."

"I didn't shoot your pa if that's what's got you riled."

The confession came so swift Ryan felt his breath leave him in a rush. "Then you must know who did."

"Reckon you plugged him already."

Skinny Bonnet. "Who ordered it?"

Jay swallowed and frowned. "Now that would be telling."

Fury ate at Ryan's calmness.

"You've got my daughter all twisted up inside. Her loyalty should be to her father."

"Her loyalty, Sattler, should be to the side she chooses to believe."

"You killed a man."

"It wasn't my shot that put Bonnet in the dust. If there's any question of his innocence, then we kept his boots as evidence. When the marshal rounds up Bradley, we'll hand all that over."

"Just you remember that my hands are clean. I don't want no trouble."

"But you'll be glad to give trouble to others."

Jay's jaw went hard. "I just want what's mine."

Ryan gripped his knife tighter. "When a man proves up a claim, it's his. That's the law. You can't take land or what's found on it just because you think you have a right to it." He forced himself to relax. "You started somewhere. Why can't you give that chance to others?"

Jay stared toward the horizon. "Things change."

"Things change people—for the better or for the worse. My father thought you were a good man. A good neighbor. What happened?"

"This from a hotheaded kid who went off on his own? Who're you to give me life lessons?"

"I'm the son that wouldn't listen, who pulled a knife on his father because I felt he was making me work too hard. I'm not proud of that, and I've never forgotten it, but I have learned from it." Ryan felt a weight lift from his shoulders, as if giving voice to his past wrongs was a cleansing. "And there are other things, too. Things life has taught me about morals and fairness."

He saw Jay's gaze shift and felt a presence at his side. His mother's hand held on to his arm. "I am sorry about Lily, Jay. I'd like to visit her sometime. Maybe I can help her do the needlework she was once so fond of."

The man's lips trembled, and his eyes reddened. He spun away and stomped back to his horse then stopped, reins in hand. "That's right kind of you, ma'am." He grunted into the saddle but sat still. The horse pranced a bit. "Laxalt."

Ryan met his eyes.

"You find Livy. Tell her—" His voice caught. "Make her happy."

Chapter 40

When the wagon crested the hill and the cabin came into full view, Ryan caught sight of Olivia and Lily sitting side by side at the edge of the pond, their hands clasped together.

"It's like a ghost," his mother whispered. "After all these years, to find out Lily was here all the time. No wonder that poor girl was so devastated."

Olivia heard the rattle of the wagon before Lily did. He could see the smile on her face even from the distance that still separated them. He'd been headed out on the mustang when he'd crossed Cody's path coming in. He learned from the cowhand that he'd followed Olivia out to a cabin. Ryan had known right away where Olivia had gone and the reason. He'd returned for his mother and to exchange the horse for a wagon while his mother gave Cody supper.

"She looks happy," his mother said.

He didn't know if she spoke of Olivia or Lily, but both women did look happy. If only Jay Sattler could see his women together. When he brought the wagon to a halt, he took the bag from his mother and helped her down.

Olivia guided Lily toward them. The younger woman looked paler than normal. She seemed tired but happy.

"This is your neighbor, Mother, Mrs. Josephine Laxalt."

Lily tilted her head, and her smile revealed a dimple. Her skin was smooth and pale. "Have you come to be a friend to me?"

"I have. This is my son. He's a special friend of Olivia's."

Lily giggled. "I have a special friend, too. He comes to visit me sometimes."

Ryan heard Olivia's gasp. "Yes, a tall man with a red beard?"

Another giggle. "Yes. He tells me I'm pretty, and he brings me peppermints."

Olivia's eyes filled, and she stared out over the shallow pond.

"Why don't you two take a walk while I show Lily what's in my bag?" Josephine suggested. She opened the bag wide, and Lily looked down inside. "Do you know how to use these?" Josephine asked.

Ryan turned toward Olivia and touched her arm.

She fell into step with him. His chest tightened when they were alone. "Tell me what just happened back there."

"She recognizes my father. He said it had taken her years to let him get close." She stopped. "There's so much to tell you, Ryan."

He opened his mouth. "We'll have time for it later." The pond shimmered. It was a peaceful place. "Your father said you ran off."

She gasped. Stopped. Reached out to clasp his arm. "Ryan?"

"He came for a visit."

Fear crept into her eyes.

"It's not what you think."

Her breathing eased along with her grip on his arm.

"Livy." He released her hold on him and held her hand in his. He was afraid of the answer to the question he needed to ask. "Your father thinks you should be loyal to him."

"I'm sure he does, but you know I can't, Ryan." Her lip trembled, and she bit it. "I think mother's illness shattered something deep inside him."

"Then maybe we can help bring him back to the light."

"I don't know. He's gotten so hard."

"We'll work it out. Little by little the Lord will guide us along the way." He held her shoulders and smiled into her eyes. "Can you believe that?"

She nodded.

He sucked in the warm air and raised his hand to her cheek then touched the tip of her sunburned nose. "Your father told me something right before he left. We didn't agree on much, but on this we did." Her eyes were round with curiosity. "He told me to find you. To make you happy."

Her eyes were luminous, and a veil of tears bore out her relief. "Oh Ryan."

"There's more." He held her chin and brought her hand up to his chest. His heart raced. "Could you care for me, Olivia? A Laxalt?"

She took a step closer. "I love you, if that's what you're asking."

"I want to court you. Proper-like. Long rides. We could come out here to be with your mother. Whatever you want."

"Cowboy style."

He laughed and took in her eyes, the curl of her lashes, and the brightness of her cheeks and nose. "What more do I have to do to take care of you?"

"You could buy me a hat that fits."

Her soft smile encouraged him. His finger traced along her lips, and he leaned forward to kiss the sunburned freckles on her nose. She moved closer and tilted her head. He lowered his lips to hers.

A laugh echoed across the water to them and shattered the moment. He turned to see his mother and Lily watching them closely. His mother was holding up a ball of yarn. Something was tied to it that looked like. . .

Olivia's eyes went wide. "A baby booty?"

Ryan pulled her back into his embrace and kissed her nose before releasing a laugh. "Or we could just fast-forward to the wedding."

Valley of the Heart

Dedication

I had the privilege to know and be loved by an amazing mother and father. Thank you, both, for your sacrifice, your example, your wisdom, and your steady guidance.

Chapter 1

Fear settled a heavy mantle over Maira Cullen's shoulders. Her throat swelled from the heat and the hurt of the many things gone awry in the last few hours, and the burgeoning realization that there was absolutely nothing she could do to change things. Except pray. And search.

Her legs trembled with every step, her mind growing hazier with each water-deprived minute. Another thing to chasten herself over. What woman, or man for that matter, in her right mind would take off in this heat without a canteen?

"Levi?" The word slipped out on a sob. She swallowed the emotion as she had for the last desperate hours she and her foreman had searched the ranch house and outbuildings. If she broke down now, she wouldn't be able to continue. Just keeping one foot in front of the other took such effort. "Levi!"

Where could he be? Where would he go? He was such a small boy. So sad and sweet and sincere. Maira's heart wrenched with fresh despair. She blinked up at the hot sun from under the brim of her hat and plucked at the material of her blouse to stir a billow of air against her skin.

"Levi!"

All she had going for her was the angle of the sun and the fact that the air would eventually grow cooler, but the sun's slow fade into the western horizon heralded her greatest enemy—darkness. She couldn't let her mind go there. Not now. By the angle of the sun she still had three hours of light. Desperation burned through her, and her mind cleared enough to realize she had no choice but to return for water. If not for herself, for Levi. He would need it when she found him. Food, too.

"Levi?" With one last shout and the remote hope that she would hear a feeble response, Maira strained for sound. Only the breeze answered her call. The sun continued to beam down on her, and the sheep in the far pasture startled, then stared. But she had no time to coddle the woolies. No time for anything except returning to the house and gathering the few things necessary to continue the search beyond the ranch. Decision made, she felt more settled and focused. She had to think. And blow the dust off her prayer life and petition God. Surely He cared about Levi.

❧

Carrot Timmons led the group down into the crevice where a longhorn brindle bull stared at them in bovine defiance. Tanner Young admired the leader's work ethic but hated the man's inability to handle a situation without calling out every cowhand on the ranch.

"You get over to him, Tanner. I'll rope his horns and pull. He's got to budge somehow."

The bull let out a sound more grunt than moo. No wonder. The bull had been hassled all morning by Carrot and Fletcher.

"All you need to do is get in there and make a ruckus." Tanner lifted his hat to allow cool air to sift through his hair. "Not much to it."

"Or you could make use of that gun and shoot him between the eyes," Fletcher grumped. "Don't reckon we'd miss him much."

"It's about making money," Carrot reminded him. "It's a good bull."

"And you're a top hand," Fletcher groused.

Carrot's eyes flicked over the man. Tanner knew the foreman's temper and saw the dawning of a tantrum. A vein throbbed on Carrot's neck, and his eyes stabbed at Fletcher. Tanner decided it was time to get the bull moving. He drew in his horse, a good mount with an even temper, nothing like the cow ponies that never quite grasped the idea of carrying a man in submission. The piebald plunged into the tangled patch of weeds. Screaming his throat raw as he came up behind the bull, Tanner palmed his gun and let off two shots into the air to add to the commotion. The bull lunged as if to turn. Tanner kept his horse moving, dodging the less agile bull's weaving head. The bull went still, his eyes blazing his rage. Tanner kept up his screaming and fired another bullet. The bull hesitated and planted one hoof ahead of the other in reluctant retreat from his prickly paradise. Fletcher stood in the path of the animal a moment too long and had to scramble to get out of the bull's way.

Tanner moved away from Carrot's withering gaze and Fletcher's shouted words of praise. Praise was the one thing Tanner avoided. Didn't do anyone any good to have it heaped on a body, and it was way too easy for a man's head to swell when it was.

"Waste of ammunition," Carrot bit out.

Ignoring the goading remark, Tanner spurred his horse into a proper gallop. If he'd thought of it sooner, he'd have avoided riding along this edge of the XP Ranch. Better to avoid the cattle and the rough men Walter Price had hired.

He breathed deep and hunched lower in the saddle as the horse's momentum blew hot air through his beard and against his skin. He yanked off his hat and let the wind caress his head, drying the sweat on his cheeks and ruffling through his hair. He brought the piebald down to a trot. No use wearing Cupid out before they reached the ranch house. He licked his lips, amused at the reaction of trail-toughened cowboys should they learn of his horse's secret name. But the horse's heart-shaped patch on his flank had brought the name to mind, and it had stuck. He dissembled by calling the gelding Cue for short in the presence of others.

Leaning forward over the saddle horn, he stroked the animal's neck and whispered sweet nothings to the only companion he'd had for years. Not that it bothered him none; indeed, he preferred it that way. Stalking cats and coyotes along the perimeters of the XP offered him plenty of time to himself, and he seldom longed for people.

As Cue took him closer to the ranch house, Tanner saw his boss on the porch watching a young man working to break a bronc that held fire in its eyes. A lone, old man, Walter Price was a force to be reckoned with. His sharp eyes watched Tanner's approach as if nothing were amiss. Tanner noted the man's stance—leaning against a porch column, eyes squinted, furrows in his brow as deep as irrigation ditches—relaxed. Walt's hair was the color of old linen, with long strands brushed forward to cover his baldness, giving the man a comical appearance if not for the cold flint of his eyes. Tanner had forgotten how hard those eyes were, and how cold they became when there was work to be done and money to be made. It was the reason Price had hired him after a pack of coyotes had taken a pocket of cows in the north range over three years ago.

"Get down off that horse and we'll drink."

"Don't drink," Tanner reminded him, swinging his leg over and ground hitching Cue.

Price raised his chin but said nothing more as Tanner followed him inside and took his seat across the wide plank table. "There's about to be a change in your duties." The old man raised his hand to the young woman who skidded into view, cheeks flushed, plucking at the hairs that fell into her eyes. She was a beauty who Tanner had never seen before at the XP. That and the fact that Walt Price had never married was not lost on Tanner now. Walter shifted his weight and grunted. "Ana? Drinks" was all he said to her before she scurried off, never once lifting her eyes to acknowledge his presence.

Upon first meeting Price, Tanner had realized that the man desired, above all else, to be seen as the ultimate boss. A rich man. A cattle baron. Price breathed cattle and drives, profit and loss.

"You've done a fine job of keeping prey from my herds. But a little problem has cropped up west of here that I want you to take care of."

Tanner accepted a glass of amber liquid from Ana. She never quite met his eyes. When he thanked her, he thought her hand trembled ever so slightly. He took the time to absorb the woman's red-blond hair. A thick spray of freckles along her nose and cheeks gave her a little-girl appearance, but her eyes, a beautiful hazel with long lashes, and the rest of her corrected any predilection that she was a child.

When Tanner returned his attention to Price, the man's scowl let him know he hadn't appreciated Tanner's perusal of Ana. Walter tossed back his drink and slapped the squat glass on the table with a *thunk* that made Ana jump. At the wave of his hand, Ana left the room.

"There's a ranch west of here. I want to you to go there and take on some work for the owner. I want to know what's going on over there, and I'm sure they could use the help."

"I'm a hunter, not a spy."

"You were a top hand, and you're a dead shot. I want you on my side, Young."

"Side?"

"Do you want the job or not?"

Tanner leaned forward and dug his fist into the table as he stood. "If it's all the same, I'll ride on. I've no stomach for such work."

"Three dollars a day, and that's on top of what you're paid while there."

He hesitated, catching the gleam in Price's eyes. The money was not to be ignored. He could buy his own cattle, build his own place, and settle down on his own spread. But the offer seemed ludicrous. Desperate. "What's the problem?"

Walter shrugged. "Just keeping my eye on the competition."

In that instant, Tanner disliked the man intensely. He schooled his features so his distaste would not show. It piqued his curiosity why the man was so interested in his competition. To put them out of business was all he could think. Sour distaste spread in his mouth. Yet. . .it would give him a break from his current routine, and if things didn't work out, he'd take his money and walk away. "I'll do it."

Price stood and offered his hand.

Tanner hesitated. "I want it written up and both of us to sign."

"Don't trust me? After all this time?"

No, he wanted to say. "It's a lot of money, and it's your word against mine. Let's call it a business contract."

Chapter 2

Entering Maira's small home was like being embraced. Even still, she worked hard to gather the supplies she would need to camp out through the night. Frank Harrison limped out of the sheep shed, his dark eyes asking questions she did not have answers to.

"He did not go far, Miss Maira. Levi is a smart boy."

Her heart ached in her chest at the reminder. She refused to think about the night creatures that prowled or the hundreds of different ways a boy could get injured or killed. Her stomach filled with acid in spite of her efforts to remain calm.

"If I could ride with you, I would."

"It's important for you to stay here. Guard the house, the sheep, and cattle. If he returns while I'm gone. . ." She drew a deep, steadying breath. "I might be gone awhile." She couldn't ask more of the foreman. Not with the twisted leg, a result of busting a bronc for their ranch hands three years ago, but how Frank had suffered, still suffered, with the injury. That she hadn't been able to pay Frank for months proved the man's loyalty to Maira's late husband and knifed the fear of losing Levi even deeper. *God, I can't lose Levi, too.*

She took her gentle old mare out this time, her mind dividing the small ranch into sections. She would begin with the east section. The section closest to the XP and the most likely route for little feet since it was flat. No matter how much she disliked Walter Price's heavy-handed and less-than-subtle hints that he wanted to court her, he had done much to help her out since Jon's sudden death. Still, the idea of marrying Walter lured her on the days and in the times when things were toughest. She ached from the burden she carried—dwindling money, dwindling herds. In the back of her mind, she knew losing the ranch loomed like a cliff she would eventually fall over. Jon would berate her worry. His faith had always been stronger.

Maira pushed Queen to the limits of the mare's endurance, a hard gallop, her eyes scanning the entire time. Half a mile out, she paused the mare and stroked her neck. Why hadn't she kept a closer eye on Levi? She knew he'd wanted to go outside, and it wasn't fair to keep him cooped up as she cleaned house and baked bread. But the pantry had been almost bare. The house neglected for too long with the work around the ranch pressing on her every waking moment.

And now this. . .

"Levi!"

Fear roared in her ears, whispering of death and injuries too terrible for Levi to endure. And buried in the images were words of discouragement and failure. *You're too late. He's dead. You should have brought Frank in the wagon. You won't find your boy. Ever.* Each crowded in on the other, pushing tears down her cheeks and rendering her voice nothing more than a croak.

She brought Queen up another half mile out and swiped at her eyes to clear the tears. This was no time for emotion. She could not waste her energy harboring the debilitating thoughts that would surely bleed her strength dry. She stared out at the spring-green hills ahead and inhaled of the hot, fetid air that belied the beauty. If only she knew where to look. What direction he'd taken. How quickly he had slipped from her side and disappeared. Rising darkness in the east meant the end of her search. She would build a fire and hope Levi saw the light. Surely her son would know that a fire meant people.

Buoyed by the idea, she withdrew her booted foot from the stirrup and swung down. She wanted so much to remove the saddle and grant Queen time without the hot, heavy contrivance, but she couldn't. If anyone approached, human or otherwise, she needed to leave as fast as possible.

She prepared little pieces of dry grass and snapped a dry stick into pieces. When she touched the flame to the kindling, it took, and she nursed the fire into a respectable blaze that satisfied. Night's heavy cloak pressed down against the light. She shivered and stacked the pieces of wood she'd gathered. If need be, she'd stay up all night to feed the flame. As her eyes grazed the wide sky, it shook her anew that Levi was lost and alone in the vast landscape. Maira curled into a tight ball and watched the flames, fighting tears, praying. The fire was her only hope in the darkness of night.

❧

Tanner noticed the smoke. A thin stream of light gray against the darkening west sky, unnoticeable to those with dull senses but second-nature to a man who lived his life tracking four-legged beasts and men. His heart raced with anxiety. He didn't trust Walter Price and wouldn't put it past the man to have someone out there waiting to shoot him dead. Maybe he'd found out about Tanner's propensity for asking questions of the surrounding ranchers. He sat back in the saddle, scanning his surroundings. Nothing stirred except the night cries and an unusual purring. Whatever lay ahead, his survival depended on keeping out of sight and the advantage of surprise.

Wheeling Cupid, Tanner worked his way north. The smooth grass and patches of late-spring wildflowers could hide dips and holes that would cripple the horse and could kill him as well, should the animal's hoof find one. He kept Cue's pace slow, straining to see in the dark. He listened hard for the screaming of a cat or the howl of coyote, but the pervasive sound was the mewling cry. It grew louder, and with every step he became more sure that it was an animal, perhaps shot or wounded, dying its last.

He could see the dull orange dot of fire on the dark horizon to his left. Coming up behind whoever waited there would allow him to assess the danger and whether it was a trap or simply Price's men out on the range for the night. That didn't make sense though, not with the XP less than a four-hour ride. Still, there was no accounting for a cowboy's desire to sleep under the stars.

He came to a stream, not more than a trickle, and dismounted for the horse to rest and drink. He tilted his head in the direction of the sound. It was close. A raccoon, maybe. Nothing bigger than that by the pitiful, weak sound of the mewling. He ground-hitched Cue and followed the stream until it widened into a small pool of water, not deeper than six inches, the dividing line between the XP and the Rocking J. With his eyes, he followed a well-worn path used by wild creatures to access the pond. He sloshed through the water and up the far bank, swiping the muck from his boot along the clean grasses. The path led into a grove of aspens, their white bark like skeleton fingers in the night. From there he was close. It tickled at his senses that he should turn back, but his curiosity would not be pushed aside. Besides, if the animal was dying, he could shoot it and put it out of its misery. No use making it suffer longer than necessary.

A hollow between two aspens showed a blur of light color. Yellow or white, he didn't know which, but the sound seemed to emanate from the ball on the ground. Tanner went still. On quiet feet he drew closer. As he stood beside the bundle, his senses were assailed by the tight fist of knowledge. He wasn't looking at an animal; he was looking at the small, crying form of a child.

"Hey."

The cries turned to a sharp gasp; the head snapped up, eyes round.

"I won't hurt you." He put out a hand, amazed. A boy. A very small boy. The wonder of his discovery brought a smile to his face. "Are you lost?"

Shuddering shoulders; wide, dark eyes; and a lip that quivered as tears fell communicated the boy's confusion and fear.

"Do you need to go home?"

This time he got an enthusiastic nod. "Peez."

"Are you hurt?" He had to ask, though Tanner's scan of the child didn't show insomuch as a torn sleeve. "We'll need to get back to my horse." He held out his hand to the child, encouraging him to rise to his feet.

The boy did so, bounding upward and smearing a sleeve across his cheeks and nose. Even in the darkness, he could see the sleeve of his shirt already sported a wet spot from previous wipings. Tanner grinned and gripped the cold little hand in his own. "I've got a blanket we can wrap you in. Do you have a name?"

A huge nod and the boy pointed to his pants, his little legs clad in denim. "Lee-vi."

"What was that?" Tanner hunched to hear the boy's answer, feeling the exhale of breath against his ear as the boy repeated the name.

"Lee-*vigh*."

He chuckled and stroked his hand over the boy's hair, a sense of protectiveness gripping him hard. How had the boy wandered so far, and where had he come from? He'd not had much to do with the ranch where he was headed, tucked as it was between two steep hills. He'd heard rumors of a man and woman running it and wondered if the child might have come from that direction. . .or maybe he'd wandered from the campfire.

When they got to the stream, he picked the boy up in his arms and stepped across the water, setting Levi back down on the other side. He took a minute to swipe the mud from his boots. Levi remained silent and still next to him, except for those big, dark-brown eyes that followed his every move as if the child feared he might disappear.

"Mommy's praying," Levi claimed as Tanner took the boy's hand again.

"She is, huh?"

The head bobbed, and Tanner didn't feel any need to discount the boy's pronouncement.

He unlatched the leather laces that held the oilskin-wrapped blanket behind his saddle, draped the blanket over the boy's shoulders, and put him in the saddle. At least Levi showed no fear of the horse; that would have created a terrible problem. Tanner pulled the reins back and over the gelding's head and joined Levi in the saddle. He hunched himself around the boy to provide more warmth. Whatever fears had plagued the tyke earlier must have washed away, for within minutes Levi's head slumped back against him.

Chapter 3

Maira woke with a start, noticed the fire waning, and staggered upward to place another block of wood across it. She chided herself for nodding off. If she let the fire go out. . . What if Levi had wandered close and she'd missed him? Bile burned her throat. She stooped to collect a good-sized branch and tried to bend and break it. She threw it down in frustration. She gulped, irritated at the delay. *God, where is Levi? Lord, please, please, keep him safe. For me.*

She spun away and swatted the fresh tears coursing down her cheeks. Air caught in her throat when she saw a shadow move in her periphery. She jerked that direction. Cold dread suffused her body. Straining to see through the darkness, she edged closer to the fire's protection. Even as she became aware of her proximity to the heat, she monitored the place where she'd seen the shadow. Another sound. Low. A shuffling of sorts, and her hand went to her throat. Queen, standing three-legged, radiated equine unconcern. If the horse heard anything amiss, her ears would prick. But the horse was old and maybe hard of hearing. Maira moved toward the mare and unsheathed her Winchester. With quick fingers, she found the ammunition and loaded the rifle, her heartbeat picking up, aware of her vulnerability should anyone or anything leap into camp. The anxiety made her fingers stiff, and she dropped the last bullet before she could shove it into place behind the others. Turning, her eyes roved behind her, her anxiety gentling somewhat as she cocked the rifle and held it close.

Nothing moved.

"Levi?" She so wanted him to pop into the ring of firelight. To see his brown eyes and the patch of hair that never lay right. Her throat closed. "Levi, is that you, honey?" she croaked, swallowing against the swell of tears.

Another shuffling sound. Less than the wind through tall grasses, yet something. Almost a sigh. She took a step forward and raised the rifle to her shoulder, keeping her finger out of the trigger guard to avoid an accident. She had to know what was causing the sound.

Queen buzzed her lips, and Maira's heart slammed hard. If the horse was alerted. . . But Queen's posture told Maira the mare was more bored than anything, probably wondering what had her owner so excited.

Maira blinked; a silent shift of the atmosphere tickled at her. Whatever had changed in that moment when she'd glanced at Queen. . . Straight ahead, she saw it. The dark shadow, arms extended. A big person.

"Come out here so I can see you, or I'll shoot you dead."

When the shape didn't move, Maira realized what had changed. She relaxed her finger on the trigger, the knots in her muscles easing away. In the changing light from the rising sun, she mistook a stump for a man. It made her laugh, but the sound was strained. Her legs gave way, and she slumped to the ground. Equal portions of relief and despair warred within her. She laid the rifle across her lap and cradled her head, feeling lost and more alone than she'd felt since Jon's death. Emptiness swelled; and a dark void threatened to swallow her whole. She needed Levi. It was the only part of Jon she had, surely the good Lord wouldn't take him, too. Her fist pressed against her lips to squelch a sob. She forced herself to take deep breaths, to focus. She could not afford to sit and give in to defeat. If Levi was out there, she would find him. She would not leave him alone as Jon had been alone in his dying moments.

❧

Breaking up his small, fireless camp, where he'd stopped to give the boy a chance to eat and sleep, Tanner helped a groggy Levi into the saddle then slid up behind him. The campfire in the distance had dwindled over the last couple of hours, evidenced by the ever-thinner curl of smoke in the air. He started that direction again, hoping to catch the men off-guard and in the middle of a deep sleep. At the base of the hill Tanner dismounted and touched the boy's thigh, indicating he should also dismount. He steadied the boy's descent and held Levi's shoulders, hunkering down to come level with the boy's dark eyes.

"You leaving me?" Levi whispered, a tremble in his voice.

"I'm going right over there to that hilltop. There's a fire been burning on the other side, and I aim to see who's sitting around it." Levi listened with solemnity. Tanner put steel into his voice. "Stay right here, you hear?"

He looked so small to Tanner. Like a little man trying to be so brave and failing miserably. The quivering lip gave it away. He could imagine that the hilltop he'd indicated must seem like a long way away for one so small. Tanner released a sigh as he shifted his attention to the horizon. Tinges of pink were lighting the sky, wrestling back the black of night, and that's when he heard something. Someone talking or yelling. A strange voice. Soft. Tanner decided he could risk getting closer; if he stayed within eyesight of Levi, maybe that would assuage the boy's fears.

He put his hand on Levi's head. "Let's get you back up in that saddle. We'll ride closer."

Tanner dared only take Cupid within a hundred feet of the hilltop. He risked the boy even this close and debated simply riding on, but if there was danger hunting him, he needed the advantage. He touched Levi's head, pointed to the rise, and put a finger to his lips. At least the boy didn't look nearly as uncertain about him walking away. Relieved, he patted the boy's head. Large brown eyes made him swallow hard. He crept toward the top of the hill, stopped before he reached the crest, and turned to wave at Levi. The boy stood stoic but gave a little wave in return. As he edged near the top of the hill, he turned his mind to his surroundings. Any movement could mean a guard posted to keep watch.

Tanner got down on his belly and crawled. His elbows dug into the soft, cold ground, morning dew soaking his shirt, clammy against his skin. He raised his head to see down into the camp. The fire was indeed low, and a lone figure sat balled next to the dying flames. Tanner pulled his body forward and squinted harder. The body didn't move, and he wondered if the person was hurt. A horse stood three-legged, unconcerned of the person's distress. That the person might have fallen asleep sitting up wouldn't surprise him, but what did surprise him dawned in slow degrees as the sun stretched over the horizon, its rays bringing illumination to the form. Dark hair, the slender back. Even as he watched, the woman stirred, revealing a rifle across her lap. Tanner ducked lower.

"Levi!" He heard her stress in those two syllables. He dared to raise his head. She'd come to her feet, her face lifted to the east. A sleeve to her face yanked a smile. Like mother, like son. He stayed still for a moment longer, dividing his attention between her movements and the surrounding area. Satisfied that no one other than the woman was present, Tanner rose to his feet and ran back to Levi.

"Did you hear that? That was your momma."

"Mommy?" He picked the boy up in his arms and felt the child's breath against his neck; his chubby hands against his cheeks demanded Tanner's attention. "My mommy." It was a statement.

"Your mommy. We're going to see her."

Levi's head bobbed, and his whole body bounced in Tanner's arms. "Hold still."

Levi stilled, and his arms slipped around Tanner's neck, head resting against his shoulder. Tanner swallowed hard and spread his hand against the boy's back as his long strides took him to the top again. The woman was kicking dirt on the fire, the rifle a few feet away from her.

"Missing someone?" He hollered down.

She jumped and spun.

Tanner was already heading down the hill. Levi lifted his face from his shoulder and bounced in his arms. "Mommy! Mommy!"

The woman's face transformed from fear to hope and joy. She spread her arms and met them at the base of the hill. Levi practically jumped from his arms to hers, her hand holding his head tight against her shoulder. Tanner felt the woman's relief like a physical caress. Strands of her dark hair tangled around a delicate, heart-shaped face. Remnants of her long night were visible in the dirty track on her right cheek and the grip she had on Levi.

When she opened her eyes, pools of emotion sparkled in their luminous green depths. "How can I thank you?"

Tanner opened his mouth but could think of nothing to say.

"Where was he?" She peeled Levi from her embrace, her relief bleeding into concern as her hands explored the boy's fragile frame for injury.

"Little hollow by a stream, curled into a ball. I made sure he was fine first thing. Cold, maybe, but the blanket and grub helped warm him up."

She brought the boy in close for another hug, and Tanner Young's past rose like a hibernating bear searching for a meal. Caught in a rush of regret and remorse, he spun on his heel, the voice of another little boy in another time stabbing at his mind.

"Please, come to the ranch for a meal." Her words stopped him cold. "It's the least I can do."

He didn't turn. "I don't need thanks, ma'am."

"Do you know what this means to me? I thought he was dead or. . ." Her voice caught. "Please."

Her words sucked at him. If he didn't escape soon, he would be drawn into a boiling cauldron of memories that would leave him mentally writhing. He couldn't bear that burden again. "Take care of your son," he bit out.

Chapter 4

Maira traced the path the man took up the hill with her eyes. Levi's arms loosened their grip around her neck somewhat, and she tucked her chin to glimpse the sleepy face cradled in the crook of her neck. The slow sweep of long lashes against his cheek told Maira all she needed to know.

Home. With Levi in her arms the word felt sweet again, nothing like the hollow grief before the man had brought her son to her. She breathed deep of Levi's little-boy smell and whispered in his ear how much she loved him.

"We need to get home. Frank will want to know you've been found."

Levi's head bobbled a fraction. She set him astride Queen and surveyed the camp. Her firelight of hope had been extinguished, smothered beneath the layer of dirt she'd kicked on top of the weak flames, but it had worked. *Thank You, Lord.* She nestled close to Levi and gave Queen her heels. Within a few hundred yards, she could easily see the man who had rescued her son, heading west just as she was. If not for Levi's limp form in her arms and the fear of him falling, she would have trotted up to introduce herself and at least learn his name. After a while, she forgot him altogether, as the lull of motion cast its spell and her eyes, too, became heavy. Remembering where she was and what she was doing jostled her awake, and she straightened in the saddle. She noted the man in front of her, his horse a beautiful piebald with bold black spots. He must know she was behind him, but he never turned.

If she hadn't known better, she might have thought him headed to their small ranch. But within the last half hour, where the steep hill ended and her ranch spread out, he swung his horse north. She ached to call to him and express, again, her thanks. She remained silent instead. In the circle of her arms, Levi stirred a bit, and she swapped the reins from her right to her left to relieve the ache of supporting Levi's limp weight. The warmth of the little body close to hers put her at war with her own weariness.

Queen finally rode in, and the haze of Maira's exhaustion lifted somewhat. Frank was there at her side, touching her leg, accepting the weight of the boy into his arms, exclaiming over Levi as she knew he would. He'd taken to the boy like the grandpa he should have been.

"I'll take Queen for ya. You take the boy inside and get that much-needed rest. I'm guessin' the details can wait some longer."

Maira smiled her gratitude. Levi looked ready to drop in the dirt. She leaned to pick him up, savoring again the feel of his little arms around her neck. Would she ever tire of the feeling? It reminded her of the time when he was only nine months and during a sickness spiked a fever. She'd panicked over him then, praying for mercy, afraid that she might lose him as she'd lost Jon. Frank had encouraged her to get some house help, but she'd known as much as he that she could not afford it.

Maira divested Levi of his clothes and slipped his nightshirt over his head. She tucked him into her bed then slipped from her dirty, wrinkled skirt and blouse and put on a fresh nightgown. Being ready for bed would help her sleep sounder. As soon as she lay down, Levi backed his little body up against her. She should put him in his own room but couldn't deny herself the precious sweetness of his presence and drew him close, a knot of emotion forcing a fresh wave of tears from her eyes.

❧

Cupid quivered beneath Tanner, restless to either get moving or bed down for the night, he guessed. The horse wasn't used to late-night rides. Or early morning, for that matter. He leaned forward to rest his weight against the pommel, squinting down at the sight before him. An older man walked out to the stable guiding the horse of the woman whose son he'd rescued. Tanner had arrived from the opposite direction to appear as if he hadn't just come from the XP. He'd secluded himself in time to witness the old man pluck the little boy from the saddle and hug him close. A touching scene. But he wondered where the woman's husband was and why he hadn't gone after the boy. The old man might be excused from consideration based solely on age and the twisted limp in his right leg. If the owner was down in the pastures or away on business, it explained the absence of a younger man, but gut feeling told Tanner what he was seeing was the truth.

"Well Cue, guess there's no use me sitting here guessing." He nudged the horse forward and out of the evergreens he'd used as a shield. The old man came from the stable. He raised his hand in welcome.

"Light and sit."

Tanner reined in Cue and relaxed his hands against the saddle horn. "Looking for some work."

"Not hiring."

Tanner inhaled slow, letting the rush of air expand his lungs and buy him time. He nodded toward the fields behind the squatting ranch house. "What kind of ranch is this?"

"They run sheep and a few head. Name's Frank."

Tanner leaned to accept the man's calloused palm against his own, surprised by the strength of that grip. "Tanner. Tanner Young. Owner around?"

He could see Frank's jaw clench in vexation. Apparently he did not like being so quickly dismissed. "I speak for the boss."

Tanner turned his gaze to the buildings. Roof shingles had blown off, and the doors to the stable sagged. The ranch house showed a broken window, and the bunkhouse listed to the right. Walt had been right in that the ranch would probably welcome extra help. He shifted in the saddle, communicating his intent to dismount. Frank gave him some room. The man's hair was more gray than dark; his beard covered his lower face. He let the silence grow long. Frank didn't flinch, cautious. Tanner could feel the steel of the spine that held the man upright.

"I'll work for food." Frank's scrutiny told him the man did not trust the offer, probably too good to be true. And it would have been if not for one thing. "I was the one who found the boy. She invited me for a meal. By the looks of things, she could use some help."

Frank's expression softened. "You found Levi?"

For a split second, Tanner hated himself for using the incident to secure the man's approval, but he could think of no other way. "I did."

"It's a generous offer." Frank chewed his lower lip and stared at the ranch house for a full minute of silence. "Reckon Maira won't mind feeding an extra mouth for the help."

"Should I meet her husband?"

Frank's eyes flicked from the fields at his back to his face. "He's not here." He wheeled, motioning Tanner to follow.

Tanner ran his tongue over the corners of his mouth then bracketed his fingers on either side to smooth the mustache. He had two ears and one mouth for good reason. Whatever the story with the husband, at least the woman had found her son. Frank showed him some tools in the barn. Feeling the need to get started fixing things up, Tanner chose the sagging gate as his first project.

"Pull up on that rope," he directed Frank after twenty minutes of analyzing the problem then putting his solution into practice. Frank took up the slack of the rope, and Tanner adjusted the counterbalance until the gate swung without dragging. He finished the project with a daub of thick grease on the hinge. "Good as new."

"Better than new," Frank trumpeted in glee. "Never could get that thing right by myself."

"Some things take two."

Frank nodded and rubbed his shoulder. "Reckon that's so." He chuckled deep in his throat. "You take care of those stable doors, and Maira might cook up that last ham she's been holding back."

"Ham, huh?" How long had it been since he'd had a meal cooked by someone other than himself? A pretty someone, at that. *Maira*. . . "I can shoot some game if she's running low." He scanned the yard, taking note of the buildings, the cellar doors. "Could build a smokehouse right over that cellar."

Frank's head bobbed faster and faster. "Been meaning to do that. Leg makes it hard to do steps. Wanted to smoke some of the fish from the stream."

"There's a good supply of wood and nails." Plenty to work on the projects that needed immediate attention and still enable him to build a smokehouse. "Is there something other than these doors and that roof that need doing?"

"Nothing that can't wait for the smokehouse. It would be a relief for Maira to have meat on hand."

Tanner opened the sagging barn door, taking stock of what he would need to fix the problem. A couple of longer nails sank into the frame. An easy fix, until he realized the holes were too worn and would not hold. Replacing the entire frame was the only solution. He took up the claw Frank handed him and set about yanking as many nails as he could. No sense in losing them if he could reuse them. His daddy had taught him to be frugal with all things. He stopped when the weight of the doors began bowing the old frame and pulled out the rest of the nails without any further effort on his part. "Beats having to pry it loose."

Frank nodded and helped him lift down the big doors. After all the years spent by himself on the edges of the XP taking down the predators that could destroy Walt Price's herds, Tanner enjoyed the quiet camaraderie of working beside the old hand. That the man didn't feel the need to fill every empty spot with words relaxed him and reminded him of his pa—a man slow to speak, but when he spoke, whatever he'd said had been worth hearing.

Within an hour he had the new frame set snug and the doors back in place. Sweat beaded along his brow. He wiped it away with a kerchief from his back pocket.

"Maybe you should take a look at the bunkhouse. . . . Get yourself settled in while I talk to Maira."

Tanner analyzed the problem of the sinking foundation in a glance. "Needs the floor shored up. Is there a place to get rocks?"

"A creek down yonder."

Tanner nodded and crossed to Cue. He slipped his saddlebags from the horse then raised a brow at Frank. "Bunkhouse?"

"Yup. I'll turn your horse out into the corral before I head inside."

As Tanner crossed to the sagging building he'd call home for a while, he heard the slight offset of Frank's steps and Cue's cautious whinny as the stranger neared. Cue's distrustful nature made Tanner smile. The door to the bunkhouse squealed open, and he lowered his bags to the nearest narrow bunk. A long row of framework supported sleeping platforms stacked three high. Frank's belongings were strewn about, a frayed blanket haphazardly covering a bottom platform. Made sense the man would choose a low bunk, what with his bum leg.

Back outside, he lay down on his belly and inspected the foundation. It was just as he'd first assessed. The caving floor inside reinforced what he was seeing. It would be a big project, mostly shifting rock, but he would need wood and nails. Maybe more than Frank had on hand.

"She aimed to get the repairs hired out," Frank stated, startling Tanner with his sudden reappearance. He didn't like that he'd been so intent he hadn't heard the man coming. He frowned and sprang to his feet, leaning to slap the dust from the knees of his trousers, working hard to mask the flare of anger at the dullness of his senses. Frank's voice lowered. "But there's been little money, and Maira doesn't have the know-how."

Tanner straightened. "Any work needin' done with the cattle?"

"Some branding to do. Roundup and all."

"Who does she usually hire?"

Frank squinted and shrugged. "Men from the ranch east of here. Can't ride myself, on account of the leg. I take care of the sheep and the boy when she's needin' to be about."

He didn't know a thing about sheep. Had seen some men in the Big Horns herding the meek little animals, but most of them didn't speak English. Cows he could handle. Tanner jerked his head toward Frank's bum leg. "You get caught up in a burrowing hole while on a horse?"

"No. Busting a bronc. He twisted on me and keeled over backward. Pinned me good."

Tanner winced. Good cow ponies had spirit, but their uneven temperament meant they could turn on a man in seconds. "I know a man who insisted on sticking his bronc between two trees before he'd mount him."

"Got into breaking them when I was young," Frank offered. Tanner circled the bunkhouse as the man talked. "Didn't have the sense God gave a goat to know I'd suffer for it down the road." Frank gripped his opposite elbow and rubbed to punctuate his statement. "Some days I just hurt all over."

"You say she hires from the XP?"

There was that strange hesitation again. As if the older man knew something or was suspicious of him. Tanner couldn't read him.

"Frank?"

The quiet voice got their attention at the same time. Tanner watched her from over Frank's shoulder. The boy slipped from her arms into Frank's, who sent the boy into the air, pulling a giggle from Levi. Tanner ripped his gaze from the man and boy back to the woman. Either it was the way she'd combed her hair, damp curls still pressing against her face, or maybe the safe return of her son that gave her skin a rosy glow, but whatever it was, Tanner saw a depth of beauty he had been oblivious to in the breaking dawn.

Levi bolted toward him as soon as Frank set him on his feet. The small figure slapped into his legs, his little arms hugging tight. Tanner let his hammer slip to the ground and pressed his hand to the boy's head. "Hello there, little cowpuncher."

"Lee-vi." The wide, dark eyes shifted up to him and a flow of warmth spilled through Tanner's heart. He touched his hand to the boy's head and knew with a sickening realization that he could never do what Walt Price needed him to do.

"I'm so pleased that you changed your mind and decided to come," she was saying. She extended her hand and he took it. As if from a great distance, his mind registered the delicate feel of the slender fingers, the green of her eyes. "Tanner Young," he managed.

Her eyes swept over the buildings behind him, quietly assessing all that he had done. "I can't thank you enough for your generous offer, but I'm afraid I can't. . ."

Tanner witnessed the subtle shift in her mood. She averted her eyes. Levi released his legs and went to the corral where Cue stood, nostrils flared, staring at the group.

"Now, Maira," Frank said. Tanner couldn't tell if his tone was a reprimand or a warning.

"Frank showed me the tools, so I got to work."

Her nod was stiff. "I noticed."

"That ornery gate is already fixed," Frank cut in. "Sure wouldn't hurt for him to stay a couple days. He's wanting to put up a smokehouse, too."

"I would consider the work for food a favor," Tanner said.

She jerked her head back to him, lips a thin line. "You've already done me a great favor, Mr. Young. I can't imagine the lure of staying here and doing all this work only for a free meal. You're not on the run from the law, are you?"

Chapter 5

No ma'am."

Maybe the tall rider had had a change of heart after his terse good-bye in the first light of dawn, but Maira didn't think so. The appearance of the man seemed too sudden, and she couldn't help but question his motives. What man offered to do repairs for food with no hope of cash? He'd wanted to ride on bad enough earlier. Why not just come claim the meal she'd offered and be gone? By the looks of him he wasn't starving, and the guns around his hips were in a holster worn with use. Which meant Tanner Young was either an outlaw on the run, or. . . She sighed. She didn't know. Jon often told her you couldn't tell much by the looks of a man. But Tanner Young had saved Levi's life. Being alone made her paranoid. If Frank liked the man, then she had no reason not to.

"We'll eat at noon and again at seven. I have a cold biscuit and some bacon from yesterday if you need something right now." She would have to get out the ham. It was the last of her meat, but she could shoot something. Having a smokehouse would be a blessing, and Jon had intended on building a smokehouse before his death.

"That'll be fine." He nodded at the doors. "I'll get back to my work then."

Levi let out a belly laugh over something Frank had said. She caught her loyal hand's eye and put all her concern over Tanner Young into her expression. Frank glanced at Tanner and straightened. Frank's silent, somber nod didn't fill Maira with confidence, but she knew the man would keep a sharp eye.

"Any problem with that ewe?" she asked.

Frank's grin came easy. "She's fine. Gave birth to twins last night with no problems."

News that made her smile. "Two blessings in one night."

"Three, really," Frank countered and tousled Levi's dark hair.

She laughed and held the wonder of it all close to her, savoring the moment. Five sets of twins this spring, with this last set occurring much later than most births, but no less a victory. Now if they could just get a handle on the cattle. She hadn't told Frank about the cut fence, or the clear imprints in the sandy soil by the stream. He would only fret over his inability to ride for long distances and tell her she needed to hire someone. A conversation they'd had too many times to count and one that she had no heart for. Jon had always handled the cattle and sheep herds. She'd had to rely on Frank for his knowledge of the latter and try herself to get a handle on the cows.

She would have to send cattle to market to keep them afloat, and she couldn't continue to rely on the good graces of Walt Price to provide cowhands for another roundup, blessing though it had been. His biting criticism of Jon had rubbed her wrong, and she'd taken the man's offer to supply his hands to round up her cattle at no charge as his way of apologizing for maligning Jon's name. Jon would never have stolen anything; she didn't care if that miner's gold had been found on his body or not.

Maira closed her eyes. No use going over it all again. Tomorrow she would need to start gathering the cattle. Already she had waited too long, and Levi's disappearance had further crimped her plans. At least she could rely on Frank. He was always watchful of the boy and knew exactly what to do to keep Levi occupied, even going so far as to encourage her son to take his naps in the stable like the horses, all so he could keep an eye on him and still work.

She owed Frank so much and didn't want to owe anyone else. Especially not the tall stranger who had rescued Levi. Yet one meal seemed like nothing compared to the bone-shattering grief of a future without that part of Jon. Her own thoughts condemned her. She could not begrudge the man a month of meals, and the work he was doing would be an added bonus. She should be grateful.

From her safe distance, Maira watched as Tanner disappeared into the lean-to beside the barn and returned with fresh boards. She didn't want to notice the way his shirt stretched across his back as he raised the middle board into place. With one hand he hammered as the other held the board, his height a distinct advantage. Jon had always needed to stand on something for jobs requiring him to stretch too high. Tanner finished nailing and steadied another board along the side.

Her eyes slid to Levi, absorbed in pounding a few nails into the ground with a rock. When Maira raised her face, Frank was watching her, and she knew by his look that he'd seen her watching Tanner. Shame rushed through her and she wondered what he must think; but what she wasn't prepared for was his smile and nod, as if he approved.

❧

"You're a worker, son. That's a good trait."

Tanner turned with an armful of split wood as Frank limped up to him.

"Been meaning to cut more, but it's hard to swing when I don't have the balance."

He didn't think for a minute that Frank's statement was a bid for sympathy. Stacking the wood, he listened as the old cowhand continued. Frank might be his key to information.

"You've done more in a day than I could do in a month. And there's more to be done. Much more." It was the tenor of the man's voice that changed. The way

Frank stood, weight shifted to his left leg, loose and unthreatening, belied the bite to his words. "If you've a thought to stay and work, we'll welcome it; but you best know that meals is all you'll be getting, and them will be scarce on meat. Last night's supper was the last meat on hand. I've got me a vegetable garden that's just starting and we're lower on provisions than a hibernating bear." Frank paused, eyes hard.

"I'll go hunting."

"And I can cut it up and get it in that smokehouse you're building."

Tanner slapped his hands together as he straightened. Something was eating at Frank, but the old man wasn't saying what was really on his mind, just giving him another verbal list of things that needed to be done. More of the same warnings about not getting paid and the meager supply of meat. He wondered if the man's warnings had anything to do with the whispers of Maira's and Frank's voices on the porch last night. He'd heard the murmur of their talk from the bunkhouse, and he'd bet anything he was the subject.

"The cattle can't wait though. It's already later than it should be to round them up."

As Frank fell into step with him up to the ranch house, the smell of food intensified. Levi bounced out onto the porch then ran back inside, hollering, "Coming. They're coming!"

Frank chuckled as he took the first step with his left foot first. "He's a good boy. Just curious is all."

Tanner waited for Frank to reach the landing, not seeing a need to voice an opinion he hadn't really formed. The screen door opened smoothly. Maira stood at the cookstove, a towel of some sort tucked into the waistband of her simple blue skirt. She turned as their boots announced their arrival. "Won't be five minutes. Levi, did you get water for the men?"

The boy bounded off through a doorway and reappeared with two mugs. Tanner sat across from Frank and watched as the boy scooted a stool over and climbed up on it. He placed the mugs on the work surface and ladled water from a bucket into the first. He picked it up and scooted around, face scrunched in concentration. Tanner almost offered a helping hand but decided against it. Work was something the boy would be used to, and not having any siblings meant he'd probably learned real fast how to get things done in spite of his size.

Levi shuffled up to him first, his face lighting in a huge grin as Tanner took the mug. "Didn't drop none. You see that?"

"I sure did. You did real good."

Maira crossed to the table with a covered basket of biscuits and a crock of butter. "Ham gravy and biscuits."

"Sounds good to me."

She exchanged a look with Frank that the older man intercepted and interpreted, but whatever the silent message, it was lost to him. If it was the food, he wasn't sure why she would feel such an offering would be lacking. He ate far less on most days when he got tired of his own cooking. And the previous evening's ham, for him, had been a luxury he seldom enjoyed. No man turned his nose up at leftovers. Is that what was troubling her? The ham would stretch to sandwiches for lunch and beans for supper. He admired frugality. She could boil the bone with potatoes. . . .

Maira placed a pot full of thick gravy and a platter of biscuits on the table. She sat and bowed her head. Levi did, too. Tanner glanced at Frank's bowed head just as the man's voice filled the air with a simple thanksgiving. On the final syllable of the amen, Frank reached out for Levi's plate and filled it with a biscuit and a dab of gravy. He did the same for Maira, giving her a bit more, then stretched his hand for Tanner's plate. Frank returned the plate with double what he'd given to everyone else, not missing the skimpy rations he forked up for himself.

"I don't eat quite as much as you might think," he offered.

"You work hard. Eat up," Frank said.

Maira ate in slow, measured bites, as did Levi. The boy chattered about the nails, the cows, the sheep, nothing about his experience getting lost. His mother didn't offer much, though she listened in rapt attention and offered a comment or two. Frank asked the boy about weeding the garden, and Levi went still and somber.

"Don't like weeds."

"But you want the corn to grow. Nothing like sweet corn on the cob. Got to take care of things, or we won't have anything."

Levi sighed and snapped off a chunk of biscuit with his teeth. "Guess so."

"You promised to help Frank," Maira inserted. "You know he can't get down like you can."

The boy nodded as he chewed. When his eyes settled on Frank, he pointed with his biscuit toward Tanner. "He can help, too."

Maira's eyes shone with humor when she met his gaze. "I think Mr. Young has already helped quite a bit."

"I'll be building a smokehouse tomorrow. If it's all right with your momma, you can help me. Then I'll go hunt for some meat to put in that smokehouse."

Levi broke off a chunk of biscuit and ran it around his plate to sop up gravy. He popped the morsel into his mouth and slumped back on his chair. "Can I play?"

Frank leaned toward the boy. "Why don't you help me clear the table and clean dishes? Your momma needs a few minutes to rest."

"I'm fine, Frank. Really."

The old man's expression clearly showed he wasn't convinced.

She sighed, much as her son had sighed moments before. "Maybe a little tired."

"If you're going off after those cows today, you'll need some rest."

Tanner forked a chunk of biscuit into his mouth. He stared at Maira then Frank. "You're rounding up your cows?"

She shared a glance with Frank then nodded.

So that's what Frank had been trying to ask but couldn't get out.

Frank scooted on his chair. "Told her it's not safe for her to do it alone."

Tanner realized Frank was silently asking him to help her. Begging, really, his dark eyes pleading. "I could help with that. It's dangerous, hot work." *Not fit for a woman,* he wanted to say but bit his tongue.

Maira shook her head. "You've done enough. I won't ask it of you." She glanced at Frank, defiant. Then she shot from her seat and bolted out the door. Frank shrugged then gathered the platter and pot of gravy. "Don't be feeling badly," he said, his gaze on him. "She's a tough one."

Chapter 6

Maira calmed herself by saddling up Queen. The familiar procedure eased her worry. When Levi did not appear, she knew Frank already had the boy busy doing something with the breakfast dishes. After Levi's birth, in that first month when the haze of Jon's death collided with the joy of a newborn, Frank had taken on everything, and only when pneumonia strangled his breath did he relent to rest. Then the bronc had busted him up, and it had been Maira's turn to care for Frank. It had cemented their roles to each other, like father to daughter and daughter to father. But they both knew they needed more help. That the situation was growing desperate.

She mounted Queen and rode by the front of the house to squint through the screen door to make sure Levi was safe. A dark shadow rose up in front of the door a second before it rattled back on its hinge, and Mr. Young appeared. He cleared the steps and was within a few feet of her before she gathered her wits enough to say anything.

"I was checking on Levi."

"He's fine," the man said. "If you're going to look things over, I'll join you."

She wanted to tell him no, to give Queen a taste of her heels and leave the man behind, but she couldn't. Or she wouldn't; she wasn't sure which.

In minutes he had his piebald saddled. He nodded at her to lead the way. It felt strange leading out ahead of the man, and she wondered at the foolhardiness of going too far away from the house with a virtual stranger. Still, he had rescued Levi. Didn't that at least show he held no evil intentions? Her qualms won out and she kept close to the house.

"There's no need to go too far the first day," Tanner said, as if he hadn't heard a word of her earlier protest. "We'll start rounding up close to the house anyhow."

He drew abreast, and she felt his gaze on her, a silent challenge, but he said nothing else. Whenever she glanced his way, she used the opportunity to watch him, taking note of what she saw. Besides the rifle in the scabbard, he wore his guns, a precaution against running into wild bulls or coyotes. Sourness coated her mouth. She'd not even thought to bring her shotgun.

Tanner held up his free hand to indicate caution and stopped his horse. Her heart pounded, yet she didn't see anything until he slid the rifle free and held the weapon to his shoulder. The tight pack of deer moved, tails flicked. She blinked and realized what a good eye the man had. Queen tensed, and Maira stroked the horse's side as the rifle barked. Tanner levered out the spent shell and fired again before she could draw a full breath. The deer were running now, tails flagging their fright.

"Two of 'em." His voice held a triumphant ring.

A swirl of smoke wafted upward in front of her face before she could see the evidence of his shooting.

He worked the piebald up into an excited little dance and grinned over at her as he slid the rifle into the scabbard. "I think I just earned my keep."

She matched his smile with one of her own. "I guess so."

And with that, he gave his horse his head. She took Queen in at a more sedate pace, watching as the man dressed the deer. Steamy entrails hit the ground. Maira smiled. Having come west to marry Jon, she remembered those first years when she'd grown ill watching this process. Now it was a way of life, a means to an end, and venison steaks would be a welcome dish. She ground-hitched Queen and yanked up her sleeves. Tanner turned the carcass in his arms and lifted it bodily.

"Must weigh a good hundred pounds," he grunted.

Maira took the knife he'd left and found the breastbone of the other deer. Inserting the blade, she slit the skin downward, careful not to puncture the entrails. The smell hit her hard. She pushed on, struggling with the legs, wishing a tree were closer so she could do as Jon had done to make the process easier and hang it from a limb. Her hands, slick with blood, struggled for purchase. Tanner knelt across from her, his mouth a grim line but his eyes glittering with unsuppressed amusement. He leaned forward and held out his hands. She handed over the knife and watched as he, with sure strokes, dispensed with the grim duties. Maira rose, the smell sticking in her throat. Deep breaths cleansed her nose and head of the noxious odor. She bent to swipe her hands along the grass and frowned at the mess on the front of her once-pristine blouse. Not her best, but her clothing was as limited as her money. It brought back the biting frustration she'd felt before leaving the breakfast table. Finding a solution to the money problems rested on her shoulders, yet she felt so weak for the task.

She shoved away the thought. One day at a time. At least she had Levi. When she returned her attention to Tanner, he had almost finished the gruesome task. She hurried back to help him hoist the deer, but he pushed away her hands with a grunt. He lifted the smaller deer with ease and strapped it behind her saddle. Straightening, his shirt bloodied with gore.

Maira couldn't resist a jibe. "Not quite the work I'd hoped to accomplish."

Tanner's lips curled a little bit. "Guess not. Sorry about that. Maybe we should take tomorrow to get that smokehouse built before we go after the cows."

He moved to her side, and she found the sun blocked by his wide shoulders. If she looked up, his face would be there, close to hers. He cupped his hand to accept her foot. She took the help with the same ease it was offered and settled onto the saddle. Queen would protest the extra weight of the carcass, but it couldn't be helped. "You're a good shot; I never even saw them. Frank's better at seeing game, but he misses more than he hits. Don't tell him I said that."

Tanner grinned over at her as he brought the piebald even with Queen. His beard covered most of his face, but his dark eyes held a distinct twinkle. "The secret is safe with me."

❧

Riding beside the woman made it harder to concentrate on his mental drawings of the smokehouse. The sky, clear blue and shot with wisps of cloud, coupled with the caress of breeze through his beard and the presence of the woman, made Tanner feel... He pressed his lips together and forced himself to focus on the design of the smokehouse. Of Frank and his thoughts about a brace to alleviate the twist and help the man ride. Of the cattle that needed to be rounded up.

"Have you been in this area long, Mr. Young?"

An innocent question. He drew in a breath. "For a while."

When she asked nothing else, he knew his vagueness had shut her down. For the first time in a long time, Tanner wished he could talk. Women liked that sort of thing, but it had been a long time since he'd been this close to one. He stole a glance at her profile, the glossy fall of dark hair. He swallowed hard and scrubbed at his beard, feeling unkempt and messy, yet safe, too. The beard helped hide him. It gave the impression of a wild, untamed man, and he was comfortable with that. A stab of anger inserted itself, and he nudged Cue to pick up the pace and take the lead.

When they came around to the barn, Frank called out from the house, "How goes?"

Tanner raised his hand. Maira went straight to the front porch where Frank stood. She would fill him in on the deer. Tanner led Cue to a tree, where he flung the coil of rope into the air and over the lower branch. He made quick work of knotting the end of the rope around the deer's forelegs and cinching the knot tight. Releasing the leather strips he'd used to keep the deer in place, he pulled on the other end of the rope until the deer dangled off the ground a good eight feet.

Maira rode her horse closer. He noted the streaks of blood on the front of her shirt. If not for the smile on her face she might look as if she'd just murdered someone. She turned the full effect of her smile on him, unaware of his dark thoughts.

"Frank's a little jealous, I think."

"No need to be." He worked the other coil of rope over another sturdy branch and motioned her to bring her horse closer.

Maira hid a yawn with her hand.

"Best change before Levi sees you."

"Frank already got him down for his nap, so I've got a few minutes anyhow."

He debated as he tested the knot whether he should bring up the subject foremost in his mind. Judging by the way she'd manhandled—*woman*-handled—the deer, this gal had spunk. But she didn't have strength, and whether she realized it or not, rounding up cattle took time, patience, and more than one person. "You'll wait for me to help with the roundup then?"

Her heavy sigh was out before she must have realized how telling it had been. "Yes," came her firm answer.

"Lot of work," he grunted as he tugged on the rope. The deer rose in increments from behind the saddle with every tug.

"I know."

"Walt isn't sending any of his men this year?"

She turned her face toward the sun, exposing a long column of pale flesh that forced him to look away. "I don't know. He never says, just rides through here and. . ."

Tanner didn't press. Though Walt's help had been generous, Tanner wondered about such an offer. A deeper question gnawed. Tying the deer into place, Tanner debated his response.

"Would you like some coffee?"

Her offer surprised and pleased him.

"Frank will have a pot made, I'm sure." She stared down at the ground then back up. He caught her uncertainty.

"Let me change my shirt and get cleaned up," he said.

His statement made her blink and frown down at her blouse. "Yes, I guess I'd best do the same."

Chapter 7

Maira struggled to stay awake. Her coffee had long ago gotten cold, but she enjoyed this time of the evening. Jon used to call it "catch-up time," and she'd found it to be true. With all the work to be done, it was the only part of the day reserved for sitting and thinking, or talking, as they liked to do. Having Tanner Young join them around the table had felt right. Like he belonged. It took great effort for her to remind herself that he did not and that his stay was temporary. She should be relieved. Without his presence everything would return to normal. He built a fire in the fireplace, and the ache of that action echoed through her. Jon had loved the sound of the fire crackling. Frank often built fires, but seeing Tanner haul in the wood and stack it carefully, his shirt stretched across his back, had taken her breath away.

She collected her hair in one hand and closed her eyes as conversation between Frank and Tanner moved to the smokehouse. Having a pantry full of meat would be wonderful, and she could not deny the fact that the burden of another mouth to feed was offset by the man's skill with a gun. She'd admired the skeletal structure of the smokehouse as Tanner had worked on it throughout the afternoon.

". . .bed?"

She blinked her eyes at the hesitation in conversation, realizing that all eyes focused on her. Frank's brow was folded into lines of amusement. "I'm headed that way," she said before giving a tired smirk. "You just want to talk behind my back."

Frank chuckled. "Then just sit there and turn yourself around."

Maira collected her cup and rose, nodding to them both. She doubted she could sleep knowing they were out here. From her room she would hear their voices, if not their words. Jon and Frank used to use the late evening to talk about the herds and Jon's hopes for expanding. For weeks they'd talked about the benefits of buying a sheep wagon and the price of shearing the flock themselves versus paying to have it done. Everything came down to dollars and cents, a subject that exhausted Maira, and even more so now when there were more cents than dollars.

She opened the front screen door, aware of Mr. Young's lingering look on her. Their gazes met and held, until she shut the door and blocked the sight of eyes the color of chocolate drops. Lifting the only window in the room, a breeze shot through and held her in its clutches, making her shiver. Chocolate drops. Her breath caught at the chill. Sliding the window down, she angled the stick to hold it open a crack and shrugged from her clean blouse. The bloodstained one was draped across a chair. What had she been thinking? Wrangling a deer, trying to prove herself. Why? She'd ruined a good blouse and she only had two others.

Peeling back the covers, she sat on the bed's edge and braided her hair, then slipped under the comforter and curled close to Levi. His warm little body brought comfort even as it stirred the ache of her loss. Jon's presence seemed strongest when night descended. Through the door, she could hear Tanner's voice, deep, resonating. Despite herself, she felt safer for his proximity. Frank's presence was security, but his limp and age made him as vulnerable as her. She turned her face into her pillow, dreading tomorrow. The cows. With Tanner getting so much work done on the smokehouse, they'd decided over supper to ride out for half a day, starting early in the morning, and return before dark so he could finish the building. She grimaced. She didn't even know how to throw a rope. Jon had meant to show her how, but her pregnancy had put those plans on hold. Permanently. All she would do tomorrow was ride around on Queen and scream at the cows to move, not knowing a fig about getting them out of tight areas or rousing them from scratchy shrubs. Frank must have laughed on the inside when she declared her intentions, but the man had remained stoic, even concerned. Could be he feared for her sanity.

Maira knew then that she would not sleep. Not with the men talking and her mind whirling and the unpleasant task ahead of her. Easing from the bed, she reversed her earlier process, pulling on the clean blouse and regular skirt. She finger-combed strands from her face and left her hair in the braid. With her hand on the door latch, she took one last glance back at Levi. A sliver of moonlight skimmed his cheek. Maira smiled, heart twisting in gratitude for the gift God had given her and the mercy of Levi's return.

When she opened the bedroom door, she was surprised to see Frank coming in the front door and Tanner by the fire, his eyes on her. Chocolate drops. She smiled. "I can't sleep," she declared.

❧

Her smile tripped Tanner's heartbeat. He groped for his coffee and sucked down the rest of it like a bear sucking honey. Though stone cold, the brew was bitter and the acid of it burned his throat. Frank made the stuff so strong it would melt iron, or at least shake the vision of Maira from his head. The effect wore off as soon as he set the cup aside. She was there, taking her seat at the head of the table, and he couldn't deny himself the chance to stare. At the silky shine of her braid, the slight wrinkle pattern on her cheek, the great green of eyes that were, in turn, staring back at him with a mix of puzzlement and amusement.

Frank brought a fresh pot to the table and filled Maira's cup, and still they were locked in a silent stare-down. His hand snaked out for his mug, and he cleared his throat. He was dimly aware of Frank moving behind him. Maira's presence held him spellbound. He squeezed his coffee mug, lifting it, and he heard Frank yelp and felt heat sear his hand. He jerked his hand and shook it as white-hot fire continued to burn. A chair scraped, and Frank slammed the pot onto the table. Fierce red etched a path along the side and back of Tanner's hand. Maira was beside him in an instant, guiding his hand to the bucket of water, where the coolness soothed the fire. He released his breath. Frank mopped up the mess on the table.

"Woolgathering?"

Tanner saw Frank's grin, more a smirk.

"If you knew he wasn't paying attention, why didn't you say something?"

"Didn't expect him to jerk it up so quick."

Maira's brows lowered at the old man. Frank shrugged, nonplussed.

"You leave your hand in there for a while." She leaned forward to gaze into the bucket, the braid of her hair slipping over her shoulder, snaking down to the tabletop.

"I'll be fine," he said.

She touched the arm that dangled over the bucket. "I'm sure you will, but the water will help. I just wish I had some ice."

Frank slumped into his chair and leaned his elbows on the table. "He's a big boy, Maira. Any cowpuncher worth his salt is used to pain. Guess it's a woman's right to fuss a little though." Frank's smile squinted his eyes. "Men tend to like it, too."

Tanner kept his eyes on the table and his mouth shut. It wasn't the fussing that bothered him; it was getting used to the fussing that was the problem. And with Maira's hand on his arm, he thought he could do just that.

"I'll be fine," he repeated. "Why don't you finish your coffee before it gets cold?"

Her hand left his arm and she took up her spot at the head of the table.

"Probably wasn't so hot anyhow," Frank piped up. "It'd been sitting for almost twenty minutes."

Tanner begged to differ on the temperature but didn't comment. He pulled his hand from the bucket and dabbed the tender spot dry with the towel Frank had used. It began to sting again, but he tuned out the discomfort. "We need to talk about the cattle."

Frank's gaze flicked to him, to Maira, then back to him.

What he was most grateful to see was the open curiosity on Maira's face. "I know you want to have a part, but it's no place for a woman without experience. I think I have a plan, if Frank's willing to hear it."

"Got my ear, Young."

"You said you can't ride, and I don't doubt it must be uncomfortable, but what if I built a custom brace for your leg? You could get on your horse by standing on something."

Frank buried his chin in his chest.

"If you can rope and peg, I can do the mounting and dismounting so you can stay in the saddle."

"Might work. I'd have to look at that brace, and what about that smokehouse? Now we've got meat that needs tending to. Shame to let it go to waste."

"The way I see it. . ." He paused, realizing Maira still had not said a word. Not even a protest. Maybe she did know how foolhardy her plan really was after all. He cleared his throat. "We'll work on the smokehouse and get the meat put up. The cows can wait another day." He turned to Frank. "I'll work on your brace in the morning, too. Shouldn't take too long, and it'll give you a chance to get used to it."

Still no reaction from Maira. He licked the corners of his mouth. "With everyone pitching in on the smokehouse, it should finish up real quick. If you're willing, ma'am, er. . ." He realized in that moment that he didn't know her last name and wasn't quite comfortable calling her by her first. "Uh, Mrs. . . ."

"Cullen."

Cullen. His eyes snapped to hers as that news penetrated deep. Jon Cullen's widow. Why hadn't he considered that before? Because it had been such a long time since he'd first found the body and begun his private examination of the accusations against the man. Accusations he could put to rest with ease. But revealing what he knew could also put her in danger.

He'd allowed a lull in the conversation for too long. Maira leaned forward, eyes round with dawning realization. Frank cleared his throat. "That name mean something to you?"

"You know something about Jon," Maira pressed.

Her statement buzzed in his head. He chose his words carefully. "Heard about him being found."

If she'd hoped for more, the slump of her shoulders trumpeted her disappointment.

"Jon Cullen was a good man." Frank folded his arms and glared. "He wouldn't steal."

Tanner weighed his words. "Some are quick to accuse a man, especially when he can't talk back."

Maira ran a hand down the length of her braid. The gesture gave off the impression of a young schoolgirl. Vulnerable and uncertain.

Words pushed into his throat, but he hesitated. They were things that would confuse her, as they most certainly had confused him. There was a game being played here by someone against Maira and Jon Cullen. He was sure of it.

Maira pushed from the table and rose to her feet. As Tanner watched, she opened her bedroom door then hesitated. She turned, and their eyes met. He caught the sheen of tears along her cheeks before she shut the door. If Tanner had set aside his doubts about the death of Jon Cullen, Maira's crestfallen expression, coupled with evidence of tears, renewed his determination to uncover the truth.

Chapter 8

There's a full moon coming up. I'm gonna head out and start work on wrapping meat for smoking and salt the rest. There's a stream west of here that we've used to keep things cool," Frank said. His voice revealed nothing. No curiosity. Nothing except the desire to work instead of sleep.

Tanner rose to his feet, too. "I'll help you get started. I'm not feeling tired."

"Been thinking about extra wood for that bunkhouse. There's an old shanty near the stream that can be torn down. Should supply the need."

Tanner nodded and swung away from the table. His hand burned where the coffee had hit. He made a fist, pulling the skin taut and increasing the discomfort. Opening and closing his fist didn't help, but he pumped it until Frank stood beside him, his brown eyes amused. He lifted the lantern high. Tanner could better see the raging streak of red across the back of his hand.

"You won't let it slow you down none."

Without responding, Tanner continued to the front door. A part of him wondered if those tears he'd seen in Maira's eyes now saturated her pillow, if she lay silent and sobbing or if sleep had claimed her and wiped away the hurt and pain. He was grateful Frank did not push the subject of Jon Cullen's death. No doubt many knew of the accusations against the man. Walt Price had crowed to all that Jon's body had been found with the gold on it. Gold he'd stolen from someone in order to buy more cattle and get a leg up on Walt. Price had painted Jon Cullen as a desperate man.

Together Frank and Tanner hauled the deer to the stream in the bed of the wagon. Frank stretched out his leg and kept hold of the two lanterns they'd use for light. At the stream, Frank sectioned the deer and began cutting and rinsing the meat while Tanner hammered at the shanty, tearing off boards and reclaiming the nails. At the end of an hour, the shanty was nothing more than a rough stone foundation and a pile of boards. Frank had washed and put the meat in a barrel, layering in salt.

"I'm starting to feel it." Frank stretched upward and massaged his right leg before lowering himself by the stream. A groan crossed his lips as he leaned forward to let the water wash the blood from his hands. "Maira will make sausage, and we'll smoke the rest." Frank sat back. "You're pushing yourself pretty hard, Young. All for nothing. Guess it makes me wonder why."

Tanner hesitated. "Can't a man ride in, see a need, and want to help without arousing suspicions?"

"Sure. I'm a God-fearing man. Believed in miracles most my life."

Shame washed over Tanner. His presence was a miracle? Is that what Frank thought? And Maira? He'd attacked the work at the ranch, even the shanty. Yanking boards and ripping into the work because of. . .what? The specter at his heels? The new things stirring in his heart and mind when Maira was near? Tanner tugged the rope holding the back hooves of the carcasses away from Frank and tied them to the back of the wagon. "I'll take you back," he offered.

Frank rose to his knees and straightened in slow degrees, hand to his hip. "Getting down gets me every time."

Tanner put the lid on the barrel and hammered it down tight, then stooped to shoulder the burden and shove it onto the wagon. Frank heaved himself into the bed of the wagon behind the barrels. They rode back to the house in silence. Exhaustion weighted Tanner's body, a harbinger for sound sleep. After driving a ways from the house, he cut the ropes and let the carcasses lay in a stand of aspens in the bright moonlight. The trip back had more of the same silence, and when the horse reached the side of the house, Tanner left the barrels in the wagon and followed Frank to the bunkhouse. He unrolled the blanket he'd tossed down earlier and removed his boots, scrubbing at his beard, thinking.

"You gonna take it off?"

Tanner caught Frank's dim profile in the dark. The older man had already stretched out, boots still on his feet. "Thinking about it."

"Jon Cullen was a clean-shaven man."

He wasn't sure what to say to that, afraid to explore the implications of the suggestion.

"When you reckon on telling her?"

Tanner worked off a boot and let it drop before he answered. "Tell her what?"

"Cullen is a familiar name to you. You knew Jon Cullen, or knew of him. And by my best guess, you know more than what the rumors brought to you on the wind."

"It's a long story" was all he offered.

Frank let out a loud yawn. "Well, I won't stay awake to hear it tonight."

And that was it. Within minutes he heard the man's deep, even breathing. But sleep did not come quite so quickly to Tanner Young, and by the time weariness threatened to swallow him, Frank's new handcrafted brace sat in the corner of the bunkhouse.

❧

Arms aching from the lifting and tugging and the heat radiating from the boiling water, Maira did her best to put on a smile every time Levi, from his perch at the kitchen window, gave a report on what the men were doing outside. Just before three in the afternoon she took out the last hot jar from the boiling water. She felt boiled herself, having hovered over the steaming pot all morning.

Grateful to be done, she held out her hand to Levi. "I think it's a good time to check up on the men."

Levi scampered to his feet, barreled by her outstretched hand, and ran through the kitchen to the front door. "I wanna see Tan-wer's face."

Maira sighed and quickened her pace to keep Levi in sight, not sure what to make of his comment. Tanner's lower body was the only thing visible as he stood inside the door to the smokehouse. He'd ridden out before she woke that morning and hadn't been in to eat at breakfast or lunch. Outside, Frank was grinning at the smokehouse as if he'd built it himself. Maira knew from Levi's updates that Frank had practiced all morning on horseback with his new brace. Frank's enthusiasm was contagious, and she wondered if Tanner knew the enormity of the gift he'd given the old cowpuncher.

"Levi tells me you've been up on Queen."

Frank grinned down at the wooden brace enclosing the bottom part of his leg. "It helps keep it from twisting so much." He stuck his leg out straight and pointed. "He even put a wedge on the heel to weight my foot to turn the right way."

She nodded at the contraption. "It doesn't look comfortable."

Frank's grin went huge. "That's where the sheep's wool comes in handy. I stick it in the places where it pinches. Other than that. . ." He shrugged, as if to say nothing else mattered. And, indeed, Maira knew that for Frank, to be back in the saddle made his world complete.

Levi tugged at the man's hand. "Can I straighten those nails for Tan-wer?"

"Mr. Young," Maira corrected.

Tanner ducked out of the smokehouse in time to hear the correction. "It doesn't bother me none."

"Well, it bothers me. . . ." She searched for air and couldn't draw any into her lungs. Tanner Young had shaved off his beard. Handsome didn't quite cover her first impression. A tilt of his lips told her her reaction hadn't gone unnoticed.

"Your face is bare, Tan-wer!" Levi crowed.

Maira snapped to attention. "Levi, you will not call an adult by their first name." She arched a brow at Tanner. "Is that clear, Mr. Young?"

"Yes ma'am." Tanner leaned down to Levi and spoke in an overloud whisper. "I'll call you Mr. Cullen."

Levi giggled like a madman. Maira crossed her arms and glared, and when Tanner tilted his face up at her, the impact of that full smile and the cleft in his chin, not to mention his shining dark eyes, starved her lungs for air all over again.

Frank broke into the moment. "We should get that meat hung and the fire started."

Tanner turned as he stood, "Mr. Cullen, if you'll gather some kindling..."

Levi dashed off toward the woodpile, laughing like a maniac. Maira ignored them and ducked into the smokehouse. Great holes allowed sunshine to beam through. She frowned and backed out. "Should there be so many holes?"

"That's where the smoke escapes. Has to have some way to get out," Frank said.

Tanner returned with slabs of meat covered in material, ducked into the smokehouse and began hanging them from the pegs that covered the inside walls. Frank handed more cuts in to Tanner until everything was hung and Tanner reappeared. Frank started the fire, adding some chips he'd soaked in a barrel overnight. "Keeps the smoke going," he explained to her as he threw them on the fire.

Smoke began to collect and billow out of the various cracks in wisps. The sight and smell made Maira feel rich. Richer than she'd felt in a long time. Her throat swelled with emotion when she considered the man who had made all that meat possible. In less than three days he'd changed so much on the ranch. Levi wiggled in beside Tanner with his rock, picked up a nail, and mimicked the man's movements as Tanner pounded bent nails straight again. Her heart twisted in a knot of familiar grief. She swallowed over the emotion and ran her hands down her skirt. "Clean up and come on in, and we'll have an early supper."

Levi stood tall and rubbed his stomach. "You hungry, Tan-wer?"

"Reckon I could eat some." His gaze went to Maira. "What're we having?"

She smiled, putting every bit of her happy emotion into the expression. "Why venison steak and gravy of course."

Chapter 9

Tanner rode the fence line to the west of the Rocking J before the sun was up next morning. He felt more in control than he had since arriving at the ranch and gazing into Maira's green eyes. Frank's horse pulled abreast of him.

"How's the leg?"

"Good. Feels real good. Being in the saddle again is like coming home after a long winter away."

Tanner understood. Eyes to the ground, he watched for prints that meant cows nearby, or hoofprints that gave away the presence of rustlers. He'd investigated allegations against cattle rustlers before and had learned that the bigger the ranch that did the accusation, usually the smaller the ranch on the receiving end. Something about seeing the little ranchers stomped on set his blood to boiling. Things were brewing beneath the surface at the XP. Price had become greedy for land more than cattle, though the two almost always went hand in glove.

There was a sweet irony in learning that Walt wanted him to spy on the widow of a man whose death Tanner knew was a murder. Beneath that calm exterior, Maira Cullen was a tough bronc, but telling her that Walt had sent him to spy might make her turn on Walt. Or on him. He had to buy himself time. Let Walt think his little game was still running smoothly.

The path they followed took them to the same corner of the property where Jon Cullen's body had been found. "And look there." He pointed for Frank to see. "Hoofprints."

"Horse."

He talked to Frank that night, away from Maira and Levi, trying to discover answers to the questions crowding his mind.

"Walt's tried real hard to get Mrs. Cullen's permission to court her." Frank answered Tanner's first question as they sat on the porch following supper. Maira's concentration on Levi gave him the opportunity to draw out the older man.

Somehow the news of Walt's desire to court Maira didn't surprise him. Walt's kind would marry for richer or poorer, preferring the poorer kind in order to keep them under his heel while he absorbed all they'd worked for. Or—Tanner's mind went black with rage—he'd be the kind to keep a girl on hand. Like the little maid. Some women might fall for Walt's tricks, but he doubted Maira would.

Frank laughed. "Maira keeps her own counsel though. Seen too much heartache in her youth to trust easy. Took offense that Walt asked her so soon after Jon's death and never forgot that he had. I'm guessing old Walt didn't reckon on him having a woman as a neighbor, and not one so stubborn as her."

"Hard to live with, is she?" He knew the question was invasive and probably bordering on inappropriate.

Frank pursed his lips and chewed hard on his lower lip. "Depends on whether you're asking for yourself or for some other reason I'm needing to be knowing about."

"Just wanting to know what kind of boss I'm working for."

The old cowpuncher didn't quite hide his knowing grin. "She's a good woman. A lonely soul." Frank rubbed at his right thigh. "Jon Cullen and I met years ago. He was a young man with no family and nowhere to go. I took him in and taught him some things. Got him a job clerking at the general store. He saved his money up, bought a ranch. Kept tabs on me for a few years, I guess. Then he started coming back into town. Asked if I would ride with him to buy some head. He was good to me. Treated me good, and the offer came at a time when I needed a distraction. We worked well together."

"How did he meet Mrs. Cullen?"

"Maira?" Frank chuckled. "She'd come from the Midwest. Was a kid with a chip on her shoulder, but he charmed her. Drew her out and got her to marry up with him. They had a good marriage."

"A chip on her shoulder?"

"Jon found out she was an orphan. Got passed over when couples came looking for children to adopt. That kind of thing is hard on a kid."

He couldn't imagine what it must be like to be abandoned by your parents, though he knew all too well the ramifications of doing the abandoning.

"Apparently a couple decided to take her home but returned her a year later. Orphanage turned her out when she was sixteen, and she hitched her way west."

She was tough. He'd learned that in the week he'd been there. To have grown up being rejected, only to be loved, then lose that love...

"She pours herself into their son. Spitting image of his pa, that one. Not in looks, mind you, but in the way he does things. Runs off real quick when he gets curious about something. That's what happened that day. Maira was plowing the garden for me, and Levi started chasing butterflies and flying pests."

Frank's talk lulled him. He couldn't help but picture a petite version of a younger Maira. Alone and rejected at an orphanage. "You get to town much?"

Grunting, Frank leaned forward. "I've tried to encourage Maira to go to some singings or to church, but she only turns the tables on me. Says I should take my own medicine and get myself into a pew again."

"Was Jon Cullen a church man?"

"Had our services here."

"He led them?"

Frank frowned. "If'n you gotta know, I led the services. Used to be a preacher."

"Isn't that something you always are? You sound like you gave it up."

" 'Bout did, until Jon set some fire under me."

There was a story in there somewhere, but Tanner knew he needed sleep. Frank did, too, and they still had some things to figure out before getting an early start. "You know what we're seeing isn't matching up to what should be there."

Frank's eyebrows knit then cleared. "You mean the cattle."

"There's precious few young ones. Did Maira keep close tabs on Walt's men while they sorted the cattle then merged them with XP for the drive to sale?"

"She done the best she could, but it was Jon's territory, if you get my meanin'."

"So it wouldn't have been hard for Price's men to take advantage of Maira's limited knowledge?"

"Guess not. I blame myself. That first year I was down with this injury. . . ." Frank stared at his hands. "Took me a long while to get myself together after that."

"Does what we're seeing match up with what you knew from the days you rode?"

The cowpuncher worked his hand across his jaw, eyes distant as he considered.

"Doesn't it seem strange that Walt sends his own men over here and pays them to work for Mrs. Cullen?"

"Did it as a favor to her after Jon passed."

"Was murdered, you mean. And Walt Price was the one who spread those rumors about Mr. Cullen stealing that gold and produced that miner who vowed that his gold had indeed been stolen." Tanner clasped his hands. "Why would the man who accused your husband of stealing then turn around and send his hands to round up your cattle?" Several possibilities came to his mind. The lies would isolate her from the townsfolk who might otherwise be sympathetic to a widow. If Maira thought they all agreed with Walt's accusation against Jon, it would give her more reason to stay clear of town. Then there was the idea that he wanted to court her. . . .

"If Walt's men show up while I'm gone, it's best to let them ride on. Tell them you'll be merging your herd with some of the smaller ranches for the drive."

The twist of Frank's jaw and the redness of his lower lip showed the man's consternation. Frank didn't like having a process questioned that he'd sanctioned "Might be I'm getting too old. Pride's not as easy to swallow when you've got young ones questioning what you've done all your life." He raised his chin and gave Tanner a nod. "You do what you think is right."

Sleep would not come for Tanner though. The bunkhouse still perched on the boards he'd used to hold up that end, the foundation of rocks growing, but he needed another load before he could finish the project. He turned over, sleep eluding him even though his body begged for it. Someone was rustling, and if they weren't doing it in the day, maybe they were doing it at night. There was only one way to find out.

❧

Frank was worried, and Maira knew it. If not for the sudden disappearance of Tanner in the night, she might not have thought a thing about Frank's show of distress; but the man had grown snappish, a trait she had seldom seen in him. Levi had grown clingy, sensitive to Frank's mood. She gave Frank space after they finished garden work, and he went off to piddle with the fire in the smokehouse. She kept Levi occupied indoors, the tension stretching her nerves taut.

When she had to explain to Levi for the third time the reason he could not play in the pile of nails outside, she ushered him into their room.

"Want to see Tan-wer."

"That's 'Mr. Young,' and you'll have to wait. I need to talk to Frank." She pointed to the bed. "Serious talk."

"I'm not tired," he pouted in a low mutter.

"Then rest quietly."

His lower lip pooched out and his eyes filled. Maira hated this, the tug of war, her desperate need for quiet and adult conversation. To know what it was Tanner was thinking and why he'd left without explanation.

"After your nap, I'll let you play outside for a while."

"With Tan-wer?"

"If Tanner is back, then yes."

"You mean Mr. Young?" Levi's tears cleared and his mouth quirked in a little grin up at her.

"Yes" She pointed again, boosting him up to the mattress. "Mr. Young."

"He likes to be called Tan-wer."

"Yes. I'm sure he does."

"Then why can't I call him that?"

"Because I said." She pointed to the bed. "Lie down now!"

He slunk under the covers, and she pulled them up to his shoulders. She tried to collect herself, but she was so tired. Worried. She just wanted everything to be good again, like it was when Jon had been alive. She leaned over and pecked Levi's forehead, not missing the wetness on his cheeks. She would have to make it up to him. Somehow.

When she reentered the kitchen, Frank had scraped the leftover food into the slop bucket and rinsed the plates in a pan of tepid water. He half-turned toward her. "Would you like another cup of coffee?"

She shook her head and sank into the chair nearest Frank.

"The garden will do well this year," Frank said.

Her back ached from the hoeing and planting they'd done, and she leaned forward to stretch the kinks from her muscles. "Yes, I think you're right."

"Levi will be quite the farmer," Frank added. "He's a good boy, Maira."

She basked in his words, feeling the little knots of tension easing a little. Since Levi's disappearance and the fear she might have lost him for good, it had been too easy to question her mothering skills. Being a mother to him was normal and natural. Yet she wished he had the benefit of Jon's presence. Her throat tightened and tears burned. She needed to be thankful that Frank filled some of that role and that Tanner was a good example as well.

"Tanner should be back soon. He wouldn't leave the bunkhouse unfinished unless it was important."

"Tell me what he's out there doing, Frank. You know, don't you?"

"He thinks. . ." Frank finished the last plate and set it, still wet, on a hemmed dish towel. "He thinks Walt Price is up to something."

Maira's deepest worries swelled. "The XP?"

"We don't get out much, you and me. Could be there's something going on we're not knowing about. Walt's got a big place, and he was the first to make the accusation against Jon. . . ."

He grimaced. "At first I had a hard time with what Tanner was saying, but the more I got to thinking on it, the more I wonder."

"We don't know him very well. He just rode in here out of nowhere and started doing things."

Frank's gaze went hard. "He came with a mind to work and has done an awful lot for us."

"So did Walt's men. For days," she reminded him.

The fact of the matter was she didn't know Walt Price either. Other than sending two or three cowhands to round up the Rocking J herds every spring and at his expense, what did she know of the man? He'd been quick to accuse Jon when gold was found on Jon's body. She tried to remember if her husband had said anything negative about their neighbor to the east. Jon had been more worried about building his herds, scraping to buy each and every cow and ewe he could. But what if the worry she'd perceived wasn't over just money problems and buying cows and sheep? What if Jon had been troubled over an issue with Walt?

"True," Frank said, "but I also know that when Jon was alive, we were doing well. The herds were growing, and we were making some profit. Not much, mind you, but based on that, and the fact that the weather's been mild the last couple of years, we should have made more. Lots more."

"Did Jon mention Walt to you? The XP?"

Frank's round face pinched in thought. "Don't recall much other than getting some XP stock off our property once or twice during that drought. His cows were pushing the fence down to get to the stream."

It wasn't much, Maira conceded, if indeed it was anything at all. Yet Frank's words showed a desperation. If the XP needed another water source, it might lead the man to underhanded methods. Price's accusation against Jon stuck hard in her stomach. She hadn't wanted to consider the truth of Walt's hard words or the miner he'd produced to prove the story true. Jon would never have stolen gold. From anyone. He had known what it was like to grow up poor, as she had, and neither wanted anything more than steady growth in the herd and a home of their own.

"Young will be back soon. We'll know more then." Frank stood to his feet, moving slower than normal, his right leg probably stiff from working in the garden.

"Are you sure you'll be able to handle rounding up cattle with your leg?"

Frank's stare bordered on a glare. "I'll do it because it needs done." He stood on the top step, his back to her. "Young's right; it's not any kind of work a woman should be doing, especially not alone. Levi needs you, and with this brace, I can ride." Without a backward glance he went down the step and headed off toward the bunkhouse.

Chapter 10

Tanner rode Cue in quietly two days later and under the cover of dying daylight. He watched Frank cross the distance between the house and the bunkhouse. Cupid was done in from the long day and strained forward. Maira Cullen's mare watched them from the corral. Frank stopped to stroke the mare's nose, speaking to the horse in low tones. Tanner was tired. He wanted nothing more than some hot food and a place to sleep. He petted Cue's neck to keep the gelding calm until Frank moved away toward the bunkhouse, his swinging gait more pronounced than usual. Must be having trouble with his leg.

When Frank went inside, Tanner led the horse from the shadow of the lean-to and over to the corral. The horses touched noses before Maira's mare galloped away in a playful show. His fingers felt thick as he loosened, then removed, Cue's cinch strap and stripped the saddle and then the blanket from his horse's back. He opened the gate to the corral, mulling another dose of jerked venison against wandering inside to see if there were any cold biscuits left from supper, when he felt a presence a second before Maira Cullen's voice broke the silence.

"I think they've missed each other."

He caught the mirth in her voice and turned with a grin, his hand going to his chin. Four days had done away with his clean-shaven look. He wondered if she noticed. Funny how he never thought of his appearance until she was there. But the thought wiped away his humor. Or maybe it was the sight of her. In that time of day when the sun had slunk away but the stars had yet to shine, her eyes were luminous. Her hair blew around her face as if an invisible hand tousled the strands. She was beautiful.

For the first time in a long time, Tanner Young wanted to forget the ache of being in the saddle or always being on guard against predators of the night. Watching Maira Cullen stirred a desire for something softer, sweeter. The light of a hearth and promise of a warm meal and arms that would welcome him with soft embraces and whispered words. A world of his own.

"Have you eaten?"

He realized he stood there with his hand on the open gate. Cue had already gone in to chase and nip at the mare, both animals oblivious to the beckon of freedom his reverie offered them. Heat crept up his neck and he cleared his throat as he swung the gate closed. "I was wondering if you might have a biscuit or something left over."

Maira's gentle laugh stole his attention. He couldn't think what he'd said that was funny.

"Come on up to the porch and I'll bring you some coffee. Levi is asleep, and Frank just headed out to the bunkhouse."

"I saw him go."

She seemed surprised. "He's been pretty anxious to talk to you. Irritable, if you want to know the truth."

As she took the steps to the porch, Tanner watched the way her skirts swung right then left, mesmerized by the movement. Or maybe by the woman. He stood on the porch, unsure where to sit. She chose the rocking chair. He dragged his gaze from the vision of beauty and gentleness she created. He'd expected her to be angry with him for leaving for so long with no explanation, but she seemed unaffected. With the setting sun, cold stabbed its fingers into the night. As if those fingers lay against her neck, she shivered and shot to her feet.

"Coffee. I almost forgot."

He waved her back into the chair. "I'll get it. Why don't you rest?" The words sounded awkward, but her small smile showed her appreciation though she didn't sit back down. "I'll need to get my shawl. It's getting chilly."

She stood beside him, head tilted back, an open, friendly expression lending softness to her face. "How's that hand?"

Like a child, he held it out. Her forehead wrinkled as she examined the skin. She ran her fingertip along the back. It tickled. He swallowed and kept his eyes on the glossy crown of her hair, the straight part in the center and the combs that held the glorious waves in place. He took a breath and wondered if he'd been holding it or if being this close to her just made it hard to breathe. She lifted her face, eyes luminous. "I don't guess you babied it much."

"No ma'am, Mrs. Cullen."

"What a mouthful. Maira will do." She turned and led the way through the door and into the warm room. A small fire crackled and sputtered in the fireplace. She knelt beside the stone mantel and put the poker to good use on the crumbling log.

"Why don't I add some wood? It's going to be cold tonight."

Her head tilted, and she nodded. "I hope Frank doesn't catch a chill." She set the poker aside and stood. "His leg begins to bother him if he does."

"If you have some extra blankets, I'll make sure he has one."

She bit her lip and stared off, lost in thought. "I shouldn't have allowed him to take the woodstove out of the bunkhouse so fast. He doesn't like it in there spring and summer. Takes up too much room, he says."

Tanner had to acquiesce. The bunkhouse was narrow, and the spot where the woodstove sat would make the center aisle crowded. "It's just him and me, and the cold snap will pass." He laid another log on the fire, poked at it, then put another on top. She returned then, blankets piled high in her arms. She set them on the table as he stood.

"That should keep you both warm. If you need more, you'll tell me?"

Her look was so earnest. So open and eager to please. It rose in his mind to tell her how he'd come to be there and to reassure her of his motives, but the telling might lead to other revelations he was not prepared to make. His only safety was that he remain tight-lipped.

Maira's eyes held a question. Her lips parted as if she might speak; instead she turned and lifted the coffeepot.

Tanner grazed her profile, wishing he could follow the path of his eyes along her cheek and neck with his finger. He drew in a long, slow breath and nodded toward the open shelf of dishes where three coffee mugs perched. "Will those do?"

"Yes. Coffee's hot." She took a mug from his hand, filled it, and passed it back. When she reached for the other mug, their fingers touched. She didn't seem to notice or be affected by the contact, her green eyes brewing mischief as she laughed up at him. "You'll want to be careful."

Heat from the mug felt good against his fingers. Too much roping, fence repair, and the hundred other tasks he'd undertaken while riding the fence looking for signs of rustlers. One entire section had been cut, the hoofprints fresh. Not more than a few days old. She glanced back at him, chin on her shoulder, eyes alight. He sucked in air at the impact of the innocent glance coupled with the flick of a smile. A gentle smile, both shy and relaxed. He didn't feel relaxed though. Not at all. His heart beat hard in his chest as he picked up her mug and followed her back out onto the porch. When she took her seat, he passed her the coffee, doing his best to ignore his feelings and focus on what he'd found out on the range. Best to think of the things he knew something about.

❧

She felt Tanner's eyes on her and dismissed the implication of his awareness as absurd. They were little more than strangers, and good-looking men abounded in this country. When he'd passed her the coffee, she accepted, trying hard to ignore the brush of their fingers, refusing to look at him. She leaned back, cup nestled in her hands, and sipped the strong brew. Frank's coffee was enough to make a woman grow facial hair. She smiled at the thought and almost shared it, as she would have with Jon, but something stopped her. Tanner Young seemed the sober sort. Jon had taught her an appreciation for humor and wit, but this man might not think it funny. It made her miss Jon. They'd sat out on the porch every evening, sipping Frank's coffee, discussing the coming baby, trying to settle on names. At those times he would share his plans for their future. At those times she'd simply listened, content to let him handle the logistics of growing the ranch, while her body grew their child.

Maira released her breath and squeezed her eyes shut. Jon was a long time ago. Still, it felt strange to be in the same spot but with a different man. When she opened her eyes, the moon silhouetted Tanner. He leaned on the railing, cup in hand, one foot on the bottom post of the porch railing. A position Jon had often struck. Fresh grief washed through her.

She had yet to ask him about his long absence, but thought she knew already based on Frank's comments.

"Tensions are mounting between big and small ranchers. It's getting dangerous."

She stilled, the pinch of grief seized beneath Tanner's words. "Tensions? You mean Walt Price?"

"Guess it's time you knew something of me. I've done some work in the past investigating allegations of rustling."

"You're a lawman?"

"Not really. I was a good tracker." He straightened, took a sip of the coffee, and settled into the chair across from her. "Your cattle seem in good shape, but they're older stock, hardly any one- or two-year-olds among them. Most of the babies are from older cows, and there weren't many of them. Could be your herd's being rustled."

"I. . ." What was there to say? Her body went cold. Speculation was one thing, but to have it confirmed was another. Jon would have been furious. "Does Frank know this?"

"Some."

It at least explained the man's irritableness. He probably blamed himself because it was a burden he could not and had not been able to physically shoulder since his accident.

"Frank said Walt was trying to court you."

The surge of heat shook off the chill. "He's old."

Tanner's eyebrows rose. "Doesn't matter much out here. You're a beautiful woman. He's a lonely old man. Some marry for far less."

Anger rose hot. "I would never marry him."

Tanner held up his hand, a crooked grin on his face. "Didn't mean to imply *you* would, just repeating what I'd heard." He took a long swallow of coffee and folded himself into the rocking chair opposite hers. His eyes lingered on her, sweeping over her face and hair and shoulders. She felt the probe with an excited reluctance, afraid to allow herself to be flattered by the admiration in his eyes.

"I took the favor of the men Walt sent because he offered. He tried to suggest we should go to town for a social, but Levi keeps me busy, and I. . ." Her throat closed, her voice breaking. "I still miss Jon."

"So he stopped asking?"

She shrugged. "Every now and again he'd visit to check on us."

"Frequent visits?"

"No, not really. Frank was always nearby. I think the two don't hold much affection for each other."

He rocked forward and stood, his back to her. "You don't have family to help out?"

Family. The word itself mocked. She could tell him about her parents leaving her, or the people who hinted at adopting her only to take her back to the orphanage. No. The only family she'd ever known had been Jon and Frank, then Levi. But Tanner didn't need the weight of her past. He sought a simple answer, and that was the one thing she could give. "Just Frank and Levi."

"Jon?"

He'd always wanted children. She'd known it was his way to fill the void left by his own shattered family. "His father left him and his mama when he was young. His mama died years back."

Tanner faced her. "So you're alone. An easy target for a big rancher with a lot of money."

Her spine snapped straight. "That's not true!"

A smile slipped across his lips. "It wasn't meant to get your dander up. It was the observation of a man thinking like another man might."

"Walt Price."

"That'd be the one."

She eased herself back against the chair. "I don't know what to think."

"I understand it might be hard to know what to believe, ma'am. When we go out to round up head, I'll show Frank what I found."

"So you've been out looking for evidence. What did you find?"

"Some cut fence. Prints. I just don't know who is doing it." He glanced out toward the corral when a whinny rent the stillness of the night.

All she'd thought was true was being turned on its head. She should have known better than to trust Walt's offer. He accused her husband yet, oh so smoothly, offered to help the "poor" widow. And what of Tanner? What did she truly know of him? "Maybe it would help if I knew who you were. Where you came from and where you're going." Her cheeks heated at the boldness of her statements. He'd asked for nothing except some food, accepting her and Frank at face value, and she was asking for him to reveal everything.

He took another gulp of coffee, and a grim smile etched across the one side of his face she could see. When his eyes met hers, shadows flickered there. "Done a lot of things. Been a top hand, run cattle, worked at a livery, and done investigative work tracking for rustlers, like I said. But I'm not running from the law."

"You're a drifter."

"I'm a man who values solitude."

She understood that. Some people needed other people like they needed water. Some didn't need anyone. "Where are you going?"

"Nowhere for now."

"But you will leave? You'll go somewhere else. Why not settle down?" She hated that she'd asked such a thing. It sounded desperate, and it was none of her business what he did.

He whisked the back of his fingers against his jaw. "Reckon all the land is taken up 'round here, or I might."

"You don't have family?"

He stared up at the night sky, dotted now with the blinking white of stars against a cold, black background. "I did. Once. Long ago. Left out young." He laughed, a brittle sound. "Was thirteen years old and thinking myself a man."

She judged him to be in his late twenties. "If I'd had family, I would want to be near them. Have you ever gone back?"

He searched her face for a moment before his eyes hardened, and he stared out into the darkness.

"They're your family," she whispered.

"Were." He thrust the empty mug toward her and went inside. When he returned, the blankets in his arms, his expression was cold, distant. "If you don't mind, I'll be turning in. It's been a long day."

"I thought you were hungry," she called out to him.

"More tired. Good night, ma'am."

Chapter 11

Sleep claimed him until early morning when he woke with a start, unsure what shook him awake until Maira's questions began a slow march across his mind. Her questions pecked at the wall built by the passage of time. He didn't want to remember those days before he left. His stepfather's presence had turned his world upside down. Again. His father's death had been the first horrific episode, his mother barely escaping the attack by Indians. She'd carried his father into the house, and the two of them had watched the life seep from him as surely as the blood soaked the blanket beneath him.

Tanner's cheeks puffed out on an exhale, and he dug his fingers into the hollows over his eyes and rubbed. When his mother married again within four months, he'd hidden his resentment for four years. Eventually his stepfather's heavy-handed attempts to tame his saucy mouth made the decision for him. Tanner had headed out under cover of night. He took the horse his father had given him and rode for miles, days, with little more than corn mush sustaining him. He'd ridden into Montana, as far as he could go on the little he'd taken with him from his mother's staples. His size had brought him offers of work, but it had been hard work that required more strength than he had. He'd pushed himself to gain the strength, knowing it would lead to the better-paying jobs. He learned to track from an Indian he worked alongside on a ranch in the Powder River Basin. And then, when he turned eighteen, it all had begun to feel hollow.

Thanksgiving found him sitting in a tent outside of town. Alone. And he'd made a quick decision to head home. Surprise his mama and let her know he was alive. Instead, he was greeted by the news of her death.

He pushed his feet into his boots, careful to move slow and easy on the bed lest the groan of the wooden platform wake Frank. Cold air swirled around him and, remembering Maira's concern, he draped his blanket over Frank's already well-covered form. Taking up the lantern, he lit it outside, the baaing of sheep a soothing sound in his ears.

He crossed to the barn with nothing more in his mind than the desire to work on one of the myriad projects still needing attention. A hole in the stall wall needed patching. He found a board and some nails, hung the lamp nearby, and set to work.

Maira's predicament galled him. He wrestled with what to do and hoped that the ranch hands Price would send showed up before he left on the roundup. He had a few questions for them. He'd already determined to ask Frank if he could see the logbooks. Seeing the figures would help him know better what to look for among the cattle.

He placed a nail with his left hand and raised the hammer to strike. In two blows the nail was sunk. Maira hadn't known about the tension between big and small ranches. He'd expected that. Hemmed in as the Rocking J was by the sprawling XP and, to the south, Ted Ranger's R7, there would be little communication with the group of smaller ranches on the opposite side of the XP. With every blow of the hammer, Tanner knew Walt Price's interest in Maira's doings had less to do with concern for her and more to do with timing. Rustling the younger cows from Rocking J stock would ruin Maira. Walt Price understood that. If she married him, all the better. If not, who would the law believe if she were to bring accusations, Walt or a lone widow woman?

Tanner sat back on his heels and tested the board for soft spots indicating another nail was needed. He found none. As he rose, the row of halters came into view. His saddle. He could ride out of here. Ranches needed hunters all the time. He didn't have to get mixed up in Walt's underhanded ways or the problems of Maira Cullen.

Jon Cullen's face swam into view. The man's surprised expression, the coolness of his skin, the stiffness of his limbs that told their own story when Tanner found his battered body. Even for the stiffened form of a man he knew more for the length of time it took to hand over some gold than for any lifelong connection, Tanner had vowed to find the truth behind the pattern of hoofprints that proved that Jon's death was forced. How he wished he'd exercised more caution and not let that mountain lion scare him away from Jon's body. At least he'd been able to examine him first. Jon Cullen had been armed, but his gun was still in its holster. And he'd been shot in the side, as if he'd turned just in time to eat the lead of his enemy. That he'd fallen from his horse was evident by the indentation in the dirt next to the hoofprints made by a standing horse. Jon Cullen had stopped for a reason, and he'd been shot for a reason. And it all happened at that back corner where XP property met the R7.

Little Levi deserved to know the truth. Maira, too, and Frank.

Tanner didn't like how Walt Price's name kept rattling through his mind, but with the cattle rustled from the Rocking J, Jon's death and the accusation against him, and the big cattle baron's lust for more land, the three events dovetailed.

❧

Levi bounced on the bed. Maira did her best to ignore him, her body pulling for more sleep.

"It's mornin'."

She cracked an eye open to see out the window and smiled. "Barely. Why don't you settle down for a bit and give Mama some more time?"

"I'm hungry!"

She rolled toward him and extended her hand for a tickle.

His laughter spilled over until his eyes rounded and he pushed at her hand. "Gotta go."

Maira giggled as he scooted off the bed, nightshirt flapping around his heels, and ran out of the room. She heard the slap of the outhouse door and hurried into the kitchen to keep an eye on his return, arms poking for the holes of her dressing gown as she went. On his return, Levi snuggled up to her at the kitchen table, his cold hands buried between their bodies, his toes tucked in the folds of her nightclothes. "I need to start the fire and get the water."

"I'll get it," he said, teeth chattering.

"You've got to get dressed first."

With that, Levi launched himself from her lap and scampered back into the room, reappearing in seconds fully dressed. She didn't have the heart to let him know he'd put his shirt on inside out, or that the buttons didn't quite line up. There would be time for such things later, but for now she needed his energy and enthusiasm. She'd slept little the previous night, wondering about Tanner Young and Walt Price, wrestling with a faith that held a thick layer of dust. Yet God had spared Levi, sustained them through the last three years, and brought Tanner here to help them. Jon would believe that. But that was Jon's faith, not hers. It was the disappointments she couldn't stand. The reversal of bright dreams.

Sunlight spilled over the horizon in a strong, single ray. Within minutes the entire sphere would be shining its face on the world. "Make sure Frank is up to help you."

"Or Tan-wer?"

Her heart squeezed. He'd been so hopeful Tanner would come home soon. Frank insisted Tanner would return, but she had seen that hope die a little more each day in Levi's face. She could smile now. "He came in last night."

Levi whooped and did a little jig. His eyes rounded with hope and a silent plea.

"I really need that water, and Mr. Young needs his rest. They'll be in shortly."

Levi's head bobbed in happy agreement as he scooped up the water pail. Her heart squeezed at his sweet face. All he wanted was to be with the men. Helping around the ranch like Frank did, and now Tanner. Levi held tight to the rail as he went down the side steps; a giant leap from the bottom one planted both his feet in the dirt and sent up a small cloud of dew-damp dust. Frank chose that moment to come out of the barn, milk pail in hand. Frank handed the bucket over to Levi and clamped a hand to the boy's shoulder. She sank away from the open door, aware that Levi's chores would be done soon and she didn't have the first biscuit whipped up.

"Good morning."

She started; her heart slammed hard. Tanner Young stood at the front door, eyes bright with ill-concealed amusement. She sank back against the cookstove. Fire fanned her cheeks. Even though she was fully covered, a man seeing her in her nightclothes was unforgivable.

"I was just coming to see if you had any more of those biscuits and bacon."

"I'm not ready quite yet." She forced lightness into her voice. "I'll be sure to call you when everything is done." She stared at the cracks in the flooring, wishing he would bleed into a lump and drip through those cracks, taking every thought of having seen her with him. Her hair! She raised a hand to touch the mass of tangles. She must look terrible, like someone who had spent the night in the throes of a nightmare.

"I'll wait for your call then."

As soon as the front door shut, she raced back to her room, glanced in the mirror, and gasped. Having slept on her right side had caused a part there and pushed the hair into a hump against the side of her head. Bedbug hair, Jon had called it, because it looked like the bedbugs had congregated then had an all-out war within the strands. Crease lines from her pillow still displayed on her skin.

Aggravated, Maira determined to be tidy when the men came in for breakfast. She scrubbed her face and neck until the skin shone as much from the cold water as from the friction. Her hair was tamed with a liberal douse of water and several hard strokes of the brush. She checked over her skirt from the previous day and rejected the article when she found a stain. Another skirt was quickly donned, along with the blouse she reserved for trips to town and had last worn at Jon's graveside. Her last clean blouse. She would have to do laundry as soon as possible.

By the time she'd dressed, the coffee had come to a boil, releasing a rich scent that beckoned with invisible fingers for her to pour herself a cup. A splash of the hot brew was all she allowed herself as she considered breakfast food options. Opting for hotcakes and venison sausage, Maira whisked up the batter and had a stack ready within fifteen minutes. When she glanced out the front door, Frank was nowhere in sight. Neither was Tanner or Levi, so she used the bell Jon had fashioned for such purposes.

As she slid the tray of sausage onto the table, Frank and Levi shoved through the doorway. Already, Levi had mud along his knees.

"Let me see your hands."

He held them up for her inspection. "Frank made me wash 'em."

She hid her smile. "Water isn't a rattler, Levi."

The boy tossed her a mischievous grin that choked her with its familiarity. Jon had grinned at her like that when up to something. Frank bent over the boy, sliding a small box beneath Levi's rump so he could reach the table better.

"Smells mighty good," Frank said.

She flipped the last hotcake and waited for a few seconds before sliding it from the cast-iron skillet to the stack, taking the whole plate to the table.

"Tan-wer will be here later. He was showvring."

She lifted an eyebrow to Frank. "Shoveling the stalls," he explained.

"Oh." She accepted the platter of sausage from Frank.

"He's my papa."

The words yanked a gasp from her. She could only stare at Levi.

"What makes you say that, Levi?" Frank asked. "You know your papa went to be with the angels."

Levi's lip pooched, and tears built in his eyes.

Moving from her place, Maira sat beside him and gathered him close. He was so still, his face buried hard against her shoulder. Only the sound of sniffs let her know he was crying. She didn't know what to say or where he'd gotten such a notion. "He's a good friend to you, isn't he, Levi? But Tan—Mr. Young is only staying here for a while."

"I can 'tend," came his muffled reply.

" 'Tend?" She tried to catch what he might mean, finally realizing. "Pretend?"

His head nodded against her shoulder. Maira drew a deep breath, glancing at Frank for help, but the hand's expression held only pinched sorrow.

Chapter 12

Tanner walked into silence. His gaze went from a distressed-looking Frank to Maira's sober expression and Levi's head cradled against her shoulder. He shut the door behind him, but his boots against the wood floor brought Levi's head up. The boy wiggled from Maira's embrace. He barreled into Tanner's legs, his arms tight around his knees.

"Hey there, little cowpuncher."

Levi's grip grew tighter. Tanner lowered his hand to the boy's head, unsure what to do or what he'd walked in to. In desperation, he looked to Frank and Maira for explanation. Maira would not meet his gaze, and Frank's mouth was a grim line. Tanner leaned over and tried to remove Levi's arms. He knelt, and as soon as he came eye level with the boy, Levi clamped his arms around his neck. Tanner's heart warmed with the show of affection, but worry plucked at him, too.

"Sure smells good in here. Why don't we go eat?"

Levi pulled back at that, his hands raising to pat Tanner's cheeks. "I'm 'tending you're Papa."

Tanner chuckled at the earnest stare of brown eyes. Warmth flowed through him at the words and the feel of the boy's hands against his face. He swallowed and glanced over Levi's shoulder at Maira. She averted her face, blocking his ability to see her expressions. Frank nodded toward them, as if encouraging him. Tanner licked his lips. "Well, little cowpuncher, cowboys need to eat, and I'm hungry."

Levi nodded and dashed back to the bench. Maira helped him onto the box, rose, and went to her own place at the head of the table. Frank said a prayer, and though the food had lost most of its heat, it tasted good to Tanner.

He licked his lips and forked a piece of hotcake into his mouth. Still no one spoke. He let the silence go for another bite then caught Frank's eye. "My guess is we'll use the first few days to wrangle those closest, returning here at night." He nodded toward Maira.

Her head bobbed. "I'll make sure to have something hot."

"Thank you," he said, unsure what else to talk about.

Levi leaned forward and grabbed for another piece of sausage.

"Levi, what do you say?" Frank admonished.

"Sausage?"

"Sausage, please."

Frank scooted the platter closer to the boy. "The brace works well. No rubbing."

Tanner nodded and forked another bite of hotcakes. Syrup coated his tongue.

He wanted nothing more than to capture that moment forever. The taste of the food, the warmth of the fire, the presence of people he had come to care for made it feel more like home.

"Tanner, I go, too."

The little boy's insistence dragged out a smile. "You can ride a horse, little cowpuncher?"

Levi nodded.

"Lee-vi," came Maira's voice, heavy with warning. "Do you think that's the truth?"

He nodded, unconcerned. "Frank made me one."

Frank guffawed. "A stick with a rope," he enlightened everyone.

"Treeflower!" Levi offered. "He's fast!"

"You need to stay here with your mother this time," Tanner told the boy in as firm a voice as he could muster. "What if someone comes to the house and she needs your help?"

Levi stuffed a piece of sausage into his mouth, his brow bunched into a knot. He nodded at his mother.

"I'd be lonely without you," Maira said.

"Treeflower and me'll carry water."

Frank rose from the table first and held out his hand to the boy. "Why don't you come with me, and I'll show you what needs done in the barn while I'm out with Tanner."

Levi stabbed a forkful of hotcake, ran it through some syrup, and popped it into his mouth, his body sliding to the floor as he chewed and followed Frank out the door.

"He's a good boy, Maira. Your husband would be proud." It wasn't what he wanted to say. He knew it. She knew it.

"I don't know where it came from, Tanner," she blurted. "He's never said anything like that before."

"Guess he misses his pa." It came to him that Levi probably didn't see many other men, isolated as he was on the ranch. Tanner let the minutes pass as he stared down at his almost-empty plate. He knew nothing of children and their ways. He scraped a piece of sausage around his plate to sop up syrup. "Looks like children are easier to say what's in their hearts and heads than we are."

Maira licked her lips and pressed a napkin there. "With you here he must realize something is missing."

He tilted his head up to look at her. "I'm not meaning to cause trouble."

She smiled, and it was the sweetest smile he'd ever seen. Despite the neatness of her hair, he thought he preferred the way it had looked earlier. He buttoned his lip on the subject. Judging from her reaction to his presence then, he knew he'd not only startled her but embarrassed her as well.

"Trouble? No, Mr. Young." She turned, her face in profile, hand at her throat.

"I just want to help, and then I'll move on and be out of your way."

She gasped and flinched, eyes wide with something akin to panic, probing his. She stood as if the chair seat had a spring. "You can't tell me that you just ride around looking for people to help. Rescuing widows and finding lost little boys, repairing things, and. . .and. . .then you just leave?"

Words failed. He stood, too, unsure how to answer her questions. Or was it an accusation? She averted her face, and he saw her swallow.

"Maira?"

"I don't need your help." She shot him a look filled with desperation. He thought of a little girl sitting in an orphanage, waiting to be loved.

"Probably not, but you've got it, and I'm here."

"I appreciate what you've done."

But the words sounded brittle.

It beat at Tanner's mind to walk away. Fulfill her request to be out of her life. The Rocking J was not his mess. He clenched his fists and stared at his boots. But it was. Riding away this time was turning his back on more than a woman in need. It was his duty to stay and help.

Her eyes were wide with expectation, but he had no answers to give as everything became a jumble in his mind. Only one thing was clear to him. She needed help. Despite her words, she needed him. And he couldn't leave her to Walt Price or his men. And something else. . .

He crossed the room until he stood in front of her. Her gaze was pleading. He could feel the fear within her because it mirrored his own. He raised his hand to her hair, touched the taut strands pulled back so hard, wanting nothing more than to take the fear away, to give voice to the tumble of emotion she stirred in him. "I prefer it loose, with a few curls to remind a man what softness looks like."

❧

Maira wanted to plead with him, to suck back the words she'd already released. When he drew close, she went still. There was no threat in his eyes, no anger. She felt the draw of being close to Tanner Young as much as she felt love for Levi. When Tanner lifted his hand, she held her breath, afraid of what this moment might mean, even as the blood pounded through her veins with the discovery of something fresh, yet fragile. He touched her hair, his eyes searching hers. She didn't know what he was looking for. Permission? Rebuke? She could bring herself to offer neither. She searched his face, concentrated on the cleft in his chin and the lips that formed words that didn't quite penetrate. And then he stepped back.

"I had no right to. . ." His thought drifted away.

Her heart slowed, and she drew a breath, his admonition finally penetrating. She should find every reason to be offended, but the emotion did not flare and burn. With effort, she turned away from him, collecting her plate, fighting for something to say to bring equilibrium to the situation. "Please keep Frank safe."

He said nothing, the mark of his path only the sound of his receding footsteps and the latch on the front door catching. Maira held the plate tight and closed her eyes. What was she doing? She hardly knew this man. He was attractive, yes, she could admit that, but Levi needed more than a fly-by-the-seat-of-your-pants cowboy. He needed a father.

She cleaned up the dishes and left them to dry, absorbing the silence of the house, hating it. More than anything she wanted to ride with the men. She could cook for them out there, but there was Levi to consider. He needed her, and a roundup would be no place for a boy—a smile crept up her face—even if he did possess a trusty steed. Three years of being alone. Was it so wrong for her to be attracted to a handsome man? She knew it was not; it was what she did with that attraction. Where she would allow it to lead her. She had a son and a ranch. Tanner was offering his help. She would continue to take him up on his offer. But she would be careful. She had known of women who married out of loneliness. She wanted to marry for all the right reasons.

"God needs to be our center." Jon's words. Spoken long ago. At a time when she thought the Bible was a book of rules and Jon's faith would protect her.

Levi shuffled in an hour later, looking defeated and tired, and she knew the men were mounting up to leave. He knelt at the kitchen window, where they were visible. Tanner had Queen tied behind his horse as an extra.

"Tan-wer's horse is big."

"Do you know his name?"

Levi looked up at her matter-of-factly. "Tan-wer."

She chucked him under the chin. "No. His horse's name."

"Cue-pid, cause he's got a heart. See?" His little finger stabbed at the horse. The black heart was visible for all to see. "He calls him Cue."

They were getting a late start. Levi waved to them as they pulled out, but neither of the men saw the boy. Though he fought the idea, she put him down for a nap, arguing that he would be up later that night if he wanted to see Tanner and Frank when they got back. He needed no further prompting. Her eyes fell on the Bible next to their bed. Jon's side of the bed. She grazed its cover with her fingers. Her eyes fell on the blood-soaked blouse. She would have to read the Bible later.

She used the time to soak a smoked venison roast and set it to simmering for stew. As she waited for the water to heat for laundry, she sat down with the ranch's books and tried to figure out the notations Jon had made, then Frank, and most recently, Walt Price's men. At a glance things seemed fine, but Tanner's warnings stuck in her head and stirred fear. If she lost the ranch, it would be her fault for leaving the oversight to men she did not know. Jon would never have done that. Maira shut the books and shoved them to the center of the table. When Tanner and Frank returned, she would have them look over the figures.

Chapter 13

Thirty head. Tanner felt tired in every muscle as they led the cattle into the front pasture, closest to the house. He stayed back as Frank drove the cows past the gate. Tanner dismounted and swung the gate shut. Frank wheeled his horse and cantered back and out of the pasture.

"A good day's work," Frank said as he knuckled his hat back on his head.

"Tomorrow will be tougher. You holding up?"

"Right as rain."

"Getting down will be the test."

"You fuss more than a mother."

Tanner let loose a laugh. "Just reminding you to go easy."

"I'm old," Frank sniped. "Thanks for the reminder."

Whether Frank realized it or not, his face showed the effort it took for him to lift and work his leg over the saddle to dismount. Tanner pretended not to notice when the man leaned against the horse for several long minutes to get his feet under him. Tanner stripped the saddle from Cue and hung it on the top rail, turning the gelding loose into the corral.

The old man still leaned against his horse, and Tanner threw off all pretense. "Best get yourself horizontal and check for swelling. I can bring you a plate from the kitchen."

"I don't need coddling." But the words were more a groan.

Tanner went to Frank and yanked up his right arm, settling it across his shoulders. "If you won't listen, you won't be able to work with me." With careful steps Frank moved back from the horse. At first Tanner knew the man was determined to bear his own weight, but he could feel the will leaving as every step siphoned blood from his face, and he leaned a little harder. He shouldered open the bunkhouse door, and Frank sat down with a long, low groan.

"I used to be able to do this."

"It's been a long time. You'll toughen up."

He leaned over to work the leather buckles and tugged away both brace and boot. Yanking up Frank's pant leg, he saw raw marks along the man's leg but no signs of swelling. "You rest. I'll get something to put on those patches and bring you some supper."

"What? Now you're a doctor?"

Tanner frowned at Frank. "If that's what I need to be, then yes."

Frank angled his face away. "I hate getting old."

"It'll happen to us all. The greatest gift is in knowing someone will help care for you."

"Fuss, you mean."

"Is that such a bad thing?" He pulled the pant leg back down. "I'd think it better than being alone."

When the man didn't answer, Tanner left. Let Frank stew; he'd certainly done more than his share for a day. But deep down Tanner worried. If it came down to Frank being unable to help, he would be forced to get help from somewhere.

After taking care of Frank's horse, Tanner rested against the top rail, weary to the bone and dreading having to do it all again the next day. He pulled in a cleansing breath and stared up at the heavy gray blanket of night rolling toward the west as the sun tucked in for the night.

"Tanner?"

The voice was soft, and the sound of it put an immediate snap into his spine. Maira stood on the porch. When she knew she'd gained his attention, she waved him over. He did his best not to appear too eager, but truth be told, the prospect of the hot meal meant less to him than seeing her. She waited for him at the top of the steps, backing up when he gained the porch. A welcoming smile curved her lips and lit her eyes.

"Was it a good day?" She stared out into the night. "Is Frank coming in?"

"He's resting. The brace rubbed his leg raw."

Worry clouded her eyes. "I've got some salve."

"I told him to stay put, that I'd bring him something to eat."

They weren't moving. She was watching him with those wide, intriguing green-gray eyes. He couldn't help but notice how her hair cascaded over her shoulders in a dark mass of soft waves. His mouth went dry with the sight of her.

❧

"I'll take him a plate," Maira said.

Tanner didn't move, and neither did she. It was a beautiful, clear night. She'd been sitting on the porch when they rode in and had seen Frank's weakness. It had scared her to see him rest for so long against his horse's side. When Tanner had helped the man into the bunkhouse, Maira's heart had been touched by the show of kindness.

"It's a beautiful night," she whispered, her words pitched low. Stubble darkened Tanner's skin now and, for a heartbeat, she wondered what it would feel like against her palm, or his lips against hers. Shamed by the dip of her thoughts, she retreated a step, breaking the reverie and leading him inside. "I'm sorry." She motioned him to the table. "I'm sure you're hungry." She reached for a bowl and ladled a helping of stew into it. Three biscuits and a tin of water completed the meal. She turned, almost colliding with him. He put a hand to her arm and pulled the stew from her grasp as it sloshed in the bowl.

"I'll run it out to Frank."

She nodded and handed him the water and napkin full of biscuits. He balanced it all, and she swept past him to open the front door, leaning against the plank when she closed it behind him. What in the world was wrong with her? She pressed her hands to her cheeks. She was acting like a tumbleweed in a high wind. As fast as she could, she ladled out another bowl of the stew and filled a plate with biscuits for Tanner. She set his place at the table and poured a cup of coffee. She would head out to the porch as soon as he sat down. After such a long day, he would probably like some quiet time, and she could at least give him that. Besides, tangling herself up over him wasn't in her plans.

Tanner did return, but when he sat down and she picked up her coffee and headed toward the door, his words stopped her. "You're not going to join me?"

She turned, feeling like a startled deer. "I thought you would want some quiet."

His hand scratched at his ear. "Had enough of that to last a lifetime."

Chocolate-drop eyes pleaded, and she found herself slipping into her regular place. He picked up his spoon and sunk it deep into the broth. After a few bites, he took a biscuit and crumbled it into the stew, a sheepish grin slanting his lips. "Always liked it best this way."

"Jon used to eat his like that, too."

"He was a good man."

Something about the way he said it. . . He stared down into his bowl, working the chunks of biscuit into the broth. It was on the tip of her tongue to ask him what he meant when Tanner spotted the ranch logbooks.

"You've been studying the records?"

She hesitated, unsure if she wanted to let his statement go unquestioned. "I found them today." She shrugged. "I don't know much about such things. It was hard for me to make out what the marks meant."

"Tally marks show the number of head total then separate them into male, female, yearlings. . ." he began explaining, then hesitated.

He reached across the table and pulled the book closer, raising his face to her, eyebrows arched in silent question.

"Please, go ahead."

Tanner's long fingers opened the cover. She could tell by the way his eyes darted across the pages that he skimmed at first, but as he leafed, his pace slowed, and his finger began to trace the entries, brow creased in concentration. His stew grew cold, and still he kept reading, flipping the pages forward, then back. Her nerves stretched taut.

At last he closed the book and slid it back across the table. He picked up another biscuit and took a huge bite, chewed slowly, swallowed, took another bite. She thought she might just scream with the tension. Instead, she picked up her coffee and filled her mouth. Its cold bite made her want to gag. She gulped quickly then coughed.

Tanner passed her his napkin. She pressed it over her mouth and coughed until her eyes watered. He set water in front of her, and she drank deeply of the liquid.

"No more coffee for you."

She gasped a breath. "It went down wrong."

"I noticed."

"What do you think about the books?"

Tanner sat on the edge of the bench closest to her. He leaned forward, his nearness invading her space and stealing her thoughts. His face was serious though. "We got thirty head today. I'd like to wait until we're done before drawing a conclusion. The cows look good so far." He tilted his face toward her. "Does that help ease your mind for now?"

She couldn't find her voice to form an answer.

Tanner leaned away and stretched to his feet. "Could use another cup of coffee if you don't mind."

Glad for something to do, she sprang upward. Tanner collected his plate and bowl and stacked them for her, polishing off the last biscuit as he went back to stare out the front window. "I might have a problem of another sort." He took the coffee she offered and jerked his head toward the outside. "I hear it's a beautiful night."

She took her place in the rocker, and Tanner resumed his position of the previous evening, foot braced against the bottom rail of the porch, elbows on the top, the coffee held between his hands. "A problem?" she prompted.

"Frank. He won't say it, but I'm not sure he can ride tomorrow. It might be good to give his leg a day to adjust before he tries again."

"I can take his place."

Tanner turned his head toward her and chuckled low in his throat. "I think we went down this road once before." He shook his head. "I don't think it's a good idea—"

"I can do it!"

His chuckle grew to a laugh. "Always knew you were one spirited woman."

She didn't know if the discovery pleased or disgusted him. Judging by his laughter, she thought it amused him more than anything.

He sipped his coffee and muttered something she didn't quite catch. When he straightened and settled into the chair across from her, she could see the white of his teeth flash in the night. "We'll give it a try."

Chapter 14

Despite Frank's protests and Levi's pout, Maira knew she had to do this. Tanner asked her if she knew how to rope and peg. She didn't. And with every question he put to her, to learn what skills she possessed, she wondered if he grew more disheartened at taking her with him.

He ran a hand over his head and down his neck. "Do you even own a hat?"

"I do!" She felt such victory over being able to say yes to something, though she supposed it must seem lame to him.

"Well, at least you can sit a horse." His eyes ran the length of her. "Though that's quite a getup."

"My riding clothes." She stroked her hand down the thick leather of her split skirt, glad for the extra protection the material offered in the saddle. Briars and bugs would be deterred.

"You'll get hot pretty fast."

His prediction came true, and Maira found herself struggling to keep up and keep cool. Tanner worked with an ease that bespoke of his time as a cowpuncher somewhere other than the Rocking J. He encouraged her to watch what he did that first day. No matter what, it seemed the cattle they ran into were all born of the same stubborn mother. Tanner lassoed and tugged, coaxed and hollered, circled and pegged, and the whole time Maira felt like a fool. His sweat-soaked shirt clung to his back, his face flushed with his efforts. One bull turned on him and lowered its head, horns poised. When the animal charged Cue, Maira's throat closed in terror. But Tanner wheeled Cue and landed his lasso around the bull's horns, giving out rope as the animal fought and strained.

He trotted Cue over to her and handed her the rope. She followed his instructions, grateful for Frank's gloves covering her hands. Tanner threw another rope over the bull's horns, and they kept the animal between them. By early evening the weariness was beginning to show in Tanner's face and the continual swipe of the handkerchief across his brow.

"Ten head."

Just the tone of his voice let her know how disgusted he was with the day's count. "I'm sorry."

Tanner rode in close to Queen, a crooked smile on his face. "Actually, I should be pleased. For the places we had to work, that's not bad."

She wanted to touch his face, wipe away the dirt streaking from eye to jaw, but it was neither the time nor place. Her question from the previous evening slipped into mind. "Last night, you said Jon was a good man. Did you know him?"

He winced. The horses kept pace with each other, allowing her knee to almost touch his. His face was a stone carving, a coldness that scared her.

"Jon got that gold from me."

Maira gasped. "You?"

"I met him. We talked. He needed money, and the bank wouldn't extend credit. I told him I had some gold."

"You knew him?" She tried to reconcile what he was saying to his sudden appearance, his rescue of Levi, and what he'd said about Walt Price. "But Walt said. . ."

"Walt's a liar!" He dug his heels into Cue's sides. Maira let him go, stunned and fumbling for what to say or even how to take what Tanner had revealed. He knew Jon. Had loaned him gold. Walt's miner was a sham, which meant the owner of the XP was not just a liar, but also a cunning liar bent on ruining Jon's reputation.

If she believed Tanner.

Maira sighed down at the saddle horn, focused on Queen's mane, reached to touch the coarse tangle of hair. Why hadn't she known Jon needed money and that the bank had refused him credit? Because she'd never asked and he'd never offered the information. She'd been too content in her little world, especially after becoming pregnant. She tried to remember times when Jon had appeared excessively stressed and could remember nothing out of the ordinary.

Tanner slowed as they approached the ranch. Frank and Levi came out to greet them. Whether Frank's limp had lessened or he was making sure to walk smoother on purpose, Maira couldn't tell. Her slide from the saddle was only a fraction more easy than Frank's had been the day before. Every muscle in her legs and lower back ached.

Tanner's boot caught her eye where she stared down at her feet, just trying to be still so nothing hurt. "Not being used to riding for so long will do that."

She scowled at him, letting every bit of her anger and frustration shine through. "We need to talk."

He nodded at the horizon. "Later. Not much sunlight left for me to teach you how to rope."

"I don't want to learn." She bit out the words, tears burning her eyes. She felt grimy and sore, and his revelation only nettled her all the more.

He leaned in, close to her ear. "We have an audience. Rope now. Talk later."

"Talk now. Rope later," she tossed back.

He nodded toward something over her shoulder.

When she turned, she saw Levi and Frank. The older man set Cue's saddle into Levi's outstretched arms. He stumbled beneath the heavy weight, and the saddle settled into the dust at his little booted feet. Frank's laughter punctuated the moment.

Biting back her anger, she nodded. Tanner strode away and picked up his rope. She'd seen him toss it out so many times, never missing the mark, always smooth and sure, but she wasn't ready to put aside her anger even if she saw the wisdom of his suggestion.

"Where'd you learn to rope?" Frank asked, suggesting he'd been privy to their conversation.

"Practice mostly." Tanner sent Maira a knowing grin. "You don't get to be a cowpuncher without knowing how to rope."

Levi clapped his hands together. "Me, too?"

Frank nodded down at the boy. "I'll teach you myself. Let your mama learn tonight."

"Now?"

"Tonight," Maira said, sending Tanner a superior grin. "After supper."

"Can I watch?"

"Did you help Frank today?"

Frank's hand went to Levi's shoulder. "He worked in the garden most of the morning and hauled water; then I showed him how to gather eggs, and we worked on milking the cow together."

"I got squirted!"

"With milk," Frank added. "But I told him we couldn't waste milk on the barn cat."

Levi's head bobbed in solemn agreement. "Got a bucket full of it!"

"Barn cat?" Maira teased.

"Milk!"

Tanner joined them, tapping Levi on the head. "Last one to the house has to drink cold coffee."

Levi's eyes widened. He glanced at his mother. "You, too."

Tanner came to her rescue. "Best leave your mom out of this. She's pretty sore from riding."

Still, Levi looked uncertain. "Go ahead," she encouraged, and he flashed a grin at Tanner and took off, little legs pumping. Tanner loped along, pretending to be running for all he was worth, arms pumping, but his legs were taking hops. Levi started laughing. Tanner scooped him up and swung him around until Levi was giggling.

"Does the heart good," Frank murmured.

Maira felt such a ball of uncertainty; yet watching the scene, she had to agree. Even as reluctant as she was to acknowledge the nudge of satisfaction.

❧

Levi talked as if it was his goal in life to use every word in the English vocabulary at least ten times. Tanner listened to the boy's chatter with both ears while keeping one eye on Maira and one on Frank. As Levi talked, he tried to assess Frank's injury. He seemed better. It sure would help to have him out on the range. His know-how was invaluable. Maira tried hard, but he'd been afraid to overexert her, and he could tell by the way she rode that she wasn't comfortable in the saddle. With each additional head he discovered and rounded up, he appreciated the quieter moments spent riding beside her, glancing over to see her soft profile, the way her hair swayed with the horse's rhythm, or the delight with which she tilted her face to the sun only to toss him that gentle smile that bloomed with contentment. Like a barn cat in the sun.

And then everything was spoiled when she had held his feet to the fire about his slip of the tongue the previous night. How he'd hoped she hadn't noticed his referral to knowing Jon. But she had, and her temperament and grief would never allow the situation to rest until all her questions were answered. He couldn't blame her, but telling her too much would be dangerous. He snatched a glance at her, surprised to find her watching him in return. He gave her a smile. She responded in kind, though the smile quickly faltered.

He continued to listen to Levi's jabbering as Maira set a plate full of roast venison on the table. Frank put a piece on Levi's plate and cut it into bits. If the old cowhand could ride, Tanner would need the man's expertise to get the cows rounded up as fast as possible. The back grazing land would be toughest, and he would save it for last since it would be easier to spend the night on the range. He entertained an idea he thought might work as Levi explained why he chased the cat from the barn.

"I told him he a bad cat. Frank said—"

Frank nudged the boy. "Best not say what I said. It wasn't nice, and I shouldn't have said it. Your mama would be mad at me."

Maira nodded at Levi, trying to look serious, but Tanner saw the hint of her smile before she took a bite of potato.

He poked at a carrot on his plate, enjoying the hot meal and the boy's chatter.

When Levi finally took a bite, Tanner speared a piece of roast and held up his fork. "You're a good cook, Frank."

"I try to help out."

"He does much more than he lets on." Maira sent a fond look at Frank. A sudden longing for her to look at him that way squeezed Tanner's chest.

"Mama, 'member when he burned the corn bread?"

"Lee-vi."

The boy lowered his eyes, then cut them to Frank. "Sorry."

The older man leaned close, a smile on his face. "Sometimes we have to remember the good things more than the bad things."

Maira pushed back from the table. Levi's eyes followed her movement with the look of certain doom. She held out her hand, and the boy's sigh could be heard around the room. Frank helped Levi to his feet.

"I think you've probably worn yourself out talking." Maira grinned as she picked him up in her arms. His little arms went around her neck as she carried him into the room and shut the door.

"I've never heard him talk quite so much." Frank shook his head. "Reckon he's trying to prove to you what a little cowpuncher he is. He's talked about you most all day."

Tanner didn't quite know what to say to that. He touched the corners of his mouth. "Not picking up my bad habits, I hope."

"You haven't got any bad habits I can see."

"It's not the ones on the outside that haunt a man."

"We've all got a few of those. Sometimes a man has to find a way to put the past to rest in order to get any pleasure in the here and now."

"Sounds like religious talk."

Frank's brows rose. "God wants us to be free on the inside to enjoy what's on the outside. It's simple, really. It's a hard country; we have to be hard men to survive. But in the midst of being hard, we lose sight of what it is to let people in." He upended the box Levi sat on and got to his feet. "I think she could love you."

Tanner cut his eyes to Frank. "That's not what I'm here for."

Frank's round face lit. "Isn't that how it works though?"

"I wouldn't know."

"I'll be ready to ride in the morning. I'll let you show Mrs. Cullen how to rope without being a fifth wheel."

Tanner did his best to ignore the implication. "You could add what you know to the lesson."

Frank laughed as he refilled his mug. "I've seen you, son. You know 'bout all there is."

The door to the room opened, and Maira came out. "I think he went right to sleep." She faced Frank. "You must have worn him out."

"He worked hard for a little guy."

"Probably talked himself tired," Tanner said.

Frank held up his mug in silent good-bye and went straight to the front door.

Maira held up the coffeepot. "Would you like some more?"

"I'm good." He slid his chair away from the table. "Should we head outside or. . . ?"

She cupped the mug in her hands as if drawing heat from it. He wondered if her fingers were cold. "Once Levi is asleep, he doesn't wake up until morning." She bit her lip and glanced at the closed bedroom door. "But I stay close just in case."

"We can practice right outside the front door."

"If you don't mind, I'd like to sit for a spell. I'm..."

"Tired?"

Her smile was small. "Fighting a headache."

"Ouch. Too much sun."

Her face disappeared as she sipped the hot brew. "I'll be fine. Nothing that a hot bath won't—" She halted, sucking in air. "I mean..." Her cheeks burned with the embarrassment of having said something so intimate.

Tanner stared down at the tips of his boots, feeling some heat on his own neck. "Maybe we should wait to rope when you're feeling better."

"No." The word came so quickly it startled him. "I'll be fine. I can do this."

"Frank will ride with me tomorrow. You can stay here and...take it easy."

"But his leg..."

"I was thinking he could do tomorrow, and you the next day. Until his leg gets stronger."

She bit her lower lip as she stepped past him. He held the front door open for her, aware of her stiff gait and the way she held her lip between her teeth. His announcement hadn't made her happy. "I thought that later, when we work on the back of the property, we might take the wagon out."

Maira set the rocker into motion. "The wagon?"

"You and Levi could sleep there. Cook for Frank and me while we're out...." He'd seemed so sure about the idea, but now he didn't know. The thought might offend her sense of propriety.

She leaned forward, excitement shining in her eyes. "You mean it? Levi would have so much fun."

"We'd be gone most of the day. It might get. . .lonely being out there in the middle of nowhere."

"I'll take him for walks. He'll have a great time."

Tanner felt his chest tighten. She would be near him. Not close. But nearby. Somehow the long days in the saddle would be so much easier knowing she would be there in the evenings.

Chapter 15

The last sip of coffee went down cold. She'd let it cool too long, but the evening was one to enjoy. With her soreness, sitting still had its attraction. She almost hoped Tanner wouldn't press to teach her to rope because it meant moving, and she wanted to talk more than move.

"You're going to get sore the longer you sit."

She grimaced. "I was just hoping you wouldn't notice."

His dark eyes lit with amusement as he straightened. "Uh-uh. Time to get up and get going. Can't have the little filly stoving up on us."

He moved to her and held out a hand.

"Can't we talk first?"

His brow creased, but he didn't withdraw his hand. "Can you give me some time?"

"Time for what?"

"There's some things I need to get a handle on before we have that talk."

She put her hand in his, let him pull her to her feet. She felt lightheaded so close to him. His nearness was too much like an invitation. Those long fingers. The expectant look on his face. She wondered if hope could be renewed so easily and love come so quickly. No, of course not, she chided herself. She didn't know him, not the deep-down parts that mattered. That took time. She also knew that she would not deny herself the opportunity to enjoy his presence or the evening. Being way out from town afforded her little contact with anyone, and Tanner offered companionship. She didn't understand his reluctance, but her heart wanted to trust him. "Then we'll talk later."

His smile was beautiful. Gentle and kind. "We'll rope."

She groaned. "What about resting?"

He chuckled as he collected his rope from the porch post, where he'd hooked it before heading in to supper. "Too much right now won't be a good thing anyway."

She wanted to stomp her foot and snort like that bull had earlier; instead, she grabbed for the rope he held.

He held it away from her grasp. "Nope, not yet. First thing to learn about roping is you got to get used to the roughness." He caught her wrist and raised her hand, spreading the fingers. "Your palms are too soft, so be careful of the rope burning your skin."

As she stared up into his face, she felt the protective net of his words surround her like a shawl draped gently over her shoulders.

"Are you sure you want to do this?"

"I guess I don't have a choice."

"You do. Maybe you can just watch me."

She knew she should pull her hand away, but his eyes melted over her, and she basked in the warmth of his gaze and his touch.

"You do look tired."

Impossible. How could she look tired when she felt such energy? She reached to shove his chest. Taken by surprise, he stepped back to balance himself. She darted around him and down the steps. And then she stopped, feeling foolish at her burst of exuberance.

His boots were a blur as he took the steps. "Guess you do have some spunk left. I'll put up the horses, grab some gloves, and be back."

His horse nickered from the corral. He entered the enclosure and slipped a rope around Cue's neck. The piebald followed him into the barn. He came back and repeated the procedure with Queen. Frank was nowhere to be seen. When she spied the light coming from the bunkhouse, she wondered if the man had left the two of them alone on purpose or if he truly was suffering. Tanner returned from the barn with an extra coil of rope. He handed the second one to her.

"Now stand here beside me, and hold it the way I do."

She planted her feet as he did, even imitating the angle of how he held his hands. If anyone could teach her, he could. She'd admired that every time he'd thrown the rope, it had landed true along the horns or head.

He held out his right hand to draw her attention, the rope grasped with the palm facing out. "It should slide through real easy like." He demonstrated, pulling so that the rope slipped through the knot with ease. "We can start with a small loop." He pointed. "This is your spoke." He indicated the length of rope between the knot and his hand, "And this is your lead. You want about a coil's worth."

She mimicked his every move, absorbing his approving smile like hot sun on a puddle.

"Now you just. . ." He flicked the rope back and forth over his hand. "You see what I'm doing? Then we're going to grow the loop some." He slipped the knot down until the loop sagged almost to his feet.

She did the same, not quite understanding the reasoning but doing it nonetheless.

"Now you want to do this." He began to spin the loop over his head, easy and slow. He stuck his elbow out at an odd angle. "Don't do this or. . ." The loop sagged downward as it turned, creating the illusion of wobbling.

Drawing a breath, she let out her rope and began to spin it over her head. It dropped behind her.

"Careful or you'll catch your horse's tail. That's a good way to get thrown off."

He demonstrated what she'd done wrong. "You're doing fine; this is the most important part. Don't be shy about swinging your arm right off." Again, his loop was smooth and perfect.

She lifted her arms and did the same.

"Good. Much better. Now keep at it until you feel the rhythm of it."

Once, she looked up to see what the rope looked like in the air. It immediately started to wobble.

Tanner chuckled as it collapsed around her shoulders. "That's the way to rope yourself!"

Maira scowled at him.

"Whoa!" He reached in close to help her work the lasso up around her shoulders. "No use getting mad; it happens."

"I guess I'm not as patient as I'd like to think I am."

"You're patient with Levi."

She smirked. "And his endless questions?"

Tanner shrugged. "He's a good little boy. Curious is all. I'd rather have them curious and asking than sullen and. . ."

His pause made her curious. He took the rope from her and coiled it, twisting it with a flick of his wrist before adding another coil to his left hand. "You were saying?"

He grimaced. "Some kids don't appreciate all that they have."

"Sounds like you speak from experience."

Tanner took a long time coiling the rope. Much longer than necessary. Finally, he handed it over to her. "Try again."

She took the rope and held it like he'd told her, noting the shadows cast by the angle of the setting sun. When she met his gaze, his eyes were as dark as oil.

❧

Tanner squinted at the ranch house. The front door. Coming to know Levi slapped every moment of his reckless youth across his face and left a bruise on his heart. Maybe this is what it means for the past to meet you in the present.

Maira was game, but she was tired and sore. "You can stop."

"Good." She stretched and winced, holding out the rope. "I'm just too done in. All I want is a cup of tea."

He placed his hands together, collecting the rope from her and rolling it into one coil. Those green eyes glittered at him, a promise of warmth and comfort and companionship. "Coffee for me." He stuck his arm through the coil and rested it on his shoulder. "I'll meet you on the porch?"

"Sounds good."

He was never more aware of himself than he was walking toward the barn to return the rope. He wondered if she was watching him. In the darkness of the barn, he hung the coil on a peg, thinking about her. Her stiff muscles. He glanced into the darkened corner of the barn. He'd spied it on his first day there, as he'd taken mental inventory of the tools in various places around the barn, and now, as he approached the deep tub, an idea formed. He ran his hand around the lip and along the bottom. The bottom was worn, thin and rusting in places, but he would clean it up. It would do the job just fine.

Tanner shouldered his prize and carried it to the side door. He peeked inside and set it down as quietly as he could, waiting for that moment when Maira would head out to the porch. When she glanced toward the cookstove that stood by the door, he ducked back and turned sideways to avoid detection. Gathering a bucket of water, he returned to the side door and glanced in again. All was clear. For now. As quietly as he could, he slipped the deep trough through the door and into the kitchen. The front corner stabbed into the cookstove, causing a ringing sound. He frowned and cut his eyes to the front. Maira stood in the doorway, hands on her hips.

"You scared me to death," she chided as her boots tapped across the wood floor. When she cleared the table and saw what he had, she frowned and shook her head. "What is that, and why are you bringing it into my kitchen?"

Tanner could feel the heat creeping up his neck. "I thought... That is..."

Her lips curled upward in slow motion. "A bath." Her gaze went to the trough, then back to him, her voice soft now. "Thank you, Tanner."

"I've got some water. Thought if you got it to heating now it might be ready after. . .your tea." He gave the trough another shove until it came even with the table. He jerked his head toward the door. "I'll get that bucket."

"I'll stoke up the fire and put on the big kettle."

He ground to a stop and turned. "Let me get that for you."

"I can handle it. I have all these years."

How could he tell her that he didn't want her struggling with heavy things? He didn't understand it himself. "I wouldn't be a gentleman if I let you lug that kettle around."

"Then I'll stop being stubborn." She motioned him into the pantry. "It's in there. My back thanks you."

The fire snapped and popped as he put on another log before settling the kettle on its hook. He dumped the first bucket, eyeballed the trough to estimate how many more he would need to fill it. Eight buckets later and he thought it must be enough. Upending the bucket by the side door to drain, he reentered the kitchen and glanced through toward the front window where she sat in her rocker. He couldn't wait to join her.

Something vibrated and he raised his head, catching a strange sound. Hoofbeats. At the front window he watched as Walt Price rode his pinto into the yard, followed by two men Tanner recognized. Ducking away, he traversed the kitchen, shot out the side door, and slipped toward the porch, where he hid in the shadow to listen.

Chapter 16

Good day, Mrs. Cullen. Carrot and Fletcher thought you might could use the help again this year. At my expense of course."

Maira's voice held just the right mix of confidence and kindness. "You know how much I appreciate your offer, Mr. Price, but I've a strong hand working for me." Tanner heard the slightest hesitation in her voice. "We're doing quite well."

Leather creaked. Tanner straightened, poised to make his appearance. Walt would want to know if he'd discovered anything, and Maira would wonder where he was. If he tarried, she might ask the reasons for his absence. He strode out from his place. Walt's eyes snapped to him first thing.

"Young, how're you doing?"

He wondered if Walt was aware of his slip. He did his best to cover. "Walt. How's the XP?"

"Roundup is underway."

Tanner stopped at the base of the porch steps, giving a curt nod to Fletcher, then Carrot.

"We came to see if Mrs. Cullen needed some help with her herd this year. She said she'd hired someone. If I'd known it was you, I wouldn't have worried so much about her." He turned to address Maira. "He's a top hand, ma'am. You've done well."

"He's been a godsend, Mr. Price. Already he's taken care of so many repairs."

Tension knifed his spine. If Maira opened up the subject of his suspicions...

"He is looking into some problems with the cows." Her bright tone showed the level of confidence she had in him. Walt Price, Tanner knew, would not miss that.

Walt raised a hand to his men, shifted his weight, and dismounted. Dust climbed to his shins then settled. Carrot and Fletcher set spurs to their horses and moved off toward the entrance gate of Rocking J. "Why don't I leave Carrot and Fletcher here to help out?" Walt's voice purred as he drew nearer. Tanner felt the man's gaze on him, hard and measuring. "It would make things go that much faster. There's a dance in town next week." His gaze shifted to Maira. "While the hands are working cattle, maybe you and me could slip away to town."

"Take Ana," Tanner suggested.

Walt's eyes narrowed at him. "Ana never wants to go anywhere." He laughed, but the sound was grating, even unpleasant. His head swiveled back to Maira. "What do you say, Maira?"

"An invitation." Maira's voice revealed nothing.

Tanner dared not react, though he couldn't deny the splash of disgust that sliced through him. This was not his fight. He had no claim on Maira, or anything for that matter.

"Sure. You keep cooped up on this ranch more than is good for any widow."

"It is my home, Mr. Price. My son needs me."

Walt's head bobbed as if he'd expected that argument. "I'm sure Frank can watch over him. Since he can't sit a horse anymore, he's little better than a nanny."

Steel came into Maira's voice. Tanner didn't bother to hide his smile. "Frank is a dear friend and loyal hand."

Walt put a boot on the lower step and swept his hat from his head. "My apologies, Mrs. Cullen. I didn't mean to offend."

The rocker ceased moving. Tanner turned in time to see her rise to her feet, her face a mask. "Your apology is accepted. Now it is late, Mr. Price. You are welcome to bed down in the bunkhouse before you return in the morning."

Walt's face went rigid. "I was just trying to help you out, Mrs. Cullen."

"And I have expressed numerous times my appreciation. However, I no longer need to take advantage of your good graces. Thank you and good night."

She pivoted, and the screen door slapped closed behind her.

"I guess that's that then." Tanner said as he met Walt's eyes. He knew the man, or thought he did. Walt disliked being crossed, but the black rage on his face spilled fear into Tanner's gut. Fear for Maira.

"She seems quite taken with *you*."

He felt the accusation behind that last syllable.

Tanner turned and walked away. Walt could rant and rage all he wanted, but he'd hired him to come to the Rocking J. He'd only been doing his job. As he'd hoped, Walt followed him away from the house.

"Tell me what you've learned."

"I learned that the man I thought to be the 'owner' of the ranch wasn't a man after all."

Walt's lips trembled in a sneer. "Women have no right to property." Walt's voice went oily. "You must be doing a good job. Gotten yourself a position in the house yet?"

Anger flared hot. "Shut up."

Walt's sneer melted into a knowing grin. "Touch a nerve, Young?"

"I changed my mind. I don't need your money."

"You aiming to be a problem for me?" His voice had become harsh. A warning.

"You sent me here to spy on a woman who has lost her husband. I'm here because of you, but no longer. I quit." More came to his tongue, begging to be spoken, but he would be better off biding his time.

"You're setting yourself up against me."

"It's not my ranch; it's hers."

"But you want it, don't you? Just like you want her?"

He didn't miss the way Walt's arm tensed over his right gun. "No. That's *your* game."

Walt's eyes glittered like those of a snake. "Never thought you one to turn traitor."

"I ride for the brand I believe in; it just doesn't happen to be the XP. If that rubs you wrong, that's your problem."

❧

Maira spent several long minutes and an entire cup of tea reining in her anger. Walt Price had nerve. His put-down of Frank prickled the hair on her neck. She could only be grateful Frank had not been present to hear it. But Walt Price would never have said it to Frank's face. No, he was the type to talk behind a person's back, a fact his comment had proven beyond the shadow of a doubt. How the man would ever think himself attractive to any woman was beyond her. Though she could see someone being attracted to his wealth. A shallow, silly woman.

How dare Walt trot in on his horse offering his men again as if she would never catch on to his game. She wrapped her hands around her mug and pressed it to her forehead. The heat soothed. Her anger cooled. If not for Tanner, she would never have known of the missing cows. The herd would have been whittled down to nothing until she would have been forced to sell the ranch. More than anything, it fueled her desire to ride out with Frank and Tanner. To be a part of gathering and assessing the herd.

Setting her cup down, she folded her arms on the table and pillowed her head there. Her confidence in Tanner had grown with Walt's acknowledgment that the man was a top hand. She wondered how the two knew each other. She sighed. The ache in her muscles, loosened a bit by the roping, had returned with a vengeance. Heat from the fire warmed the room, embracing her as Jon used to embrace her. She could have that again. With Tanner. She wanted to experience that closeness. Lifting her head, she surveyed the room. He'd brought the trough in and then the buckets of water. For her. A smile filled her heart to overflowing. Would he come in for the promised cup of coffee? Remembering the mugs, she stood. If Walt was still in the yard, she wouldn't put it past him to make another play for her affections. He had been persistent enough.

The scene that greeted her reeked of tension. Walt stood, his shoulders tense, hand hovering over his gun. But it was Tanner's stance that most worried her. He seemed unaware of the other man's anger. Fletcher and Carrot, too, had become suddenly alert. Their faces intent, gazes hard on Tanner and Walt. Murder in Walt's eyes.

Jon. Her throat closed with the vision of her husband. Alone and dying.

She barreled down the steps. Her mouth opened, but nothing came out. Tanner turned to face her, his relaxed expression becoming a mask of horror. Walt pivoted, his hand raising, something in the palm. Her legs pumped harder. Hoofbeats vibrated in her ears. Tanner's leg swept out, and Walt's mouth gaped in pain as the muzzle of his gun flashed.

Chapter 17

Tanner caught sight of Maira's body hurtling toward them, hand raising her skirts to free her feet. He pivoted toward her, but Walt was turning, going for his gun, spooked by the unexpected movement. Tanner crouched and hooked his leg behind Walt's. The bark of Walt's gun rent the night air before the man collapsed, landing hard on his side. His gun slid away.

Hooves pounded toward him. Tanner straightened as Carrot's horse skidded to a stop beside him. "Back off!"

Fletcher added something Tanner didn't hear, but the man was off his horse, kneeling by Walt, and beyond him, another crumpled body.

Tanner stumbled forward, mouth dry. His knees gave out beside her, the sight of blood stealing his ability to draw in air.

"Tanner!"

He didn't know who said his name. Didn't care. Someone groaned. He slipped his arms beneath Maira, rolling her toward his chest, lifting. Her head snapped back, the mane of dark hair spilling toward the ground. Another groan, and his mind spun to another time, another place, when an Indian woman's dark hair had spilled over his lap. She'd died because he hadn't acted fast enough. His fault.

He felt a hand on his arm.

"We need a doctor." Frank's voice.

"I'll ride." Fletcher.

Leather creaked, a horse whinnied.

"I didn't see her." Walt's voice was gravelly. "Thought it was Frank. She shouldn't have run—"

Shouldn't have run. . . Shouldn't have run. . .

As the copper smell of blood filled his senses, Tanner's mind shredded one layer after another—to a time when the same words spilled from someone else's lips as the man laughed and shot holes into the innocent. Tanner hadn't acted fast enough to stop the massacre. And then there was his mother. A lone woman. Cold and hungry. Dying by herself when she should have been surrounded by family. He should have been there for her, and for the Indian woman.

❧

Maira struggled toward the light. Her arms couldn't quite touch the halo that she knew, somehow, would grant her the ability to return. Levi's voice. Crying. Warm hands. And underscoring the normal sounds was a river of pain. Dull, sharp at times. Hands moved over her side. Weakness held her limbs pinned to the mattress.

She struggled against the confines. Levi's tears needed to be wiped away, his fears assuaged. *I'm here, Levi.*

Her world tumbled and spun. A knot of nausea fisted in her stomach. She turned her head aside, body heaving, acid rising. A hand stroked her hair, touched her face, rubbed her cheek. Damp coolness on her brow eased her restlessness. She was not alone. *Please don't leave me alone.* Loneliness plagued her. She was at the orphanage, so alone. So afraid. Hopeful when rumors spread that a couple would be coming, looking for a child to adopt. Oh, the hope that always flowed through her. Through them all. But they never wanted her. . . .

Jon did. His face, so earnest. Gone. . .

Pain stabbed. She thought she heard Jon call out. It must have been like this for him. To die alone. Each drop of blood—slick and hot—sliding her closer to an abyss. Blackness beyond comprehension. She fell, groping. Darkness choked her. She closed her eyes, opened them. It made no difference. Black was black. Cool air shifted around her then blew away as hot breath washed over her. Sweat popped from her pores. She writhed, trying to escape the heat. When she thought her body might explode, she spun and fell flat, exhausted, spent.

She drifted. Memories touched her. So vague. She wanted to capture them, bring them into focus. She thought if she could touch them with her fingertips, they would bloom and grow. Instead they faded, writhed and twitched, and slid into the abyss with her.

Chapter 18

It had been a shaken Walt Price that had answered the sheriff's questions as the doctor worked over Maira. Levi's frantic tears had jerked Tanner from his daze. He'd pulled the fragile form into his arms, Levi's tears wetting his shirt front as the boy gave vent to his fear just as he had the night Tanner had found him. It seemed so long ago now.

After the doctor finished with Maira, he took Levi in to see his mother. He relished both the warmth and the connection the boy showed to his mother. "Will she be better? I want Mommy to wake up." He'd collapsed into Tanner's arms then, sobbing, and asked questions. Tanner answered every one of Levi's questions as best he could. And all the while he kept the boy close, soothing as he had never been soothed. Finally, he tucked Levi in next to his mother and cautioned the boy to be careful not to jostle her.

Levi slipped his hand beneath Maira's. Tanner left him like that, knowing he had yet to face the sheriff's conclusion on the entire matter. He had a few things to say about Price. He opened the door to see the men at the table. All eyes landed on him as he moved to the head of the table. Maira's spot.

Doc was saying his peace as Tanner sat. "...Not a bad wound, but she lost a lot of blood. Time will tell."

Sheriff Miller made the suggestion first. "I think, Price, you should plan on having your men pitch in on the roundup. Was your actions that put this grief into motion." He turned his head as Tanner entered. "You'll be in charge of the men. You and Frank can make the decisions Mrs. Cullen would normally make."

Frank agreed to the offer without hesitation. Tanner's suspicions came to the forefront. "They'll be watched at every turn. We've had some problems with our numbers, Sheriff." Though he addressed Sheriff Miller, his eyes were on Walt. The man's face blanched.

"What are you trying to say?"

He swung a leg over the bench and settled himself before responding. "You've sent men since Jon Cullen's death. You want this ranch, Walt. You said as much to me, even sent me to spy on the owner in hopes you could use information against the rancher. Against Mrs. Cullen. A widow."

Sheriff Miller's brows raised, his hazel eyes settled on Walt. "Heard as much in town that Carrot and Fletcher been working the cows here."

"Ask them about it, then. Maybe they know something." Walt seemed to deflate. "I wanted the ranch, but I wouldn't steal her head."

"You have proof of this, Young?"

He nodded toward Frank. "He can verify that Walt's sent men over since Jon Cullen's death." He leaned forward and accepted the cup of coffee that was set in front of him, then in front of Frank. "I'm waiting for the final count to figure what's been lost over the years."

"Your men honest, Price?"

" 'Course they're honest. Wouldn't hire 'em if I didn't think so."

Tanner leaned forward. "Timmons has a chip on his shoulder about something."

"He's used to being boss."

He held the rancher's gaze and narrowed his eyes. "Time for him to learn to take orders."

Walt inclined his head. "I'll tell him he'd better not cause problems."

"How soon can you get your men out here?" Sheriff Miller asked.

Walt took a gulp of coffee and swiped a hand across his mouth. "I'll send two more out. Carrot and Fletcher can stay here."

"If Mrs. Cullen doesn't make it, you might be looking at time. I'll have my deputy stay close to this area tonight and tomorrow." The sheriff's eyes shifted between Frank and Tanner. "Can he stay here?"

"Plenty of room in the bunkhouse," Frank offered.

"It's the best I can do under the circumstances." The sheriff lifted his hat with a finger to scratch his forehead. "Does this satisfy the two of you?"

Frank agreed. Tanner couldn't bring himself to reply. He scooted the bench back, anger notching up with every footfall. His shirt rippled in the night breeze, stiff where Maira's blood had drenched the front. Her rocker sat empty. He touched the front of his shirt, rubbed at the bloodstain there. He wanted to take back the moment when he'd faced Maira as she'd barreled toward them. If not for his reaction to seeing her, Walt's nerves would not have shattered, and the bullet would never have been fired.

The spring on the door hummed a warning. He glanced to see Sheriff Miller. "From all I've heard, it was an accident. Walt's remorseful. I can't haul him in on nothing, Tanner. You know that."

He pressed his lips together. "I know that."

"You want to talk about what's eating you? The rustling?"

He drew air into his lungs. "Jon Cullen."

"Jon. . . ?"

Tanner turned at the surprise in the man's voice. "He was murdered."

Miller stayed quiet.

"I found him right after it happened."

"What's to say you didn't shoot him and are trying to place the blame elsewhere?"

Temper flared then waned. No matter what he thought, Miller was right.

"Who and what makes you think it was murder?"

"He was shot in the side. Hoofprints were everywhere."

"You out hunting?"

"Yeah. Had seen some cut fence, thought I'd look into it while I watched the XP cattle."

"This cut fence have to do with the rustling of Maira's herd?"

"I don't know."

"You're assuming Jon wasn't involved."

"Cutting his own fence?"

"Framing his neighbor to get compensation."

"Not Jon."

"You seem certain of all this." The big man shifted forward. "This needn't become a vendetta against Price. You worked for the man to investigate your own theories?"

"Part of the reason."

"And the other part?"

"Jon Cullen was my brother."

❧

Beneath gentle hands, Maira struggled to open her eyes. She'd felt the hands on her side, then her face and forehead. She wanted so much to know who attended her with such gentleness. Jon? No. Jon was gone. Levi? He could never be silent for that long. Even as the longing swelled, the little bit of strength she possessed receded. Her side burned. She remembered the shot, twisting in the dirt, the numbness that permeated every inch of her before her mind blanked. She tried to move her fingers to touch the place that sent such heat through her body. Gunshot. Her mouth felt as if she'd inhaled the dirt stirred by a late-summer wind. She sighed. Nothing seemed to be working like she wanted, not her fingers or her mouth or her legs. And the terrible pain was swelling again. She winced as it crested. Heard a mewling sound. Then silence.

She woke to a touch against her forehead. The same hands she'd felt earlier. But no, these were different. Rougher. Heavier somehow. There was something like a sob. Her hand was encompassed in warmth and rubbed against something rough. Wetness. She felt it and wanted to turn her head that direction. It would be Tanner. Had to be. There was a pain deep down inside him, and she wanted to know what it was. They'd been about to talk about it that night. Or had it been afternoon?

"Tan-wer."

Levi.

Her lips were dry. She moved them and felt a glorious victory for the effort. Words lodged in her throat but would not come. Her hand was released, and she tensed. The pain swelled. "Mommy, wake up!"

Levi's little hands touched her cheeks, patting as he often did.

"Sh, you want to let her rest as much as possible. She'll get stronger if she sleeps."

Little sobs reached her ears.

"Shhh. . ." Tanner's voice soothed the boy. "Let's see what Frank has for us to eat."

"Not hungry."

"You need to eat, Levi. Your mommy would frown at you if she heard you say that."

The voices faded, and she didn't know if it was because they were leaving the room, or if she was.

Chapter 19

Tanner stood on the porch, coffee in hand. Frank had tried to get him to eat breakfast, but all he could think of was Levi, sitting on his little wooden seat, eyes red with the evidence of his worry. He had sat next to the boy and encouraged him to eat every bite Frank had set in front of him. Carrot and Fletcher had arrived as Frank scooped the last bite from his own plate into his mouth. At the presence of the men, Levi's mood had perked. Tanner left the boy to help Frank get breakfast for the XP cowhands.

He mulled his options, which were nonexistent. The boy was too small to take with them on the roundup, and someone had to care for Maira anyway. He dug his fingers into the point along his hairline where pressure mounted every passing minute. Frank had assured him he could ride and would be the eyes and ears to keep the XP hands honest, but Tanner feared Frank's leg could only take so much.

That Maira's injury had been his fault plagued his every breath. He wanted to ride out. Needed the action and the distraction. He had no choice. Frank would go out alone with the men Walt sent. He would stay behind with Maira and Levi. He drank long and deep of his coffee, breathing in the steam, feeling the pressure in his head ease somewhat. Pale gray dawn gave off a cold light. Around him was stillness. He squinted into the distance, catching movement. XP hands were riding in. He straightened, his mouth sour from the coffee.

"You wanting to go?"

Tanner jerked around to see Frank standing in the doorway. The cowhand let the door shut behind him, his tired eyes meeting Tanner's. "I can keep watch over them as well as you. Been doing it for a long time."

"Riding might not be good for your leg."

"Is this about my leg or about something else?"

Tanner frowned. "I don't know what you're talking about."

Frank crossed his arms and leaned against the porch post. "You think that bronc busted more than my leg? That he busted my head, too? I can see how much Maira taking that bullet bothers you. As well it should. Maybe you should have been honest with her from the first you were kin."

He shouldn't have been surprised that the sheriff had told Frank about his relationship to Jon Cullen. What the sheriff still did not know was the reason for his arrival on the Rocking J. That Walt Price had sent him over. Or maybe he did know. Walt might have told the sheriff to get the glare of the spotlight off himself.

Anxiety bunched the muscles in his neck. He flicked his wrist and sprayed the remains of his coffee into the dirt of the yard. "What do you know?"

"Probably not enough."

Clouds were moving in. Dark clouds, heavy with rain. Along the horizon he could see dark dots. Riders coming in. Three of them. Strange, hadn't the sheriff only asked for two others to be sent? But Frank's statement needed an answer, and he wondered if he should tell all or fabricate a story that would ensure Maira's protection. Frank could be trusted. As he let his gaze fall over the older man, Frank's brows lifted high.

"Better make it a good lie, or, better yet, just give me the truth."

"I didn't lie."

"Nor did you tell the truth."

"I have no evidence that Jon was murdered or that Rocking J cattle have been stolen. Still don't."

"But you didn't think it important for Maira to know you were Jon's brother. That seems like something mighty important."

"Half brother. And I didn't know at first she was his wife or Levi his son."

The cowhand's mouth drooped. "How could you not know?"

"I haven't seen Jon for a long time."

Frank's jaw worked hard. "What makes you think he was murdered?"

Tanner suddenly wished he hadn't tossed out his coffee. He wanted something to drink. An excuse to delay talking so he could order his thoughts first. "Jon went to town that day. When I met him, I thought something was familiar, but I hadn't seen him since I was thirteen and he was five."

"You left home?"

Home. Is that what he was supposed to have called it? The old bitterness of his mother's remarriage so soon after his father's death soured his mouth anew. But he had no right to be angry. It had been his mother's choice. A wrong choice, maybe, but age had given him the understanding that a woman alone meant trouble. And she'd had him to think about. "You needed a pa, and I needed someone to shoulder the load or we'd lose the farm" had been her explanation the one time he'd asked her about it. Those words branded resentment into him, fueled further by the tongue-lashings his stepfather had freely rained down on his shoulders.

"Jon begged me not to leave. He was five at the time and the apple of his Pa's eye." Despite their different fathers, Tanner had loved his little brother. He'd enjoyed having the boy toddle after him, then pester him to play games. He told Frank of the affection he had for Jon, but the pressure of his stepfather's dissatisfaction with him had been a burden his young shoulders could no longer bear.

"It took me a few minutes to realize who Jon was. When I asked him about his growing up years, that's when I knew. Had me a beard then." Tanner rubbed his sideburns and jaw. "Figured he would never know unless I told him."

"But what was he there for? And did he talk about needing money or gold?"

"I had some gold. I gave him a pouch of it after realizing who he was. Figured our mama would approve. Told him to buy some head."

"He didn't tell you about Maira?"

"Never said a word. I didn't even know where he lived."

He'd followed Jon out of town for a couple miles, getting a general direction for where his brother lived. He'd returned to the XP, to that corner of the property that met the neighboring ranch where he'd been tracking coyote when he found Jon's body, the gold still on it.

"I knew he'd been shot. Murdered. That Walt Price's story was nothing more than a lie. Maybe he didn't rustle cattle, but he helped fabricate that story to cover for whoever was doing it. That he stole the gold and that his horse got scared and bucked him. That hole in his side was from a bullet."

Frank winced. "Why didn't you bury him?"

Tanner laced his fingers and cracked his knuckles. "Two things. One, I had a mind to pick up signs, hoping to track whomever pulled the trigger before rain set in and wiped everything away, and two, a mountain lion appeared on the scene. Never gave me a chance to do much of anything except get off a shot and light a shuck out of there. I heard about the find the next day, which meant I was too late to do anything."

"Price told the sheriff you worked for him."

Tanner drew air into his lungs, eyes on the riders, every second making them more distinct. He could feel Frank's disbelief and could understand the man being reluctant to trust what he was saying. "He hired me to come and spy on the owner of this ranch. I had no idea whose ranch it was. The money was good, and I was ready for a change."

"Funny how that detail didn't make it into his explanation to the sheriff."

"That he sent me to spy?"

Frank shifted his weight, glanced over his shoulder. Levi stood there, shirt soaked with water. Frank's eyes cut to him, then back to the boy. How much had Levi heard? "You're supposed to wash the dishes, not take a bath," Frank said gently.

"I can't get more water."

"Let me help you." Tanner followed Levi back to the dirty plates and grabbed up another bucket of the warm water. "You be careful you don't burn yourself."

"It feels good."

Tanner chuckled. "Well, you're supposed to clean the dishes, not yourself."

Levi lifted a dirty dish and plunged it into the water. Tanner leaned forward and grabbed a bar of lye. Using a knife, he scraped some into the water. Levi plunged his hands in to stir everything around, making it clear how he got so wet. Tanner tousled his head. "I'm going to talk to Frank again."

The boy nodded over at the tub scooted into a corner of the kitchen. Maira had never gotten her bath. "Can I take a bath in that?"

"Tonight."

He went back outside and sat across from Frank.

"That boy. . . He could be yours."

Tanner exhaled, licked his dry lips. Frank's gaze held his, and he knew in those few minutes he'd been gone to help the boy, the ranch hand had made his decision to trust Tanner.

"God put you here, son. Plain and simple. Spy or not, you're here, and you've helped, and it's plain that you—"

"I told Walt I wasn't doing it," Tanner spit the words. They felt bitter on his lips. "That I quit. It's what got him riled."

"Reckon it would." His eyebrow went up. "What made you change your mind?"

Maira. Levi. His relationship to them both. The old guilt gnawed at his backbone. He swung his eyes back to the horizon. "We've got company."

They were too far out to allow an immediate distraction. Tanner left the porch anyway, crossing to the corral to work on saddling the horses needed for the day. Frank stayed put on the porch. He felt the man's presence without turning to make sure he was right. When the XP riders entered the yard, Tanner left off saddling horses to greet them. A young woman was among them. For long seconds, Tanner tried to remember where he'd seen her. Strawberry hair. A thick layer of freckles across her nose. Ana. Walt's "maid."

"Walt told her to make herself useful here" was Slim's introduction as he and the other cowhand dismounted. "This here's Roger and Ana." Only when Roger was beside Ana's horse did she dismount, but despite Roger's proximity, the hand didn't do a thing to help her down. Slim frowned at Roger and kept talking. "Price thought we should bring her out. He don't want trouble, and Ana can care for the boy and the woman."

"Those your words or his?"

Slim was a wiry fellow, as his name suggested, affable and remote most times that Tanner could recall being around the XP hands. Tanner noted the way the cowhand watched the young girl, his expression a mix of sadness and longing.

Ana climbed the steps with quick movements as Carrot and Fletcher joined Frank on the porch. The XP hands grinned at the girl, lecherous smiles that slammed a fist in Tanner's gut. She stopped in front of Carrot.

Slim motioned him closer. "She can do whatever needs done, mister. Ana's a good worker."

Carrot guffawed in a way that darkened Slim's countenance. "Shut up, Carrot," Slim grumbled.

"Only Walt would say she was a good worker," Fletcher snickered.

Tanner waded into the group on the porch. "Mount up and move out. Frank will lead off." Tanner turned toward the older man. "Queen is in her stall." He'd left the mare there on purpose. At least there Frank could mount up without having everyone stare at his awkward movements and the brace.

Frank nodded, glanced at Ana, Tanner, the men, then back at Tanner. His unspoken question was obvious.

Tanner took in the girl's appearance, the dirty shirt and dowdy split skirt. Clothes that did not become her. "Can you keep an eye on a little boy and—"

"Mr. Price told me what needed done."

He nodded. "Nothing more will be required of you."

"Cooking. He said I should cook for the hands."

"There is that, yes." Tanner glanced at Frank. The older man shrugged and turned to follow the rest of the men. Slim stayed behind, but far enough away he couldn't hear their conversation, his eyes on Ana. For all of the man's tactics to appear otherwise, Tanner knew the cowhand was not only interested but maybe even wary of Ana being on the porch with another man. He decided to put the hand out of his misery. "Slim!"

The young man's head snapped up.

Tanner motioned him to the porch.

"What is it?" Slim asked, his gaze shrugging over Ana.

"I want you to stay here with Ana."

Slim's jaw dropped; his eyes cut to the girl's. "Mr. Price would have my head if I did that."

"Why? There's a lot of work needin' done. Wood to be chopped and I don't have time to do it. Ana might need you."

"You stay then."

"It's my responsibility to keep tabs on the others."

A wash of red streamed up into Slim's cheeks. He rolled his eyes toward Ana, then away.

Levi came to stand in the doorway, hair askew. Eyes, round as pies, stared up at Ana.

The girl's lip trembled as she reached out to the boy. Levi took her hand and smiled real big. "Are you going to help my ma?"

He tugged her inside. Ana gave a last, fleeting glance over her shoulder at Slim, then Tanner.

"I came to round up cows" was Slim's comment.

Tanner descended the steps to stand next to the lanky cowhand. "There's something wrong with Walt Price having this young woman work for him. He doesn't treat her well."

A muscle jumped in Slim's jaw, anguish twisting his expression. "He treats her like a dog. She's his—"

"Then it's your duty to stay. Show her it doesn't have to be the way it is."

❧

"Your toast, Mrs. Cullen."

For Levi's sake Maira kept a straight face at the single piece of toast with jam Ana set on her lap even though eating was the last thing she wanted to do.

Levi gave a little bounce. "I'll eat it!"

Doing her best not to move too much and wake the sharp pain that liked to jab up her side, Maira held out her right arm in invitation to her son. He crept close and tucked himself under Maira's arm. When he rested his head against her chest, tears collected in her eyes. Thankfulness. She felt stronger now, and with the rain pummeling against the roof and Levi tucked close to her, life tasted sweet indeed. Ana's shy, sad eyes concerned her. The girl hadn't said much of herself, though Maira had heard her chatting with Levi throughout the dismal, rainy afternoon.

"I can't tell you, Ana, how much I appreciate you coming."

The young girl nodded.

"Ana says she came because she had to!" Levi offered.

Ana's hair blocked her expression, but her bowed head said much about the young woman. Maira patted the side of the bed. "Why don't you tell me what you and Levi did this afternoon?"

Like she was wooden, Ana perched on the edge of the mattress. Maira reached to touch the young woman's arm. "I heard the two of you laughing."

"Ana is funny!"

The young woman's face tilted upward, a small smile pulling her lips upward before the whole effort was wiped away and her head fell again.

Levi tensed to say something. Maira silenced him with a squeeze to his shoulder and took a bite of the toast. "I'd like to hear what Ana has to say." She touched the girl's arm again. "Please, Ana. Tell me about yourself."

At first, she didn't think the girl had heard. Her concern grew with the silence. "You work for Mr. Price?"

"I'm his maid."

"You enjoy your job?"

Ana shrugged. A hollow sound rang out, followed by the creak of wood. Maira turned toward the window. "What is that?"

"Slim. He's cutting wood just inside the barn door to keep dry," Ana said.

"Tan-wer had him stay."

Maira rolled the information around in her head. She didn't buy that the young woman was shy. Hearing her with Levi earlier had convinced her that Levi was having fun. Maybe the girl felt more comfortable with children than with adults. Walt Price was not this young girl's father. He wasn't married. Another thought rolled into her mind. She'd been the recipient of Walt's oily stares once too often not to believe the idea could happen, but stating it outright seemed bold, and there was Levi to consider. "I think it's time for a nap." She smiled down at her son.

Ana leaped to her feet, as if her spine had been jerked taut by a string. She made her exit on soft feet, closing the door quietly. Maira's heart squeezed at the girl's distress.

"I'm tired," Levi snuggled closer.

"You like Ana?"

"She smiles sometimes."

Funny the way he said it. Even Levi noticed the girl's solemn nature. "Smiling is good."

"I tried to make her smile lots."

She smoothed her hand down his cheek. "Let's rest now. We'll keep each other warm."

Levi giggled a sleepy giggle.

The rain on the roof combined with the food she'd just eaten and Levi's warm body pulled at her. She heard the front door slap open, then Ana's soft voice answered by a deeper one. She opened her eyes and tried to focus on the conversation but could not. She blinked, then blinked again. It would have to wait for another time.

Chapter 20

Tanner rode hard through the day, as did all the hands. Even Carrot seemed to curb his sullen attitude. They watched the dark clouds build throughout the morning as they worked to free eight head that had become bogged in the mud of a wide stream. Everything was a muddy mess. Rain puddled along the brim of his hat and dripped in a thin stream from the front. He tilted the hat back on his head, feeling the icy stream against his clinging, wet shirt. The rain could not touch the coldness in his soul, a barren thing ever since Maira had taken that bullet and Levi had spent that first evening tucked in his arms, sobbing. What they needed was someone who could love them without failing. They needed Jon. His brother had life burdens, but Jon lacked the specters that rose to torment on a moment's notice.

He fought to think, the rain so cold on his arms. He twisted in the saddle and worked the buckle of the saddlebags with hands already stiff from the slashing rain. He shook out his oilskin and poked his head through. It was too late to keep him dry, but it would at least lend a modicum of warmth.

Frank roped a stuck cow, pegging the bull in place. Tanner moved behind the animal, beckoning Fletcher to do the same. A whoop went up from another XP hand as a cow found its footing and climbed the bank to the other side of the wet-weather stream.

Even as Tanner dismounted to help a mud-caked cow, the rain came harder, faster. Slipping along the muddy bank, his boots offered no barrier against the water. Another step sunk him into muck up to his knees. Fletcher caught his dilemma and backed up before he, too, became mired. With Frank holding the bull, Fletcher used his horse and rope to pull Tanner free. The mud clung. Tanner bunched his toes within his boots to prevent the thick mud from sucking them right off his feet. As soon as he could, he let go of the rope and gained his footing.

Lightning spliced the dark clouds. Thunder roared seconds later. Like a great, dark veil, the rain was moving toward them. Carrot yelled, trying to move the herd back from the water, Tanner gained his seat on Cue and rode toward the lead cattle.

"Another bolt like that..."

Tanner understood what Frank meant. In a flash, lightning sizzled from the sky and struck a lone tree a hundred feet from the cows. Within seconds, they were moving, en masse, a ball of angry, frightened energy, their bawling becoming a cacophony. Tanner saw the threat. He stretched out his hand and slapped Queen on the flank. Frank's face registered surprise as he tried to gain control as Queen lunged, her hooves digging hard into the ground. Tanner rose in the stirrups, yelling, hoping to turn the angry, frightened animals. He pulled his gun from its holster and shot into the air. *Turn! Turn!* Another shot. But they came, undeterred, eyes rolling in their heads, the ground vibrating.

"Tanner!"

He knew it was Frank. Fletcher was motioning to him. Frantic.

The lead cow roared closer, hooves churning, a ball of angry bovine behind him. Tanner gave his heels to Cue's side, but the horse balked, quivered. He could feel the horse's fear. He yanked on the reins and dug his stirrups into the horse's sides. Rain slashed at him, cold and hard. More like balls of hail. Cue's muscles bunched hard. Tanner's fingers curled tighter on the reins. Any minute and he would be done. He talked to the horse in a calm voice he did not feel. Cue straightened out and heaved forward, jerking Tanner along. They cleared the middle of the stampeding animals when Tanner felt the jerk and slant of Cue's gait. He pitched forward and rolled over the animal's head. His right foot hung him. Suspended from the right stirrup, he kicked out. The cows were close, their hooves a roar in his ears. He gave a vicious kick, the cows almost on him. Cue righted himself just as Tanner pulled his foot from the boot and rolled to his feet.

He turned to the column of cows. A hundred feet. Seventy five. Tanner sank to the wet earth, moisture wicking through his pants. His hand dropped to his right holster. Gone. He'd lost the gun. Palming the left gun, he took aim at the first cow. His finger, cold on the trigger, seemed to have a mind of its own. One by one, six shots, and five cows went down in front of him. Tanner balled himself behind the shield of dead carcasses. Waited. The pounding of hooves heavy in his ears. He tensed for the feel of the first hoof on his back, imagined the piercing pain of the hooves pummeling him. Minutes stretched long, his heart slamming hard.

He heard a scream. Frank's voice. Coming closer.

Fletcher was at his side first, helping him to his feet, clamping him on the back.

"Go." He breathed hard. "The cows."

Fletcher gathered his reins and bolted after the departing herd.

Cue stood far off, in a grove of trees. The animal's knees were skinned, and lacerations on his right shoulder bled freely. Tanner's hands went over the horse. He didn't want to ride. Didn't want to think. The cold rain pounded at him. He stared out at the pile of carcasses. Those cows had saved his life. Maira's cows.

"Sit down." Frank was beside him now, anger in the man's eyes. "You have a death wish?"

He'd never thought for a minute the man could yell so loud. It reminded him of his stepfather. Of that last argument. The hail of hard words that had sucked away

Tanner's desire to stay home another day.

"Sit down! Now!"

Tanner leaned against Cue, but no, the horse was injured, too. Was he hurt? What was wrong with him? Frank was saying something else, but he couldn't understand the words. He sank to his knees and took deep breaths, but they didn't help. His teeth chattered. He hugged himself, nausea building. Driving rain slapped his neck and poured icy fingers down his back and chest.

"Tanner?" Frank's voice, gentler now but still a rough edge that wouldn't allow for stubbornness.

He raised his head, gulping a breath as the icy rain smeared along his face. His hat?

"Can you stand, son?"

He saw Frank's hand reach down, noted the man's stern expression. Reaching out, Tanner caught the man's hand in a firm grip. Frank kicked his foot free of the stirrup. Tanner stabbed his boot into the hollow ring, seeing, for the first time, that his right foot was bare. In a disjointed way, he wanted to laugh; instead, he leaned forward and dragged himself upward, every muscle rebelling against the effort.

❧

Tanner held his head as Frank slid a cup of coffee in front of him. Frank draped a blanket over his shoulders and took a seat across from him as he ran a linen over his head, then hooked it around his neck. He took in the interior of the crude little shelter under a jutting ledge of stone. Nothing more than a very shallow cave, but it was dry and warm.

"What did you call that?" Frank growled.

The words hit hard. He shoved the cup of coffee away. Frank pushed it back. The first bloom of anger raged. "It's not like I started that stampede."

Frank pressed his lips together, nostrils flared. "You risked your life."

"At least she'll have plenty of roasts and steaks."

"That wasn't funny."

Tanner cradled his head. "Wasn't trying to be. I was only trying to. . ." Why were they having this discussion? "If you'll recall, I saved your life."

"And then you sat there and wasted time shooting off your gun."

He cupped his hands around the coffee. "I was trying to get them to swerve."

Frank dug his thumbs against his closed eyes and released a sigh. "I can't tell you. . ." His voice was soft now, more controlled. "How afraid I was when Cue went down."

"Everything worked out."

The cowhand shifted and grimaced, rubbing a hand along his right leg. "It was a foolish risk. Getting yourself killed won't help Maira or Levi. That boy has come to love you."

Tanner absorbed those words, the worry that he saw in Frank's eyes. "I didn't do it on purpose."

"Didn't look that way." Frank clamped his jaw and lowered his eyes. "You scared me."

"I thank you for your concern."

"If you'd died. . ." As if doused with a cup of anger, Frank's eyes flared again. "But taking those risks. . . That bull could have turned and gored you. It was like you were doing everything possible to put yourself on the line."

"Can I just drink my coffee in silence?"

Frank's eyes were penetrating, and Tanner felt as if his skin was being stripped from his body. Like Frank wanted to see to his soul.

It's too black in there. You wouldn't want to see it.

"You're right."

Tanner gripped the coffee cup tighter. Had he thought that, or said it out loud?

"Finish your coffee." Frank plunged his hat on his head then struggled back into the saddle, using a boulder for a stepping-stone. "I've got to find out what happened to the men. We'll save this for later. You get on back to the ranch."

He watched Frank disappear knowing now he should have stayed at the XP hunting animals or, better yet, roaming from town to town, doing odd jobs. No commitments, no relationships that doomed him to certain failure.

Restlessness surged through him, smothering his need for a warm fire, hot coffee, or even food. He needed to be free again. Feel the wind in his hair and the steady rhythm of the horse's gait beneath him. He'd done his best for Maira. He could at least figure out the things he needed to for Jon.

Stripping the blanket from his shoulders, he stared down at his stocking foot. One boot. Almost laughable, except for his need to get moving. To be done with this thing.

Chapter 21

Maira thought she might drown in Levi's tears. She touched the center of his back, absorbing every shaking sob, her own mind reeling from the creeping reality of Tanner's absence. Frank chomped on his lower lip as his palms traced a path up and down the legs of his denim trousers.

"I told him to come back here."

She nodded, unable to put together the pieces of the puzzle. At supper, the whole crew had shown up at the table, except Tanner. Frank had come to her, explaining their last conversation. "Seemed to have something stuck in his craw. Might be he went back for his boot."

A flimsy excuse. She knew it. Frank knew it. It mollified Levi though. "He lost his boot?"

The cowhand nodded and chomped his lower lip harder. "Saved my life." He reached to pat Levi. "Chin up, boy. Tanner's a smart man. He'll turn up."

"But we don't know where he is."

Maira stroked Levi's back. If only she felt stronger. Her deepest fear gnawed. He'd left. For good.

The scraping of chairs signaled the meal was coming to an end. Boots scraped against the floor as the hands filed out. Through the closed window, Maira caught the distinct belch of one of the men.

"Really!" Maira made a face. "Like they were born in a mud pit with the pigs."

Frank shot her an amused look and extended his leg out in front of him, expression sobering. "Do you want me to take some of the men to look for him?"

Levi had quieted, but Maira knew his ears were attuned to her every word and expression. "You've all had a long day. Give the men some time and rest. Tanner will probably ride in soaked to the bone and wanting some coffee."

Frank glanced at Levi and inclined his head. "I'll tell Ana to keep the pot on for him."

Levi snuggled close to Maira's side. "Is it time for bed?"

Frank jabbed the boy's shoulder. "How about we play some checkers first? Then I've got to help butcher those cows. Plenty of jerky in your future."

"Yeah!"

Bless you, Frank. Maira smiled her gratitude at the man as Levi slipped from the bed and ran into the kitchen.

As the loyal cowhand turned to leave, she caught his hand. "Tell me. There's something you're not saying."

He leaned forward and rubbed his leg, voice low. "It's probably nothing. . . ."

"It is if it worries you."

"Does it show that much?"

She grinned. "Yes."

He sighed. "I used to hide these things so well."

"Frank. . ."

"Tanner took everything." He chewed his lip. "His bedding is gone. Had himself an extra pair of boots. They're gone, too. All of it."

"Tell me what happened out there."

He looked at the doorway, then sank down onto the chair. "I don't know. . . . It's like he was driven. He insisted on being out front, being in charge."

"Isn't that what he was supposed to do?"

"It was different."

"Maybe it's for the best." She clenched her teeth, throat suddenly raw.

Frank's eyes narrowed at her. "Who are you trying to convince?"

"I'm just saying it's better for him to pull up stakes now. Levi will forget him. We'll go on as before."

"And that will be better? For who?"

She tried to form an answer. On the tip of her tongue were the words she wanted to say, but she lost the impetus to launch them with that last stomach-clenching question.

"You can't stop loving because it hurts."

"I'm not."

"Yes, you are. I think we both are, though in different ways."

It was in Frank's face, the confusion and uncertainty. She'd never known him to be at a loss for words. Slow to speak, yes. But Frank's wisdom went deep. Jon had depended on that wisdom. Maira turned her head to glance at the old Bible, dusty and unused.

"Jon had an interest in religion, and I was doing my best to put distance between me and God when he asked me to come on here. Mrs. Jackson made sure I met Jon. Said he was looking for religion."

Maira ran her hand over the thick quilt covering her. The beautiful quilt she'd sewn herself with the help of Mrs. Jackson in town. She'd almost forgotten the patient owner of the lone boardinghouse. All those nights they'd spent together, Mrs. Jackson's gnarled fingers working the needle with precision, working so Maira would have ample bedding for her pending marriage. She'd heard Mrs. Jackson had died a year back, but she'd not gone into town to the funeral. She couldn't at the time, not with Levi so young and the ranch in such bad shape and her heart still breaking over the loss of Jon.

She pushed away the grief to focus on Frank. "You were a preacher."

"People got to talking about my marriage. Married me a mulatto woman. Good woman, but they didn't like that when they found out. So I stopped preaching. Mrs. Jackson called me a coward." Frank's mouth curled into a rueful grin. "Jon helped me see how close to the truth she was. I couldn't pull away from God just because people hurt me."

"I didn't know you were married."

"She died of fever before I ever came to town."

"You and Jon used to talk all the time about God and the Bible."

"And when he died, it was like another hurt on my rock pile."

His words paralleled what was in her own heart. She stared at the Bible.

"Tanner's hurting, too," he continued. "That deep-down hurt that's got us all pulling up lame."

❧

Tanner had never been so glad to see the moon. After two nights of rain, the glowing white orb surrounded by bursts of starlight comforted him. Despite the cold, the fire had kept much of the chill of night at bay. He set his boots as close to the fire as he dared, relishing the warmth and the last of his jerky. Cue whinnied from the cover of the rocky overhang that had sheltered him after the stampede, content to be dry and fed at last, his lacerations eased with the salve. He'd made sure to pamper the horse a bit. About a mile out was the place where he'd found Jon's body, the point where the XP and R7 ranges met. He would go over that area again. Try to remember. Leaning back, Tanner focused on the day ahead. He had to have a plan. He'd found Jon's body so long ago, and yet only he knew the truth. Jon had been shot in the side, riding away from someone or something. He wasn't simply robbed. No one had seen the gold change hands.

When morning sun lit the sky in the east, he saddled Cupid up and dragged himself into the saddle, weary from his restless night. In fits and starts he had dreamed, vague images that made little sense but left him uneasy. More than once he'd jerked awake, thinking he heard the sound of someone crying. First a child's cry, then a woman's, and though the face had been nothing more than a blur with dark hair, he had known it was that moment when Maira had taken lead. He shook his head and scratched along his heavily stubbled jaw. Could be his age was factoring into his inability to sleep, or maybe it was the shattered sense of peace and place that being on the Rocking J had given him. Cue, at least, seemed reinvigorated by the night's rest.

He breathed in the cool, fresh air and sat forward in the saddle, longing for a cup of hot coffee and a piece of sausage. At least he had left Frank, Maira, and Levi with meat. His cheeks puffed out on a heavy sigh. It didn't feel like enough.

No matter what he did, it would never be enough.

Each placement of Cue's hooves echoed that thought back to him. Punishing. Pushing with its spectral finger against his failures.

A slow spiral of smoke writhed skyward in the distance. He guided Cupid that direction, curious. Judging by the distance, it would be property beyond the reach of the XP or R7. It was a small fire, almost imperceptible, shielded by a staggered range of rises, too little to be called hills. He rode on, Cupid's ears alert, twitching as he drew nearer. No doubt the animal smelled the smoke, maybe even something else that his nose could not make out. He passed the place where he'd found Jon. A slope that overlooked the XP before dropping downward toward the Rocking J. On the opposite side, the smoke writhed into the air.

A sixth sense brought him up short. Cue chafed to continue the forward trek, but he held the gelding steady, eyes alert. He tried to superimpose the image of Jon's body with the lay of the land. Jon's body had shown marks along his lower arms. He recalled a tear in his brother's shirt that hadn't made sense at the time.

Not if Jon had been riding.

He traced the road that led toward the Rocking J, then the perpendicular path from the road out to the place where the smoke weaved like a beckoning finger. There was no road here, but a light trail, as if little but consistently used. More worn than he remembered. Tension snaked along his spine as he gave Cupid his heels, and the horse moved forward. He scanned the ground. A lone hoofprint and bushes with the tips of their limbs snapped off, the evidence that guided him in the direction of the rider who had built the fire. He didn't know quite how far he had passed, a mile, two, maybe three if the windy way could be physically straightened. The sun was heating the ground and beginning to draw sweat around the brim of his hat. Cue climbed the rise in terrain, every muscle in the animal's body tensed with effort. Tanner sat easy in the saddle, amused at the pitch of the deceptively shallow rise, even more astonished as the earth opened up below him with every step. The terrain gave way to a canyon, narrow and rough, but a surprise.

And not a surprise.

He realized two things at almost the same time: that the milling brown and white beasts below him were surely the yearlings missing from the Rocking J, and that he was a perfect silhouette against the sky. The unmistakable bark of a rifle brought Cue up straight before the horse willingly heeded Tanner's heels and launched a mad gallop down the rise and out of the gunman's sight.

Tanner's heart staccatoed. He condemned himself for having ridden right into showing himself like some kid with no experience. He'd suspected rustlers, and now he'd found them and shown his hand; and now he had no doubt he was riding for his life. Just as Jon had probably done, except he wouldn't get himself killed. He should have been paying attention to that telltale fire. Whoever was down there clearly had a guard. And that man had seen him long before Tanner had reached the pinnacle of the hill.

Cupid's stride reached for more ground, and more, eating up the sloppy ground like a destructive tornado. He slowed the horse for the last three hundred feet to the base of the rise, the most treacherous footing, expecting a bullet in his back at any moment. Everything becoming crystal clear. The angle of the bullet that killed Jon. The scratches on his arms from wading through the scrub to get to that pinnacle, probably leading his horse. . .

Tanner dared to stop Cue at the base, turning the horse. The gelding fought him, terrorized by the bullet. He put a hand to the horse's neck, feeling the hard bunch of Cue's muscles. He turned the horse sideways and slipped to his feet, slapped Cue on the rump, then leaped and dug his shoulder into the ground. He rolled to his stomach and palmed his gun. He squinted into the brightness lining the horizon. He searched for the telltale glint of sun off a rifle even as he scooped a handful of dirt to rub along the shiny barrel of his own gun. The muddy grit against his fingers took the shine off with each swipe of his hand. He blinked then blinked again, panning the area around him.

Nothing moved.

Chapter 22

The picture no longer brought a choking swell of pain. Maira marked the Bible with the worn photo and closed the pages. It was a shame to her to see the thin layer of dust surrounding the space where the Bible had lain on the dresser. She hadn't forgotten God; she just hadn't made time for Him. Levi kept her busy, the ranch, the worries of it all. . . .

Jon's strength had been her crutch. The leather cover, cracked from age and wear, was from his handling of the Bible. He'd been haunted by his mother's passing, his father's desertion. The two events had formed the conviction that he needed to make a secure future for himself and those he loved. That she had been the recipient of his love had been her greatest blessing, with Levi a beautiful extension. She tested the weight of the volume in her hand and considered a life without God, her deep-seated distrust of others. It didn't mean she couldn't trust Him, did it? Jon would want Levi to know a faith in God.

Maira set the volume aside, her finger lingering over the words printed on the front cover, *Holy Bible*. She'd locked herself away from the world after Jon's death, and in the process she had locked Levi away as well. Did God understand? He was merciful, yes, but she didn't think He would abide being neglected. Crowded out. And she needed Him. It had become too easy to rely on herself for her needs. The bullet could have missed her side and entered her heart. Levi would have become an instant orphan. Frank a lost cowhand riding for a brand that would cease to exist.

A black abyss opened up in Maira's mind. The blackness brought a chill. She closed her eyes. God wanted her to give Him her heart and for her to teach Levi of Him. But where to begin? A small smile curved her lips at the answer that whispered across her mind. She began with herself.

The Bible fell open on her lap and she began reading in earnest, until the rising sun stretched its golden fingers through her window. She read of Christ in a garden, crying, going back to His friends only to find them asleep. He would wake them and tell them to watch and pray, asking of flesh and blood to help Him. And they failed each time.

People failed Christ.

His friends. Those closest to Him.

Maira's hands shook at that revelation. How often had she, as a child, put her trust in others only to have them fail her? Yet she never realized God wouldn't fail her. People would fail, again and again, but God would not.

The house stirred with wakeful sounds. Ana moved around the kitchen. Levi slept on, his cheeks flushed with deep sleep. Her heart had broken over Levi's tears when Frank had finally suggested that Tanner might not return. It made sense that Tanner would gather all his belongings if his intention had been to give himself some space.

Disappointment flooded her, sucked the joy from the morning and the long hour she'd read through the Bible. The final story flowed to the front of her mind. People failed. Tanner had left her. She would not go on in her own strength. Couldn't. The hurt flowed too deep. *God, I need You to ease this hurt and help me. Help me to help Tanner. Somehow.* She sighed at the absurdity of such a prayer. He would not return, and she really needed to focus on herself, not Tanner.

Pushing herself up, she groaned at the spike of pain. She scooted to the edge of the bed and let her feet dangle, flexing the muscles in her legs and calves, rotating her feet to wake the muscles. As soon as she shifted her weight to her feet, her knees wanted to buckle. She stumbled sideways and gripped the bedpost, rattling the bed. She caught her breath, afraid to jostle Levi awake, but he only shifted and slept on. From post to post, she shuffled around the bed, careful steps marking her passage. Pleased with herself, she sat back down and reclined, amazed at the weakness that still held her in its grip.

A knock on the front door brought her alert. Tanner! But the name wilted when she realized he would never knock like that. Ana's footsteps echoed her path to the door. A strident male voice that she didn't recognize grated. Ana's reply, quicker, scared, seemed out of character. Maira pushed to her feet again, moving to the door, strength drawn from a rush of curiosity and anger. Hand on the door latch, she heard Ana gasp, a scuffle. She swung the door open, and a man loomed there, as if he had just been about to kick her bedroom door in.

"Good morning, Mrs. Cullen. We've heard you've not been feeling well."

"Where's Frank?" was all she could think to say, afraid what the man's presence meant. She knew him. The red hair. Timmons. Carrot Timmons from the XP.

"Frank's out on the range with the others. We'll take care of him later."

Carrot was one of the men Walt had sent. Why, then, was he here and not with Frank on the range? Fresh fear set her nerves on fire. She took a step back, reached for the door to slam it. Carrot wedged his foot in the door and lunged forward. His hand clamped onto her arm. She lashed out with her other hand, her injury spitting fire and making the blow she intended nothing more than the batting of a kitten's paw. His free hand caught her arm and spun her toward him. The long length of him became a wall of fury, his voice a snarl. "You want us to treat that boy of yours real nice, now don't you? Just listen real close. I don't take with the thought of hurting a woman. All we need is some time."

Her chest rattled with the pressure of suppressed sobs. Levi sat up and rubbed his eyes.

"Tell the boy to get dressed," Carrot's voice rasped.

"Levi." She steadied herself. "Levi, you need to get up and get dressed."

"Good girl, Mrs. Cullen."

"Who's that?"

"No matter who I am, kid. Do what your mama said."

Levi's dark eyes rounded. His chin trembled. "Mama?"

Carrot's hand gripped her arm harder in silent warning. Maira looked intently at her son. "Just do what I asked you to do, Levi."

Her son stared at her, then at the man behind her. Maira whispered a prayer and pleaded with her eyes, until, finally, Levi slid to the floor. He grasped his pants and did his best sticking one leg in, then the other, but he got the legs backward. She guided him with her voice, aware that her arm below Carrot's grip was going numb. When Levi had worked himself into his shirt, Carrot Timmons finally relinquished his grip on her arm a fraction.

"Come here, boy."

Levi was on the verge of tears; she could see it in the way he held himself, shoulders squared, his gait slow, as if planting each foot carefully took priority. So like Jon. Even Tanner walked that way. Confident. Sure. A rolling gait that was at once limber but alert for anything.

Levi stopped in front of her. She stroked her hand down his face. All at once, Carrot shoved her forward. Her toes tangled in the hem of her gown, and she stumbled to her knees. She twisted, gasped at the stab of pain. Carrot held Levi close to him. "Mama!"

"Get dressed, Mrs. Cullen." Carrot demanded. He yanked Levi back against him and slammed the door.

❧

Tanner waited in the dust for half an hour, afraid to move, eyes growing weary from the constant vigil. He'd discovered them. They knew it. He knew it. They must also know they had not hit him, and if they had decided not to come after him, then they had another plan in mind. But what?

He debated the question as he breathed the smell of musty wetness radiating from the ground. Sweat poured down his face and into the growth of whiskers. His disadvantage was he still had no idea who was running the group of rustlers. When he could stand the stress of inactivity no longer, he let out a low whistle and waited. He whistled again and heard a sharp whinny. Cue was near, too scared to come close. Crawling on his belly, Tanner came to his knees behind a clump of brush with the first hint of new growth. Cue stood off two hundred yards. He whistled again, and the horse crept closer, one cautious step at a time.

"Come on, boy," he murmured. He brushed at the front of his shirt and slapped his hat against his leg. Cue picked up his pace, trotting up to him. They'd taken off then, toward the place he knew would be most vulnerable. If the band knew Jon Cullen and had been the ones to plug him, then they must know of Tanner's presence at the Rocking J. They would go there first to look for him.

Whatever nervousness the animal harbored was lost in the grinding gait Tanner enforced with his spurs. "Go, Cupid. Fly, boy. Fly!"

Chapter 23

Maira pounded her fists against the locked door. Levi's shuddering, exhausted sobs leeched away her composure. "I'm here, baby. I'm here."

"Mama! I want you!"

"Levi, hush. Listen to me."

But his sobs were too shuddering. Too afraid.

She put a wall up around her shattering emotions and lowered her voice, talking to him as she did before bedtime. Low and soft. When she knew nothing else to say, she pulled the Bible from the table. Hazy memories of a boy's fight with a giant came to her. Levi loved stories. He would love that one. But her fingers fumbled over the pages, and she couldn't remember the book or chapter or verse. *Oh Jon, help me! God, please, please. . .* The pages slipped through her fingers, one book after another. Leviticus. As she searched, she told Levi how much he needed to be brave. Joshua. Judges. Ruth. Levi had quieted, and a question balanced on her tongue. She hated to ask it. Didn't want to stir Levi's fear, but she had little hope other than to see what Levi was seeing.

"Levi?"

Silence.

"Mama, I'm scared."

"I want to read you a story." She continued to turn. "It's about a boy and a big man." Her fingers turned another page, and she saw the name at the top. First Samuel. With shaking fingers she scanned down the chapters, until she came to the story.

"Big man?"

"Like the one who held you."

"He left."

She drew breath into her lungs, pressed her hand against the trembling smile and the answer to the question she hadn't even needed to ask.

"Good. I want you to listen to this. It's a good story. Your father used to read it to you when you were"—she choked at the memory—"you were in my tummy."

"Big man?"

"Yes, yes, honey. A big man and a little boy."

"Like me?"

"A little older. Now listen."

The door rattled as Levi settled his weight against it. She could picture him, ear to the door, head bowed low. She read about David, her voice weak, aware of the quiet outside, of the fact that the "big man" could return at any moment. The words flowed, and when she finished, Levi didn't say a word. Her fingers longed to touch him, to smooth the hair from his brow and look into those chocolate-drop eyes.

Chocolate drops. . . Tanner.

"You are a brave little boy, Levi."

"Like David?"

The burn in her throat birthed a single tear. "Like David."

She heard the distant pounding of hooves and tensed. At the window she saw Carrot dismount. He headed toward the house. She scooted to the locked door, wincing at the tightness in her side.

"Levi." She blew a breath. "The big man is back. You are a brave boy—"

She heard his boots, heard the door slam and his raised voice. "Come here, boy!"

"Mama," he whimpered.

"You're a big boy. Be brave and. . .Levi, I want you to pray to God. Ask God to help you. Just like David did."

Fresh shame washed over her. Had she ever prayed with him before this moment?

"Like David."

Carrot's boots stomped across the floor. Levi whimpered.

"I'm taking your boy, Mrs. Cullen. He'll buy us some time. If he's good, we'll return him."

She capped a scream, pressed her palms flat against the door, weak, vulnerable to the threat on the other side of the door. "Please don't. Let me out. Take me."

"We could do that, but women can be a handful."

Maira leaned her forehead against the door, all her fears bunching a knot. "Oh, please. . .please, no."

Levi let out a surprised screech. Maira jammed her fist against her lips to keep from crying out in protest, not trusting what the man would do if antagonized.

A shot rang out. Panic surged, sucking her breath away. Levi howled.

"Levi?"

Hard footsteps, a muttered curse. Carrot's voice, another shot, closer this time. "Stop right there."

She had to know. *"Levi?"*

Little feet came running, the press of something against the door, a rush of ragged breathing. "Tan-wer, Mama! He's home."

❧

Tanner watched the man descend the steps. Carrot, foreman of the XP. The man's terse command and the unblinking eye of his gun slowed Tanner's advance toward the house. He was too late to protect Maira and Levi. He lowered his still-smoking gun, biding his time, hoping to draw Carrot away from the house.

"You've got some cows of ours."

Carrot's chuckle held no humor. "Thought it was you Casey saw."

"Nice little deal you've got going. Jon Cullen was on to you."

"Not me, but to the fact cows were disappearing. He found our little hiding place, but Casey saw him first." Carrot stroked his chin. "Never liked the idea of him poking around. Or you for that matter. Sorry Casey missed."

"Jon was my brother."

"Don't matter none now. It's time to round them up and move them out. I'll cut some from the herd to sell and use the rest to build up my own spread."

"It's all about you, is it?"

"My men will be well paid." Carrot spit into the grass and smirked. "I'm an honest rustler."

"The sheriff will gather a posse."

"Nope. Because the way I see it, Young, you're going to let me out of here. I'm taking the boy. You follow me, he dies. The sheriff comes after me, he dies."

"And you'll let him go. . .when?"

Another dry chuckle. "When I'm good and ready. Might make him a partner." Carrot swiped his free hand across his mouth. "If he squalls too much, he'll become a silent partner."

The door behind Carrot hadn't latched and was swinging open. Tanner was about to use the movement as a distraction when a small figure barreled through the open door, plunging, hitting Carrot behind the knees. The man staggered forward, lost his footing, and tumbled down the steps taking Levi with him. The gun flew from Carrot's fingers, landing in the tall grass.

Tanner lunged for the weapon and caught it. A scream rent the air. He glimpsed a face in the front window—Maira's room. Levi lay still on the ground. Tanner cocked the gun and dug it deep against Carrot's neck.

"Get down flat."

With slow moves, Carrot lowered himself flat against the ground. Tanner adjusted his position accordingly, edging toward the boy, heart in his throat. He crouched, keeping the gun in line with Carrot's back as he touched Levi. Before his fingers grazed the boy's shirt, Levi stirred. Tanner's breathing came easier. The boy sat up and squeezed his eyes shut, then opened them.

"Hey little cowpuncher."

"Tan-wer?" Big brown eyes blinked up at him. Eyes unlike Jon's but very much like his own.

Levi got to his knees, before jumping forward, clasping his little arms around

Tanner's neck. Tanner spread his hand on the boy's back, warmth rising in his chest. "You saved my life."

"Like David."

"Let me take care of this man—"

"I took down the giant!"

Levi pushed from his one-armed embrace and ran to the porch, waving at his mother as if he'd just roped the biggest steer in the world. Tanner chuckled as he came to his feet and dug his boot into Carrot's side. Sure looked like Levi had done just that.

Chapter 24

Maira?"

Even before the second syllable was out of his mouth, Tanner saw Levi crouched at the door to Maira's bedroom. He didn't doubt that the man had locked her inside somehow. He scanned the simple latch. No sign of any lock at all. Levi got to his feet, face anxious as he pointed.

"Can't get that out."

Tanner kicked at the wedge of wood lodged to trap Maira in the room. He worked it free with his fingers, and the door swung inward. Maira stood there in a simple skirt and blouse, her hair tousled and untamed, her face pale. Levi plunged into her arms. Tanner caught her grimace when she took Levi's weight. They shared a look over the boy's head. Tears sparkled in her eyes. "I've never been so scared—" She lowered her face and sniffed then stiffened, green eyes wide with panic. "Ana!"

"Out in the barn. They tied her up and left her. I told her she might want to sit awhile to recover from the blow Carrot gave her." He shifted his weight and laughed. "That's the most riled I've ever seen her."

Relief smoothed the tension from Maira's brow. "Carrot?"

He swallowed, his mouth suddenly dry with the desire to do more than stand beside her like they were strangers. "I tied him up and put him in the barn. The other man rode away, probably back to the canyon."

"I'm not sure that I understand." Her eyes were on his, a silent question there.

His attraction to her was like the pull of air when a tornado ripped through. In that second he wanted to believe things might work. Maybe he could shake the past and settle down with hope and happiness. Maira would be his wife, Levi his son, and there would be more children. A ranch. He had a chance. The invitation was in every facet of her face, even if there were no words, until she looked down at Levi, ran her hand over his head. She bit her lip and leaned to pick the boy up then gasped, lips pressed tight.

"Best not." Tanner brushed away her hands and lifted the boy into the cradle of his arms. Levi clung. "Sit down, Maira."

She brushed past him and went outside to the porch. Her hair was in disarray in the back, the part showing where she'd been lying against pillows. Her dishevelment tugged out a grin and pleased him somehow. As if by witnessing it she was allowing him to get close. To know her on a new level, or maybe with all that had happened she simply had forgotten.

He watched as she sat in the rocker, her sigh more a painful gasp.

"Lying down might be better."

She ignored his words and gestured for him to turn around. He bent at the knees and twisted his upper body so Maira could see Levi's face over his shoulder. Levi felt warm in his arms. It felt right for him to be there. His hero.

"He's sound asleep," she whispered.

Ana stepped from the barn. Tanner quirked an eyebrow at Maira, who followed his gaze. Ana drew closer, eyes rimmed with red. "I'm so sorry, Maira."

"It's not your fault, Ana." Tanner gave the answer. "They've been doing Mrs. Cullen wrong for a long time. It just so happens we caught up to them. Slim must have ridden out with the others this morning?"

She nodded.

"You'd do well to keep that man close. He loves you, you know."

Ana's head tilted up at him. "Mr. Price..."

"He has no hold on you, only the hold you give him. I'm sure Mrs. Cullen would love to have you stay here. You'd be safe, warm, and if I don't miss my guess, you'll be married before too long."

A deep redness pushed into the young woman's cheeks. She took the stairs and held out her hands to take Levi. "I'll tuck him in."

Tanner exchanged a secret smile with Maira as Ana lifted Levi close. She pressed her lips against the boy's cheek.

"Mr. Young is right. I'd be delighted to have you stay. I wouldn't be able to pay you—"

"Mr. Price doesn't pay me...." She bit her lip and glanced at Levi, then at Maira. "I'd love to stay, but if Mr. Price comes looking for me..."

"You have nothing to worry about. Slim and I can handle Price, Ana."

She stared at him a full minute before she gave the slightest of nods. "You're right."

❧

Throbs of pain stabbed along Maira's side. She did her best to relax the muscles. To sit still. She wanted to talk to Tanner. Share all that she had learned in the night. Instead, the question foremost in her mind slipped out. "Where have you been?"

"I needed to move on."

"But you came back. I deserve a better answer, Tanner."

He nodded and scratched at the stubble of dark beard along his jaw. "There were some things I needed to think about."

"You were leaving us for good?" She did her best to keep the plaintive note from her voice. "Frank said you took everything."

"I did." He turned his face in profile, his boot catching the lower post of the porch. She felt like she'd seen him stand that way a thousand times.

"I found what I think got Jon shot, Maira. There's a canyon about three miles beyond XP and R7 land. It edges the place where I found Jon." He paused, stared over at her.

"You found. . .Jon? But when they found him, he was. . ." She lifted her face. "I don't understand."

Tanner straightened and came to stand in front of her. "He was my brother, Maira. Jon and I met for the first time in years that day he went into town. He suspected someone was rustling his stock and came to hire an investigator. I was that man. When I saw him, I knew he was my little brother."

She tried to remember. To connect the loose ends of the conversation. "Jon?" She saw it then. The planes of his face, those eyes, the same color as Levi's. Physical similarities ended there. "Then you're. . ."

His lips curled upward. "Family."

"You didn't tell me."

"I didn't know at first. Only when I heard your last name did it dawn on me that you were his widow."

So many questions. "What brought you here? What took you so long?"

Tanner drew a deep breath and squinted out into the yard. He told her about finding Jon that day. He'd set out behind his brother to begin investigating Jon's allegations. Only by accident had he stumbled upon Jon's body. Maira processed every word, beginning to understand the depth of Tanner's isolation.

"No one likes you much when they know you're investigating them. I hired on at the XP as game hunter before I knew about my brother. It was a good cover for what I really did." He inhaled long and deep. "If someone was willing to kill Jon, then the likelihood of Jon's accusations being correct increased. I just had to figure out all the details and put together evidence, but the rains washed everything away, and a mountain cat came on the scene. . . ."

She shuddered and turned her face away, and he saw her swallow.

"I'm sorry."

"No, no. It's all right." She hugged herself. "Jon didn't tell you about us?"

"He told me very little about himself before our time was cut short by a scuffle that broke out. I gave him some gold." He swallowed hard, the muscles in his jaw working. "A gift."

She gasped. "Walt said he stole it! I knew it was a lie, but the miner said it was true."

"I wish now I'd talked sooner, but there were those rustling allegations to investigate."

"What about this canyon?"

"Found it by tracing Jon's body. It's well hidden. Someone shot at me, so I rode back here figuring they'd come looking for me. I detoured to Frank and the other men. Told them to check out the canyon."

"They're out there now?"

He nodded. "When I got here there were two men, Carrot and one other. The first one took to his saddle pretty quick. I expect he went back to warn the others."

"What about Frank? The men?"

"They've got their guns; they'll figure it out."

"Tanner—"

"Enough talking. You need to get in bed and rest." His hand was a light pressure on her arm. He gave her time to move at her own pace, and she took it, slow and easy, not entirely because of the pain, but because of the closeness his arm offered. Her brother-in-law.

She caught his hands, suddenly afraid for him to let go. She hated this, her vulnerability. It was time to put her trust in God. If He wanted this man for her, it would work, but she had to know. "Will you stay?"

His eyes searched hers. "I'll be here when you wake up."

And it was enough. For now.

Chapter 25

Tanner clamped the arms of the rocker Maira had just vacated. He'd given his word, and he would stay, but for how long? The ranch needed more work. She needed help. Frank couldn't do it all, as evidenced by the shape of the place. If he didn't stay, it would only be a matter of time before the Rocking J went under. Rustlers or not, Maira didn't have the resources. Cowpunchers might agree to deferred payment, but it gave the ranch a reputation that might make it harder for her to get help.

Old fears rose to the surface. Maira had taken a bullet because of him. He was no good. Too quick tempered. Too easily provoked. He'd wanted to believe he had matured. He heard a light scuff and turned to see Levi. The boy said not a word but came to him and crawled up in his lap.

Tanner relaxed his fist and spread it over Levi's back, his other arm securing the small body against him. "Couldn't sleep?"

"I got scared."

"Is your mama asleep?"

No answer.

"Levi?"

"I wanted you."

It was like a punch to his heart, shattering all the negative thoughts. Lodging warmth into his cold world. How many times had Levi done this? Shown him a love that knew no fear? Tanner's lip trembled, and he bit it hard, his throat burning with emotion.

"Tan-wer, you scared, too?"

He couldn't see Levi's face, nestled as it was against his shoulder. "No, son. I'm not scared."

The boy's hand reached out, touched his cheek. Tanner felt the smear of wetness. "Then why you cryin'?"

He dug his fingers against his eyes to wipe away the tears.

Again Levi's hand touched his cheek. "Like sticky hay."

Tanner's smile shone through. He looked down into Levi's face, taking in those wide brown eyes and long lashes. "What if I shave it off?"

Levi nodded against his shoulder, his eyelids sweeping downward, lashes brushing his cheeks then opening.

"Can I stay here?"

Tanner swallowed hard. "You can stay here."

He waited for the boy's eyes to shut before securing Levi's position against him.

For an hour he wrestled with himself. Deep down inside, Tanner knew he couldn't risk staying. He handed Levi over to Ana and watched as she took him into the spare bedroom. Maira's closed bedroom door gave him pause. He could say good-bye. It was the least he could do, but dangerous to his determination. Even as his boots crunched across the front yard toward the barn, he picked up his pace. He'd never admitted to Maira why he'd left the first time, and he wouldn't this time either. He needn't answer to anybody. He disappeared into the shadows of the barn. Cue nickered a welcome as he passed and went to the room built into the back. He opened the door and was met with the scowling face of Carrot. He shut the door again, anger surging at all the grief the man had brought on Maira and the Rocking J. But he was done.

He had to cut the tie to the Rocking J, and fast. He remembered the hopelessness of watching his father die in his mother's arms. How he had wanted to stop the bleeding, to keep his Pa forever. The line between his father's death and his own bleeding emotions smeared. Maira was coming into the barn, slow, clutching her side. He could hear the whisper of her feet and the soft movement of her skirts. God help him, he could *smell* her. A light scent of spring grass and wildflowers.

"Tanner? Are you. . . ?"

"Got to leave."

"Why?"

"Nothing more to do. Things should go better for the J now. If I don't miss my guess, Ana and Slim will stay here and help out, at least for a while."

"And then?"

He didn't want to face her, to give in to the pressure of her hand on his arm. "You'll figure something out."

"I love you, Tanner. Is that what you're scared of?"

He closed his eyes and drew air into his lungs. "I didn't mean for this to happen."

Her hand on his arm, the challenge in her words. She loved him. It matched that moment when, sitting at the table, he'd seen Maira whisper to Levi, their heads so close together and their affection so apparent. A crest of emotion had gripped him at the sight of mother and child. Two people he had come to care for more than any others. He couldn't stay and risk it all. It hurt too much.

"Jon told me you left home."

The way she said it, her head tilted at an angle, her expression earnest, her eyes knowing.

"He said your mother never forgave your stepfather for driving you away."

Tanner couldn't face her. He ground his teeth, trying to distance himself from the memory.

"When your stepfather left, she lost the ranch. Jon went out on his own in hopes of making enough to help them, but he couldn't. No matter how hard he tried."

His chest rattled with pent-up emotion. "If I'd stayed, I could have helped."

"But you didn't."

"Don't you think I know that?" he ground out.

"What happened isn't your fault."

"I could have helped." He faced her then. "I'm partly to blame for it all."

Her green eyes searched his. "Talk to me, Tanner. Don't leave until we've talked. You promised me that once."

Cue whinnied, as if reminding him of his original intention. Maira raised her hand to his cheek. Her fingers grazed lightly along his jaw. "I don't know how it was that I didn't see the resemblance sooner."

"We don't look alike."

"The eyes. They're Levi's eyes if not Jon's. You must have taken after your mother."

She cupped the side of his face, and he leaned into the warmth of her smooth palm. She was killing him. Those eyes. Her touch. The pleading of her heart. Even the small talk, easing him off the cliff of his own emotional turmoil. "Jon resembled his daddy," was all he could manage.

Her lips curved upward and her hand fell away, stroking down his arm until she held his hand. She turned, steps sure, and he followed her to the bales of hay. He waited for her to sit, heard the little gasp of pain that parted her lips. "Maira. . ."

She patted the bale next to her. "My pain will heal."

His had festered.

"When Jon died, I was so alone." She looked at him, a penetrating, serious stare. "I'd been alone most of my life. My parents left me at the orphanage when I was little. One day. . ." She lifted her face to stare at the ceiling. He could hear the tears in her voice, and though he knew the story, he didn't stop her, wanting to hear it from her lips. "One day a couple came and took me home with them. They said they wanted to adopt me, but I wasn't enough for them. I never worked fast enough or hard enough. They took me back after a few months."

He didn't know what to say.

She sent him a tremulous smile. "I was so angry. I became the 'problem child,' the one hard to place, and I didn't ever want to be placed again. I wanted nothing more than to be left alone, but being alone meant enduring a very different type of pain." She rubbed at her side. "When you left, I felt that way all over again. Abandoned. Hated."

"I don't hate you."

Her grin was cheeky. "I know you don't." She glanced away, growing serious again. "Jon didn't get back in time to help your mother either, and for a long time he blamed himself."

She was offering him an opening. In the silence, he weighed his choice to take it or to ride away and, for once, he didn't want to leave. Not now. "I went back years later. The house had been burned down. The neighbor told me my mother had lived at her house for a year with no money and no food. They'd done their best to help her. They said. . ." He choked, pausing to regain his composure. "They said they had to go get her. That she was starving by that time and very weak."

"I wandered for a long time after that. Picked up some work when I joined a posse, and the deputy discovered my skills at tracking. We stumbled upon a group of Indians. One woman in their midst. The man I was with pulled his gun and started blasting away." He remembered it so well. There'd been sightings of Indians, but the posse had been gathered to trace the escape of rustlers. They'd been out for blood though, and he'd known it. Even as they'd ridden up to the Indians, the man in charge had wanted an excuse to fire his gun. He'd felt the man's need. Heard it in his voice, and when the Indians had been silent to his questions, he'd pulled out his gun. Tanner's throat tightened.

"The Indians started running, and he laughed and told them they shouldn't have run but that cowards needed to be shot. Then he blasted into them, the others joining in some strange, secret bent to massacre." He remembered the leader's laugh as they scrambled away from the sudden assault. The Indian woman had been the last to react to the threat of the drawn guns. She'd twisted away, catching a bullet low.

He'd lost it then. Every bit of reason had left him as he drew his gun and fired at the leader, his shot sending the man's gun flying, shattering his wrist. But they'd stopped shooting, letting the rest of the Indians go. As he'd slid from his saddle and cradled the squaw's head, they'd left, one by one. He'd buried the woman and kept riding, always searching for something he could not understand.

"When Walt shot you. . ."

She leaned forward and touched his knee. "It was a mistake."

"He could have killed you."

"But he didn't, Tanner." Her laugh was unexpected. "I really shouldn't have just bounded down those steps like that, but I was scared. For you."

"It's easier to be alone."

She nodded. "In some ways, but think of what you're missing."

Hadn't that been the very thing to spark his fear? Feeling the comforts of the Rocking J, of having a woman around, and Levi. Even Frank's friendship. Wanting more than that was the problem. Wanting Maira as his own, his wife. Levi as his son instead of his nephew. It would be so easy.

Maira was moving. Her skirts rustling. She slipped to her knees in front of him, her lips compressed. He held out his hands to steady her, and she accepted the help. "What are you doing?"

She settled herself, standing on her knees, putting her face almost even with his. She crept forward, her face coming closer, her hands slipping around his waist. Tanner gathered her close, his arms hungry for her touch. He buried his face in her hair, breathing deeply of her need for him. All that she offered shone like a bright star. Why had he felt the need to escape her? In the circle of her arms, it all seemed so silly, unnecessary. Leaving would hurt her and Levi. It wasn't about him any longer; it was about the woman who held him.

He pulled back just enough. "Maira?"

Trust lit her eyes. Fragile in his arms, she shifted away, lifting her hands to his face. "You don't have to say anything, Tanner, but I needed to tell you how I felt. If you choose to leave, then I'll be here for you when you return." She pulled from his embrace and used his leg to get to her feet.

"Where are you going?"

She stood in the doorway of the barn, her body a dark silhouette against the sun. "If I kiss you, it will only make things more difficult, and my love won't heal what ails you."

Chapter 26

Tanner held no illusions about his choice or about Maira's feelings for him. The two were at odds with each other, but her wisdom shone through when she told him her love would not heal him. He didn't know what would heal him. If anything. As he tied Cue to a hook in the wall of the barn, he slipped the saddle on the horse's back. The gelding would at least be ready to go. When Frank returned, he'd fill the man in, show him the prisoner, and let him take control of the situation. He tightened the cinch. Arching his neck, Cue took a playful nip at his sleeve. He batted the horse's nose and smiled.

"Where should we go next?"

He stroked the horse, thinking. He should say good-bye to Levi. The boy deserved at least that. And to Maira? Tangled emotions balled his gut and filled him with dread. He strode out into the evening air and noted the light coming from the front window. Restless with his indecision, Tanner kept busy. Repairing harnesses, feeding the cow. He turned the horses out for the night and gave grain to the chickens. The smokehouse was full of the meat from the slaughtered cows. The men had taken care of all that without him. It filled him with confidence that life would go on here without him. They wouldn't notice his absence.

But this time the lie didn't work. He would be empty inside. He would miss Levi and Maira. All that he had come to know in his short time there.

A whistle rent the air, and Tanner left the smokehouse. Frank and the group of hands were returning. The older man waved as they drew closer. "Get me that stand."

Tanner returned from inside the barn with the box Frank used to help ease his mounts and dismounts. "Leg hurting?"

"Like fire."

The men surrounded them, laughing, covered in mud. Pants were ripped and caked with sweat and grime. "We got 'em," Slim crowed, motioning to the last horse coming in and carrying two men, both bound hand and foot to the saddle in some way, a rope held by the men who rode on either side of the prisoners. "Got a place to keep 'em for the night?"

"Were you able to check the brands on the cattle?"

Frank grunted as his feet hit the box. "Most of them were unbranded stock. We'll go back for Rocking J cows tomorrow and let the others know where they can get theirs. Some XP in the herd."

"Stealing from his employer."

Frank raised a brow.

"Carrot Timmons was leader of the rustlers. You can put those two with him in the barn." He glanced at the other two men, not recognizing either of them. "Guess he'd recruited his own men to take care of the herd."

"Grass was getting low in that canyon. They needed to move on, and fast. Otherwise they wouldn't have made it through the summer." Frank lifted his head. "How's Maira?"

"Better."

Frank's eyes swept over him. "Thought you'd gone for good."

"It's a long story."

"As soon as I get this brace off, I'll have all the time needed."

"I won't."

Cowhands swarmed around them as they stripped saddles and halters from their horses, drowning out conversation. Roger opened the gate as the rest of the hands started their mounts into the corral. As the gate closed, the noise receded, and the men shuffled to the main house for supper. Frank rubbed his knuckles against his vest. "I'm guessing there's no need for me to be privy to the reasoning behind those words."

"No need."

"You hurt Maira, and I might chase you down."

If Tanner had expected the man to protest, he'd never expected it in such a manner. "She's a strong woman."

"Had to be. Being mama and papa to that boy." Frank grunted as he rubbed his leg. "You being the brother and all. . . Seems only right that you stay."

There it was. Verification of his responsibility. "Nothing like a little guilt." He turned away.

"There's a ghost riding on your back about something, son."

"I'll deal with it."

"No, it'll deal with *you*, just as it has all these years."

Tanner pivoted, anger overflowing. "You don't know me."

"You're right, but I know something's riding in the saddle with you. You ride away and you'll break Maira's heart."

"I love you, Tanner. Is that what you're scared of?"

He focused on Maira. On Frank and Levi and what he was leaving. When he'd left his mother, it had been to escape his stepfather's overbearing ways, and he'd carried the guilt of her death for so long.

"You rode in here and started fixing things, and now you're content to ride out?"

It was more than that.

"Maira and I were talking while you were gone. She needs to get back to church and so do I. We've secluded ourselves. Want to know why?"

Tanner leaned to pick up the stand, roiling with the question. Did he? What did it have to do with him?

"Seems we've let ourselves become reclusive. It's been hard for us to let go of the past hurts. Maira at the orphanage, me and the problems I faced with being accepted. Guess we decided after Jon's death that it was safer here on the ranch, away from people, but you know what?"

Tanner ran his fingers over the smooth wood of the step stool.

"If we'd been involved in town, we might have seen sooner that our cattle was being rustled. We'd have heard about it. Known more about the people there. Been less afraid to reach out when we needed help. We'd have formed relationships. Let people know we wanted to talk and be talked to."

"I don't know what you're talking about." Tanner set the stool inside the barn door. He ran his hand over Cue's nose, then the reins.

Frank limped up beside him then frowned. "You wanting to leave is for yourself. To protect yourself. From what?"

Tanner's gaze snapped to Frank's.

"Wanna know what I think?"

"No. I really don't."

The old cowhand's nostrils flared, his eyes hard. "I'm going to supper then, but I want to say one more thing first. You said awhile back that the greatest gift was someone caring for you. You remember that?"

He did.

"It makes me wonder why a man would turn his back on that kind of gift."

Chapter 27

In the room full of men, at the long table groaning with food, Tanner felt lost. Aloof from the jokes and ribbing comments. He tucked into his food as soon as Frank set a plate in front of him. Talk turned to his heroics, the carcasses they'd dragged off after they'd settled the stampeding herd. Tanner said nothing. He had nothing to add and didn't relish the way they spoke of him. As if his actions were heroic. He'd done what needed to be done, and it had saved his life. There was nothing more to it than that. He noticed that Frank presided over the table, that Maira, Ana, and Levi were nowhere to be seen.

"We'll be using tomorrow to catch up." Fletcher directed his comment at Tanner. "Frank said you'd be going somewhere else tomorrow."

"Yeah, I guess I will." In slow motion, every cowhand's eyes turned to him. He felt the weight of their anticipation and curiosity.

"We've all been talking about staying on here," Slim said. "Price isn't a good man to work for, and I think we all agree that Mrs. Cullen needs the help more than him."

"You won't get paid," Frank reminded them as he motioned for Roger to pass his empty plate.

"We'll go back and settle up with Price. Should keep me going for a season if I'm careful." Fletcher passed his empty plate down the table and held up his mug. "More coffee?"

Frank jerked his head toward the pot, hands full. "Help yourself."

Tanner pushed back his plate, contents congealed, his appetite gone. That was it, then. He was no longer needed.

They lingered over coffee until Frank suggested they take their conversation to the bunkhouse. "Got another round of mouths to feed." As Slim, then Fletcher, passed him on their way to the door, they pounded him on the back, wishing him luck on his ride. Unaffected by the loss of him on their team. Roger lifted his hand in silent farewell. Tanner nodded at the men, saying little. It was the way of cowhands not to get too attached, knowing a man could move on at any time and for any reason.

Frank busied himself at the cookstove. The side door of the kitchen opened and Slim stuck his head inside. "Ana around?"

"No use lurking in the doorway. Come on in before you let the critters in with you," Frank fussed.

Slim stood there looking like a chastised schoolboy. He'd donned his hat and slicked his hair.

Frank shot Tanner a look then rapped the back of his hand on Maira's door. "Supper's on, and there's a young man interested in talking to Ana."

Levi yanked open the door, cheeks flushed. "I'm hungry!" His large brown eyes landed on Tanner. "You leaving?"

"Levi!"

Maira's chide caused Levi to duck his head. "You said he was."

"I said I *thought* he was."

Levi turned into her skirts. "Don't let him leave, Mama."

Ana squeezed around Maira, her face hot with a blush as she glanced at Slim, then knelt beside Levi and whispered something in his ear.

"Outside?" Levi asked.

"Can't have a picnic inside." Ana smiled.

Frank handed over two plates to Slim, with Ana taking two cups of water. Levi stopped in the doorway and looked from his mother to Tanner before he followed Ana and Slim out the side door.

Before Tanner realized what was happening, he caught on to the fact that he was alone in the kitchen with Maira. And Frank.

He swallowed hard. "I guess I'd best be leaving, too."

Maira searched his face, her gaze skimming over his cheeks, his hair, his jaw. She nodded. "If that's what you want."

His breath caught as she turned from him, settling herself in her chair, accepting the plate Frank put in front of her. She bowed her head, raised her fork to her lips, all without acknowledging him. His breath came fast. He wanted to make good on his words, but he couldn't move. He was a coward. Afraid to stay, scared to leave. All because he'd never known, never allowed himself to know, exactly what Maira's presence had taught him. She loved him, and though he didn't know much about loving a woman, he thought his feelings might match hers.

"I'll. . ." He flinched at the sound of his own voice, paused, and tried to collect his thoughts. "I'll be out on the porch when you're done with supper."

❧

Roast beef never tasted quite so good as that last bite Maira chewed. She could see Tanner waiting for her, leaning on the railing as he always did. He hadn't left, and her heart soared with the hope of his waiting figure.

"It's a good sign that he's waiting," Frank started.

"I know," she assured the man as she handed him her plate. "Thank you, Frank. Pray for me."

The man's smile stretched wide. "I'll be doing just that."

When she stepped out onto the porch, the night air swirled around her, carrying on it the sound of Slim and Ana's conversation. She couldn't see them but suspected they were just around the corner, enjoying the rising moon and peaceful sound of the crickets. Tanner turned to face her as she moved farther out onto the porch, closer to him. As close as she dared. Why had she been so reluctant to see him as more than a passing cowboy who'd rescued her son? Her love for him had crept up on her, heightened each time he'd done a kindness to her or Frank or Levi, with no hope of repayment. Even if his motives had started out untrue, he had proven himself to her time and again. People had failed her in the past, and he might fail her even now, but God would be her rock.

"You..."

The way he looked at her made her mouth go dry. Devotion spilled from his gaze. Yet there was that knot there. She dared to reach out and splay her hand against his chest. "Why is it so hard for you to accept love?"

All the affection seeped from his gaze. He stared down at his boots, and she could feel the twang of his heart, like a blacksmith's hammer on an anvil.

"Tanner?"

"Getting too close is like being near a fire." His jaw worked, and when he lifted his eyes, she saw his torment. "I've never put much stock in feelings."

"I won't burn you."

Tanner's hand crept upward, covered hers. When he lifted his gaze to hers, pain peeled from him in waves. "I might fail you."

His fear became clear to her then. "You didn't fail your mother, Tanner. Or anyone else." His breath came, ragged. He turned his face away, but she caught his chin, framed his cheeks in her hands. "Do you hear me?"

"If I hadn't left..."

"You did what you thought right at the time. I think the question now is, can you forgive yourself? Your mother would want you to be happy and whole, not running from people because..." She didn't quite understand his need to run. But he did. Maybe the suggestion of her words would be enough for him to fill in the blank.

"I want to stay."

His simple statement spilled through her. "I want you to stay. I love you, Tanner. I love who you are, the heart for people that you have."

He drew her close, his hand splayed on her back. She pulled his head down to her shoulder and held him there, swaying with him in her arms, as she had once rocked Levi.

❧

The Indian woman's blood spilled over his lap once again, accusing. He saw his mother's sad face, the disappointment she must have felt in him when he left. All of it soared into his mind with Maira's quiet question. Could he forgive himself? He'd done his best. Endured what he could endure with his stepfather. Tried to protect as best he could the vulnerable Indians. He'd had no way of knowing what the leader would do. No way of foreseeing his stepfather's abandonment. He should have gone back sooner, sure, but he hadn't. He would learn from the mistake, hold those he loved closer and be more aware.

He'd once heard a man talking of God's forgiveness. *Please, God, I need it so bad.* The pressure in his chest eased, like a fist finally relaxed. He could commit to Maira. To Levi and the Rocking J. He would enjoy the closeness, Maira's gentleness, and coming home to her at the end of a long day repairing fence. He'd tortured himself long enough, and Maira was right: His mother would want him to be happy.

When he raised his head and stared down into Maira's upturned face, he measured the consequence of what he was going to do next. He held her shoulders, bent his head, searched her eyes, wide now with expectation. When his lips touched hers, he felt like a man finding color in the bend of a creek bed. The moment was pure gold. No streaks of other sediment, just beauty and tenderness. He breathed in the scent of her hair, kissed her forehead, tilted her chin for another kiss on her lips. And then he held her, unsure if his sense of balance was off because of her or him or the hope that came on the wings of the realization that he was in love. This was love.

He pulled back. "Maira, I love you."

Her eyes filled with tears and she nodded. "I figured that out."

S. Dionne Moore is a historical romance author who resides in South Central Pennsylvania, surrounded by the beautiful Cumberland Valley and lots of historically rich locations. Find more about her books at www.sdionnemoore.com.

If You Liked This Book, You'll Also Like...

Brides of Ohio
by Jennifer A. Davids
Author Jennifer A. Davids has spun three stories from historic Ohio where hope has been shattered for three women. A Southern belle's life is displaced. A widow takes a risk to save an old friend. A spinster librarian harbors a secret. Between past hurts and present trials, is there room for love?
Paperback / 978-1-63058-152-7 / $12.99

Brides of Iowa
by Connie Stevens
This historical collection explores hope and healing in the heartland of Iowa. Will God use Gideon to heal Tessa's shattered heart? Will an estranged son's anger undo Hubert's and Pearl's dreams for love in their later years? And does Tillie dare hope to convince Everett of her love—despite his disfiguring scars?
Paperback / 978-1-62836-235-0 / $12.99

Brides of Idaho
by Linda Ford
Three historical romances from bestselling author Linda Ford take readers into the rough mining country of Idaho. The three independent Hamilton sisters struggle to make a home and livelihood for themselves, and they don't have time for men they can't trust. Can love sneak in and change their stubborn hearts?
Paperback / 978-1-63058-798-7 / $12.99

Find These and More from Barbour Books
at Your Favorite Bookstore
www.barbourbooks.com

If You Liked This Book, You'll Also Like...

The Rails to Love Romance Collection

Nine historical stories celebrate a spirit of adventure along the Transcontinental Railroad where nine unlikely couples meet. From sightseeing excursions to transports toward new lives, from orphan trains to circus trains, can romances develop into blazing love in a world of cold, hard steel?

Paperback / 978-1-63409-864-9 / $14.99

The California Gold Rush Romance Collection

Nine couples meet in the hills of California where gold fever rules hearts and minds from the lonely miner to the distinguished banker, from the lowly immigrant to the well-intentioned preacher. But can faith and romance lead these couples to treasures more valuable than gold?

Paperback / 978-1-63409-821-2 / $14.99

The Valiant Hearts Romance Collection

In nine historical romances from beloved Christian authors, brave men and women endure some of life's hardest mysteries, challenges, and injustices spanning from war in the 1860s to Prohibition in the 1920s. Will the bonds they form and the loves they develop lead to lasting legacies for nine couples?

Paperback / 978-1-63409-672-0 / $14.99